PRAISE FOR KATI HIEKKAPELTO

'Hiekkapelto's brooding debut, a large-scale police procedural set in a small Finnish town, tilts heroically at such vexing ills as racial prejudice, alcoholism, and domestic abuse … tough and powerful crime fiction' *Publishers Weekly*

'Hiekkapelto provides an unsentimental account of Finnish society and its cultural traditions, in particular the Finnish obsession with hunting and guns, which means that, in theory, virtually anyone could be the killer on the rampage' *Irish Times*

'Crisp and refreshing, with a rawness that comes from a writer willing to take risks with her work' Sarah Ward, CrimePieces

'For a first novel *The Hummingbird* delivers a lot. The perspectives on immigration feel genuine and are insightful and the writing is atmospheric and absorbing. The two police investigations, one official and one not, are balanced well and the characters are rounded and appealing such that you want to know what will happen next in both their professional and personal lives. A second instalment is on the way and I look forward to following the careers of both Anna Fekete and Kati Hiekkapelto' Live Many Lives

'It's like reading Henning Mankell, when Senior Constable Anna Fekete works on several tricky cases in the icy-cold winter of Northern Finland while contemplating the harshness of life' *Helsingin Sanomat*

'She has a wonderful natural style and narrative flow, as well as a talent for creating memorable, intriguing characters. I will look forward to Anna's further adventures and the blossoming of her relationship with her colleagues' CrimeFictionLover

'As the plot keeps deepening, Hiekkapelto turns out to be incredibly skilful at carrying off a complicated story … the suspense feels real and the writing flows nicely' *Savon Sanomat*

'Hiekkapelto really treats her readers like royalty. The plot – with all its twists, its humorous yet wise narration – guarantees a perfect reading experience. I'm sorry for the superlatives, but I believe *The Defenceless* is the Book of the Year for me' *Literary Blog Rakkaudesta Kirjoihin*

'If you're a fan of Swedish crime queen Camilla Läckberg, you'll love Hiekkapelto' *Kaleva*

'A confident, thrilling crime novel that credibly depicts the everyday life of the Finnish police' *Me Naiset*

'Hiekkapelto knows how to get under your skin' *45 min*, MTV

'Kati Hiekkapelto delivers a knockout punch in the fight to be top dog in the Scandi Crime wave with her debut crime thriller *The Hummingbird*. It has everything you need: three interwoven stories, the dark noir, the defective detective, the racist detective, all in the north of Finland as summer turns to the darkness of winter. This thriller will really get under your skin as the imagery is striking and at times stark and haunting like some of the landscapes can be as the changes from summer take place towards the Arctic circle' Atticus Finch

'A few other Finnish authors have surfaced in English since Antti Tuomainen appeared in 2013, but Kati Hiekkapelto is one that truly stands out' Crime Fiction Lover

'There are plenty of twists in the investigations to keep the reader guessing' *Book Oxygen*

'The twin investigations provide *The Hummingbird* with its narrative spine, but much of the story, which is translated by David Hackston, is engaged in exploring what it means to be Finnish, a place where "people were expected to unflaggingly present a play directed by market forces, a performance called Western civilisation"' Crime Always Pays

'Hiekkapelto does not forget to develop a decent plot and the crimes here are both complex; requiring a good deal of investigative shoe leather … I am already looking forward to the next installment of the series' Reactions to Reading

'I am really enjoying this burgeoning crime sub-genre of "social realism", in which I include British authors such as Eva Dolan, Rob Wilson and Stav Sherez. Hiekkapelto looks set to be joining their ranks with her debut novel … a writer with a wonderful imagination and use of language' Vicky Newham

The Defenceless

ABOUT THE AUTHOR

KATI HIEKKAPELTO is a bestselling author, punk singer, performance artist and special-needs teacher. She lives on an old farm on the island of Hailuoto in Northern Finland, where she is currently setting up a retreat for writers and artists in danger. Hiekkapelto has taught immigrants and lived in the Hungarian region of Serbia, which inspired her to write her highly regarded debut crime novel, *The Hummingbird*. Shortlisted for the Petrona Award, *The Hummingbird* has been published in six languages to date. *The Defenceless* won best Finnish Crime Novel of 2014. Kati is currently working on the third novel in the Anna Fekete series. Follow Kati on Twitter @HiekkapeltoKati or visit www.katihiekkapelto.com.

ABOUT THE TRANSLATOR

DAVID HACKSTON is a British translator of Finnish and Swedish literature and drama. Notable publications include *The Dedalus Book of Finnish Fantasy*, Maria Peura's coming-of-age novel *At the Edge of Light*, Johanna Sinisalo's eco-thriller *Birdbrain* and two crime novels by Matti Joensuu. In 2007 he was awarded the Finnish State Prize for Translation. David is also a professional countertenor and a founding member of the English Vocal Consort of Helsinki. David has translated both titles in the Anna Fekete series. Follow David on Twitter @Countertenorist.

The Defenceless

KATI HIEKKAPELTO

Translated from the Finnish by
David Hackston

ORENDA
BOOKS

Orenda Books
16 Carson Road
West Dulwich
London SE21 8HU
www.orendabooks.co.uk

First published in the United Kingdom by Orenda Books 2015
Originally published by Otava, Finland, as *Suojattomat* 2014

A catalogue record for this book is available from the British Library.

ISBN 978-1-910633-13-7

Typeset in Garamond by MacGuru Ltd
Printed and bound by CPI Group (UK) Ltd, Croydon CRO 4YY

Orenda Books is grateful for the financial support of FILI, who provided a translation grant for this project.

SALES & DISTRIBUTION

In the UK and elsewhere in Europe:
Turnaround Publisher Services
Unit 3, Olympia Trading Estate
Coburg Road, Wood Green
London N22 6TZ
www.turnaround-uk.com

In USA/Canada:
Trafalgar Square Publishing
Independent Publishers Group
814 North Franklin Street
Chicago, IL 60610
USA
www.ipgbook.com

For details of other territories, please contact *info@orendabooks.co.uk*

For Robert, Ilona and Aino

A humid wind blew through the pass, pushing back the hazy threat of the Afghan borderlands up ahead. The air shimmered in the glow of the sun; everything was silent. Something appeared from behind the horizon, at first only a speck, growing rapidly. It was a car, a jeep full of men. The barrels of rifles, deadly Mosin-Nagants and Kalashnikovs with bayonets, jutted like extensions of the men's silhouettes towards the sky, hidden behind the thick gauze of dust and sand kicked up behind the vehicle. The jeep was getting steadily closer and now, from amongst the men on the trailer at the back, a smaller figure came into view; black and slightly hunched. The jeep came to a halt. Two men with rifles jumped to the ground; one of them held out his hand and helped a woman shrouded in a burqa down from the trailer. She cautiously lifted her veil, a sliver of black lace covering her eyes. She didn't look around, simply followed the riflemen towards a whitewashed building.

Finnish Foreign Ministry
Pakistan: Travel Briefing

Violence and terror attacks possible throughout the country, particularly in the Afghan border regions. Visitors should avoid unnecessary travel to the area.

The situation in Pakistan remains unstable, and violence may erupt around the country for political, economical, social or religious reasons.

The risk of terrorist attacks, political unrest, violence and mass protest is particularly acute in Karachi, Peshawar, Lahore, Islamabad, Quetta and other large population centres. The risk is even greater in the Afghan borderlands, which travellers should avoid at all costs. Violence has escalated in Karachi in recent weeks. Travellers should exercise extreme caution throughout the country.

Travellers should not attempt to visit the tribal areas in the northeast of the country (Fata, including the Khyber Pass, Peshawar and the Swati Valley) or the province of Balochistan.

Pakistani blasphemy laws are extremely strict; contravention of these laws is punishable by death.

1

SAMMY HAD ARRIVED in Finland in the same manner and using the same route as the heroin that he knew so well, smuggled in to feed the hungry veins of Western Europeans: hidden in a truck belching thick exhaust fumes and driven across the endless steppes of Russia, illegally.

The heroin had continued on its way; Sammy had stayed put.

He applied for asylum, settled down in a reception centre, tried to kick the heroin and almost succeeded. He waited two years, four months and a week. Finally he received notice of his deportation. That's when he went underground, on to the streets – and discovered Subutex.

Beads of cold sweat glinted on Sammy's forehead and he could feel a headache coming on. He counted out his money: a measly banknote and a few euros in coins from the church's homeless fund. That should get him something, then he'd be able to think more clearly about where to score some more. Money always turned up, if you knew where to look. He collected bottles, worked unofficially at a pizzeria, cleaning and running errands for the owners. At least he hadn't had to sell himself, at least not often, and he hadn't resorted to real crime. He wasn't a criminal. He hated people who stole from the elderly, who broke into other people's houses. That's what he hated the most. Burglary. You shouldn't touch other people's houses. A home is a home. It's a place where you should feel safe. If he had been left in peace in his own home, if he had felt safe, none of this would have happened. He would be putting himself through school, planning his future career. On Sundays he would go to church and steal glances at the girl that was already arranged for him. She was beautiful. Her full, curved eyelashes cast shadows on her high cheekbones as she sensed his gaze and demurely lowered her own. The hint of a smile flickered on the girl's elegant face. It would be spring. Outside the air would be filled with the sound of birdsong; it would be warm, and the thousands of trees in the valley back home would be in full bloom.

A biting wind blew right through Sammy's clothes. The frozen ground was slippery and uneven, making it hard to walk. Earlier that day the sun had warmed him a little. He'd trudged around the edge of town, closed his eyes every now and then and raised his face to the sky, felt the glimmer of warmth on his cheeks. But in the evening winter mercilessly gripped him again and the temperature plummeted. The duffel coat he'd been given at the Salvation Army flea market wasn't very thick and he'd never heard of dressing in layers. He'd been on the streets for two months and it had been freezing cold the whole time. Did the winter and the cold never end? Where could he sleep tonight?

But first he had to find some subs. Bupe. Orange guys. *A dear child has many names.* In one of his Finnish classes they'd gone through Finnish proverbs and tried to come up with equivalents in their own languages. Sammy didn't know if there was any such saying back home, and the teacher had gently pressed him to think back. It felt like an eternity since that class.

Sammy trudged towards the Leppioja district. He'd met a dealer who lived there. A Finnish boy, a user himself, the same age as him. Sammy didn't much like Macke; there was something tense and volatile about him, something frightening, the agitated craziness of a substance abuser. But Macke almost always had some gear. Maybe Sammy could get a small discount. Maybe he could spend the night there. His headache was getting worse. Sammy quickened his step. The district was pretty far away, nothing but a few low-rise blocks of flats and a couple of isolated terraced houses in the middle of the woods. Not your average junkie area – there wasn't even a corner shop to rob. Sammy liked the silence; for some reason he was more afraid of being arrested in the city centre than anywhere else, though he realised he attracted more attention in areas where you didn't see all that many immigrants. The city's largest suburbs – Rajapuro, Koivuharju and Vaarala – were the best places. There was always plenty of gear about, and friends, even some of his compatriots. In the suburbs he could disappear altogether, and in a way these too were quiet places. Leppioja wasn't a big place. Maybe Macke's parents owned the flat and allowed their son to live there. Sammy couldn't think of any other reason for the flat's location, or why Macke hadn't yet been evicted.

The outer door was locked, of course. He couldn't let Macke know he was coming because he didn't have a mobile phone. This made scoring a fix pretty difficult, but Sammy was prepared to go to extra lengths, because, more than running out of Subutex, he was afraid of being caught by one of the police narcotics officers. One misplaced phone call or text message and he would leave a trace on the police radar like a hare's paw print in fresh snow. He had learnt to identify hares' tracks. There were lots of them around the city at night, a city that to his mind was nothing but an insignificant clearing in an endless forest right on the edge of the Siberian taiga. The city he had left behind had over a million inhabitants. Besides, constantly changing his phone and SIM card was expensive and brought with it another risk: visiting shops. Sammy didn't want to show his face anywhere that there might be a security camera.

This time he risked it. He waited by the front door. Maybe someone would turn up and he'd be able to sneak inside. He tried to remain calm but kept glancing around restlessly. Could anyone see him? The adjacent low-rise building wasn't very close. Between the buildings there were a few thick spruce trees and bushes coated in frost, a children's playground and the ground, frozen and hard. The few lampposts weren't powerful enough to light the whole garden. People in the surrounding apartments were still awake, but from their lit windows they wouldn't be able to see down into the yard.

Sammy wasn't entirely hidden in the shadows. The bright, hexagonal lamp above the door to the stairwell was like a searchlight. The hue of the light made his warm, dark skin look blue.

He felt as though he were on a stage and started to feel uneasy. It had been too long since his last hit. He had tried to keep his usage under control, injecting just enough to help him cope with the constant fear and the freezing nights. He would quit as soon as he got things sorted out. It would be easy, because he wasn't really hooked. But now he could feel the tremors starting. It was so terribly cold. He felt like smashing the window, shouting out. He had to get inside. Macke would sort him out. Just then, the lights in the stairwell flickered into life. Sammy stood up straight, took a few steps back and tried to affect a friendly, carefree expression, though he knew it was pointless. Out here he would never blend into the crowds, just another part of the blissfully identical pink-skinned masses; his black eyes and dark skin dug into Finnish eyes like a spike. And that's precisely why it was important to try and look friendly. Even the slightest inkling of danger from someone like him would have people reaching for their phones and calling the police.

A man appeared in the stairwell, not very old but not young either. It was so difficult to gauge the age of Finnish people. The man was stylish, tall and wearing a dark woollen jacket and hat. But he didn't look particularly wealthy. His clothes were old. Sammy had been watching people for such a long time, indeed, his whole life, that he'd learnt to smell money and friendship and danger. And this time he smelt danger. Just as the man was about to open the door, Sammy forced a smile to his face and stepped up to the door as if he had just arrived and was still fumbling in his pocket for the key, though he was afraid he looked like he was about to vomit. What a stroke of luck. And a very good evening to you too. Godspeed to you and your family. He would have said something, if he'd been able. He settled for a smile and hoped his tremors weren't too obvious. The man glowered at him, said something in a gruff voice. Sammy pointed upwards and smiled like an idiot. The man stood in the doorway staring at him sceptically. Sammy noticed the man's hesitation. The sense of danger evaporated. Again he pointed upstairs, this time plucking up the courage to say the word *friend*. The man glanced into the stairwell just as the automatic light switched off. As if expelled by the dark, he pulled the door wide open, strode outside and disappeared without looking back. Sammy slipped into the darkness of the corridor.

Vilho Karppinen was tired. He had felt terribly queasy all evening and had almost fallen asleep in front of the television on more than a few occasions. He had forced himself to go to bed, but now he couldn't get to sleep because of the infernal din going on somewhere nearby. He couldn't make out melodies, but the thump of the bass was so powerful that it seemed to travel through the girders of the building, along his bedposts and straight into his ears. It was as though the whole bed was trembling. Sometimes the noise stopped and Vilho almost nodded off, but then it started up again and wrenched him from sleep once again. It had happened before. Vilho had expected that the troublemaker would eventually get a warning, but apparently that hadn't happened. The cacophony went on and on, not every night, but now and then. Didn't it disturb anybody else? These damn kids get to keep everyone awake through the night without anyone batting an eyelid! Well, this time it's going to stop. He would go down and tell them to switch off the racket – you couldn't call it music. If they didn't listen to him, he'd call the police. He decided to make an official complaint to the housing association first thing in the morning. The noisy kids would be evicted and he'd be able to sleep in peace and quiet. He needed the little sleep he got – and as an old man he was more than entitled to it.

Vilho gingerly got up and sat on the edge of the bed. Again he felt a dizzy whirr in his head. It'll settle down, he thought and stood up, pattered into the hallway and groaned as he pulled on his slippers. Why did he suddenly feel so doddery? When had this started? Only a few winters ago he'd been skiing at the cottage. Or was it longer than that? Dressed in his pyjamas he went into the stairwell, left his door ajar, didn't switch on the lights and listened to hear where the noise was coming from. It was one floor down. Probably the apartment where that young tearaway lived. Vilho didn't know the boy, but he'd seen him in the corridor once or twice. The boy never said hello and never looked him in the eyes. Suspicious lad. But at least he's in the same stairwell, Vilho thought with relief; he wouldn't have to put his coat on.

Vilho took the stairs down to the first floor and gave the doorbell a resolute ping. The door opened and in a flash he was yanked inside. A fist gripped his nightshirt, pulling the fabric so hard that it tightened around his back.

'What the fuck you doing creeping around out there, Grandad?'

The young man held Vilho close to his face. Vilho caught the smell of alcohol and saw his neighbour's eyes for the first time, their pupils nothing but tiny black dots. He knew this had been a mistake. He should have called the police straight away instead of trying to play the hero. Sometimes he simply forgot his age, no matter how dizzy he felt, how weak he had become or how often he looked at the grey, shrivelled prune of a man staring back at him from the mirror.

'Could you turn the music down a little?' said Vilho. 'I need to get some sleep. That's all.'

'But we're trying to fucking listen to it,' the boy replied and began dragging Vilho further into the living room. Vilho tried to resist. He felt faint. He tried to pull the boy's fists loose, but he was powerless against the strength of youth, now so buoyed up with chemicals. Vilho tried to hit him, but his own fists were like leather gloves dried on the radiator: useless, pathetic clumps. Amid the chaos of the living room, the boy released his grip. Vilho gasped for breath. He saw another boy sitting on the couch, a dark boy with languid, good-hearted eyes, not threatening at all. Perhaps he'd get through this after all.

'I don't mean any trouble,' said Vilho. 'I just wanted to come and say that the music is disturbing me because I live right above you.'

'Shut it, old man. Think you're the boss in this house, do you? Always spying on other people. Never a moment's peace round here, the fucking codgers are always breathing down our necks.'

The boy on the couch said something in a limp voice. Vilho didn't understand a word, but he noted the boy's conciliatory tone. This would all work out. He turned to leave. Just then a wave of dizziness came over him and his legs buckled beneath him. Vilho grabbed the first lad for support. The boy bellowed angrily and clocked him in the face with his fist. Vilho fell to the floor, knocking his head on the edge of the table. Blood gushed on to the stinking living-room rug, forming a pool between an empty syringe and a can of beer.

'Shit, I've killed him!' said the boy and started to snigger. Vilho's consciousness gradually began to fade, but he had time to see the boy stare at him, first with a look of amusement, then more seriously. The boy searched for Vilho's pulse but couldn't find one.

'He's fucking dead!' he hollered at the boy on the couch. 'We've got to do something. Get up, you Paki bastard, move your stinking arse. We've got to do something. Fast!'

2

THE EARLY MORNING was still dark. Senior Constable Anna Fekete had woken with a start; she'd been dreaming about something terrible, but now she couldn't remember what. Her sheets were damp with clammy sweat. Anna took a hot shower and made herself some tea for a change; she drank quite enough coffee at work. Sipping her tea, she sat reading the morning paper, listening to the sounds of the building wakening around her. Her neighbour was in the shower; the sound of rushing came from the pipes next to the kitchen. There was a thud somewhere. It occurred to her that she didn't know any of her neighbours. People in the stairwell greeted her, polite but distant, but who were they, what did they do for a living, what kind of dreams did they have, what moments of joy, what pains? Anna knew nothing of their lives. She couldn't even connect the names on the letterboxes to the right faces. But it was fine by her. She had no yearning for communal living, she had no desire to take part in shared gardening activities or local committee meetings held in the building's clubroom.

For Anna, community spirit was nothing but an illusion, and an over-rated one at that. The only people that actively sought it out were people who had never experienced it first hand. In the West it seemed that mercilessly scrutinising other people's business, sticking your nose into private matters, and people's often violent attempts to preserve their personal freedoms were considered charming forms of care and concern without which all social ills flourished. Anna found it irritating. It wasn't long since the greatest concern for Finnish people was what others, neighbours, relatives, people in the village, thought and said about them. People had allowed their lives to be shaped to fit society's expectations; they were afraid of rejection, and in their fear they had accepted a fate imposed on them from outside. How many people had spent their whole lives suffering because of this? Is that what we should go back to? If her brother Ákos returned to Serbia, would he be more depressed than he was now, Anna wondered, more of a drunk? Was that why he wanted to stay in Finland?

Anna glanced at the clock, pulled on a pair of skinny jeans and an old hoodie, and decided to cycle to work despite the biting frost. She put on a thermal jacket, her hat and gloves. It felt crazy, the habit people round here had of cycling to work come rain or shine, of risking the freezing weather and potentially fatal, slippery roads, balanced precariously on two thin wheels. Her family back home would be shocked if they knew, but Anna had come to enjoy cycling in the winter. With a good set of studded tyres and a helmet, the snow didn't slow her down at all. It did her good to get some fresh air before starting work, to wake her limbs, still stiff from sleep.

'Anna, I've got a special assignment for you,' said Chief Inspector Pertti Virkkunen at the morning meeting of the Violent Crimes Unit.

'What's that?'

Esko Niemi fetched his third cup of coffee of the morning, Sari Jokikokko-Pennanen was eating a sandwich and doodling along the margins of her notepad, Nils Näkkäläjärvi was drinking a cup of tea. Virkkunen's expression was stern.

'We've picked up a Hungarian girl.'

'Oh. What's she done?'

'We'll be investigating this as a case of causing death by dangerous driving. She ran someone over last night.'

'Oh dear. Had she been drinking?'

'No.'

'Drugs?'

'Nothing that showed up in the patrol officer's initial breathalyser. We've sent blood samples to be tested.'

'Was she speeding?'

'We don't know that yet. In any case, she doesn't speak a word of Finnish, and her English is pretty weak, so it's best if you take care of the interview.'

'Of course!'

A tingle of nerves rippled through Anna's stomach. A Hungarian girl. An interview in Hungarian. Would she be able to do it? How did you say 'injured party' in Hungarian? What about 'involuntary manslaughter'? There were so many words in her native language that she couldn't remember or that she'd never even heard. Where could she find all the relevant technical terms and phrases? Her mother knew a lawyer back home; perhaps she should contact him.

'Well, get going then. We can't keep her locked up forever.'

'What? Right now?'

'Yes.'

'Who's the deceased? Where did the accident happen? When? I can't go in there not knowing anything about the case.'

'Last night, just after midnight, near Kangassara on the road leading out of the city, right on the edge of town. The victim was an elderly man. He was only wearing his pyjamas. We still haven't got an ID on him. Sari can start looking around to see if anyone matching the description has been reported missing. Here are the initial photographs from the scene.'

Anna looked at the photographs spread out on the desk. The body and the blood spatter looked horrific; she doubted whether she would ever get used to images like this. Which was worse: to be so numbed to violence and the sight of bloodied corpses that you didn't feel anything, or to be distressed by it every time?

'There's an old folks' home out near Kangassara, isn't there? The victim could have wandered off in the night.'

'Maybe. Things like that happen all the time, but they don't usually end up under a car.'

'Normally they freeze to death,' said Sari.

Esko hadn't said anything. Everyone in the room had noticed his reddened eyes and the faint tremor of his coffee cup, but nobody said anything, not even Virkkunen. Perhaps he'd worked out how long it was until Esko's retirement and decided it was too late to change him. Besides, Esko always did his job and wasn't in the habit of taking days off sick, though nobody understood how this was possible given how obvious it was he'd been hitting the bottle. Anna had started to think that maybe some people simply needed alcohol to survive, to postpone death, to make waiting for death that bit more bearable, to numb their pain, to brighten their mundane day-to-day lives, to pep them up, to splash some colour against the greyness of routine, to provide release, self-deceit, self-destruction. Not everybody could be sporty health-freaks in top physical condition. Society needed the drunk, the obese, the depressed, as examples to the rest of us and to provide statistics with which to frighten people. And to this end, alcohol was the perfect weapon.

I wonder how Ákos is doing, Anna wondered. She knew her brother had been drinking for at least a week now.

'Good job we can deal with this without an interpreter,' said Virkkunen. 'I'll call the boys upstairs and tell them to take the girl into the interview room.'

'*Jó reggelt, Fekete Anna vagyok*,' Anna introduced herself.

'*Farkas Gabriella, kezét csókolom*,' the young woman responded formally, making Anna feel awkward. Nobody had ever addressed her like that before. 'I kiss your hand'. That's what you said to old folk or people who were clearly in a higher position than you. And for the first time Anna realised that that's exactly what she was in this job. A superior, the holder of power. She had power over this person. Of course, not all power; thankfully there were laws and regulations in place to protect the rights of individuals and to define the extent of the police's jurisdiction, but in this instance, as in most other work situations, the balance of power lay with her. A simple greeting, one that she happily used when she was visiting elderly relatives back home without giving it a second thought, had suddenly revealed something about the nature of her work that she'd never appreciated before. This was the power of words, she thought – the link between our native tongue and how we understand the world. How many other things remained hidden from her, concealed behind words without a mother tongue?

Anna noticed that Gabriella was waiting. She began by recapping what she already knew about the case and asked whether this was correct. Gabriella nodded.

'Where were you going?'

'Kangassara. That's where I live. I'm an au pair with a family out there.'

'How long have you been an au pair?'

'Just over ten months.'

'And you're staying for a year?'

'Yes.'

'Where are you from originally?'

'*Budapesti vagyok. És te?*'

'*Én vajdasági magyar vagyok, Magyarkanizsáról.*'

'Cool! I have friends nearby in Erdély but I've never been to Vajdaság. Have you lived in Finland long?'

'Since I was a child. I'll ask the questions, okay?' Anna said, trying to sound friendly.

'Oh, yes, of course. I haven't spoken Hungarian for ten months, except on Skype,' replied Gabriella, a little embarrassed.

'I know the feeling. But let's get back to business. Where were you driving from?'

'The university. Well, the student village really. I was at a party.'

'And your breathalyser test was negative.'

'That's right, I don't drink if I have to drive. I don't drink much anyway.'

'And had you taken anything else?'

'No. But I was listening to music.'

'Well, that's certainly not illegal.'

'I was completely lost in it. Hungarian folk music,' Gabriella said quietly.

'Tell me in your own words, as carefully as you can, exactly what happened.'

Gabriella seemed to stiffen. She was clearly holding back tears, didn't look Anna in the eyes but stared off into the distance, breathing in fits. Then in an anxious voice and swallowing back her tears, she explained how she had seen the man lying in the road but that the car hadn't obeyed her, how it had continued sliding forwards. It felt like it took an eternity, though in reality the whole sequence of events must have lasted no longer than a few seconds. How the man seemed to get closer and closer, and she was unable to do anything about it. The sound of the thump as he struck the car. How she momentarily lost control of the car and feared more for her own life than for that of the man.

'Will I go to prison?' she asked, by now weeping.

'First we'll have to establish how fast you were driving. If you weren't over the speed limit, there's probably nothing to worry about. Of course, you should bear in mind that the speed of a vehicle should always be regulated according to the prevailing driving conditions. The roads were very slippery last night.'

'I'm not used to driving in weather like this, but they told me the car had a good set of winter tyres.'

'Whose car is it?'

'My host family's second car. I'm allowed to use it to get about. Will I ever get home? Look at me, always thinking of myself instead of others.'

'You'll have to stay in Finland for the duration of the investigation and possible trial. Let's think about that once we know which … charges are going to be pressed or whether you'll be charged at all.'

Anna had to think for a moment how to talk about pressing charges. I must get myself a legal dictionary next time I'm at home, she thought. *A büdös fene*, I don't even know how to tell her she's suspected of reckless driving! At worst, I could be found guilty of misconduct. I should have insisted on an interpreter – and at the same time I might as well admit to my colleagues that I can't speak my own mother tongue any more.

'At least he was an old man,' Gabriella woke Anna from her thoughts. 'If it had been a child, I don't think I could bear it. I'd kill myself.'

'Well,' said Anna, 'thankfully it wasn't a child. But you say the man was already lying in the road when you noticed him?'

'That's right.'

'So he wasn't walking along the road?'

'No, he was lying there. At first I didn't even realise it was a person, it just looked like a dark heap in the road, a pile of gravel or something, a rubbish bag.'

'Was he moving?'

'I don't know. Probably not. At least I don't remember him moving.'

'Do you remember how the man was lying before you hit him?'

'No. It was so terrible, so unreal. All I knew was that the heap was getting closer and that it was a man after all. Wait, he might have been lying on his side. I think I remember seeing his face; it was like he was staring me right in the eyes. But I'm probably wrong or I'm just imagining it. Who was he?'

'We don't know that yet. It's likely he was a dementia patient who had run away and got lost. You see people like that wandering about in strange places.'

'Did he have a heart attack?'

'Perhaps, or he might have fallen over. The autopsy will tell us what happened.'

'The relatives are going to hate me.'

Anna didn't have the heart to tell her that this was very likely.

'But I can't believe you're Hungarian too. How great is that!' said Gabriella. 'I'd never get through this if I had to try and speak English.'

'You would be assigned an interpreter.'

'You're far better than an interpreter. I want you.'

Though she might have wanted to, Anna was unable to say anything in reply.

Esko Niemi was standing outside the police station smoking a cigarette. He was thinking of the case the National Bureau of Investigation had assigned him. Jesus Christ. Working as a dogsbody for those idiots in suits annoyed him. He didn't want to take orders from anyone but Virkkunen, and even those orders generally pissed him off. Things had started to irritate him more and more recently, and Esko didn't really know why. Something was bugging him, something he couldn't put his finger on. He felt as though he'd been driven into a corner, trapped in a cage. He'd felt troubled like this before, though he didn't want to think about that, let alone admit it to himself. What if he just sold his apartment, bought a house in the woods, withdrew into the peace and quiet? He didn't need all that much in the way of modern conveniences. Running water would be good, he'd need a small kitchen and a place to put his bed, a sauna and a fireplace.

Living without electricity might be a bit too basic – he wasn't moving to a Siberian gulag. Maybe he could install a few solar panels; they were fairly cheap, though the people that normally bought them were generally your typical green-fingered eco-warriors. He could give it a try. There were a couple of small panels at Virkkunen's summer cottage too. Esko visited Virkkunen there at least once every summer, and together they went fishing and relaxed. Those panels were enough to run a couple of lamps and charge up the laptop. A boat on the shore, a decent barbecue, a simple life far away from everything. Damn, it would be great. Esko felt a burning in his chest. He rubbed the spot with a clenched fist. The pain seemed to singe his dreams. He was no longer a young man, but surely he still had time to do something other than wading through the endless mire of the criminal world. But before that he would show the rookies at the NBI how an experienced policeman does his job, Esko thought. This case would be his grand finale. Then he could disappear, ride off into the sunset, leaving the dust to settle behind him. Esko smoked his cigarette right up to the filter, stamped the stub into the ground and lit another one. After finishing it, he went up to Anna's office.

'Pack your lipstick and tampons. We're off to investigate the scene of an accident,' he said.

'Come up with something new, will you?'

'I'm trying,' Esko grunted. 'You know I am,' he muttered more to himself than to her.

Anna and Esko took the lift down to the depot beneath the police station, checked out a light-blue Ford civilian car and drove into the city. The sun gleamed in the cloudless sky. Exhaust fumes gave off steam in the frosted air, the silhouettes of buildings rising up majestically against the radiant blue of the sky. The tall piles of snow at the side of the road were dirty and grey. That's what my lungs will look like when I'm older if I don't quit smoking, Anna thought. Still, we all have to die of something, so why not lung cancer? She tried not to think unpleasant thoughts of hospital beds, painkillers and oxygen masks, but focussed on watching the crowds of people, which became sparser as they made their way out of the city and headed towards Kangassara. The urban landscape turned to forest, and after a bend in the road they saw the car that the police had moved to the verge during the night. The area was cordoned off with police tape. They pulled up by the side of the road, far enough away from the scene of the accident not to disturb any evidence.

Anna stepped out of the car. The icy surface of the road glinted in the bright sunshine. Seen from a distance, the car Gabriella had been driving didn't seem to have sustained any visible damage, but any closer investigation was a job for one of the vehicular specialists on the traffic-accident investigation team. What a job title, thought Anna; compared to that, senior constable sounded almost human. The car would soon be transferred to the MOT inspection office and all imaginable data regarding the road surface, the friction force, the condition of the tyres, any braking marks and damage to the car would be collated and compared to the injuries and impact marks on the victim, and to the photographs and sketches of the scene taken by forensics, after which the investigation team would sift through the data, analyse it on their computers and give a statement about the sequence of events. Anna often wondered how the police seemed to have so much specialised expertise at its fingertips. She found it fascinating and was continually taken aback by it, perhaps because it gave her a tantalising sense that her career was in constant development, that it would never stagnate.

The thick spruce forest was silent, the dark-green gloom of its branches extinguishing any light reflected from the snow. Anna looked closely at the forest. Nobody would be able to walk through that thicket, she thought. The man must have been wandering along the road.

'I'll drive on a kilometre or so and walk back to meet you,' said Esko. 'Let's try and work out what direction the old boy was coming from.'

'Okay. Then we'll examine the ground in the immediate vicinity.'

Esko glanced at the dense spruce wood and sniffed. 'Nobody could walk around in there,' he said, repeating Anna's own summation, before getting back in his car and driving off.

Anna stood on the spot for a moment. She listened to the fading hum of Esko's car but could no longer hear when it stopped and when Esko slammed the door shut. He must have driven quite a distance, she thought. I wonder if I should go back a bit. She quickly strode about half a kilometre back towards the city, turned and began slowly walking forwards, closely examining the road as she went. Every now and then she saw animal tracks in the soft snow on the verge. The surface of the road was so icy that someone out walking a dog wouldn't have left any footprints – or had the dog been loose, a runaway, just like the old man might have been? Then two footprints: one in a heap of snow by the verge, the other sunk further into the drift with deep paw impressions all around it.

The snow still hadn't crusted over, thought Anna. She still couldn't go skiing across the fields. The human footprints were small. The dog had been out here with someone, a woman or a child, she concluded. The dog had caught the scent of a hare and raced off into the forest, dragging its owner with it. These weren't the old man's footprints, she thought, as she continued on her way, there's nothing here; the road is too icy. She could see the police tape up ahead. Despite the icy conditions, the car Gabriella had been driving had left skid marks, though they were barely visible. Nothing sticks to a surface like this, thought Anna and looked at the blood spatter on the ground. That had stuck, that much was certain; blood and everything that had sprayed out of the old man upon impact had soaked into the ice, melting large, dark-red pools into its surface. The blood had seeped gruesomely into the surrounding snow.

Esko soon joined her. He was visibly out of breath.

'You should cut back on the cigarettes,' she commented.

'Why the hell should I?' he snapped, fumbled in his jacket pocket and lit another one. 'Let's check out that thicket and cut the bullshit, if that's alright by Miss Moral High Ground?'

Anna laughed. She felt as though, in a very peculiar way, she sometimes even liked Esko.

They clambered in among the spruces. At first their legs sunk up to their knees in snow. Then, though there wasn't much snow beneath the trees, the thick tangle of branches made it hard to walk. There was no way a feeble old man could have reached the road this way. And there are no prints here either, not even animal tracks, Anna noted just before she saw a bounding hare's tracks in the soft snow. That's what the dog must have been chasing; it would have run off after its prey if it hadn't been on a leash. Anna examined every tree trunk for a strip of fabric, a hair, anything at all. But she could see nothing.

'It's odd,' she said to Esko, as they returned to the road and dusted the snow from their legs.

'What is?'

'Well, the fact that there are no tracks round here. Nothing to suggest where the victim was coming from.'

'I don't think it's all that odd. If the old boy was doddering around in the road or on the verge, there wouldn't be any tracks. Everything's iced over, and ice is pretty damned hard.'

'I suppose. But it's still odd.'

'You'll have to apply for more details on the Hungarian driver,' said Esko. 'Virkkunen's orders.'

'How am I going to do that? I don't know how to apply for details like that.'

'For crying out loud, you know how to use the telephone and you can stammer something in your own language. Either that or send an email.'

'Back at the station I could barely remember how to say "press charges". And who am I supposed to call? There are probably more police officers in Hungary than there are people in this city.'

'Ask Virkkunen. You'd better check out her residence permit while you're at it.'

'Listen, you're perfectly capable of doing that yourself. Any news on the identity of the victim?'

'Sari just sent a message saying she'd come up with nothing. Nobody matching the description has been reported missing. She's ringing round all the local hospitals and care facilities.'

'Judging by the photographs, the man's pyjamas weren't issued by a hospital. Besides, surely these places would notice if someone has gone missing?'

'You'd be surprised at the things people do and don't notice in these places.'

'I'm not surprised at all, sadly.'

Anna thought of her own grandmother, who lived with her father's sister, Anna's aunt. Grandma drank a small glass of home-made *pálinka* every morning. Apparently it helped her circulation and kept her mind in good order, and Anna certainly had no reason to disagree. Grandma was over ninety, she'd survived the wars, she'd seen plenty of sorrow in her life, not least the loss of her son, her grandson and her husband, but somehow she always managed to remain happy and content with her life. Back home people didn't hide their old folk out of sight, didn't send them to care homes to lose their minds. Back home they were treated with respect and greeted with the words *kezét csókolom*, 'I kiss your hand'.

'It's late and I'm starving,' said Esko. 'What say we go back to town for a bite to eat?' he suggested.

'Good idea,' Anna replied. She hadn't eaten a proper meal all day.

A match flared in the darkness. The ember of a cigarette began to glow, then another. Jenni and Katri, both ninth-graders at the Ketoniemi secondary school, peered behind the tree to make sure nobody was coming. Jenni had stolen the cigarettes from her mum's boyfriend and sent a message to her best friend Katri, who lived next door. The girls had told their parents they were going for a walk. Pinching the cigarettes had been easy, Jenni explained. Mum and her boyfriend had been watching TV; the boyfriend's jacket was hanging in the hallway and the fags were in his pocket. To top it all off, the packet was suitably half full. If it had been full, two missing cigarettes would have been obvious, but if it had been almost empty, taking two would have cleaned it out. A half-full packet was best; nobody would notice a thing. Jenni knew this all too well, because she'd been caught stealing cigarettes from an almost empty packet before.

The girls dragged hungrily at their cigarettes in the woodland just behind their houses, gossiped about their stupid teachers, the cute guy, Ilari, in their year and all the other important things that fifteen-year-olds talk about. They spat in the heaps of ploughed snow. Once they'd finished their cigarettes, they decided to hang out at the shopping mall, see if there was anyone there, though they doubted it. It was dead on Thursday evenings. In fact, it was always pretty dead at the mall. The youth centre had been closed due to cutbacks and the only people at the shops were families with little kids and the local drunks loitering outside – there was never anyone around. But they needed to get rid of the smell of smoke before going home, so they had to take a walk somewhere no matter what. They decided to walk through the woods, though the snow made walking quite difficult, their toes froze and their Converse trainers were soaked.

'What's that?' said Katri and stopped in her tracks.

'What?'

'That on the ground.' Katri pointed towards a large pine tree. Something lay on the snow beneath the branches.

Jenni stepped closer.

'Oh my God,' she shrieked. 'Look at this!'

It was a knife. Not just a normal breadknife, but a weapon with a curved blade. It was covered in blood.

'Look,' Katri whispered and pointed at the ground about two metres from the knife. A cloud of steam billowed from her mouth into the frozen air.

The snow was soaked in blood. In the darkening evening it looked almost black.

'Has someone been killed?'

'D'you think we should call the police?'

'I'll be fucking grounded if my mum finds out we've been out here smoking.'

'So what are we going to do?'

'I don't know. Let's go to the mall and think.'

'Oh God, I'm scared. What if the killer is still here?'

The girls stood listening to the darkening forest around them. At first it was perfectly quiet, all they could hear was the sound of their frightened breathing. There came a crackle from the trees, then another.

'Let's get out of here,' Katri whispered, terrified.

The girls broke into a sprint. They ran through the woods, paying no attention to the branches slapping against their faces. Jenni tripped in the snow and began to cry; she shouted for Katri to wait, but got up quickly and continued running. Back to the safety of the houses and the lights, out of this terrifying forest where a crazed killer was on the loose. Soon they were standing in the yard outside the shopping mall. They ran up to one of the pubs, because it was the only place with people around, leant on the wall and glanced around, gasping for breath. Nobody had followed them out of the woods. The mall was deserted; there was nobody in sight.

'What do we do now?' asked Jenni.

A drunken woman staggered out of the pub and lit a cigarette. Soon afterwards a man appeared and began hitting on the woman.

'Let's go to my place,' said Katri. 'We can think what to say about this. If we talk to my mum first, then maybe your parents won't start asking about the cigarettes.'

Anna's studded trainers gripped the icy path. The frosted air tingled pleasantly at the back of her throat. The running track through the woods behind Koivuharju had been turned into a skiing track, so Anna had to run along the cycle paths. She enjoyed skiing too, but for that she needed a stretch of ice covering the open sea and the sight of a distant horizon, the bright, clearly defined contour of the skyline. Anna didn't like pre-prepared skiing trails through the woods. The aimless freedom of vast expanses of ice, that's what she wanted to find on her weekend-morning skiing trips that took her kilometres from the shore.

Her run that evening was fast and short: half an hour at full pace, then home to shower and smoke a cigarette. She'd managed to keep her New Year's resolution – only one a day – though she'd made the promise with a cigarette in her mouth, tipsy with champagne, as the fireworks from the town hall in Kanizsa crackled and fizzed above her, diamonds, balls, glitter and coloured stars all exploding across the sky, people laughing, hugging and wishing each other a happy New Year. Réka's circle of friends, many of whom Anna had known since they were at nursery school together, had organised a party. They had reserved a pub on the outskirts of town, ordered food from a catering service, played hits from the 90s, danced and drank the night away. Just before midnight they had gone into the town centre to watch the fireworks, like most people in Kanizsa on New Year's

Eve. Her mother had been there too, with her own friends. Anna had never seen fireworks this spectacular in Finland. In Kanizsa there were sometimes displays of fireworks in the middle of summer. For Anna it was one of the most exhilarating things in the world, an unexpected set of fireworks on a warm, dark summer's night. She hadn't seen Ákos among the partygoers.

At the party she'd also met Béci, a boy who used to hide Anna's satchel and pull her hair when they were in first grade. Béci had been living in Budapest for the last ten years and Anna hadn't seen him since she'd left; until that moment she'd forgotten he existed. But he had remembered Anna. After the fireworks had ended they bought some beer from a kiosk and walked down to the chilly banks of the Tisza and sat on the old swings suspended on metal chains, garish flakes of red, yellow and green paint flaking from the wooden seats. They reminisced about their childhood as the rusted bolts gave ear-splitting shrieks beneath their combined weight. When Anna began to feel cold, they'd snuck back to Béci's parents' house and up to the boy's bedroom on the top floor, a room that hadn't been decorated in at least ten years. The next morning Béci's mother had insisted on cooking breakfast and Anna couldn't bring herself to decline. It was embarrassing. It felt like being fifteen again.

Anna nervously crushed the stub of her cigarette into the ashtray and wanted to light another one. She'd had to go home with him, hadn't she? Now Béci had tried to contact her in Finland, too; Réka had given him Anna's email address and telephone number. *A fene egye meg.*

She forced herself to forget the idea of a second cigarette, went back inside and agonised over whether or not to call Ákos. Eventually she called him. Her brother was drunk, but not too much, and said he was at home by himself watching TV, the television Anna had given him. Anna couldn't hear the sound of the television. She asked whether Ákos had remembered to apply for his unemployment benefit, whether there was food in the cupboard and whether he'd had a shower. Yes, yes, everything was fine, Ákos was just cutting down on his drinking, he'd almost stopped altogether, he hadn't drunk much, everything was fine. *A kurva életbe*, Anna cursed under her breath as she ended the call. I've become a mother to my own older brother.

3

'SEEMS THE OLD MAN hadn't run away after all. I called all the local care facilities yesterday,' Sari told Anna.

It was five past eight. The Violent Crimes Unit was starting its daily work, the photocopier whirred into life, the coffee machine gurgled, office lights switched on one by one, computers booted up. On the surface it was like an average day in any office. There was nothing to suggest that in these drab offices, with their non-descript furniture, people spent their time investigating acts which had their roots in the darkest recesses of the human mind.

'That means he must have wandered off from his own home. I hope a relative notices something soon,' Anna replied.

'Let's hope so. It makes me think of a few old people we've found mummified. They'd been lying dead for years and nobody noticed a thing.' Sari yawned. The kids had woken her up at five and started playing.

'Cases like that are rare exceptions. Let's give it a few days; someone's bound to call us worried that their grandfather has gone missing. They'll probably call today.'

'I hope so. I visited Rauno yesterday, by the way,' said Sari.

'Oh. How is he?'

'He's on sick leave until the end of April, goes to physiotherapy a few times a week. He's coming along well, though it's a long road to recovery. Apparently his left knee is in constant pain, and it'll be a weak spot for the rest of his life.'

Senior Constable Rauno Forsman had been seriously injured when his car collided with an elk the previous autumn. Anna remembered the sight of her colleague, battered from the crash, as he lay in intensive care; how she'd wished she could be in his place, in a coma, forever. She gave a shiver. At the time, she had been suffering from acute insomnia and was so tired that she'd started to wonder whether she was even capable of carrying out her duties as a police officer.

'So we can forget the Achilles heel; from now it'll be known as Forsman's knee,' commented Nils as he walked into the staffroom. His dark hair was still tousled with sleep. Nils was actually quite cute, Anna noticed and stole a glance at the golden ring gleaming on the ring finger of his left hand.

'What about Nina?' asked Anna.

'She wasn't at home. I didn't want to pry. Still, you wouldn't believe how the girls have grown. Rauno sends his regards to everybody, and said you should all pop in some time. Make sure you do; the poor guy seems bored to tears.'

'I'll have to stop in,' said Nils.

'Yes, me too,' said Anna, though she knew she wouldn't go.

'Where's Esko?' asked Nils.

'He was here before seven this morning, working that case the NBI was asking for help with.'

'What case is that?'

'Some foreign street gang that's trying to establish itself round here,' said Sari.

'That's all we need,' said Nils. 'I hope I won't be drafted in to help them.'

'I doubt it. We've got our work cut out with our own motorbike gangs, don't you think?' said Sari with another yawn.

Anna went into her own office and switched on her computer. She had to write up a few reports, then later that afternoon conduct interviews about a suspected assault. Nothing special; she'd get it all done in good time. But what should I do this evening, she wondered. The idea of a lonely Friday evening in her lonely apartment wasn't appealing. Should she go into town, to a pub? She might ask the pathologist Linnea Markkula to join her.

Anna hadn't gone out once in her free time since the Christmas break. This looked like it was going to be the start of yet another weekend when she would do nothing but exercise and wait for Monday morning to arrive. Was she really going to be only thirty-one that summer? She felt much older, with one foot in the grave of her suburban apartment. She yearned for Réka's uncomplicated company, everyday chat about everyday things, long walks across the *puszta* that opened up between Zimonić and Velebit, the *járás* as they called it, a place where sheep grazed, herded by a shepherd skilfully using his dogs to guide them. The view could have been a hundred years old, if only the shepherd hadn't occasionally been seen playing with his mobile phone, listening to music with a set of in-ear headphones, and if their walks hadn't been cut short by the ploughing that tore the plains open, making them impossible to cross on foot. Churned fields were swallowing up the *puszta* one strip at a time; farmers were still ploughing the land in December. The pastures were getting smaller and smaller, and the wild animals no longer felt at home in the industrialised landscape; even the shepherd used his mobile to look for a better job.

A knock at the door brought Anna back to the here and now. Virkkunen stepped inside.

'A squad car was called out to the woodland behind Ketoniemi last night. They found a knife and a lot of blood, as though an animal had been slaughtered.'

'Is this another job for us?' asked Anna.

'Maybe. Forensics are on the way there now.'

'Perhaps someone killed an animal out there? Or there was a fight and someone got hurt?'

'We haven't had any new reports of an assault.'

'If this was a fight between two drunkards, I doubt they'd come down to the station and press charges.'

'Still, it's not a place you'd expect drunks to hang out.'

'Surely people go out there drinking sometimes?'

'Call round the hospitals all the same and ask if they've seen anyone injured in a stabbing. And check the health centres too.'

'Sari has just called them all regarding the old man in the traffic accident. If only we'd known, she could have asked about this too.'

'The information just came in. Could you get on to this today?'

'Very well.'

'How are you otherwise?'

'Excuse me?'

'In general. Work, life?'

Anna felt awkward. She didn't consider Virkkunen a particularly close acquaintance, though she'd had to tell him things about herself that she hadn't wanted to share with anyone. Once her position had been made permanent in January, Virkkunen had asked about her sleeping problems, the panic attacks she'd had as a child and all manner of other things: her past, her plans for the future. Indeed, what *were* her plans for the future, Anna found herself thinking long after the conversation.

'Everything's fine,' she said with a smile. It's true enough, she thought. There's nothing the matter with me.

Anna's mobile beeped. An unknown number was flashing on the screen. Virkkunen left the room with a wave of the hand.

'Fekete Anna,' she answered in an official mode.

'*Szia, Anna. Itt Gabriella, emlékszel?*'

Remember her? How could Anna have forgotten her? She had interviewed Gabriella only yesterday. The girl had been released soon afterwards. Initial tests had revealed her speed at the time of the crash to be around eighty kilometres per hour, far too fast given the weather conditions but still within the speed limit. Gabriella's shocked host family had picked her up at the station. She had been advised not to leave the country until the investigation into the crash was completely wrapped up. She seemed visibly relieved when word came that she had been driving within the speed limit. She'd promised to call Anna some day; Anna hadn't expected the call to come quite so soon.

'*Szia, Gabi. Hogy vagy?*'

'I've felt better. Thankfully Tommi took the day off. That's my host father. I'm still not in any shape to look after the children. I couldn't get to sleep.'

'That's perfectly normal; it's a shock reaction. It'll last for some time, but it'll pass eventually.'

'I can't stop wondering why the man was lying there. Why did I have to go that way? Why was I listening to music?'

'Gabi, calm down. It looks as though this was all an accident. You weren't speeding, there was no alcohol in your blood, no drugs. You haven't done anything wrong; you just had some bad luck. If you hadn't run over that man, someone else would have done it.'

'There was nobody else on that road. Nobody.'

'Then he would have frozen to death.'

'What if he was already dead?'

'Gabi, we've already talked about this. If he had some sort of heart attack, we'll find out in the autopsy.'

'Who was he?'

'We don't know.'

'You still don't know!' Gabriella cried.

'It's been one day. Sometimes investigations like this take weeks.'

For a moment Gabriella said nothing. Anna heard the rush of background noise, a child's voice, then a man's voice somewhere further off.

'Listen, could we meet up?' said Gabriella suddenly.

'What?'

'Off the record. They gave me numbers for a crisis counsellor and an interpreter, but I'd rather talk to you about it. Besides, you already know the facts of the case; it would be easier.'

Anna hesitated. It didn't feel like a good idea to get mixed up in the life of someone currently under investigation; more to the point it was probably prohibited. On the other hand she understood Gabriella. If she had been in her situation, she would probably have done the same thing. She wanted to help this girl who, though not exactly a compatriot, was something along those lines. They arranged to meet at the Irish Corner Bar at nine o'clock that evening.

After ending the call, she asked Sari for a list of phone numbers for the health centres and hospitals in the city and called them one by one. It took a surprisingly long time; there were a lot of numbers and she never got the information she needed from the person who first answered the phone. None of them had treated a stabbing victim in the last week. Someone must have killed an animal out in Ketoniemi, thought Anna, maybe put down their dog because they couldn't afford to take it to the vet. She looked up at the clock on her office wall. Another hour and she would be free for the weekend.

Sammy woke with a start in the pitch dark. Amazingly he'd managed to sleep for a moment, though now he felt anything but alert. The wind had whipped up last night. It had blown in from the northeast, making the icy temperatures feel even colder. The surface of the road had frozen over, and was now more slippery than before, but hidden in amongst the newspapers he had felt surprisingly warm. A windproof plastic covering and a thick layer of paper to insulate him. That's where Sammy slept whenever he was unable to find anywhere else. And that's what he'd done last night too. Paper recycling bins were warm but unsafe. You couldn't spend many nights in the same place. He was afraid that someone would notice him and call the police. A few times someone had come along, opened the lid and thrown their newspapers inside and shrieked when they noticed a young man curled inside the bin. In situations like that Sammy had tried to look as friendly as possible. *Sorry, sorry*, he repeated before running off. Two months now, nothing but running. His whole, hellish life had been nothing but running – running from the police, running from normal people, from the withdrawal symptoms, from radical Islamists. Sammy didn't know what to do. There was no one he could ask for help. Surely nobody could spend their whole life in hiding? Not in a country this cold at any rate. He felt trapped without any chance of escape, like a fox caught in the grip of an iron snare. But even that was better than the certain death that awaited him back home.

Sammy hadn't eaten all day, but he barely noticed it because the cravings were worse than the hunger. After what had happened last night, Sammy had decided to lay low for a while and stay away from the drug crowd. But he couldn't go on like this for long; he had to find some money and some Subutex. If only he could afford a dose big enough for an overdose. An overdose of bupe would be difficult; he'd need something else too, a handful of diazepam at least. Too expensive. He'd been dreaming of his final journey and made peace with his reaper, there in the shadows of the recycling bins, the corridors and basements. Sammy no longer feared death at all, but he refused to give the satisfaction of his death to the men who had already murdered his father, mother and brother.

Sammy listened to the courtyard around the paper bin. Everything was quiet, not even the sound of traffic from the nearby road. That told him it was a weekday and that it was almost midnight. He could have rested here in peace and quiet for hours if he hadn't felt so awful. The muscles in his legs were twitching, he had a headache and felt sick. He caught the disgusting smell oozing from his skin. When was the last time he'd had a wash? Sammy tried to relax. He imagined being at home in his own bed. In his memories it was softer than it had ever really been. He had shared a room with his brother, a small room with just enough space for two narrow beds. His mother and father had slept on a sofa bed in the living room. The kitchen was in the living room, too. They didn't have any other rooms. Still, even two rooms were a luxury if they were your own. And their home had been their very own; his father had worked hard, he and his brother had gone to school. In this respect their family was exceptionally well off. The whole family knew how to read, even his mother. His father had been so proud of this. Everything had been fine until a new family moved in next door. Sammy tried not to think about it; anger would only make him feel worse. He closed his eyes and listened. No footsteps. No cars. People rarely brought their rubbish out at this time of night. He was safe. He would have to leave early in the morning, before the first people hurrying to work flicked a pile of advertisements into the bin as they ran to the bus stop. But where could he go? The stinking crack dens, each worse than the next, more squalid than Macke's dump of an apartment – a place the boy's mother even came and cleaned once in a while – were all out of the question. There was no safety in those strange rooms, dimmed by drawn curtains and a collective chemical haze. Someone always lost it or tried to rob him. The police could raid places like that at any moment. At Macke's he could walk in at any moment, and Sammy never wanted to see him again.

Sammy started to feel that the only sensible option would be to go straight to the Hazileklek pizzeria the following day and explain it all to Farzad and Maalik, the whole sorry story from start to finish, the drugs, everything. He hadn't had the courage to tell the pizzeria owners about the refusal of his asylum application, though they were the only people with whom he had something resembling normal contact. He didn't want to cause them any trouble. He already felt ashamed of himself in their presence, unable to trust them. Sammy was convinced he would never be able to trust anyone on earth ever again. And yet, by himself, it was impossible to survive. He desperately needed help. He needed food and sleep. He needed to be at peace in his soul. He needed money; he needed Subutex. Oh, why had he got mixed up with the rotten stuff? Wasn't his situation difficult enough without it?

Fear and anxiety gripped him. The streets hadn't hardened him and the frost hadn't frozen him completely; his conscience never relented, though he tried hard to subdue it. He would never be able to tell the kind pizzeria owners the whole story. His nausea seemed to escalate. He felt trapped, three limbs shackled in irons, their teeth sinking deep into his shins and arms, all the while his former neighbours standing above him laughing, drooling, threatening to kill him, offering him a syringe only to move it beyond his reach every time he stretched out his free hand. In the background the face of the murdered old man stared at him through grey eyes, with a look of confused accusation on his face.

Sammy stood waiting outside the back entrance to the Hazileklek pizzeria well before it opened for business. There were people in the courtyard, but nobody paid Sammy the least attention. The pizzeria had been in the same building so long that residents were used to the sight of people with dark skin waiting at the door. The ache in Sammy's legs had worsened; standing on the spot was agony. It felt as though someone was digging a knife into his head. Muscles twitched all over his body. Sammy thought he must look like his cousin Yousuf, who had been damaged during a difficult birth and was now housebound, writhing in bed, his face set in a grimace. He had heard that disabled children could go to school in Finland, that they had to study just like able-bodied children. Sammy thought this somewhat strange, but the idea felt good. For some strange reason Sammy had always liked Yousuf. He would visit his cousin and read him books and newspapers, though his father had told him it was a waste of time, that his cousin didn't understand a thing. Sammy disagreed and so did his aunt; Yousuf's mother had taught him to indicate when he needed the toilet, when he was hungry or cold, and how to give yes or no answers to simple questions, and sometimes Sammy felt that they were able to communicate on a higher level of understanding than most people who speak fluently. Yousuf's mother had shown her gratitude by baking Sammy hearty naan bread and looked at him with, if possible, eyes more loving than those of Sammy's own mother.

Later on Sammy had lost contact with his cousin's family. They had been forced to move and disappeared around the same time that the persecution against Sammy's family had started. He'd heard rumours that they had gone to Karachi. He'd looked for them there.

'Sammy!'

Maalik and Farzad had arrived. They seemed glad to see him, shook his hand warmly and gave him a friendly tap on the back, but they couldn't hide their worried glances. They could see that something was wrong, badly wrong; they could smell the dirt and the fear. The men took Sammy into the back of the restaurant. Sammy told them of his rejected asylum application, of how he had been living rough for two months in the terrible Arctic conditions, sleeping wherever he could, of how tired and hungry, how dirty and desperate he was. He decided not to tell them about the Subutex. He hoped that the men might help him; in fact, he was sure they would – Maalik and Farzad were Muslims, but not religious zealots like so many people in Pakistan these days. They would take him in, give him food and maybe even some money. He would buy small doses of bupe, reduce his intake over a couple of weeks, then quit altogether. That's what he would do. Giving up all at once could be dangerous. Besides, he hadn't been taking big doses before now; eight milligrams had been the absolute maximum. Of course, when injected that was a lot, but as a former heroin user he could tolerate larger doses. From now on he would take only four-milligram doses for a week – he felt ravenous saliva forming in his mouth at the very thought – then one week at two milligrams, then one, then a half, then he'd be free. Perhaps the men would bring him some painkillers, Burana or Panacod; they might even have some sedatives. He could tell them he'd caught a terrible flu brought on by all the stress. He would get through this somehow. Once he'd cleared his head, he could start planning what to do with the rest of his life. Perhaps he could go to Sweden or England. He had relatives there.

Farzad and Maalik withdrew to the dining room to talk. They glanced at the clock; it was almost time to open and they hadn't even started preparing lunch. Sammy waited in the backroom, trying to resist the temptation to rummage through the bag Farzad had left on a chair. The man's wallet might have been in there. But Sammy was not a thief. A pathetic junkie and a worthless refugee, yes, but not a thief, never. And at that moment the eyes of the dead old man opened wide and stared at him from the depths of his consciousness.

Farzad called in one of the part-time staff, a young student girl who sometimes helped out at the pizzeria, and started chopping cabbage before shredding it in a large food processor. Maalik took

Sammy back to the men's apartment. Have a shower and rest, we'll give you some food, he said. We'll make up a bed on the sofa.

Maalik drove through the city centre and out towards the other side of town. Sammy looked at the throng of people in bewilderment, recalling how he had once been puzzled at the incredible silence and cleanliness in the city centre, how few people there were, how peaceful everything was. He had been in hiding so long now that it felt like a crowd.

When they arrived, Sammy started coughing and complaining of a headache, said he'd been feeling ill for a few days. Maalik gave Sammy a towel, opened the sofa bed and made it up with clean sheets, showed him what food there was in the cupboards and left a banknote on the kitchen table as he left, telling Sammy to pick up something at the pharmacy – just as Sammy had hoped. The money was just enough to get him eight milligrams, which he could then halve. By increasing the time between fixes he could probably make it last over the weekend. But where could he get his hands on some gear? Sammy knew the city and he knew the best places to score. Macke's place was closest, but he wasn't going there. He'd have to go to Rajapuro, though it was further away.

Most of the windows in the police station were dark on a Friday evening. Dozens of offices quietened down for the weekend, leaving only the duty officers and the traffic police downstairs on duty. But the lights were still on in one window on the fourth floor. Esko Niemi was sitting in his office reading about a Danish-Swedish street gang called the Black Cobras, who ran a lot of drug trade on their own territories in the suburbs of Copenhagen, Stockholm, Malmö and other large cities, and who were involved in violent clashes with other gangs. Members of the gang had now been seen in this city. Information had come through yesterday from the National Bureau of Investigation. Esko was examining lists of names, online surveillance data, criminal registers, addresses, reports, links to other known gangs, their connections to a variety of crimes and all the other information that now formed tall piles of paper on his desk. Every now and then he took a swig from his bottle of Koskenkorva, a quarter of which had now disappeared, and every time he did so he realised how much he enjoyed these lonely nights at the office. If only he could disconnect the damn smoke detectors, he wouldn't have to go up and down the stairs just to have a cigarette.

Esko's task was to investigate the recent activity of a local immigrant youth and to help the NBI establish what plans the Black Cobras had for expanding in the city. The kid in question was a Finnish citizen; he had turned up in Finland by himself ten years ago as a teenage refugee. His name was Reza Jobrani. Esko stared at the black-and-white passport photo taken a few years ago. Reza was a handsome young man with a slender face and black eyes, dark stubble on his chin, though in the photograph he must have been barely twenty years old. They're all so fucking hairy, thought Esko. The women are probably like monkeys too. He'd read in a report that Reza had visited Copenhagen four times in the last two years. Budget flights to Copenhagen and back. The first visit had lasted four days, the second and third a week each, and the latest visit, a month ago, had taken four days. Nobody had followed the boy's movements in Denmark. A month ago nobody had paid much attention to him at all; no one imagined he was responsible for anything at all. But then something had happened in Denmark: a shoot-out in broad daylight in an area of town with a reputation that made Koivuharju and Rajapuro seem positively gentrified. The boy had been 'in the hood', as they say. The police had taken him in for questioning. At first it all seemed like coincidence, the boy said he just happened to be walking past, but Esko's Danish colleagues had been smart enough to establish that Reza had in fact been staying with a guy called Mohammed, even though he'd checked into the Copenhagen Backpackers Hostel in the city centre. Of course, there was nothing illegal about this, but it so happened that Mohammed was a member of the Danish Black Cobras; not one of the leaders, but someone they trusted. Reza had denied any involvement in the shoot-out, and because spending the night at the house of a known criminal is not a criminal offence, they'd let him go. The Finnish police had been alerted to Reza, and now he was on Esko's radar.

You little runt, I'll find out everything that you're up to and put you away for the rest of your life. Let *that* be asylum for you, thought Esko with a sense of contentment, as he felt the blood boiling in his veins and the magnificent burn of Koskenkorva in his throat. Now he had to go downstairs for a cigarette.

It was a quarter to nine; Anna had arrived at the pub a little early. She'd driven straight home from work, gone for a short run, taken a shower, put on some make-up and, exceptionally, thought hard about what to wear. She'd eventually picked out a pair of jeans and a black blouse. She sensed that she'd have to wait well past nine o'clock. You didn't need to travel far to encounter very different ideas of time-keeping; in fact, you didn't need to travel at all. Different notions of punctuality had arrived in Finland, too. Anna always arrived on time and, if possible, a bit early rather than late, a very Finnish trait. Back home she'd found herself irritated by having to wait for Réka to turn up at the Gong or the Avant bars. She'd had to work hard to get over the irritation, because people who were uptight about punctuality were far more annoying. Now Anna wanted to hold on to the nonchalant attitude she'd acquired back home. She ordered a pint of cloudy ale, its taste pleasant, bitter and smoky, and sat at the counter looking calmly around; she decided not to hang around waiting for Gabriella if she was late. The pub was already full. Some of the customers seemed to have found their way in there on the way home from work, briefcases propped against their tables, their eyes unable to focus. A quirky looking older man at the other end of the bar started giving Anna the eye, but Anna didn't look at him and he soon buried himself once again in his newspaper. The barman exchanged a few words with her, asked about the weather, mentioned in passing that his shift would soon be over and that he was going ice-skating, recommended a new brand of ale. Anna decided to order that one next.

Gabriella stepped into the pub at nine o'clock sharp, Anna noticed with amusement. The girl was soon the object of many a stare. Even Anna could see that Gabriella was beautiful; long, healthy, dark hair, brown eyes and full cheeks, slim, with stylish clothes. Anna felt herself hopelessly old and bland as Gabriella sat down on the barstool next to her as lightly as a spring breeze in a fruit orchard. There was no sign of shock or grief in the girl's eyes. Perhaps youth could conceal sorrow more effectively than any foundation cream.

'*Hihetetlen*,' said Gabriella. 'I drove down here in the car. Unbelievable! And I wasn't at all freaked out. Well, I was a bit when I left, but it soon passed.'

'So it seems,' said Anna sipping her beer. She couldn't hide the note of irritation in her voice, because she'd expected Gabriella to turn up still weeping and wracked with guilt. I've turned into such a petty old busybody, she thought. Gabriella didn't seem to notice her tone of voice. With a confident flick of the wrist she beckoned the barman and ordered a glass of tonic water.

'But this time I wasn't listening to music,' she said with a little laugh. 'Do you like Sebestyén Márta?'

'I've heard her once or twice.'

'Once or twice? Oh my God!' Gabriella shrieked. 'I'll lend you a few CDs. You just have to get to know the star of Hungarian folk music.'

'I never listen to folk music.'

'What do you listen to then?'

Anna thought of electronic music, sounds made by computers, the surreal world into which she disappeared in the evenings, a world that opened her eyes to incredible landscapes, much more powerful than television, more exciting than the cinema. What could she tell Gabriella of this?

'Not much at all,' she replied. 'Classical music sometimes.'

'Liszt? Bartók?'

'Sometimes,' Anna lied.

'Haven't you ever visited a *táncház*?'

'Gabi, I've lived in Finland since I was ten.'

'Oh. Poor you. Why on earth?'

Anna finished off her pint and ordered another. What an annoying brat, she thought. She had turned up to console someone she thought was in the depths of despair, but now Gabriella was behaving as if nothing had happened, as if she wanted to get to know her, as if the words *kezét csókolom* had now been replaced by a simple 'hi'.

'Because my family moved here back then, and because at that age people don't normally leave their families. Or do they?'

Gabriella still didn't seem fazed by the sniping tone in Anna's voice. Perhaps she hadn't noticed it at all.

'Yes, yes, but why did you come here?'

'Because there was a war going on that had already killed my eldest brother, and my mother was worried that my other brother would be sent to the front. That's why.'

'Oh right, the war in Yugoslavia. I was just a baby back then, it was so long ago. Was it really awful?'

'What?'

'The war.'

'I was never in the war, and there wasn't any fighting in Vajdaság; things were fairly calm there. People just tried to get on with their lives. The only thing was that all the young men disappeared. I know as much about that war as any Finn my age. I've seen images on TV, watched a few documentaries, read a few books.'

The image of a pile of bodies flashed in Anna's mind. Panic tugged at her insides but didn't sink its teeth in. Anna closed her eyes for a microsecond, fixed the muzzle in place and tried to focus on her pint.

'You know more than that,' said Gabriella. 'Your brother died.'

Anna said nothing. She wanted to leave. The alcohol in her head felt good, but Gabriella was somehow tiresome. What if she just said she had to go home and moved to another bar instead? For the first time in a while I could have a good few drinks this evening, thought Anna.

'Okay, if that's all I think I'm going to go home,' she said and moved her half-full pint further away. 'It's been a heavy week and I need to get some sleep.'

'Should I burst into tears or something?'

'Excuse me?'

'Do I have to be drowning in self-pity for you to talk to me or even chat with me? Surely it's a good thing that I've got over the whole business so quickly?'

'The investigation is still pending. You might still be charged.'

'But it wasn't my fault. The old man was lying in the road and probably about to die anyway. The whole thing was an accident, pure and simple, so I'm not going to lose sleep over it.'

Anna felt embarrassed.

'You're right,' she said and picked up her pint glass, raised it. Gabriella clinked her glass of tonic water against it and smiled. That girl's a little too pleased with herself, Anna couldn't help thinking.

Anna drank another pint of beer, Gabriella ordered a mineral water, and they talked about Gabriella's family in Budapest, her studies and dreams. Anna made sure the conversation focussed on Gabriella. The girl was inquisitive, but like most people, she couldn't resist the opportunity to talk about herself. And so Anna learned a little about Gabriella. Boyfriends, dreams of finding a husband, the family's old stone townhouse near Városliget, her host family in Finland and their children. Anna had to remind Gabriella of her obligation of professional secrecy; her host family's arguments and the size of their pay packets were not public information. Of course, Gabriella hadn't considered this. Anna learned that Gabriella had graduated from university as a Hungarian teacher but that she hadn't been able to find work. The situation in Hungary is pretty screwed up, she'd explained. Her studies in Hungarian had included a few optional courses in related languages and she'd taken a beginners' course in Finnish, so after spending a while looking for work in her own field she'd decided to look for an au pair placement in Finland. Improving her Finnish could be useful, she'd thought, and after a quick online search she soon found herself a host family in Northern Finland. The parents were affluent, career-oriented types; they had three children, an enormous detached house, expensive hobbies and no time for the family. Gabriella had been a godsend. The children's constant need for adult attention left her feeling drained, but she had decided to stick it out despite her feelings of homesickness. In ten months she had grown attached to the kids as though they were her own. But sometimes she had to get out. Elina, the mother of the family, had suggested the university, a place where she was bound to find friends her own age and at the same stage in life. And that's what had happened, but unfortunately there were no other Hungarians around this term. Gabriella had secretly hoped to find herself a nice Hungarian boyfriend, she told Anna with a wry smile. Well, an African guy called Isaac had been flirting with her. Nice enough guy but a bit too intrusive. And he has body odour, Gabriella said with a giggle. Anna laughed too.

All in all a very pleasant evening, thought Anna as she walked home from the bus stop. A refreshing, human evening, just right for a thirty-year-old stuck in her ways. Gabriella was talkative, funny and upfront. Anna had to admit that it was more than enjoyable to spend an evening speaking Hungarian.

A cold wind had whipped up. Anna wrapped her face in the folds of her thick scarf. It's a good thing I didn't drink more, she thought. I'll go skiing in the morning if the wind isn't too strong. She heard her mobile beep in her pocket, removed her gloves and clicked open the text message with numbed fingers. The message was from Virkkunen. A quick test had revealed that the blood in the woods was human, it read. Anna took the stairs up to her apartment, washed off her make-up, brushed her hair, ate a sandwich and drank a cup of tea, flicking through the newspaper before finally brushing her teeth. The idea of working on a Saturday really grated. And there was something else bothering her too. As she climbed into bed and tried to relax in the warmth of her duvet, she realised that there was something about Gabriella that just didn't feel right.

4

THE CAFÉ WAS SITUATED on the edge of the city centre. It was decorated with light wooden furnishings with cosy tablecloths that perfectly matched the twee curtains. Pensioners and people setting off early for work sat sipping their morning coffee and reading the newspaper. The atmosphere was quiet and relaxed, unhurried.

Sitting at a table in the corner, Esko glanced at his watch. The guy should have been here fifteen minutes ago. Esko fetched another coffee and bought a doughnut covered in sugar to go with it. Was this a no-show? The little bastard had better not try his luck, thought Esko just as the door of the café opened. An unkempt-looking young man with long hair, wearing a denim jacket and tight trousers, stepped into the café looking around warily.

'Aren't you freezing?' Esko asked as the man sat down at the table. He didn't answer but blew on his nicotine-yellow fingers, now reddened with the cold. He was barely twenty-five years old, but his hands were as weather-beaten and wrinkled as those of an old man. A tough life and tinkering with a motorbike had taken its toll. Esko noticed two women staring at them from across the café, whispering to one another. What could they be thinking? A tearaway son come to ask Daddy for cash to buy more booze? That Daddy had ordered his son in for a talk, told him to pull himself together and get a job?

The young man wasn't Esko's son; he was his informant, his rat, as the gangs would call him if they knew. Every decent criminal investigator had his own snitches, and this young man had been Esko's for a few years. He was involved with the inner circle of the Hell's Angels, got himself caught up in drug dealing and smuggling, violent crimes and God knows what else, things Esko would rather know nothing about. He knew that the Angels' road captain had voted against the guy becoming a prospect member on several occasions and shagged his girlfriend at a drunken party a few years ago, though touching other members' girls was strictly forbidden in the gang's code of honour. The young man hadn't made it past hang-around membership, though in his own words he'd been faithfully serving the group 24/7, the way members in his position were expected to do. He'd swept the club floors after parties, run around town on errands for the leaders, often putting his own safety at risk, demonstrating his competence, his readiness for a fight, showing his loyalty and his desire to become a fully-fledged member in every way he could, even taking a six-month sentence for a crime committed by someone else – a full member. And still he was left lagging in the lowest echelons of the group. The old dude taking his girl was the final straw. For some reason the road captain had taken a dislike to him – and now he wanted revenge.

'Want something?' asked Esko.

'I'm starving,' the man replied quietly.

Esko stood up, fetched a cup of coffee and a baguette, took a napkin from the stand and placed everything in front of the man. He felt stupid waiting on him hand and foot, but he wanted people to fall for the father-and-son scenario. The man was risking his life coming here. Esko had no respect for a criminal ratting on his own comrades, in fact he felt a deep contempt towards the man, but the information he provided was invaluable to the police. He wanted to secure his informant's safety as long as he could. That's how it worked. Esko needed this man, now perhaps more acutely than ever.

'Have you heard anything?' asked Esko.

'I think I know what you mean. Yes.'

'Tell me.'

The young man sheepishly looked around him. Esko had chosen this café because its bourgeois surroundings were unlikely to attract the Angels or anyone else from the criminal underworld for a cup of properly brewed Darjeeling. They were sitting at a table in the corner so that they couldn't be seen from the windows, Esko could keep an eye on the front door and the man could sit with his back to the other customers. And they were right next to the toilet in case they suddenly needed to hide. They didn't meet up very often, they couldn't, and the safety measures could never be underestimated.

'A couple of guys have been hanging around. Danish. Black Cobras,' he whispered.

'Tell me something I don't know.'

'They're trying to drum up some business. They're already dealing.'

'Have they got many members?'

'I think so, because the core group was formed a while ago. It's our very own Pakis, too.'

Esko had guessed as much. The police had known for years that street gangs would find their way to Finland sooner or later, just as they had in Sweden and Denmark, and the members of those future gangs already lived here. They had grown up in frustrated suburbs in families of frustrated refugees and asylum seekers. The members were the children of those who had been granted asylum, young people who, unlike their parents, should have had the opportunity to make something of their lives. There had already been attempts to establish home-grown gangs in Finland, but they'd been foiled. Not, alas, by police efforts, but by the same motorbike gang whose runt of a henchman was sitting in front of him. Gangs were always one step ahead of the police, but this time Esko planned on being up to speed with what was happening on the street.

'Got any names?'

'I've got a few addresses.'

Esko handed the boy a slip of paper and a pen. The man scribbled down two addresses and glanced agitatedly behind him.

'Have the Angels got any plans for these addresses?' asked Esko.

'The operation is called *Annihiliation*.'

'When?'

'All I know is it's going be soon.'

'Who lives here?' Esko pointed to one of the addresses.

'Some small-time dealer trying to line his own pocket. Poor kid doesn't know what the fuck he's getting himself into.'

'And the other one?'

'That's the Cobras' nest. It's not head office, but it's an important branch.'

'Where's head office?'

'Haven't got a clue.'

'Ever heard of Reza Jobrani?'

'He's top of the Angels' hit list.'

'And where's he holed up?'

'No idea. He's gone into hiding, for sure. He knows we're on to him. These Cobras have really freaked the Angels out. Shit, man, there'll be bodies before long.'

'Okay, you and I are going to have to meet up a bit more regularly in the near future.'

'Not gonna happen.'

'Then I'll just have to look up that report that details how I found a loaded Ruger and five grams of hash on your person this morning.'

'What the fuck are you on, mate? I never carry a gun…'

'I know. Funny how things can turn out, isn't it?'

The young man's posture slumped. The scrawny body beneath his clothes suddenly seemed as though it belonged to an insecure teenage schoolboy and not a professional criminal with a lengthy wrap sheet.

Esko handed him two SIM cards and a fifty-euro bill. The man gave a cautious smile. How easy it is to keep you happy, thought Esko in disgust. Chewing tobacco had stained the man's front teeth brown.

'I couldn't have another sandwich?'

'Buy one yourself; you've got cash now. And don't forget to brush your teeth tonight,' said Esko and left the café. He called Virkkunen, who immediately issued warrants to search the two addresses.

Sammy woke up in bed. It felt incredible. He stroked the scented sheets, gripped the soft, thick quilt inside the duvet cover, looked out of the window and listened to the sounds that carried up from the street. He guessed he must have slept for about twenty-four hours. Sammy stood up, slowly stretching his limbs, stepped on to the warm floorboards and yawned. This is what it was like to be a normal person; you could wake up every morning full of energy, eat breakfast prepared by your wife, go to work. He would kiss his wife as he left, pat their son and daughter on the head. Warmth would caress his face as he walked to work, dust would catch in the sweat on his brow, the sound of people and traffic would surround him, a cow would stand chewing its cud in the middle of the road, holding up the traffic, but he would be used to everything and nothing would faze him. Friends would greet him in the street, ask how his children were doing. Nobody would look askance at him, hurl abuse, throw stones at him. Nobody would make up fatal lies about him.

The apartment was empty. Maalik and Farzad had left for work early in the morning. It was already mid-afternoon, but the men wouldn't be back until late at night. On the kitchen table was a note and beneath it another banknote. Sammy felt spittle oozing from his glands, rinsing his tongue in a constant stream. The sense of self-loathing only returned as he swallowed his spit. He was as far from normal as the outer edge of the solar system was from Earth. The message told him to eat the pizza and salad that the men had left for him in the fridge. Sammy could use the money to buy himself some clean clothes or whatever else he needed. They planned to come home early that evening; they had called in replacements at work. Then they could all discuss what Sammy should do. Perhaps we can appeal against your deportation order, said the final sentence. It felt strange for Sammy to read these familiar, curlicue words, writing he hadn't seen for such a long time and that to his eyes was so beautiful. Then he looked at the clock; it was already four o'clock. He would have time to pick up a tab before the men got back. He'd used up the eight milligrams yesterday; after all, he had to get to sleep somehow. Today he'd only need a half.

Sammy left the apartment. The glare of the sun dazzled him. It had clearly been a glorious day. The light breeze felt surprisingly warm against his face. At one of the houses he slowed his step. In the yard outside he saw children skiing, parents in winter jump suits carrying their equipment back into the garage; a half-melted snowman slouched amusingly in the garden. The sight attracted Sammy because it was at once so exotic and yet so ordinary. He felt a powerful desire to join them, to be a part of this strange country and its customs, a part of that happy family. They would probably soon go to the sauna, sit down together and eat something nice, then spend the evening lounging on the sofa, side by side, watching television.

Sammy felt a sting of envy. His thoughts jumped back home, to the girl that didn't really exist. They would sit in church, listening to the priest's gentle sermon, people would be pardoned and, at least for a moment, they would be happy. They would sing a few hymns. After the service he would sit at lunch so that he could watch the girl all the time. Their eyes would meet for a fraction too long, but their parents wouldn't mind; they would pretend they hadn't noticed. Give it a year or two; first he would have to graduate, then the priest would marry them and the girl would be his. They would have children; four, perhaps, girls and boys, two of each. The children's bubbling glee would fill their modest but clean and comfortable house. He would be a good husband and a gentle father. They would never argue. Would he never experience things like this?

Sammy walked briskly towards Rajapuro. That's where he'd bought the gear yesterday too. Just then he heard a sound he feared more than any other. He frantically looked around, but there was nowhere to hide. The sound was already too close, there was no way he could run for cover. A police car sped past him, its sirens wailing. It took all his will power to try and walk normally, not to slow down or speed up, not to lower his head or turn away, not to dive into the verge of ploughed snow. Anything like that was sure to have caught the police's attention; the bastards kept their eyes peeled even when they were racing through the city. Once the sound had disappeared into the distance, Sammy ran up to the nearest house, gripped the concrete wall the way someone drowning would cling to a lifebuoy, leant his head against its surface and breathed deeply.

The police were going to the same place as Sammy. There were three squad cars parked in the yard, their blue lights washing across the high walls of the surrounding buildings. Someone was being led out of the stairwell in handcuffs. Sammy didn't hang around to watch; he turned as soon as he saw what was happening and walked quickly in the opposite direction. There was always one officer whose job it was to watch people gathering at the scene, an officer who would notice even the smallest detail. Sammy knew his photograph was in the police records and that there was a warrant for his arrest. One of the cops was bound to recognise him. But what could he do now? It was almost evening. Maalik would be home soon. They would sort out his appeal. As long as his appeal was pending, he wouldn't be a sitting duck.

He had to find some gear, fast. Even a small amount, enough to help him act normally and sit calmly at the kitchen table with Maalik. Again his thoughts turned to Macke. Macke wouldn't rip him off. Macke lived close to Farzad and Maalik. Sammy didn't like the decision to go to Leppioja, but headed there all the same.

'Two teenage girls found the knife in the woods behind Ketoniemi the day before yesterday,' Virkkunen began. He had called Anna, Sari and Nils into work, though it was a Saturday and everyone wanted to enjoy some time off.

'Shit,' said Nils with a satisfying stretch; he looked as though he hadn't had much sleep.

'Initial tests show that the blood is human, and that's why we have to look into it.'

Virkkunen paused and looked at each of the officers present from behind his spectacles. They were sipping coffee, each of them looking exhausted. The lack of enthusiasm hung in the air.

''Do we have to investigate it right now?' asked Nils.

'Yes,' Virkkunen replied drily. 'For some reason the girls didn't tell us about what they'd found straight away, but thankfully we haven't lost too much time.'

'What were they doing out in the woods?' Anna wondered.

'Nothing in particular, they said. Forensics are already processing the scene in greater detail, and so far they've found a great deal of blood, footprints, tyre tracks and a couple of cigarette ends. I believe the cigarettes belonged to the girls; both had pink lip gloss on the filters.'

'So what do we do now?' Nils mumbled.

'Anna and Sari, I want you to examine the scene immediately. It's been a few days, but at least it hasn't snowed again. Best to give the place a thorough investigation. Nils, get in touch with these girls. Let's try and sort this out so that we don't have to come in tomorrow too.'

Anna and Sari pulled on their police overalls; they came in handy when you had to crawl around in snow-covered woodland. They took the lift down to the car depot beneath the station. The air was heavy with exhaust fumes and another smell associated with cars that Anna couldn't put her finger on, oil perhaps, dirty old rags or something metallic. Two stocky officers were giving the back of their squad car a good clean. Someone must have thrown up in there, thought Anna. She felt no nostalgia for the time when she had to do the same thing after almost every shift. Still, working with the traffic police had been much easier; the days just came and went without the burden of prolonged investigations and the sense of stagnation. In criminal cases it often felt as though the investigation wasn't going anywhere, that everything was up in the air. Her shifts consisted of looking for tiny fragments of evidence, trying to stitch them together, discarding false leads, placing good leads in their rightful place in a pattern that was still to be worked out. Her brain was constantly at work, trying to find a light at the end of the tunnel, though sometimes no lamps appeared to light up. At times it was downright frustrating, and yet extraordinarily fascinating. Because a lamp always came on eventually. Always. This Anna needed to believe.

Anna typed the location of the bloody knife into her navigator, or rather she gave the address of the house nearest to the woodlands where the knife and the blood had been found. The neighbourhood was situated to the north of Rajapuro, far away from the city centre. There were a few recently built apartment blocks, but on the whole this was an area of detached houses and families with kids, lots of surrounding nature, good opportunities for outdoor activities, a school and a shop. It occurred to Anna that she'd probably never visited the place before. The temperature had once again dropped overnight, the sky gleamed in a surreal turquoise, not a cloud in sight, the sun burned against it like a giant orange. The car thermometer showed -12°C. Spring had come to Finland.

They parked the car outside an apartment block at the edge of the woods. Nils had already arrived in his own car. The block was home to one of the girls who had found the knife. Behind the building a path led into the woods. Anna and Sari walked off along the path. The place was nothing but thicket. After only a short distance the birches and willows were so tangled that the path came to an end, though the girls' footsteps continued deeper into the woods. They had pushed their way through the thicket.

Anna and Sari followed the footsteps; the frozen snow crunched beneath their feet. The woods spread out over a large area. Anna thought of the city map. Beyond this there were no more residential areas until you reached Asemakylä, she thought, which until only a few years ago hadn't belonged to the city. If someone had been murdered out here, then it was done in peace and quiet.

Anna and Sari followed the girls' steps for a few hundred metres. They were beginning to think they had come to the wrong place when they saw the yellow police tape through the tangle of branches. Just as Virkkunen had told them, forensics were already at work. Kirsti Sarkkinen waved to them with an enthusiastic smile.

'Come and have a look, but be careful of that corner; there are some really interesting prints over there,' Kirsti shouted, pointing to the left-hand side of the cordoned area.

Anna and Sari cautiously stepped closer.

'Jesus Christ,' Sari gasped.

'What on earth happened here?' Anna asked and looked around with a feeling of nausea. The snow was churned up and soaked in blood. There was so much blood that it looked as though someone had slaughtered an animal at least the size of an elk. But this wasn't elk-hunting territory; this was still within the city limits, and besides, it wasn't hunting season.

Sarkkinen lifted up the curved weapon, now tagged in a transparent plastic bag, for everyone to see. The blood on the blade had dried and darkened.

'Any fingerprints?' asked Sari.

'We'll soon find out. But this blood is relatively fresh, a few days old at most. Those girls must have been here fairly soon after the event. Thank God they didn't turn up while the blood was flying. There are some strange prints over there,' said Kirsti and pointed to the west.

'What kind of prints?' asked Anna.

'Very likely two sets of footprints: one belongs to a man, the other to a woman or a small man. But the only prints leading away from the site are the larger ones. I guess the owner of the smaller prints was either beaten up or killed here. The knife was found right there in the middle. It's a very strange model; we should try and trace it.'

'Christ,' Sari repeated.

Anna watched for a moment as the forensics officers photographed and sketched the scene and a technician measured the position of the blood spatter. Section by section, scene by scene, they pieced together the events of this tragedy without seeing its protagonists. It was quite a task, but they were good at it.

Anna wandered off in the direction Kirsti had indicated. She was right; there were sets of footprints, numerous indentations pressed into the deep covering of snow, large ones and smaller ones.

'What's that?' Anna shouted back to Kirsti. Along the ground was a deep trail about a metre across. It had erased some of the footprints.

'Something heavy was dragged along the ground. This looks like it was made by a plastic bin liner. Doesn't take much imagination to guess what was inside it.'

'Can I go down there?' asked Anna.

'Sure, we've already documented those prints, but don't trample over them. We'll have to examine them in more detail, see if there's a proper shoe print anywhere.'

The hairs on Anna's back stood up as she followed the trail through the thicket. She walked well away from the footprints so as not to compromise them. The trail stopped at a small clearing after which was the start of a forest track cleared by a snowplough. Tyre tracks were clearly visible. One of the forensics officers was in the process of photographing them.

'Hello,' Anna greeted the man.

'Hi there. I don't think we've met. Pekka Holappa, nice to meet you.'

'Fekete Anna.' Out of habit, she introduced herself in the Hungarian manner.

'I know. I've heard about you.'

Anna felt like asking what exactly he'd heard about her, but thought better of it. His camera flashed. The man knelt down to take some close-up shots.

'Any initial thoughts about these tracks?' she asked instead.

'Not really. They're standard treads, quite thick tyres. I'd guess an SUV of some sort.'

'I doubt a smaller car would get through snow like this.'

'Well, there is a tarmacked surface underneath, and there have clearly been other cars up this way, but there's a lot snow. If I were trying to move a body, I wouldn't risk driving out here in a smaller car,' said Pekka with a chuckle.

'Get in touch as soon as you come up with something on these tracks, okay?'

'Sure thing,' said Pekka and smiled at Anna. Not bad looking, thought Anna and smiled back.

'Can I get in touch anyway?' he shouted after her once she made to leave.

Anna pretended not to hear. You're a stupid girl, she chided herself and felt the fleeting desire for a cigarette grip the back of her throat.

'Hey, don't go yet! Look at what I've found here,' Pekka called after her.

Anna turned around and went back to him. Pekka held up a dark-green card.

'What's that?'

'A cloakroom ticket.'

'Where was it?'

'In that footprint, pressed inside it. It's a wonder I even noticed it; the footprint is at least thirty centimetres deep.'

'Does it say what restaurant it came from?'

'No. All we have is the word KOFF and the number 147.'

'Someone is going to have to visit every pub in the city,' said Anna and felt a wave of resignation at the thought that that someone would be her.

His chest felt tight. No, just a twinge. A twinge in his lungs, that was all, too many smokes and too little exercise. Damn it, Anna was right, thought Esko. He reached for the packet of Norths in his jacket pocket but didn't light up. He couldn't, not indoors. He watched as a dark-skinned man in his twenties was handcuffed and bundled out of the apartment. As far as he was concerned it was the wrong guy; it wasn't Reza. No matter, they'd get something out of this one too – at least, they would if Esko was allowed to interrogate him. He knew he wouldn't have the chance; the NBI boys took care of all the tidy indoor work, while the city police were sent out any time you might have to get your hands dirty.

Esko glanced around. Far too tidy for your average junkie's pad, he thought. Most likely people didn't shoot up here; this place was just for dealing or planning. A brand new computer caught Esko's attention. It was in the bedroom on a light-brown veneer desk with piles of paper, a pencil stand, headphones and a printer all seemingly in their rightful places. A home office used to organise drug deals and gang warfare – all paid for by his taxation. Fucking hell. Esko's head ached. The sun beamed in through the windows, hurting his eyes.

'Look what we've got here,' one of the officers smirked in the corridor. He stepped out of the closet carrying a shoebox. The box contained transparent bags filled with white powder and a few packets of Subutex. Not much of a raid, but enough to prove that there were criminal dealings going on in this apartment.

'What an ingenious hiding place,' the officer laughed.

'Get a load of this,' another officer shouted from the bedroom. He was holding a clothes hanger with a black hoodie. The back of the hoodie bore the white image of a snake and the words Black Cobra in calligraphic text.

Esko flinched. So that damn Islamist gang from Denmark and Sweden really was trying to expand out here, in our city. The Cobras were an extremely violent, dangerous, nasty crowd. While the police had expected them sooner or later, the black hoodie seemed to take everyone by surprise, like a sudden storm. The officers stared at it in disbelief. An electric tension fizzed in the air; Esko could feel its ripples on his skin. These hooded youths' future plans didn't include a classroom and a shitty, underpaid job. As far as these guys were concerned, society had been unable to provide them with anything of interest. On the contrary, it had only succeeded in marginalising them. Esko hocked up a persistent clump of phlegm and spat into the kitchen sink, its rim covered in yellow scum. For a group like that, it was easy to wind up in the world of organised crime, a world of poverty, frustration, disappointment and substance abuse. It was as easy as planting a potato in soil hoed by someone else. All you needed were good contacts, of which these guys had plenty, relatives all over the place, and soon new members would be popping up like rabbits. Decent contacts, good planning, a head for organisation, and the bomb was set. Suburban wogs craved money and power just as much as business-school yuppies, and now it was on offer to them with a bit of action on the side. Jesus Christ, the police had to stop the Cobras setting up in Finland, no matter what the cost. Esko felt a quiver of excitement inside him. Drunken louts, wife beaters, burglars, shoplifters – it was all so familiar, so harmless, almost mundane crime, the unchanging routine of decades of work, serving only to fill his empty days with more emptiness. But this case, these gangs. They were international and probably better organised than Nokia. There was a sense of real criminality about them, real danger. It was a proper assignment. Stopping the loathsome expansion tactics of the Black Cobras would be the good deed of the century. Admittedly, his part would be small, very small, but great rivers run from small springs, or what was it they said? He would do his job to the best of his ability, better than any assignment he'd ever worked on – and that was saying something, because he always did his job well. Then he could think about retiring. He could do anything he wanted.

Macke didn't open right away. Sammy didn't want to ring the doorbell for too long. He felt afraid standing in this stairwell. He felt as though someone was watching him through the peephole in the door opposite; it seemed to gleam in the dim of the corridor, staring at him, accusing him. He listened, his ear up against the door to Macke's apartment; there was noise, someone was home. Why wouldn't Macke open the door? Then the sound of shuffling steps in the hallway, the glow of light behind Macke's peephole went out for a moment, the door opened and Macke almost fell into the stairwell, a can of beer in his hand. Sammy grabbed him and pushed him back inside, quickly pulled the door shut behind him. Macke said something, but Sammy couldn't make it out. He noticed a trickle of blood running from Macke's forehead.

'You hurt?' Sammy tried to ask, but it was futile. Macke didn't hear him; he was already far away.

They went into the living room. The low coffee table was covered in packets of pills; there must have been dozens if not hundreds of them. Strewn on the table there were syringes, spoons, pieces of tin foil and the cotton wool used to filter solutions of dissolved pills. Cans of lager covered most of the floor. Sammy wondered where Macke had got his hands on so much gear, but he didn't want to ask. He wondered too how Macke dared let him in, with so much stuff to pinch. Sammy hadn't said anything about his past, but perhaps Macke realised that Sammy was an exception, even for a junkie, an outcast among outcasts and therefore harmless. Sammy didn't understand, and he wasn't all that interested in Macke. As long as he got his hands on some bupe. Macke slumped on the sofa, took a gulp of lager and again tried to say something. His eyes couldn't focus. Blood still oozed from his head; Sammy saw a gaping wound on his crown. The hair around the area was dark-red and sticky. Macke chuckled incoherently and started to choke. A moment later bilious green and white vomit gushed over the sofa. Sammy felt a wave of disgust, but the packets of Subutex strewn across the table commanded his attention. They formed a wonderful little hill, almost a mountain. Macke's not just a street dealer, he must be involved in some kind of smuggling ring, thought Sammy. That's the only explanation. The apartment started to feel more and more dangerous. Gangs of organised criminals were the last people Sammy wanted to get messed up with. He knew that gang members weren't afraid of violence and carried weapons in their clothing. Best to get away, quick. Get out of here, you're not safe here, he tried to command himself as he sat down in an armchair and reached a hand towards the offerings of the table.

His fingers trembling, Sammy opened one of the packets, pressed a pill from its plastic bubble and felt its light touch against his palm. The familiar insignia of a sword looked like a cross, the tablet like a small tombstone. Sammy groped in his pocket for a syringe and other equipment and laid everything out ready. Macke had quietened down on the sofa, his eyes pressed shut. Again Sammy hesitated. Maalik would be waiting for him. They were supposed to sort out his appeal together. He could win this, easily. All human rights reports showed that his situation back home was untenable. If only he had the paperwork to prove it. Here you needed paperwork for everything. Surely people here knew about the situation facing Pakistani Christians – the erosion of their rights, the harassment and persecution, the cooked-up blasphemy charges. Surely people here had to know? His chances were good, he'd be granted asylum instantly. He would leave this shit behind, get himself clean and become an upstanding citizen as soon as the appeal was submitted. But his application for asylum had been rejected. And he had fled. If people really did know something about his situation, they didn't give a damn. He looked at the mountain of pills. He would never have an opportunity like this again. Nobody would notice a few missing tablets. He could pay Macke later, if he ever mentioned it. He wouldn't. Sammy glanced at Macke. He was asleep; he looked almost dead. The blood had started to congeal on his face; the can of lager had fallen to the ground, small bubbles lazily forming at its mouth. Sammy pressed another tablet from the packet, and a third, and ground them into a fine powder with experienced hands. Amazing, absolutely amazing, was all he could think, nothing else. Finally a decent trip.

5

MONDAY MORNING DAWNED as brightly as the day before. Anna woke up early, stretched her legs, still stiff from sleep; she had no desire to get up, but her sodden sanitary towel forced her out of bed. The sheet was stained too. Anna hated her period, the fatigue and stomach cramps in the first few days, the moodiness and pads that started to smell no matter how regularly you changed them. Anna took a shower, put on some music – AGF's classic album *Westernization Completed* – changed the sheets and made some coffee. A leisurely weekday morning was a luxury, period or not.

Gabriella had called that evening. One of her friends was interested in coming to Finland and wanted some advice. What did Anna think she should do? Could Anna help her? Anna had been perplexed. She had suggested the friend ask an EU officer at a local employment agency or contact the Finnish embassy. She couldn't help with a matter like this. She had no idea how nurses were recruited to Finland from abroad or whether they were recruited at all. The things people imagined she knew…

The coffee tasted good. Anna sipped it slowly while reading the morning paper. The news reports were a bit thin; Anna wanted more in-depth information about many things. Maybe newspapers can't afford decent journalists any more, she thought. People can't afford anything these days, and still there seemed to be more of everything than ever before. Humans will soon choke on their own impossibility; we'll gobble everything up and regurgitate it at our feet. Anna closed the newspaper and listened to the music for a moment, her eyes shut. Strange sounds. Noise. AGF's singing, their dreamlike poetry. Whenever people asked her, she could never really describe electronic music. She knew this, because Béci had asked her. The black waters of the Tisza had flowed before them, the early morning and the onset of a hangover had pressed the cold beneath their clothes. They had left the swings, walked hand in hand to the old jetty and sat down. Béci had hugged her and asked what kind of music she listened to. Anna had tried to explain. Music made by computers, music that doesn't always sound like music, sometimes it's just sound, it has a weird sense of flow and you can lose yourself in it. Béci had looked at her nonplussed. What flow, he'd asked. Anna pressed a kiss against his lips and changed the subject.

Since then Béci had sent her at least ten emails that Anna had systematically deleted without even reading. Even now she banished him from her mind, stood up and pulled on her clothes. She would go for a pizza today, she decided, and for the first time in ages say hello to Maalik and Farzad.

The phone vibrated against Esko's chest. He was lying on the sofa in yesterday's clothes. It was early morning and still dark, six o'clock perhaps. He forced himself to pick up the phone, open his eyes and answer. It was Virkkunen. The big bosses had decided to carry out a raid later that day on the other address Esko had been given and they wanted him to take part – if he was up to it, Virkkunen added pointedly. Of course, Esko stammered into the telephone, no problem. How the hell did Virkkunen seem to know everything? Esko clambered to his feet and shuffled into the kitchen. There were no flowers on the windowsill. He opened the fridge and shoved his hand into the torn cardboard box inside, gripped a frosted aluminium can and imagined a cold beer rinsing away the taste of shit in his mouth. I'm definitely going to sell this place, he resolved as he stared at the microwave standing on the worn kitchen counter, the curtainless windows and the bag of empty beer cans. What the hell have I been doing here all these years? Waiting for things to go back to how they were before?

Two hours, then I'll have to go to work, Esko thought, reluctantly let go of the can, deciding instead to take a few Buranas and a Diapam, which the police nurse had prescribed him years ago for his anxiety. Renewing the prescription was as easy as harvesting hay, as people used to say. What kind of a proverb is that, he wondered. Harvesting hay only became easy in the 1990s after the EU donated hundreds of tractors to Finland, and by that time the expression had already begun to disappear from everyday use. Nobody knew anything about harvesting hay these days, of scythes and poles and rakes, of the straw and dust beneath your clothes, the heat and the horseflies. Esko undressed in front of the hall mirror but avoided looking at himself. Half an hour's sleep in a real bed, just until the painkillers started to kick in, he thought and climbed under the sheets.

His half an hour seemed like ten minutes, and he couldn't sleep. Get the porridge on to boil, cigarette, shower – did he have any clean shirts? He'd have to do the laundry that evening. Christ, one for the road would sort me out, there are still a few in the cupboard, but no. After a bowl of porridge and another cigarette he began to feel normal again. He could do this. It was as easy as harvesting hay.

The raid was scheduled for two-thirty that afternoon. By then the last remnants of his hangover would be gone and he would be back on form. He had to prepare, go through the sequence of events with Virkkunen and the team. The meeting was at nine. Then they'd have to fetch their equipment, maybe visit the shooting range, eat something before the show started. They were in for a great day, the noose was tightening round the necks of these towel heads. You had to admit, the NBI really knew their stuff. And so did he. As he left, Esko glanced in the mirror. Jesus, I shouldn't have bothered, he thought as he locked the front door and felt his chest tighten again.

Virkkunen divided assignments in characteristically reserved fashion. Establishing the origin of the knife and the cloakroom ticket went to Nils; Esko and Sari were to take care of the raid. Preparations for the raid were rehashed in such detail that Anna felt bored. She was to spend the afternoon at the autopsy of the man in the traffic accident. She glanced over at Esko, who looked like he was in bad shape. The bags under his eyes were darker and more swollen, his cheeks were riddled with a web of burst blood vessels. Every now and then he had a fit of coughing, though as soon as the meeting ended he headed straight for the smoking area outside. Anna retired to her office to catch up on paperwork; she still had to write up a few old investigations, and she had a niggling feeling that these new cases would soon eat up all her time.

Hazileklek was almost empty. Anna recalled her previous visits when there hadn't been a seat in the house. I hope Maalik and Farzad are coping, she found herself thinking and wondered when she had turned into such a worrywart.

'Anna! How are you?' Both men dashed out to hug her. They smelt good, as always, helped her out of her coat, hung it in the cloakroom and ushered her to a table.

'I'm fine. But how are you two? I haven't seen you for ages.'

The men quickly looked at one another. Anna couldn't help notice the worry in their eyes, worry that melted into happy smiles as soon as they turned back to her.

'Lot of work. Lot, lot of work,' said Farzad.

Anna looked around the empty dining room.

'It will be busy soon,' Maalik explained. 'And Friday, Saturday, we are here until morning.'

'No time for holiday,' said Farzad. 'But that is good, no?'

'Everyone needs a holiday some time,' said Anna. 'You have other staff. Surely they could look after things for a day or two?'

Again the men glanced at one another.

'Well, we talk about it, but is difficult to arrange.'

'Nonsense,' Anna chuckled. 'You really are workaholics. It's not good for you, you know.'

'What else you do except work? Who you are with?'

Though Farzad asked this with a friendly chuckle, without the slightest trace of sarcasm, his questions felt like a punch in the diaphragm and knocked the air from her lungs.

'I go skiing.'

'The skier should not ski alone.'

'Don't tell me you've read Eino Leino?'

'What? Me?'

'Do you read Finnish poetry?'

The men burst into laughter.

'Yes, if Rumi is a Finn.'

'Or Nazo Ana.'

'Who are they?'

Again the men laughed.

'You can look it up on Google,' said Maalik. 'But yes, I know my Leino. And my Edith Södergran and Aale Tynni. Difficult poets, but good for practise Finnish.'

Anna felt ashamed. She was well aware that Farzad and Maalik were highly educated university lecturers, intellectuals forced to flee from Kabul, and that they knew about many things besides grated cheese and tomato purée. She too was regularly considered a pitiable imbecile as soon as people found out about her Yugoslav past. Still, she didn't want to tell people about her father's aristocratic background or the fate of her mother's wealthy industrial family after they lost their entire fortune to the communists at a time when most Finns were still trying to eke out an existence ploughing stony fields for a landlord. Anna was actually grateful to the communists. She had been able to live a normal life as the youngest child of a normal family; they weren't rolling in money and they didn't worship the family coat of arms, but they never wanted for anything. The coat of arms existed only in a photograph in a drawer in her father's desk. Anna, of all people, shouldn't have been surprised by Maalik's reference to the national poet. But that's what had happened.

'What you like to eat?'

'What delicacies do you have for me today?'

'I'll make anything you want.'

'What was that amazing meat stew I had last autumn?'

'Oh, let's make that. Restaurant is quiet, and we are hungry too. We eat together.'

Anna was happy; it was nice to have some company. This would give her the chance to ask why they seemed so concerned.

Soon the table was filled with rice, sauces and salads. The dizzying aroma of spices filled the restaurant. Delicious, thought Anna and sighed yet again that you couldn't find food like this back home. Of course, her mother made good *pörkölt* and *paprikás*, but restaurants in Vajdaság were monotonous and often sub-standard. The food was heavy and greasy, nothing but traditional Hungarian dishes, Serbian *ćufta* meatballs, white bread that always tasted amazing at first, because it was warm and fresh from the bakery, but made her feel bloated after a few days. Anna admired the Hungarians' unflagging belief in their own tripe and pig-trotter casseroles; there was something noble and persistent about it in an age of pizzas, hamburgers and sushi, but she couldn't bring herself to touch them. Traitor.

Maalik and Farzad asked after Ákos and Anna's mother. They asked Anna to give Ákos their greetings and tell him to pop in one day. It was through Ákos that she'd first met the men. Ákos had done a few months' work placement at the pizzeria and become friends with the owners. Once the formalities were out of the way, Maalik spoke up.

'Anna, we know we can trust you. We have problem.'

'What's the matter?'

'We must make an appeal about asylum application, but we don't know how. You know how is done?'

Anna realised instantly what their concern was about. They had a friend whose asylum application had been rejected and whom they wanted to help. Were they hiding their friend? More than likely. Anna felt a sense of pride, of satisfaction. She was a police officer. How much do people who had fled from Afghanistan trust the police? She had all the necessary powers to get a warrant to search the men's apartment. The mere suspicion of harbouring an illegal immigrant would be enough, one phone call was all it would take.

These two men knew it, and still they had asked her for help. And she would help them as much as she could.

'You'll need a lawyer,' she said without asking any details. 'A qualified, experienced lawyer. What chance do you think your friend has?'

'He will die if he is sent home. He'll be killed. No doubt about it,' said Farzad.

'But the immigration office doesn't believe it,' Maalik continued.

'Of course not,' said Anna and felt thankful once again for the emergency law enacted by Finland during the conflict in the Balkans. Their arrival in Finland had been quick and easy, everything had been almost shamefully simple. First, transportation to Munkkisaari, then to the reception centre outside the city, and before long they had an apartment – all this in just over six months.

'I'll find you a good lawyer. Keep him hidden until then.'

'There's another problem.'

Yes, she thought. There always is.

'He disappear again, we cannot find him. I don't want to say his name, but he is a young man. Could you see if someone like this has been picked up?'

Anna thought about this for a second at most.

'Of course I can,' she said. 'But first I have to visit the morgue regarding another case.'

'Anna, haven't seen you in ages. How the hell are you?' Pathologist Linnea Markkula stepped out of the autopsy room just as Anna arrived at the forensics department. She wanted to discuss any findings and a possible ID with Linnea face to face; this was always better than over the phone or via email. Linnea had left her scrubs in the changing-room laundry basket and looked like the stylish, attractive, self-assured doctor she was.

'Coffee? Let's go to my office so we can talk in peace.'

'Thanks.'

Anna followed Linnea up the stairs. Are autopsy rooms always in the basement, she wondered but decided against asking out loud.

'How are things on the boyfriend front?' Linnea quipped over her shoulder with a smirk.

'Not much to tell,' Anna replied spiritlessly.

'You're such a prude, Anna. You're probably still a virgin,' Linnea teased her.

If only you knew, thought Anna.

'I had a free weekend for once. I'm still exhausted. You've got to come out on the town with me some time. We'll find you a bloke. I can help.'

'Maybe...'

'Maybe, maybe. At this rate you'll die a spinster.'

'I wouldn't mind,' said Anna and tried to smile. 'So, what do we know about the victim?'

'He took a battering. His torso was completely crushed. Have we located the next of kin?'

'No.'

'Then we'll have to call in the forensic dentist, otherwise we'll never find out who he was. Or should we hold off a while?'

'Virkkunen said to give it a fortnight. If we haven't found any relatives by then, we'll have to work out his identity some other way.'

'Okay. More cutbacks, eh? A while ago they would have examined his teeth straight away. Was the girl speeding?'

'No. And she wasn't drunk either. She says the victim was already on the ground when the accident occurred.'

'Yes, he probably was. Otherwise the impact wounds would have been in a different area, on his legs and hips, and the man would have been knocked on to the verge or into the oncoming traffic.'

'Had he had some kind of seizure?'

'His heart was slightly enlarged, which can be a sign of high blood pressure, but it's very common in people that age. Apart from that his heart was normal, no signs of a heart attack, and nothing in the brain either. Heart attack and stroke are the most common seizures. The victim was in his pyjamas. Perhaps he was simply tired and collapsed on the road right there on the spot.'

'Could he have passed out?'

'There were no signs of alcohol in his blood and his organs don't look like they'd been pickled in gin, but of course I've sent samples off to be analysed. We'll have to wait about three weeks for the results.'

'Anything else?'

'The victim had a head wound and bruises to his face that are inconsistent with a traffic accident. To me they look like blunt-force trauma, but they were so fresh that they must have occurred on impact. Perhaps in the collision he hit his head against the icy road.'

'He was lying on his back when they found him. Could he have rolled over?'

'No, I don't think so. He was probably lying on his side and was knocked on to his back.'

'That's what Gabi said too.'

'Who?'

Anna felt embarrassed, sensed a rush of blood to her cheeks.

'Farkas Gabriella, the girl driving the car.'

'Do you know her?'

'No. It turns out she's Hungarian.'

'My sister's got a Hungarian piano teacher. Great guy and really good. I could give you his…'

'Maybe the old man had fallen over just before the accident; he could have been concussed and wandering around the woods, hit his head against something,' Anna interrupted her.

'Maybe.'

'Except that there were no footprints fitting the man anywhere near the scene; nothing in the woods or on the road, though the road was iced over.'

'He was wearing a pair of slippers. It should be easy to isolate any footprints.'

'But there weren't any prints. Not even along the edge of the road, where there's normally more loose snow than on the road.'

'Maybe he was walking down the middle of the road.'

'Maybe.'

Sammy heard music somewhere in the distance. It was getting closer, louder. He opened his eyes. It took a moment to work out where he was. He was sitting in an armchair in a dimmed living room. A mobile phone was ringing on the table in front of him. The word *Mum* flashed on the screen. He recognised that word, but not the melody. It sounded like all the music in this country: boring and American. Macke didn't answer the call. He was slouched on the sofa. Sammy tried to focus on Macke. The edges of his field of vision shimmered, and the living room, darkened with thick curtains, seemed to whirr in time with the music. Sammy untied the strip of tubing around his arm. He felt amazing, better than he had in a long time. He didn't care what the time was, what day it was, whether Maalik and Farzad were waiting for him, worried, what kind of appeal they lodged, whether it was successful, whether he was eventually bundled on to a plane for Karachi, whether he was killed straight away or slightly later. He didn't think of anything, he wasn't cold, wasn't hungry.

The armchair felt soft. He felt united with its spars, its threadbare velvet coverings. He was the armchair and it felt good, safe. Again his eyes pressed shut; he didn't try to fight it. He didn't fall asleep, but sank into a pleasant, relaxing state of oblivion so powerful nothing could make its way through into his consciousness.

Nothing except one sound. There it was again. A banging, rattling. Sammy tried to ignore it, he didn't want to open his eyes, but when a man's voice bellowed right into his ear, he had to. The room was full of people in blue uniforms. Sammy jumped to his feet. The room was swaying violently, he gripped the armchair for support, but only for a hundredth of a second, then he tensed every muscle in his body and dashed towards the hallway screaming like an animal, his arms thrashing wildly, but in vain. He had moved not even a metre before being caught in the iron grip of an enormous police officer. The powerful arms wrapped around him like pliers. He tried to wrestle himself free but didn't have the energy, couldn't match the officer's superior strength. Sammy slumped, limp, and started weeping against the blue overalls. The prey had finally been trapped; the hare had run for the last time. And as he stood there sobbing, there in the unflinching grip of the policeman's arms, for a fleeting moment Sammy felt a great sense of relief, of returning to his mother's embrace.

'Call an ambulance,' someone cried out. 'This one's not breathing.'

Sammy understood the word *ambulance*. He turned to look at Macke, now receiving CPR on the floor, there amongst the rubbish. Macke's face, his skin stained with blood, was white as a sheet. What have I done to deserve a life like this, thought Sammy. I should have stayed and defended my mother, not run away like a cowardly sewer rat. Sammy pressed himself tight against the officer's broad, safe chest. Tears and mucus stained the blue overalls.

6

'WE GOT A CALL from the switchboard. Missing person,' Virkkunen told Anna.

'Finally,' she said, relieved. 'Who was he?'

'The victim reported missing is an elderly woman by the name of Riitta Vehviläinen.'

'Oh. So why was it transferred to us?'

'Normally they wouldn't have called it in, but this woman lives in the same house where we found Marko Halttu and the illegal kid. The same floor, even: Halttu lived in the apartment opposite.'

'Quite a coincidence.'

'Indeed. It's probably chance, but in any case I thought we should have a look at her apartment too, just to make sure we've covered our tracks in case it turns out it's not coincidence after all. I thought you could take care of this while we're processing Halttu's apartment.'

'That's fine.'

'Sari can help Esko with the drugs case involving these gangs; you go through that woman's apartment.'

'Am I looking for anything in particular?'

'I can't say. Look for anything to suggest where she might have gone, but don't rule out the possibility that these gangs might be involved in her disappearance. If a woman living opposite a heroin hellhole goes missing at the same time as we find the tenant of the hellhole dead with a wound to his head and a huge stash of drugs, we have to react accordingly.'

'Of course. When was the woman last seen?'

'Here's her daughter's telephone number. She called it in; apparently she visits her mother fairly regularly. Call her and ask her to accompany you to the apartment. She'll be able to tell you if anything looks out of the ordinary.'

'Okay.'

The spasms were worse than ever. Sammy was lying in police custody, on a hard bunk in a bare cell. His whole body was trembling, the pain was excruciating and it was attacking him all over. He was sure there wasn't a single, tiny patch of his body that wasn't screaming in agony. What's more, he stank. An officer had visited him that morning, a beautiful, blond woman, and tried to talk to him. Sammy noticed how she was holding her breath, trying to hide a look of disgust. He'd understood what she was asking, his English was good, but he'd only said one word to the officer: *heroin*. He hoped she would get the picture, fast. In this country heroin addicts were given Subutex. Soon he would find relief. Maybe. Unless they didn't give subs to prisoners. If that were the case, he'd have to languish here a long time before the spasms would pass. It would be a good thing, of course. He was ready to suffer the withdrawal symptoms, he would accept it as divine intervention; that much he owed himself and his family. And the longer the symptoms continued, the longer he would remain in here. Perhaps. Perhaps they wouldn't repatriate him in this condition. His legs were cramping, cold sweat was dripping from his skin, the pain was terrible. He felt like crying out, crying to God.

The last time he had prayed was in January, at the immigration office of the police station as he went to pick up the result of his asylum application. He had done everything slowly, reached his hand out to the stern-looking officer, opened the sheet of folded paper with exaggerated dignity. He had been so sure. He had saved up money for coffee and cake at the finest café in town, borrowed a suit jacket from Ali in the room next door; he'd even thought of buying a flower to put in his buttonhole but decided it would be a bit over the top. He had resolved to apply to a carpentry course starting that autumn at the city's academy of arts and crafts. His prayer had been simple:

thank you. Thank you, Holy Lord, for this gift, for the possibility of a new life. And now he was here, in a dead end. This wasn't a stopping point on the way to hell, this was the deepest inferno, forever banished from Paradise. Everything was over, *finito*, done and dusted. The flames scorched his ravaged body, his head was caught in a clamp and a rack all at once. But he would never pray again. Never.

'The boy is called Sammy Mashid. We've had a warrant out for him for the last three months,' said Sari. She, Anna and Esko had gathered in Anna's office.

'What for?'

'He's in the country illegally. His asylum application was refused in January and he immediately disappeared from the reception centre.'

'He was completely out of it when we found him,' said Esko.

'No wonder. That apartment was full of Subutex, amphetamines and God knows what else,' said Sari.

'Didn't he say he was taking heroin?' asked Anna.

'Yes. I tried to talk to him this morning, but he just kept repeating *heroin, heroin*.'

'The hell he was on any smack. The little Paki's trying to cheat a dose of Subutex out of us. Jesus, do these junkies think we're stupid? They really think we came down in the last shower.'

'Esko, don't use that word,' said Sari.

'Why? Virkkunen's not here,' Esko quipped.

Anna felt her old sense of loathing for Esko bubbling to the surface. After the initial teething problems, their relationship had improved, and Esko's behaviour towards her had been bearable and at times almost paternal; he held back his racist jibes at least when she was around, but now Anna realised that teaching an old dog new tricks wasn't all that easy.

'Where's the boy from?' she asked.

'Pakistan. He belongs to the Christian minority and has been charged with blasphemy,' Sari explained.

'My arse! Christians in Pakistan? They're all Muslims. Liars, the lot of them,' Esko snapped.

'Esko!' Sari raised her voice.

'You saw for yourself how high the kid was when we brought him in. I don't believe a word he says.'

'Because he's a junkie or because he's a Muslim?'

'Both.'

'You really are a nasty piece of work. Virkkunen's going to hear about this.'

Esko let out a smug laugh and gave Sari an icy stare. Anna felt it too; she remembered only too vividly what that stare felt like.

'You do that, Little Miss Perfect. Be my guest. Come on, Anna. Time for a smoke.'

'No, thank you.'

'Christ alive, do you have to turn into a nagging cow too?' he boomed and left the room.

Anna and Sari were left alone.

'He's always hung over these days. What an arsehole,' said Sari.

Anna could see that Sari was really upset. Her face was red and her breath short and tight.

'Forget about it. You once told me that deep down Esko's okay.'

'What must I have been thinking? He's a fucking drunk, that's what he is. You should have seen him at that raid yesterday in Leppioja. He can't even breathe properly. He was huffing and puffing so much I thought he was having a heart attack. Even Raivio, the field officer on the operation, noticed it. I'll be surprised if he doesn't tell Virkkunen first.'

'Is this Sammy involved with the gangs Esko's investigating?' Anna changed the subject. She didn't want to discuss Esko's problems with anyone.

'We don't know yet. But Marko Halttu, the tenant, he's definitely involved.'

'In what way?'

'Esko's informant told us that Halttu had been working for the Hell's Angels and started lining his own pockets.'

'So Halttu stole the drugs from the Angels?'

'Most likely. And if that's the case, it's no wonder he ended up dead. He was on the Angels' hit list.'

Anna tutted. 'What was the cause of death?'

'We don't know yet. There were some signs of violence and the flat was full of all kinds of narcotics. You should have seen the mess; it was awful.'

Anna had seen it. Not in this particular apartment, but during her time on patrol she had visited so many crack dens that she knew they were all the same: filthy, stinking, desperate rooms full of pain.

'We're going to need all hands on deck,' said Sari.

'I know, and now there's a body too. At least in that respect, the case will be transferred to us.'

'Right. Could Sammy be involved with the Black Cobras? Perhaps he and Halttu had plans for all the drugs. The Cobras are attacking the Angels' territory.'

Anna whistled and nodded.

'That's what must have happened. When can we interview Sammy?'

'He's totally out of it, doing some serious cold turkey. The doctor will soon decide whether he needs any initial care. If you ask me, we should give him something so that we can interrogate him, otherwise it could take weeks,' said Sari.

'That might be best,' said Anna. 'You said the boy was an illegal?'

'That's right. An illegal alien, or whatever we're supposed to call people who've been refused asylum.'

Anna had a sinking feeling. How many young, male illegal immigrants could be lying low in a city this size? The reality is probably far worse than we can ever imagine, but I have to call Farzad and Maalik immediately, she thought and stepped out into the corridor. Sari remained in the office, staring blankly after her.

Anna finished the call with Maalik with a sigh. Her suspicions had been confirmed. Sammy Mashid was the friend the Afghan men had been talking about. I feared this would happen, said Maalik, when Anna told him about Sammy's withdrawal symptoms. I'll find you a good lawyer, Anna promised before ringing off.

She knew her old acquaintance Zoran had good contacts, so she called him straight away. His wife Nataša answered the phone. Her voice sounded cold and clipped. *She knows*, thought Anna.

Zoran was away somewhere and had forgotten his mobile. Nataša promised to tell him that Anna had called. Anna was doubtful. She tried to ask how things were going, but got only a brief 'everything's fine' in response. Nataša didn't even mention the kids.

Anna and Nataša had been friends when they were younger, but when Anna joined the police academy their relationship deteriorated once and for all. Or had it happened earlier, after Anna had spent that first illicit night with Zoran? Anna was convinced that Nataša had known everything from the start.

Anna urgently sent Maalik a message saying that they'd soon have a lawyer and that they could visit Sammy in the police cells if they wished.

7

THERE WAS NO BALCONY at the front of the building. The vernal sunshine revealed a faded wall, the roughcast chipped here and there, though the windows seemed relatively new. Three floors, two stairwells with only nine apartments feeding from each. This will still take all day, thought Anna as she and Sari stepped into Building A. Marko Halttu's flat was on the ground floor. There was no name on the door, only a handwritten sign reading NO ADVERTS. The Vehviläinen and Kumpula families also lived on the ground floor. Sari went into Halttu's apartment, where the forensics team had already started work. Anna had arranged to meet Mrs Vehviläinen's daughter Leena Rekola, and waited for her in the stairwell.

Halttu's apartment was depressing. It was so dirty and desolate that Sari shivered. What could go so wrong in a young person's life that they began to self-destruct? How could she protect her own children from such desperation? They called the boy's mother soon after they had found Marko. She had come in and identified her son's body. She seemed perfectly normal, cried a little and told Sari that for the last few years she had shuddered every time the telephone rang, that she'd known this could happen one day, that, as terrible as it sounded, in a way this was almost a relief. She had caressed her son's hand and told her how Marko used to bring her flowers from the yard, daisies and dandelions. 'What happened?' Sari plucked up the courage to ask. The woman raised her tearful eyes, looked at Sari and said that she didn't know.

The forensics team examined every inch of the apartment; Sari gave the place an overall look to see if she could find anything that might provide more information, something other than the piles of drugs that lay everywhere. The seizure had been significant: five kilos of amphetamines, two kilos of hashish and 4,700 Subutex pills, a total street value of at least 300,000 euros. Macke hadn't got himself mixed up with any small-time crooks. They could have got some valuable information from him, and now he was dead. Sari felt bad objectifying a victim like this, as though he didn't have a grieving mother, as though his life was only interesting as a source of police information. This work toughens you, she thought, and perhaps it was for the best. You'll never survive if you start weeping over every dead junkie. As long as I never take my hard-boiled work persona home with me, Sari thought and felt a pang of guilt. She had become angry with the children the previous evening and shouted at them over something trivial.

The small, one-bedroom flat was strangely devoid of personality, unless evidence of heavy substance abuse could be considered personal touches. There was nothing there that people normally have in their homes: no real food or cooking equipment, no dishes at all, no books, papers, plants, no decorative items or photographs. Just a few clothes, a few pairs of shoes and a computer – and empty beer cans, litter, empty microwave meal packets and used syringes. Filth.

The bathroom was disgusting. It seems substance abuse upsets your stomach too, Sari concluded. She was just closing the bathroom door, trying to hold back the urge to vomit, when one of the technicians shouted for her.

'I've got blood.'

'Where?' she asked.

'On the corner of the coffee table and on the rug.'

'Could it have come from those syringes? I bet there's blood all over this place.'

'Yes, the sofa and armchair are covered in small specks of blood, but this bit here isn't from an injection. There's too much, quite a lot actually.'

'Do you think Marko and Sammy could have had a fight? The victim had a head wound.'

'Maybe, either them or someone else. There are always fights in places like this. I've swabbed all the samples I've found here. There was plenty of other interesting evidence on the rug. We'll soon find out who's been hanging around in here.'

Leena Rekola was a youthful woman of around forty. Her slender face bore a look of worry and urgency as she pulled a set of keys from her handbag and opened the door to her mother's apartment. She explained that she'd visited yesterday and there had been no sign of her mother. She flicked on the hallway lights. A jacket and an umbrella hung in the coat rack, there was a six-piece mirror on the wall, two pairs of shoes on the floor. The long hallway rug was straight. The atmosphere in the apartment was one of calm. The ticking of a wall clock could be heard somewhere.

'Mother's outdoor coat is missing,' said Leena. 'And her winter boots. Here we only have her smart shoes and wellingtons.'

'When did you last see her?' Anna asked.

'I fetched some groceries for her last Wednesday; I saw her then. I tried to call her the day before yesterday but she didn't answer, and that's when I decided to pop in. It was yesterday morning. I called the police straight away.'

'How was she when you last saw her?'

'The same as she always was. Poorly. That's why I go shopping for her. She doesn't have the strength to carry bags of groceries.'

'Would she have the strength to go away somewhere?'

Leena Rekola laughed. 'Absolutely not. She never goes on trips.'

'Where does she go?'

'Nowhere. That's what's so strange.'

'Does she have any relatives she could be visiting?'

'My mother's sister lives down south. I've already called her. My aunt hasn't heard from her.'

'Any other relatives? Where is your father?'

'He died years ago. Heart attack,' Leena explained, holding back tears.

'Could your mother have some sort of gentleman friend and gone to his place?'

'My mother? No. She's a seventy-two-year-old old lady in poor health. She hasn't had anyone since Father died. Trust me, she never goes anywhere. She can barely take out the rubbish.'

'Fine. Let's examine the apartment. Look around, take your time, and tell me if you notice anything out of the ordinary. But please don't touch anything, just in case.'

Leena sighed and wiped the tears that had run down her cheeks. 'There was nothing out of place yesterday.'

'We'll take another look. Let's start in the bedroom.'

Leena followed Anna into the bedroom. The air was stuffier than in the hallway. Anna could smell the sheets, the nightgown, the pungent scent of an elderly woman's body. The room didn't exactly smell bad, but the air had a hint of someone spending too long between showers. Anna had noted the same thing in the homes of elderly people before. It was as if nothing should be dirty, but that soap and water shouldn't be wasted on showers and sheets. The curtains were drawn and the bedspread lay neatly folded on the arm of a chair. The sheets themselves were crumpled, the pillow lumpy and the duvet thrown to one side as though she had climbed out of bed only for a moment, to go to the toilet, perhaps, or to have a glass of water.

'Mother makes her bed every morning,' said Leena.

Anna looked at the empty bed. Then she carefully lifted the pillow and the duvet. There was no nightgown.

'Check the cupboards to see if anything is missing, clothes, for instance. In case she has gone somewhere after all.'

Leena Rekola began examining the two wardrobes in the bedroom, cautiously lifting piles of nightgowns and underwear and shaking her head. Then she went through the blouses and dresses hanging in the closet. Women with a penchant for 1960s retro would have been over the moon.

'I don't think there's anything missing. Of course, I don't know every item of Mother's clothes. Anyway, the bed shows that she was sleeping just before she left. She disappeared in the middle of the night. She would never leave without making the bed.'

'There's no nightgown in the bed,' said Anna.

'Mother used to fold it and put it next to the pillow.'

'Perhaps it's in the laundry basket.'

'I'll have a look,' said Leena and went into the bathroom.

Anna looked around the empty room. Decorative plates and the grandchildren's drawings hung on the walls in endearingly tasteless disarray. Next to the bed, a radio alarm clock showed the time in large, red digital numbers. A glass of water, half full. A jar of pills: Tenox 20mg. So Riitta Vehviläinen had difficulty sleeping. I wonder if I should try those, thought Anna.

Leena appeared at the door.

'There's only underwear and socks in the laundry. Has Mother gone off somewhere in her nightgown? I'm beside myself with worry. I'm convinced she's dead.'

'Don't say things like that. We'll find out what's happened. Where does your mother keep her bags and suitcases?'

'In the hall closet,' said Leena, and disappeared again. A clattering sound came from the hallway. 'All her bags are here. It seems she didn't take anything with her,' Leena shouted.

'There's a mobile phone here,' Anna shouted back. 'Under the bed.'

Anna looked at the antiquated mobile; its buttons were so large you could press them no matter how badly your hands trembled. The screen showed twelve missed calls.

'Would your mother go away without her phone?' she asked Leena, who had returned to the bedroom.

'No. Check the phone.'

Anna clicked open the phone log. Riitta Vehviläinen seemed to be in contact only with her daughter. All the answered and unanswered calls were from Leena. Even the calls she'd made were all to Leena. All except one, the last one.

'Your mother called someone called Villy after midnight last Thursday, but it seems nobody picked up. At least, the phone doesn't tell us how long the call lasted. Since then she hasn't made any calls.'

'Who?'

'It says Villy here.'

'I don't know anyone called Villy. Mother never spoke about anyone called *Villy.*' Leena was becoming agitated.

'Well, she clearly knows someone by that name.'

'Good God, what on earth has gone on here? I was only here on Wednesday. Everything was fine then.'

'Her text-message log is empty.'

'Mother doesn't know how to send text messages,' said Leena. 'Though I've tried to show her.'

'Let's give this Villy a call,' said Anna. 'We'll soon find out where you mother is.'

But the call was instantly redirected to the operator. *The number you have dialled cannot be reached*, a monotonous woman's voice explained.

'No answer,' said Anna.

'Send the number to directory enquiries,' Leena asked.

Anna did this, but that too drew a blank; the number was either ex-directory or it belonged to a prepaid account.

'Don't worry, we'll find out who this Villy is back at the station,' Anna tried to reassure her. Leena clasped her hands, wrung them back and forth inconsolably, restlessly shifted her weight from one leg to the other, and held back her sobs.

'Now, now. Let's take our time and check everywhere else,' said Anna and gently touched Leena's shoulders. Riitta's daughter tried to give a brave smile.

The kitchen was a bit shabby but tidy like the rest of the apartment. The chipboard cupboards, painted in light blue, were full of crockery and kitchen appliances that looked as old as the dresses in the wardrobe. Why do elderly people put up with old belongings, Anna wondered. And why is the younger generation constantly amassing new things? If the world revolved around old folk's needs, we might as well close down most manufacturing the world over. Why on earth do we need so many new things?

Anna and Leena looked in the fridge and the cupboards, the rubbish bin, the chest of drawers, but nothing seemed out of place. On the wall opposite the fridge was a small medicine cabinet. It was full of different packets: Marevan, Diapam, Propral, vitamins and three types of painkillers. A pill dispenser on top of the cabinet was full. Anna noted that all the pills with a street value were still here. And Riitta would certainly have taken the dispenser with her if she had gone away for a few days.

'Is everything here as it should be?' she asked.

'Yes. Mother had lots of aches and pains but nothing deadly. Everything looks exactly as it did before.'

In the living room was a beige three-piece suite complete with threadbare cushions, a large rug and a television, and two framed cross-stitch patterns on the wall; the shelves displayed a few books, trinkets, and photographs of Leena in her confirmation dress, as she graduated from high school, and portraits of the grandchildren on their first birthdays.

'This is terrible,' said Leena. 'Everything is normal; only Mother is missing.'

'Have you ever noticed anything strange going on here, in the building or in the yard, when you've been visiting your mother?' Anna asked.

'Such as what?'

'We're investigating a drug-related case. The neighbour living opposite was found dead in his apartment yesterday.'

'Good God, that young man? What's been going on here?'

'Do you know any of you mother's neighbours?'

'No. Well, I'd recognise some of them. There are a few old people living upstairs and a couple of families with little children.'

'Did you ever see the neighbour opposite?'

'Yes, and I could tell that everything wasn't quite right.'

'In what way?'

'I could see his dilated pupils and how dishevelled he looked. I know a junkie when I see one.'

'Did you ever see anyone with him?'

Leena thought back, then shook her head. 'I don't think so. And I never saw the young man much either. Do you think Mother's disappearance could have something to do with your other case?'

'I'm sure there's a pretty logical explanation for all this,' Anna replied. The suspicious look in Leena's eyes told her the truth: the explanation would be neither logical nor pretty.

'We will find out who this Villy is and why your mother called him just before she disappeared. Please call me as soon as you hear anything of her,' Anna continued.

'Likewise,' said Leena and wiped a tear from her cheek.

After Leena had gone, Anna and Sari visited the other apartments in the building. There was nobody in at the Kumpula household. They took the stairs up to the next floor and tried Karppinen. Nobody at home there either.

'People are at work at this time of day,' said Sari and rang the bell at a door bearing the name Lehmusvirta. The sound of steps and banging came from inside the apartment. A woman of around seventy opened the door and stared sourly at Anna and Sari.

'Police, good afternoon,' said Anna with a smile. 'We've got a few questions about what's been going on these last few days. You've probably heard.'

'I certainly heard when the police came bursting into the building. Should I have heard anything else?' said the woman.

'There was a substantial seizure of narcotics in an apartment on the ground floor and the tenant was found dead. On top of that, one of the residents in another apartment has gone missing, so we'll be asking all the neighbours a few questions.'

'Get on with it then.'

'May we come inside?' Sari asked.

'Is that necessary?' the woman sniped.

'Actually, yes. Everything we discuss is confidential; out here someone could overhear us.'

'Nobody hears a thing round here,' the woman scoffed.

'What a nice name you have. *Lehmusvirta*,' said Anna.

Again the woman scoffed. 'My old man's name. He's been dead and buried for twenty years.'

'Let's get down to business. Have you noticed anything out of the ordinary round here lately? Any strange people in the stairwell, that sort of thing?'

'Yes.'

'What, for instance?'

'There was a crowd always in and out of the flat downstairs. Sometimes they played music very loud. A terrible racket, it was.'

'Do you mean Marko Halttu's apartment?'

'Yes, I do. That boy wasn't right in the head. No wonder he's gone and died.'

'Why do you say that?'

'It's no wonder any junkie or alcoholic dies, if you ask me. What use are they to anyone?'

'How did you know that Halttu was a drug addict?'

'I didn't until you started talking about drugs, but I'd guessed as much.'

'Tell us about the crowd that was always in and out.'

'They all looked the same to me. Boys in hooded jackets. You couldn't see their faces.'

'When was the last time you saw these boys?'

'Last week, it was. They weren't here every day. Thankfully.'

'How often were they here?'

Mrs Lehmusvirta's expression soured further still. 'I couldn't tell you. I don't spy on them.'

'What kind of hooded jackets were they wearing?'

'Normal ones, I suppose.'

'Did they have any patterns on them or words, perhaps?'

'I don't know. They were probably wearing coats on top of the hoods. It is winter, you know.'

'The image of a snake? A cobra about to attack? Like this,' asked Sari and showed her the picture.

'I really do not know. All I remember is the hoods.'

'Have you seen anything suspicious going on out in the yard?'

'Nothing in particular. You sometimes see that rabble loitering in the car park.'

'Did anyone look foreign, do you think?' asked Anna.

'You look foreign.'

'I don't mean me; I mean the hoodie boys.'

'I already told you I never saw their faces. Still, I thought they must have been foreign.'

'Why?'

'They weren't speaking Finnish.'

'So you heard them talking. What language could it have been?'

'How should I know? I only speak Finnish.'

'Do you have any children?'

'Yes. Why?'

'I just wondered whether they might have seen or heard something when they visited. Perhaps they could tell us what languages those boys were speaking.'

'My children don't visit me. They both live down south and get on with their own lives. They're not interested in their mother's affairs.'

'Oh. I'm sorry,' said Sari.

The woman glared at Sari with her pale grey eyes. Her stare was bitter, hardened, emotionless.

'Don't be. They were never good children. It's best they keep their distance.'

Neither Anna nor Sari knew quite what to say.

'Well … Have you seen any jackets like this one?' asked Sari and showed her a picture of the Hell's Angels insignia.

'No.'

'Any motorbikes?'

'I doubt anyone drives a motorbike in this weather. I haven't seen any.'

'Do you know Riitta Vehviläinen who lives downstairs?' asked Anna.

Mrs Lehmusvirta snorted. 'So she's the one that's disappeared?'

'That's right.'

The woman gave a dry cackle. 'It's hardly surprising.'

'And why is that?'

'She wandered the stairwell spying on her neighbours. I doubt the druggie crowd liked that very much.'

'What do you mean, she spied on people? Do you know something about it?'

'Riitta came round for coffee sometimes. Well, quite rarely, maybe once a month. Judging by her comments she seemed to know quite a bit about what was going on in this house.'

'What did Riitta tell you?'

Mrs Lehmusvirta turned her nose up and looked at Anna and Sari with a bitter glare her eyes. 'Last time she was here she was gossiping about the constant rows at the Kumpulas' place. And she was afraid of that Halttu.'

'When was the last time she visited?'

'It's a while ago now. After Christmas, it was. I haven't seen much of her since.'

'Why could that be?'

'I told her she stank. I tried to be friendly about it, but I think she took offence. What of it? I haven't missed her. I don't give a hoot about the gossip round this place. I hope someone half-decent moves into that tearaway's flat so we can get on with our lives in peace.'

'Where could Riitta have gone? Her daughter told us she never goes anywhere.'

'How should I know?'

'Are you even the slightest bit concerned?' Anna couldn't help asking.

Again Mrs Lehmusvirta gave a dry, deeply unpleasant smile. 'People should look after their own affairs,' she said.

Anna and Sari bid her goodbye, left their contact details and continued up to the top floor, but nobody was home in either of the apartments.

Building B was home to pensioners and a group of students sharing a flat. They too had noticed strange-looking young men hanging around the yard, but because they'd been there only rarely and hadn't seemed to cause any trouble, nobody suspected any criminal activity. Nobody had seen hoodies decorated with snakes or Hell's Angels jackets here either.

'That Lehmusvirta was a right old cow,' said Sari as they drove back to the station.

'What a truly awful woman. But it's odd that nobody has seen anything going on.'

'Maybe the drugs crowd wasn't there very often,' Sari suggested.

'Yes. Perhaps Marko did all his dealing elsewhere. That would make sense.'

'But people had noticed Marko. Even the ghastly Mrs Lehmusvirta said she'd noticed something wasn't quite right. And the nice couple in the other building.'

'Yes. You notice these things if you keep your eyes open. But you're right, it's strange that that's all anybody saw.'

'And Mrs Vehviläinen has disappeared into thin air.'

'We found her mobile. It was under the bed,' said Anna.

'Under the bed? That's weird.'

'I know. And the final call from that phone was to a Villy, who didn't answer and who's number is ex-directory.'

'Sounds spooky.'

'There's something really odd about all this. I'm afraid it looks like Mrs Vehviläinen's disappearance has something to do with Halttu and the drugs.'

'You know, I feel really sorry for Halttu and all the other kids that get themselves mixed up with drugs and end up ruining their lives. It's terrible. I can't bear the thought of Siiri and Tobias ever…'

'Siiri and Tobias won't get mixed up with drugs; they have two loving parents.'

'You never know. I met that boy's mother. She said she didn't know what happened to Marko, why he turned out like that.'

'You can't expect her to open up to you, to a complete stranger, in that kind of situation. She's standing by the body of her own son, she's not going to talk about how she should have set him stricter boundaries or told him she loved him more often, how his father was a drunk and disappeared from their lives, how he left Marko without a father, how she was unstable as a child too, unsure of herself, not strong enough to bring up a feisty, sad little boy all by herself.'

'How do you know that? Have you spoken to the mother?' Sari asked, perplexed.

'I've read the statistics, so I think you can relax. Junkies don't come from happy, nuclear families living in detached houses in Savela.'

'There are exceptions. Always.'

'Very well. Your kids are probably already doomed.'

Sari wiped a tear from her cheek and chuckled.

'Having your own children turns you into a neurotic wreck,' she said. 'Sometimes I think I should have got a dog instead.'

Anna laughed out loud. She could never have anticipated hearing that from Sari's mouth.

'This job doesn't exactly bring out the brighter side of human nature. There isn't much to brag about on Facebook,' Sari continued.

'Do we ever get used to this?' Anna wondered and thought of the old man crushed in the car accident.

'On some level, we probably do, but never completely. At least, I can't.'

'Thank you.'

'For what?'

'For making me feel relatively normal.'

'Now that's saying something,' Sari quipped, and Anna laughed again.

'But Marko. Despite everything, and judging by what we've heard, he managed to live a fairly quiet life.'

'Who owns the apartment?'

'The mother.'

'How long had he been living there?'

'According to his mother, about a year.'

'If you've got a junkie dealing drugs in a small apartment block in a peaceful area of town, someone must have noticed more than this. They simply must.'

'How about we get a bite to eat and come back again after four o'clock? Hopefully the people out at work will be back home by then.'

'I'll have to call the babysitter,' Sari sighed. 'She's leaving town in the autumn, going off to university.'

'Oh, where?'

'It doesn't matter where. The bottom line is Sanna will be gone. She's planning on leaving at the end of May. Backpacking round Asia, apparently.'

'Sounds great.'

'Anna! It's a catastrophe. We'll never cope without Sanna.'

'You didn't expect a girl that age to stay with you forever, did you? To forge a career nannying at your house?'

'Yes.'

'Of course you didn't.'

'Another two months and she'll be gone. It doesn't bear thinking about.'

'Two months, and with any luck this damn snow will have melted. Have you advertised for a replacement?'

'Teemu and I have talked about getting an au pair. We've got a big house, there would be plenty of room.'

'Would you really want a complete stranger working for you day and night?'

'We'd get used to it, I'm sure, though it'll be a bit weird at first. If I knew someone who'd already had an au pair, I could ask what it's like.'

Anna thought of Gabriella and her host family. She could ask them. But she didn't want to contact Gabriella.

8

'PLEASE DON'T SEND ME HOME,' Sammy said in beautiful English with a marked Pakistani accent, looking Anna lethargically in the eyes. The boy had received treatment; the doctor had spent a long while in the holding cell and returned later in the evening to administer more medication and check that everything was all right. He had been ordered to get the boy into a condition fit for interview. When Anna and Esko walked in the room, Sammy looked sleepy, thin and gaunt, but still lucid. Anna noted his tired eyes, eyes that had seen so much and that could have belonged to a man many decades his senior. Pity wrenched her from within. The eyes were meek.

'We will be submitting an appeal to the immigration office this afternoon,' said Ritva Siponen, a stern lawyer approaching sixty. 'His life will be in danger back home.'

Zoran had returned Anna's call that same evening and asked her out for coffee. Anna hadn't wanted to meet him, not so soon after speaking to Nataša, and certainly not on a day celebrating equality and the life of the author and social activist Minna Canth. Anna had noticed the raised flags on her way to work and wondered why they were hoisted; she later heard the reason on the radio. Anna had felt a sense of great pride at her new homeland. How many countries in the world raised flags in support of equality or showed such respect for a controversial writer advocating women's rights? Not very many. Zoran had probably never heard of equality, though he'd lived in Finland longer than Anna. You couldn't simply pull up roots stuck in the chauvinistic Balkan culture, and Zoran hadn't even tried. The best thing to do would be to forget about him for good, Anna thought and pursed her lips.

Zoran had given her Ritva Siponen's number straight away. Anna was surprised that the lawyer was a woman, simply because it was Zoran who recommended her. Zoran was about as macho as a macho Serb could be; he seemed constantly surrounded by other men, especially when it came to business. Ritva had defended countless residence and asylum cases, Zoran assured her, and Anna hadn't asked any more. She never asked. The ins and outs of Zoran's business affairs were the last thing she wanted to know. Then he'd suggested he could come and pay her a home visit. My brother is here, she'd said hurriedly and Zoran had burst into laughter. Don't lie, he said. Ákos is sitting in the pub drinking, his unemployment benefit apparently burning a hole in his pocket. Zoran had helped him out by buying him a pint. Anna was annoyed. She'd hoped her brother might have finally calmed down.

'So Sammy, tell me how long you've known Marko Halttu,' she asked.

'Only a few months.'

'Have you lived at his flat?'

'A few nights, that's all.'

'Where have you been living since you ran away from the reception centre?'

'Here and there. On the streets, in rubbish bins, stairwells, with friends.'

'Ask him how long he's been using drugs,' Esko told Anna.

Anna asked him, but the answer was not short. At first Sammy didn't want to talk at all, but at Ritva Siponen's suggestion he relented and told his story in a monotonous and dispassionate voice, now with even the edge of sadness sanded away by all the sedatives. Sammy was originally from Quetta, a city near the border with Afghanistan. The first ten years of his childhood had been good. For members of the Christian minority, they had been in an exceptionally good position, because Sammy's father had always had a job. They went to church on Sundays; life had been frugal but comfortable. Of course they followed the news about the Taliban and other extremist groups raising their heads in Pakistan, though at the time it seemed they didn't have much influence in Sammy's corner of the city. Later Sammy realised that his mother and father had managed to hide their worry from the children. The sense of danger had been hanging in the air long before a group of fundamentalist Muslims moved into the neighbourhood. That's when everything started. At first it was just minor disturbances at Sunday services, interruptions and noisy protests outside the church. The priest's family had been threatened and the church no longer felt safe. Soon afterwards began a systematic campaign of terror against all Christian families in the area; even their old neighbours joined in. Sammy's family was bullied, harassed and assaulted. The man next door claimed that Sammy's father had insulted the Quran and for this he was charged with blasphemy, which in Pakistan often carried the death sentence. One day Sammy's mother was raped. This set in motion a chain of events that wrenched the last remnants of normality from their lives. Sammy's father and brother wanted revenge. Though her physical wounds eventually healed, his mother never fully recovered from the shock and the shame. When their father was kicked out of his job, it was the final straw. Sammy's father and brother went to the neighbours' house. Sammy explained how he and his mother had waited in the darkened house for their return; his mother prepared bandages, mumbled quiet prayers and boiled washing water. They didn't say a word to one another; fear had taken their ability to speak. They waited and waited, in vain. Sammy's father and elder brother never returned.

In the early hours of the morning their neighbours and a large crowd of followers arrived, broke into the house and took his mother away kicking and screaming. Sammy escaped through a window at the back of the house and ran as fast as his legs could carry him. The neighbours' relatives moved into the house the very next day; their house was quite literally occupied. Sammy was fifteen at the time. He lay low for a few days with some Christian people he knew and fled to Karachi after he heard that he too had been accused of blasphemy. Once there, he lived on the streets and in a church for almost a year. He constantly felt as though someone was watching him, following him, hounding him. The only person he could trust was the priest of the congregation, who worked in fear for his life to protect the small community of Pakistani Christians. The priest had tried to get help, approached the courts, contacted human rights organisations, but it all came to nothing.

I should have stayed there and looked after my mother, he said, expressionless. He never found his cousins, who had already fled to Karachi. Sammy tried to look for them, but asking around was difficult because he had to remain in hiding. Instead he found his way to the opium dens, and heroin was easy to come by – after all, they were right in the middle of the Golden Triangle poppy fields, at the start of the smuggling routes to the west.

The drugs helped him – at first. He wasn't safe anywhere. The grip of radical Islam seemed to be closing all around him. The local priest eventually helped Sammy to escape. He headed for Europe, a Christian land, in search of help. He found himself in Finland, Lutheran through and through, managed to kick the drugs and started learning Finnish; he was hopeful and finally believed he had a chance at some kind of normal life, though his asylum application dragged on and on.

And now he was being sent back.

'I have nothing left there. Nothing but a blasphemy charge for defaming Islam. They'll kill me,' Sammy said bringing his lengthy story to an end. His posture had slumped; his voice was hushed.

'We're going to gather new evidence about these events. I'm going to try and contact the priest who sheltered Sammy in Karachi and helped him escape. In my opinion Sammy's initial application wasn't well prepared; lots of aggravating evidence was missing,' Ritva explained in English and gave Sammy an encouraging smile. There wasn't a flicker of hope in his eyes.

Anna was shocked. She wanted to help that emaciated, innocent-looking boy. If even half of what he had said was true, it was incredible that his asylum application had been refused. Why is it that welfare is something we only give out like alms to the chosen few who meet a set of ridiculous criteria dreamed up by a bunch of bureaucrats? We don't listen to individual stories; we just look at the overall situation, the general conditions and the law in each country, and if everything seems above board officials here simply can't fathom that the law and the general conditions are not the same for everyone or that things published in writing might not necessarily be true. That wasn't even the case in Finland, let alone a country like Pakistan. Laws were created by humans and were often rigged to protect the rights of the majority. Anna sincerely hoped that Ritva Siponen knew what she was doing.

'It's a terrible story, but it's not really our concern. We've got a dangerous street gang, one drug-related death and a missing pensioner to look into,' Esko said and looked at Anna. 'Can he tell us anything about them?'

Anna almost lost her composure at Esko's indifference. Surely Sammy's story couldn't leave anyone cold, not even Esko. On the other hand, he was right: their job was to investigate a crime, not to assess the rights and wrongs of Sammy's asylum application. That was Ritva Siponen's job. Anna pulled herself together, reminded herself that she was a police officer, and asked where Marko Halttu had got his hands on the narcotics. Sammy swore he didn't know.

'Was there always so much gear there?'

'Never before. Not when I was there, at least.'

'When did you go to Halttu's flat?'

'Saturday, I think. In the afternoon.'

'Why did you go there?'

'To buy some subs.'

'What did you think when you saw everything?'

'I thought, wow.'

'Didn't it occur to you that Halttu could have been mixed up in more than just dealing?'

'Yes.'

'But you didn't care.'

'No. The cramps were terrible.'

'What was Marko's condition when you entered the apartment?'

'He was completely out of it. He fell asleep on the couch soon afterwards.'

'Marko had a head wound. Did you two get into a fight?'

'No.'

'So where did his injury come from?'

'I tried to ask him; he already had it when I arrived. But he didn't tell me. He couldn't speak.'

'You were there almost two days. Did Marko wake up at all?'

'To be honest I don't know. I was too excited by all the drugs and took quite a lot of subs.'

'So it's possible that Marko died on Saturday, right in front of your eyes, and you did nothing.'

Sammy looked at Anna. Could she see a glimmer of fear and anxiety behind those meek eyes, so clouded with medication?

'Yes.'

'Have you ever seen Riitta Vehviläinen, the lady that lives opposite Marko?'

'No. Why?'

'She's gone missing.'

Anna tried to read Sammy's expression to see if there was even a flicker of fear, of not quite telling the truth, anything to suggest he knew more than he was telling her, but the drugs had rendered him almost expressionless.

'I don't know anything about Macke's neighbours.'

'Did Marko ever mention anyone else by name? Other dealers or customers?'

'No.'

'Ever heard of the Black Cobras?' Esko interrupted them in English. So he does understand, thought Anna.

Sammy shuddered almost imperceptibly.

'No. I mean, I've heard of them, but that's it.'

'Where did you hear about them? Who told you?'

'I can't remember.'

'Try and remember,' Esko snapped.

'Somewhere in Rajapuro, I think. I've been there a lot.'

'More specific,' Esko commanded him.

'A man once asked me if I wanted to become a dealer. He was wearing a hoodie with gang emblems on the back.'

'What kind of emblems?'

'The Black Cobra emblem.'

'How do you know what the Black Cobra emblem looks like?'

'I've seen them before.'

Anna gave Esko a look of concern.

'When was this?'

'The end of January, maybe. My sense of time is a bit hazy.'

'So this happened in Rajapuro?'

'Yes, I think so.'

'Where exactly?'

'In an apartment. Please believe me, I don't remember where it was or who lived there. I was totally out of it.'

'Was the man Finnish?'

'No. He spoke English and he looked … Iranian or Palestinian.'

'Did you start dealing?'

'Of course not.'

'Why not?'

'There's a greater risk of being caught. I wanted to be as invisible as possible.'

'But you got hooked on Subutex.'

'Yes, unfortunately.'

'It's easy to get your hands on drugs round here,' said Anna, and recent statistics for drug-related deaths flashed through her mind. Most of them had been caused by Subutex. The substance had become a real nightmare. It had taken over the streets because it was so cheap and easy to get hold of. A drug originally intended to help alleviate heroin addicts' withdrawal symptoms had now hooked people who had never laid eyes on heroin. The demon had been replaced by the Devil himself.

Sammy laughed glumly. 'Yes. I'd only been on the streets for a week when someone came up and offered me some pills. Hungry and desperate in the freezing cold, it was easy to relapse. I was weak.'

'Describe this guy.'

'He was Finnish, in his twenties. Blond hair, acne. I haven't seen him for a while.'

Anna thought she might just know who the young man was.

'Where did you get money?'

'It's not very expensive.'

'You were asked where you got the money,' Esko barked.

'I did odd jobs,' Sammy replied.

'Ah, working illegally. Where?'

'Here and there.'

'At the queers' pizza parlour?' Esko ratcheted up the pressure.

'No, not there. They're just friends.'

'Did you sell your arse to them?'

For the first time, Sammy's expression suddenly changed. He was shocked.

'To Maalik and Farzad? Absolutely not. They would never...'

'Who then? Did you?'

'Yes.'

'Who to?'

'I didn't know them.'

'You make me fucking sick.'

'Esko, it's against the law to buy sex, not to sell it,' Anna interrupted.

'Yeah, right. I'd have you on the next plane to Karachi, mate, the whole fucking lot of you.'

Sammy wiped a tear that had trickled down his cheek. Ritva Siponen began gathering her papers. She glared at Esko across the table.

'This interview is over. My client is in shock and is not in a fit condition to continue. Besides, we still have to submit our appeal to the high court. And I'll have to consider how best to deal with the behaviour of Senior Constable Niemi. At the very least you'll get a written warning for this outburst. I'm going to make sure you never interview my client again. You'll never interview anyone at all, if I have my way. I've heard about your attitude before.'

Esko scoffed. Anna felt mortified on his behalf. Sammy had returned to that limp, phlegmatic state. He stood up and shuffled behind his lawyer out into the corridor, where an officer from the holding cells was waiting for him.

'Utter bullshit,' said Esko in the staffroom. It was already evening. Anna was eating the sandwiches she hadn't had time to touch that morning and drinking the bitter coffee burnt at the bottom of the pot.

'What is?'

'The kid's story about Pakistan and the rest of it. The gangs are behind all this, the Cobras and the Hell's Angels. There's a full-blown turf war going on out there,' he said and gestured out towards the city. 'That Sammy is protecting someone else's backside. The Cobras probably brought him here in the first place, you mark my words.'

'I will.'

'What?'

'I'll mark your words. Where should I write them?'

'Oh, piss off. The worst thing is that the Cobras have already been operating here for a while, and we didn't notice a thing.'

'Sammy came to Finland over two years ago. I doubt the Cobras were even thinking about coming here back then.'

'Sammy looked frightened when I asked him about the gangs. And the first time the Cobras tried to set up shop here was a few years ago.'

'I still don't think Sammy has anything to do with them. He's just had some bad luck.'

'Do you know what the Black Cobras are like? They're ruthless, and their primary preoccupation is the drugs trade.'

'I know.'

'I've read hundreds of reports from Sweden and Denmark about what they get up to. It's crazy.'

'Aren't things dying down a bit, in Sweden at least?'

'The police over there have hit them hard. Maybe that's why they want to set up here. Besides, it's all an act. In Sweden the Cobras have stopped wearing gang emblems, so their operations have become invisible. These guys' jackets and hoodies give us a head start.'

'Do you think they'd take on a Finnish boy? They're an immigrant group, after all.'

'Initially, yes, a Muslim group, but I'm sure any kid crazy enough will do. For day-to-day street dealing it's probably good not to stand out too much. Up here in the north, at any rate. There aren't that many of your lot here yet, thank God. Halttu got his hands on the Angels' gear and he had other plans for it, and I'll bet those plans involved the Cobras – and Sammy.'

'It sounds possible. But you behaved appallingly towards him.'

'I didn't say anything that old bat could use to lodge a complaint.'

'You were downright repulsive. I feel really sorry for that boy.'

'I don't feel a drop of sympathy for people like that. The kid's mixed up with an international criminal gang, he's doubtless spreading HIV and hepatitis round the city, and now he's in our holding cell having his cold turkey treated at our taxpayers' expenses. For crying out loud.'

'I really thought you'd changed.'

Esko stared at Anna with bleary eyes. His expression said it all. 'Just because I think you're okay does not mean I suddenly love all the wogs round here.'

Anna glanced over her shoulder to check that nobody else was around.

'You helped one of them,' she whispered.

'We agreed never to talk about that again,' Esko hissed back at her.

Anna's telephone rang; it was Gabriella. She pressed the 'silence' button.

'One of your boyfriends?'

'That's right, three at once.'

'Haven't you got yourself a bloke yet?'

'It's none of your business.'

'Why not? You're not a dyke, are you?'

'Esko, you sound like my mother.'

'I'm just worried about you. It's fashionable these days, being worried about things all the time. Surely I can be worried about something too?'

'No need. Have you got a lady friend?'

'You bet. Plenty.'

'With your looks and charm I bet you have to chase them off with a stick.'

All at once something flashed across Esko's face, something different from the usual arrogant, hard-boiled cop; a lonely man behind the mask. I've gone too far, thought Anna. What do I know about that man's life, about what had hardened him so much? Nothing whatsoever.

'I fancy a quick pint,' said Esko. 'That bitch of a lawyer really pissed me off. You coming?'

'Just the one. I'm going for a run later.'

'Should have guessed. Well, I'm going back to work later, so it's only one for me too.'

Anna was already on her evening run when she noticed that Gabriella had called her another five times and sent two text messages. Anna had put her phone on silent as she and Esko entered Kaarle's Bar on the outskirts of the city centre, near Pizzeria Hazileklek. Esko had three pints, Anna only one. She'd been tempted to ask about Esko's past, where he was born, why he had joined the police, whether he had any children, but she didn't have the courage. Esko didn't like busybodies. In that respect he and Anna were similar.

The conversation had stayed on safe subjects, work and colleagues, Rauno's drawn-out recovery from the car crash, last autumn's hunting season when Esko had caught four hares in one day. After that Anna had gone home and Esko had returned to the station.

Anna wondered whether she should call back. Did Gabriella have anything important to say? Anna noticed she'd received another text message from her mother. *Call soon. It's important* was all it said.

Anna turned the sound back on and called her mother straight away. Anna's grandmother had been taken ill, her mother told her. She couldn't eat properly and was complaining of pains in her back and stomach. She had gone to the doctor that afternoon and been sent straight to hospital for further tests. Her mother promised to call her as soon as she knew more.

Anna was worried. Grandma had always been there. She couldn't become ill, and she absolutely couldn't die. Grandma, that dear, wonderful, wise, warm-hearted lady who had never once moved house, but who had still lived in five different states. The borders moved, rulers came and went, names changed and maps were redrawn, but grandmothers remained constant. Or did they?

Anna burst into a sprint. She decided to run further than she had planned; it helped alleviate her distress. Sweat ran down her warm skin, though the chill pinched her cheeks. She ran back and forth through Koivuharju until her mind began to calm with the physical exertion. The phone rang in her pocket just as she was passing Ákos's house. Anna glanced up. The lights were on in his windows.

'*Szia, Anna*,' Gabriella whooped.

'*Szia*.'

'*Hogy vagy?*'

'*Jól vagyok*.'

'Is there any news about the old man?'

'*Nem*. I'll call you as soon we hear anything.'

Anna felt the sweat on her back cooling. Her moist running clothes didn't protect against the wind.

'Can we meet up?'

'I'm out running. I can't really talk.'

'You're such a sports freak! I should go to the gym too.'

'Well…'

'Can I come round? This evening?'

'Sorry, I'm going to my brother's place.'

'More Hungarians! Can I come too?'

'No.'

'Why not?'

'Another time.'

'Fine, if you say so. *Szia*.'

Gabriella hung up. Anna heard the hurt in her voice, the disappointment, the homesickness. I'm an insensitive bitch, she thought, looking up at Ákos's window and stepping into the stairwell.

Her brother didn't open the door. Anna tried to call him; she could hear his phone ringing in the hallway. As a ring tone, 'Too Drunk to Fuck' sounded even more ridiculous than on disc. Anna shouted through the letterbox. Not a sound. Either he wasn't home or he had passed out. Probably the latter. Anna wondered whether Mr Karppinen could have passed out too. Nobody had answered the door there either, not even on her second visit, when all the other residents of the apartment block in Leppioja had returned home.

The computer screen glared numbingly. Esko restlessly clicked the mouse, surfed the net, drifting from one place to the next. He didn't know what he was looking for. He clicked open an estate agent's website, looking for something similar to his own apartment. He wouldn't get much for his place. The location was crap, and in all these years he hadn't done any renovation whatsoever. Selling his apartment was beginning to seem like hard work. Perhaps he could rent it out while he was away. But then he could forget about a cottage in the woods, unless you could rent them too. Damn it, everything was so difficult. Esko moved to travel agencies' websites and began planning a summer holiday, but soon that too seemed to bore him. Why the hell should he take off to a place with rows of hotels and millions of other tourists? He'd never done anything like that before. Why won't this feeling of restlessness go away? And where would I go? What's the matter with me, he wondered nervously and felt a tight, painful sensation in his chest. He pressed his hand against the pain and rubbed his chest muscles with his knuckles. Just then there was a knock at his door and Virkkunen stepped inside.

'Still working?' said Pentti and looked at the computer screen. Esko quickly clicked the screen away.

'You too, I see.'

'Problems with your ticker?'

Esko did nothing to hide the look of annoyance on his blotchy face.

'No. I'm fit as a fiddle.'

'Of course you are. Any progress on the Reza case?'

'Nope. Still haven't got the little bastard in my sights. But I've got a feeling we'll find him soon. The Cobras have started falling into our hands like ripe apples.'

'Have you seen your informant again?'

'No. But things on the street are heating up. Big time.'

'Indeed. The Cobras are encroaching on the Angels' territory.'

'I reckon we're in for full-blown gang warfare.'

'We had an average call-out at the weekend over in Rajapuro. You know Pasi Raatikainen, young guy from patrol?'

'Yep.'

'Well, he said there was something odd going on in that apartment.'

'What?'

'There were two guys from Iran hanging about in there, though they weren't the reason for the disturbance, so they were simply removed from the property. A Finnish couple got into a fight. Standard stuff, drunken fisticuffs.'

'And what's weird about that?'

'Raatikainen only heard about the Cobras at this morning's briefing. It was his first night on duty since Christmas, so he didn't know anything about the gang investigation. This morning he realised that one of the guys had the letters B.C. tattooed on the fingers of his right hand.'

'Damn it. I want that apartment turned inside out.'

'Yes, and we'll have to bring the drunken couple in for questioning. I'll bring you up to date once we've decided when to go in. How are things otherwise?' Virkkunen asked and looked at the computer again. Christ, the man sees everything, thought Esko.

'I've been thinking about selling up and leaving.'

'That's a great idea, Esko. A change of scenery could do you good,' said Virkkunen and left the room.

9

A HUMID WIND BLEW through the pass. The grains of sand shimmered in the air. The Afghan borderlands sweated, a hazy threat electrified the air. Everything was silent. A speck burst from behind the horizon, growing rapidly. It was a jeep full of men. The barrels of rifles and bayonets, Mosin-Nagants and Kalashnikovs, jutted like extensions of the men's silhouettes towards the sky, veiled behind the thick gauze of dust kicked up behind the vehicle. The jeep hurtled forwards; suddenly it was enormous, it was going to hit him. Sammy woke with a start to the sound of his own screams. His skin was sticky with sweat, his heart was thumping, a trail of saliva ran from the corner of his mouth. It took a moment to calm down, to realise that he was safe, there on the narrow bunk in the police holding cell.

Though Sammy knew that he would soon be returned to the place that dream had come from, for the first time in a long while he felt calm and protected in this bare, concrete room. He noticed that he almost enjoyed the officers' polite knocks at his door, their gentle behaviour and the short conversations they had as they took him to the yard outside or brought him his meals. He wasn't shown love and compassion, but he was treated well. What's more, his illness, his addiction and withdrawal symptoms were being treated too. A nurse visited him, a beautiful young woman. She brought him medication and asked how he was coping, took his blood pressure and his body temperature, touched him with her warm, delicate hands. Sammy couldn't remember the last time he'd felt the friendly touch of another person on his skin. The woman's eyes were indescribably blue, her hair fair and blond like the finest wool, and she smiled at him. His five-square-metre cell with no entertainment or conveniences was heaven, a place Sammy could stay for a long time.

Sammy didn't think Ritva Siponen's appeal would be successful. She hadn't been able to locate the priest in Karachi; Sammy guessed that he too had probably been killed. Ritva had looked online for information about human-rights organisations in Pakistan; she'd found the odd scrap, but nothing to show that Sammy's family had been the victim of any persecution. The local judge had said he knew nothing of the blasphemy charges against Sammy and his father, the dirty liar. Ritva was trying her best, but Sammy had already lost hope. He knew exactly where he would go as soon as he got to Karachi, if he wasn't arrested as soon as he got off the plane. In a city of millions there were a few people who always had room for him in their cardboard shacks. It was a shame that those shacks were in the opium fields, he thought and swallowed the saliva that flooded into his mouth. Perhaps he should just turn himself in at the airport. Pakistani prisons were worse than the opium dens and the slums, but he deserved his punishment. He could have saved his mother, but instead he'd saved his own skin.

Anna sat up, wide awake. Friday morning, another weekend on its way, she thought. *Bassza meg.* She trudged into the hall to fetch the newspaper, made some coffee and flicked through the paper before brushing her teeth and her thick, almost black hair, and setting off for work. Anna often felt her repetitive, everyday routines were oppressive, making each day feel like an eventless, empty copy of the day before, the patterns of life became predictable, numbing the senses and desensitising her mind. Morning chores, work, supermarket, home, food, evening chores, bed. Why was it she so often felt this wasn't enough, that there should be something else, something greater and more exciting, something to shunt these repetitive routines off kilter and wake her up? But wake her from what exactly? And what for? After all, weren't routines a shield to protect us against life's often devastating quirks, events from which nobody was safe?

Routines forced people to hold on to their lives, to take care of their responsibilities, to swim with the current; they gave days a meaning and a rhythm.

Why couldn't she just take care of her duties and be thankful, live in the moment? Why did she always have to look far into the future, out of reach of the everyday? Loved ones die, partners leave us, we lose our jobs, but it's only when people no longer have the strength to cook food, to have a shower or take out the rubbish that they start to slip away. Was that the reason Subutex was so popular in this northern welfare state where youngsters all had an equal chance of an education lauded in international PISA reports, an equal opportunity to live a life filled with routines, a life identical to the people living next door? What else were drugs for if not to numb the tedium of everyday life and our sense of insignificance in the greater wheel of life, our exaggerated emotions that made routines feel like a noose pressing against our windpipes? In a way Anna could understand all those kids and parents that slipped into a cycle of alcohol and substance abuse. They yearned for something more from life, something out of the ordinary, but they didn't know how to achieve it. They lacked the means, the stamina and patience; PISA reports didn't say a word about people like them. Where was the fine line between success and failure? What pushed people over the edge or carried them to safety? I should learn to love my routines, because they don't stifle me; rather, they make life possible, thought Anna and decided to cycle to the station.

Upon arriving at the station, Anna learned that Gabriella Farkas would be facing charges of reckless driving and involuntary manslaughter, even though she had been within the speed limit and was completely sober at the time. The reason was that the driver should have taken the adverse weather conditions into consideration and should have adjusted her speed appropriately. At least the word 'gross' had been left off the list of charges. Anna's mother had sent her a Hungarian legal dictionary, so Anna would be able to find all the relevant terminology. If and when this case went to court, they could hire an interpreter, she thought. That's one thing I'm not prepared to do. She'd also received word from the Hungarian authorities that Gabriella had been apprehended for possession of marijuana in her first year at college. This was only a minor offence, Gabriella had got off with a fine and she had no other misdemeanours to her name, but now it made her seem very irresponsible.

Anna sighed. She felt sorry for Gabriella; she would probably receive a minor punishment, but whatever it was, the sentence would be a blow. It would be a nasty blot on her record. Would she ever get a job again? At the same time Anna felt a foul sense of satisfaction. Not exactly *Schadenfreude*, but something similar. What is it about that girl that bothers me, she wondered. Why do I think this somehow serves her right?

After this Anna began writing up yesterday's interviews with Marko Halttu's neighbours. To Anna and Sari's surprise, the working families with little kids had seen and heard far more than the pensioners who were at home all day. The Kumpula family, who lived on the same floor as Halttu, had twice complained to the housing association about the loud music, first at the beginning of February, then just recently on March the twelfth. They had been certain that things weren't going very well for their neighbour. Apparently the children didn't like going into the yard by themselves, because they had to walk past Halttu's door. Children can sense these things, Mrs Kumpula had said. But there wasn't a constant flow of people in and out of the apartment. On the whole everything had been quiet and discreet, though Mrs Kumpula remembered once seeing a logo that could have belonged to a motorbike gang on the back of someone's jacket. She wasn't entirely sure of what she'd seen.

The Vehkaperä family on the top floor had taken their suspicions a step further. They had called the police after finding a used syringe in one of the rubbish bins. The bin had been full of rubbish bags and the syringe had almost fallen out as they opened the lid. This had happened some time last summer. They didn't know whether the police had taken any action. Earlier in the winter, perhaps back in January, they had seen a scruffy, foreign-looking boy hanging around in the yard. They had assumed he was on his way to Halttu's apartment. They had seen other, similar-looking boys in the yard before and thought the syringe must have come from one of these pallid loiterers. But because they hadn't found any other evidence of drug abuse and because Halttu's emaciated guests hadn't caused any disturbance to speak of, they hadn't taken the matter any further. And how could they have been sure who threw the syringe in the rubbish bin? The Vehkaperäs stressed several times that they didn't want to think ill of people, at least not without any proof. They hadn't seen any snake logos, motorbikes or men in hoodies. Nobody knew anything about the disappearance of Mrs Vehviläinen.

Anna telephoned the caretaker, who sounded arrogant and uptight. He confirmed that there had been a few complaints about the music and that he had given the tenant in question a written warning. The caretaker claimed he had never seen Marko Halttu himself. He sounded just a little too cocky as he explained he was responsible for dozens of apartment blocks across the city and that he didn't have time to look into every single complaint that came his way, because there were plenty of them. Anna asked whether the caretaker had ever met Riitta Vehviläinen, Halttu's neighbour. He couldn't remember ever having met her. Anna then dug out the original complaint about the syringe in the police files. The complaint had been made last August. That's when I started working in this city, when I started chasing down the Hummingbird, she thought, and shuddered. She banished the brutal murders on the running track from her mind every time they tried to resurface, though she was happy that, soon after the Hummingbird had been apprehended, snow had covered the running track through the woods behind Koivuharju and made it inaccessible.

Anna realised she was hungry. She looked at the time; it was almost one o'clock. Morning had turned to afternoon without her noticing. There was no point asking anyone to join her for lunch;

everyone would have eaten already. She decided to eat by herself and visit Leppioja again, to ring Karppinen's doorbell one more time.

How the hell does anyone understand a bloody word of these Pakis' gibberish, Esko muttered to himself. He had spent hours trying to listen to the tapes he had ordered from the National Bureau of Investigation – intercepted telephone calls in which members of the Black Cobras were discussing business – to see if he could find a single conversation that might be in a language he could recognise. More specifically he was looking for a link between the Black Cobras – Reza Jobrani in particular – and Marko Halttu and Sammy Mashid. Esko was convinced Marko's death wasn't entirely self-inflicted. Gangs didn't hesitate to take out people they thought they couldn't trust. Killing someone meant instant promotion within the gang's hierarchy; members of the Angels even got a special badge on their jackets. In those circles, someone capable of killing was highly respected. But these taped conversations in foreign languages were impenetrable. They could have been talking about anything, last night's football results, anything at all. Not even the towel-heads were stupid enough to talk business on a normal telephone. Couldn't the NBI afford to have these translated?

This is a fucking waste of time, thought Esko, switched off the tape recorders and started going through the lists of phone numbers that had been in contact with one another. A few of them were legitimate numbers, registered to people with foreign-sounding names. The rest were all prepaid and probably long since discarded. One number seemed to appear much more frequently than the others – and it was registered. Esko couldn't find anything to indicate that the NBI had interviewed the owner of this number. I'll do it myself, he thought and logged into the police's telephone register. The owner lived in the Vaarala district. Esko searched for the name but couldn't find a Facebook profile or any signs of life on other social media. The owner can't be very young, he concluded. He flicked through other sites that came up on Google and found an interesting news item about someone by the same name who ran a public-health project for women and girls in the northern Iranian countryside. The article was in English and was dated three years ago. Could this be the same person? Esko looked at the image of the woman hidden behind a veil, her black eyes lined in heavy kohl. The woman's clothes made it impossible to guess her exact age, but her eyes revealed that this was a woman who had already reached middle age. He tried to read the article, but a pop-up window prevented him. I'll have to call the IT department, tell them to update our firewalls, he thought. The words *Volunteer Help* flashed across the advertisement. Against his better judgement, he clicked it open. *Do you want to work abroad?* the advertisement asked him. Not on your life, Esko answered to himself. *Do you want to help children in developing countries?* Esko scoffed. Me? *We offer thousands of voluntary positions in fascinating locations around the world. You can help make a difference. Today.*

Esko saved the site in his Bookmarks folder, asked for an interpreter and scheduled a meeting in Vaarala for the following Monday. We'll soon find out about the woman behind the telephone number.

Her stomach full of pasta and sausage, Anna steered the car towards Leppioja. At that time of day the traffic on the southbound motorway was quiet. It was overcast for a change, but the layer of snow covering the fields extending on both sides of the road still reflected so much light that Anna had to wear sunglasses. She curved into the junction and exited the motorway. An area of newly built detached houses, Leppioja had sprung up right next to the intersection. Anna took the winding road through the suburb, passing young mothers pushing prams. Rauno lives somewhere round here, she thought, and tried and failed to remember his exact address. There followed a few hundred metres of woodland, like a transition zone into the older part of Leppioja with its sparsely situated apartment blocks and terraced houses by the ditch, an oasis of peace and calm far from downtown, far from the city's restless high-rise jungles. But every police officer knows that nothing is ever what it seems at first appraisal.

Anna pulled up outside Marko Halttu's house and sat in the car for a while examining the surroundings. It was the first time she had come here alone, and now she was annoyed that she hadn't brought the keys to Halttu's apartment. Anna enjoyed house searches; they always revealed something. Perhaps not right away, but as sources of information they were every bit as good as people. A home told you about its owner and rarely lied: did the inhabitant have a family, were they lonely, tidy or untidy, what did they enjoy doing, what did they like, eat, how did they spend their time? Homes could reveal a history of substance abuse or the suffering of mental illness far more honestly than any relatives; sometimes it seemed as though walls could weep. Most affecting was visiting the homes of seasoned criminals and finding photographs of children, mothers, fathers, pets, souvenirs from abroad, a concert ticket from twenty years ago, all those small but precious items that we all have, things we use to document the important events in our lives. It was moments like this that Anna tried to think of in interview situations, when anger and personal dislike began to blur the human being sitting in front of her.

The yard was deserted. There were only two cars parked outside: an old Opel covered in snow and a newer Toyota plugged into the outdoor battery charger. The building towered above the car park; there were three small, square air vents in the gable, one on top of the other like blocks of Lego bricked into the concrete wall. Those must be the bathrooms, so the only way of looking out into the car park would be to stand right next to the ventilation grille. Only from the neighbouring house could you see anyone entering or leaving the yard. I'll have to speak to those residents too, thought Anna. To the left of the car park she noticed a row of bins, the place where the syringe had been found last summer, and tried to gauge the distance from the door of the A-building to the bins and from the bins to the road. She turned to look back the way she had come. How did people get into town from here? Had she seen a single bus stop along the way? She couldn't see one from here. Did Marko have a car? She would have to find out immediately.

A short phone call to the station revealed that Marko didn't have a car but that his mother owned an old Opel. Anna asked for forensics to join her at the scene and tried to remember when it had last snowed.

Anna still hadn't seen a soul as she walked into Building A. She looked at Halttu's door, the carefully handwritten note reading NO ADVERTS, and felt a burning desire to get inside the flat. Marko's apartment was on the north side of the building; his ventilation grille was one of the Lego blocks overlooking the car park. He therefore only shared walls with two neighbours: the Kumpulas, who had complained about the music, and Vilho Karppinen from upstairs, the man who hadn't answered the door. Anna rang Karppinen's doorbell and waited. The apartment was just as quiet as before. She rang again, louder this time. Nothing. She lifted up the letterbox and peered inside. The first thing she noticed was a pile of post and advertisements scattered across the hallway floor. At a guess, Karppinen hadn't been here for at least a week. The letterbox didn't open wide enough to let Anna see further inside, but she noticed that the hallway lights were switched on. She called Virkkunen.

'I've got to get into Karppinen's apartment,' she said.

'I'll get a warrant and send the caretaker to let you in straight away. Wait there,' said Virkkunen without asking any further questions. His quick understanding of situations and his ability to trust his officers' professional judgement were qualities that Anna greatly admired in her boss.

Anna sat down on the stairs and listened to the house: the faint sound of a flushing toilet, the blare of the television coming from Mrs Lehmusvirta's apartment. It can't be this dead round here, she thought. Nobody went in or out in the hour that she waited for the caretaker. By the time he finally arrived, Anna was beginning to get irritated. The caretaker didn't apologise for the delay. His body language reinforced the impression he had given on the telephone, that he was being forced to interrupt something far more important. Anna swallowed back her annoyance.

'Do you know the man who lives here?' Anna asked as they clambered over the pile of post and into the apartment.

'Vilho Karppinen, I think his name is. Never laid eyes on him.'

'Of course you haven't,' Anna muttered. 'You're responsible for thousands of apartments.'

Only now did the caretaker look at Anna. His uptight expression seemed to melt away. That was sarcasm, idiot, thought Anna and forced herself to give a friendly smile.

'Well, a plumber was called out a while back to look at the pipes. Karppinen was worried about noise he'd heard coming up through the drains.'

'And was there anything wrong with the pipework?'

'Nothing whatsoever. I remember it because we had a good laugh about it with the boys back at the office. You meet all kinds of cranks in this line of work.'

Believe me, you don't know the half of it, Anna almost said.

'The old boy lay in bed complaining he was dizzy and said the pipes were making such a racket he couldn't hear anything else. The racket was in his head, if you ask me. The pipes in this building are fine; they were only renovated a few years ago, and new windows fitted too.'

The lights were on in the bedroom too. How likely was it that he would have left the lights on if he was going away for a few days? Don't people normally check these things many times, come back from the front door to double-check the stove, the lights, the coffee maker?

'Vilho Karppinen is an elderly man, I assume?' Anna asked as if in passing.

'A batty old dinosaur, Kalle called him – the plumber, that is. He's got a sense of humour, that boy.'

I'm sure, thought Anna. The caretaker's presence was beginning to annoy her. She wanted to look around in peace; otherwise she wouldn't hear what the apartment wanted to tell her.

'Could you wait in the hallway, please? Preferably in the stairwell.'

'What? I can't leave you here by yourself to rummage through the old man's things. You realise I'm responsible for anything that...'

Anna pulled out her badge.

'Have you forgotten?' she asked. 'Or would you rather I charged you with obstructing an officer?'

The caretaker fell silent, turned and left the apartment. Within a minute Anna heard him talking on the telephone.

Anna went into the living room. It was small and dark with simple furnishings, a leather sofa, an armchair, a television and bookcase, and a worn, Oriental rug on the floor. Anna crouched down and ran her fingertips along the rug's surface. To her surprise she noticed that this wasn't a polyester copy but a genuine hand-made, woollen rug. This must be very valuable, she thought. Strange that such a modest apartment should contain a rug like this. It surely had a fascinating story attached to it or memories of a trip somewhere. The bookcase was full of novels, classics, collections of poetry. An intellectual, Anna concluded. The unit also contained two glass cabinets. One held expensive bottles of wine, whisky and cognac, and the other housed a collection of unusual knives.

Anna opened the doors to the vitrines. The collection comprised twelve knives, each finer and more elaborate than the next. They were clearly handcrafted; many of them had the maker's name engraved into the blade. Could the knife found in Ketoniemi belong to Vilho Karppinen's collection, Anna wondered and felt a light tingling sensation along the length of her arms. Was it possible? And what on earth would it mean? She closed the cabinet and went into the bedroom. The covers had been thrown back, as though someone had just got out of bed; the sheets, washed hundreds of times, were crumpled. The room was tidy and bare. Only a bed, a bedside table with a book of crosswords filled out in jittery lettering, and a chair with a shirt and a pair of trousers hanging over the arm. It was like a male version of Mrs Vehviläinen's bedroom. Vilho Karppinen. Anna tasted the name. Could this be Villy? Had the two of them run off together? The thought seemed good. It was the sort of thing she too might do with a fun-loving elderly gentleman.

Anna peered into the bathroom. The Lego window was high up on the wall. You could open it to let out condensation from the shower and the laundry, but you'd have to stand on a chair to look out of it. An electric shaver was in the mirror cabinet above the sink. There were yellow-and-brown streaks at the bottom of the toilet.

The stink of an old rubbish bag hung in the kitchen. This finally confirmed what Anna had feared from the outset: Vilho had not gone on a trip and neither had Riitta downstairs. Where were they? Why hadn't they come home?

A terrifying thought crept into Anna's mind. The old bypass ran behind Leppioja and headed towards Kangassara. It was about seven kilometres away, but the route was straightforward. That's where Gabriella lived with her host family. Gabriella would normally have driven along the motorway, which was quicker and more direct, but that night she had wanted to postpone going to sleep, to put her music on full blast, so she'd taken the smaller bypass instead. Lost elderly folk were sometimes found very far from home. Despite their dementia, a life of hard work often meant they were in better shape than teenagers wasting away at their computers. She had to find Vilho Karppinen's relatives, have them identify the body in the morgue and establish whether one of Vilho's knives was missing. But where was Riitta Vehviläinen?

Vilho Karppinen had a son, Juha Karppinen, a fifty-three-year-old tax officer who was currently on a skiing holiday in the north. He had been there for over a week and was due back the following evening. He agreed to come in and identify the body on Monday morning. Anna didn't want to go into detail over the phone, and Karppinen's son hadn't asked. All she said was that the body of an elderly man had been found on the old bypass at Kangassara and that the victim could be Juha's father. The road at Kangassara, the man had asked, somewhat perplexed. Then I doubt it's my father, but of course I'll come and look as soon as I get back, he continued. Behind the voice trying to sound succinct and matter-of-fact, Anna could hear the blur of alcohol. I doubt you've even taken skis with you, she thought spitefully.

It was evening. Anna was lying on the sofa listening to Vladislav Delay's *Anima* album, trying to put off going out for a cigarette, though she really wanted one. Then it would be over, her only cigarette for the day. It smouldered down so quickly, and she was always left craving for more. Gabriella had tried to visit her. Anna hadn't answered the phone or opened the door. Ákos didn't answer the phone to Anna either and didn't open the door. What the hell's wrong with us, Anna wondered and got up from the sofa, fetched her outdoor coat and went out to the balcony. The cigarette felt good, the nicotine seeped through the membranes in her mouth and up into her head, the feeling of giddiness was wonderful, she inhaled deep into her lungs and blew smoke rings into the crisp night air, its chill pinching at her bare hands. I'll have to call Mum on Skype, she thought. And Réka. She missed them both and was worried about her grandmother.

Anna smoked her cigarette down to the filter; it was already burning her fingers by the time she stubbed it out in her grandfather's old ashtray that she'd brought from home. Her grandfather had been a heavy smoker. Small items from their former home – an ashtray, a water jug, a coffee cup, the old terry towel that she'd used to dry herself as a child, worn away so much it was now almost smooth – they all created the feeling that there was something permanent outside her daily routines, they brought a continuum to her life, the sense that she hadn't drifted too far after all. Tomorrow, she thought as she stared at the crumpled cigarette end, and didn't know what to think of the feeling of sadness that the thought elicited. I mustn't give in to these stupid nicotine cravings; I'm an athlete. I want to be out running when I'm an old woman. Only one. That will have to do.

She sat down again on the sofa and looked at the white walls around her. She could already see faint cracks in the paintwork. The building was quiet, as though she were its only resident. She wondered whether to read anything or whether she could be bothered to clean the bathroom. There was a basket full of laundry that needed to be washed, but it could wait until tomorrow. She switched on her laptop, plugged in her headphones and signed into Skype. Réka wasn't online. Of course she wasn't online – it was a Friday evening. Everyone would be down at the Gong, or perhaps they'd gone to Szabadka or Szeged for the evening. Or maybe they were all at Nóra and Tibor's place. The group of friends often met up there nowadays, because it made life easier for little Gizella's parents. Anna called her mother's landline, counted five rings and hung up as the answering machine cut in. Mum had things to do too, people to see, friends and relatives, though now she was probably in hospital with Grandma. Only Anna was at home by herself, moping. What might Béci be up to? Was he getting ready for a night out in Budapest? Or was his five-year-old son spending the weekend with Daddy? Béci had divorced two years ago. His ex was from western Hungary, and according to Béci she'd never fully understood his Balkan mentality. Anna asked him what that mentality was like. Béci laughed. You know, he'd said and looked her in the eyes, and Anna felt almost faint.

She got up from the sofa, went into the kitchen and drank a glass of water. She washed up the dirty dishes in the sink: a fork, a knife, a plate and a frying pan, as if to destroy any evidence of the meal she'd eaten, all alone. Was there anything more depressing than eating by yourself on a Friday evening in a drab suburban apartment, she wondered. If I had a husband and children I'd need a dishwasher. My routines would take on a new meaning altogether. She banished all thoughts of family dinners from her mind, of children sitting around the table, of a husband that cleared up the dishes after dinner, loaded them into the dishwasher and thanked her for the excellent food with a kiss. That's not what she wanted. She couldn't deal with that. In the hallway she fetched her mobile from her coat pocket and wrote Réka a text message suggesting they talk on Skype tomorrow. At the last minute she decided not to send it. Instead she replaced the word 'tomorrow' with 'today' and saved the message as a draft. Réka won't even read the message until the morning, Anna explained to herself, though she knew that wasn't the real reason. She was ashamed of her own loneliness. She curled up on the sofa, propped the laptop on her knees and clicked open the Magyar Szó Online newspaper and used the headlines to travel back home to Vajdaság, imagined the rustle of the newspaper, their small kitchen table, always covered with a clean tablecloth, and listened to the clink of her grandmother's coffee cup.

10

THE SEA ICE GLEAMED so brightly in the sunlight that you couldn't look at it directly. Sun cream and a good pair of sunglasses were essential if you wanted to spend all day out on the ice. Anna planned to do just that. She took her skis out of the car, strapped them to her feet, slung her rucksack over her shoulder and sped out on to the ice. She gauged the direction that the wind was coming from and headed right into it. With any luck the wind wouldn't turn, and the journey back would be easier, helped along by the breeze. There were other skiers out on the ice, as well as ice fishers and people on snowmobiles, but the further out Anna skied the more deserted her surroundings became. The best thing was the speed. Working your body as if you were on skates, you could travel very fast, and that's what Anna enjoyed. This is actually better than running, she thought as she felt the sweat moistening her head and back and let the empty, barren landscape envelope her as she hurtled into it.

A biting wind blew across the ice, though there was no covering of fine snow on the surface of the ice. Any loose snow had long since become pressed into the ice beneath, and though at times it snowed again, fresh snow immediately clung to the old stuff. Just like me, thought Anna. The light burrowing into her eyes was so bright that she couldn't look at it. Although the amount of daylight increased as the days passed, this spring had been exceptionally cold. At night temperatures dropped to around -20°C, while during the day they rose to no more than -10°C or -8°C.

Anna had decided to head towards a small island situated about five kilometres from the shore. The wind blew against her face, and skiing felt difficult. Punishing her body like this felt amazing, pushing it, making it do more, last a little longer, go a little further. Without regular exercise and a good sweat I'd lose my mind, Anna thought. She knew this from experience. From a young age she'd been into running, skiing, hiking across the empty fells of Lapland, marathons. The head of Anna's high school had suggested she take up football or basketball. Anna had dismissed this with a laugh and said she wasn't remotely interested. In fact, the mere thought of it stressed her out: changing rooms, communal showers, competitions, training sessions late into the evenings, fundraising events, raffles, buses full of teammates and team spirit. The latter two were at the top of her anxiety list. She imagined she would have been able to poison the best of team spirits, would always sit at the front of the bus staring at the motorway.

The island appeared on the horizon like a blemish on the ice. Anna marched towards it, increasing her speed. The thought of the Thermos full of warm coffee and the salami sandwiches in her rucksack flickered in her mind. No man is an island, or so people said. What are we then?

Her phone rang in her bag. *A fene*, she said, braked and stopped, and looked at the screen, catching her breath. It was Gabriella. She pressed the 'reject' button, but the phone started ringing again before she could put it back into her bag. Was the girl in some kind of trouble?

'Anna.'

'*Szia Anna, itt Gabi. Jó reggelt.*'

'Morning.'

'Listen, I've been thinking about all sorts of things. I need a bit of help.'

'I'm out skiing, I can't talk right now. What if I call you on Monday?'

'I'm looking after the kids again on Monday.'

'Yes, and on Monday I'll be at work again. Technically, you're a work issue at the moment.'

'I wondered, could I come over this evening? Tomorrow maybe?'

Anna was becoming frustrated. She simply couldn't be seen to chum around with someone under investigation any longer. It was completely unprofessional, no matter how Hungarian the suspect. She could be taken off the case and given a warning. Besides, she didn't want to have anything to do with Gabriella. There was something very annoying about her.

'I'm sorry, Gabi. It's not on. Only once the investigation is over. Do you understand?'

'What if I give you a call later this evening?'

'*Nem.*'

'*Miért nem?*'

Anna could feel the chill. The sweat was drying on her skin and the bitter wind was freezing the hand holding her phone.

'I'll call you on Monday,' she finally said.

'Fine then. Monday it is,' Gabriella responded, hurt, and hung up without saying goodbye.

Bassza meg, that girl is getting on my nerves, thought Anna. She went back to her skiing but couldn't find the same rhythm or speed as a moment ago. Even the ice stretching out towards the horizon seemed dreary now. The wind had eaten away at its surface, forming dips and lumps that knocked against her skis and almost toppled her. The wind had blown the soft covering of snow on to the shores in the distance. The ice was hard and unforgiving. Anna curved along the shore of the small island and looked for a sheltered dune of snow; she unrolled her outdoor mat and sat down to eat her sandwiches. The sun warmed her. She made out the faint buzz of a snowmobile. Gradually she calmed down.

Back home, the River Tisza never froze over. There were rarely sub-zero temperatures, and even if there were, the current in the river was too strong for it to freeze. She'd told her friends that people in Finland go winter swimming. Zoli and Ernő had wanted to try it out, and as their friends stood shrieking on the shore the boys went swimming in the 4°C waters of the Tisza, roaring and only feeling the chill afterwards. Anna told them about the health benefits of winter swimming and the men decided to take it up as a hobby. After that, the same group of them had gone down to the shore every day. Réka, Anna, Nóra, Tibor and their three-year-old daughter Gizella remained on the jetty, cheering on Zoli and Ernő as they splashed around in the water, enjoying being the centre of attention, like little boys. Then they ran to the Gong for coffee, beer and a pizza. Anna smiled. The spontaneous ability of her old group of friends to have fun was something invaluable. Anna didn't know whether they always behaved like that or whether her rare visits brought out a little extra fun-loving spirit. She looked at the impressive contours of the horizon in the sunshine, watched the speck of a distant skier gliding along it. She looked at her watch. There was still time to continue, to do a really long round trip. Or she could go into work. The thought of returning to her lonely apartment wasn't appealing. She could pay another visit to Leppioja, talk to people in the house next door to where Halttu and Mrs Vehviläinen lived.

Anna watched her steps as she walked across the frozen yard. The gritting had become embedded in the ice and her feet slipped. Someone had built castles and horses in the snow. So there really are children here, she thought, and not just bitter old folk. But again the yard was empty. During the week the children were at school and nursery, where they were taught how to obey orders that over time would stymie their free spirits. Now they were spending Saturday afternoon with their families. The only people at home in the neighbouring block were a retired couple and one poor soul who could barely see herself in the mirror. Naturally none of them had noticed anything, and they didn't know the people living in the building next door. Anna asked the retired couple to let her in; she wanted to look out of their windows to see what the yard looked like from up there. The couple eagerly agreed. They wanted to make some coffee, but Anna declined. She looked out of the windows for a long time. There wasn't a good view of the car park. It was already so dark that the few streetlamps were unable to light the area completely. This is the perfect place for dodgy dealings, Anna thought. No one can see a thing.

There was nobody home in any of the other apartments. The old couple guessed their neighbours had gone skiing for the weekend. Anna felt frustrated. Why was this so difficult? She dropped her card through each letterbox with a note asking people to call her. She didn't want to come out here again unless people had something to tell her.

The beer can opened with a hiss. My favourite sound, thought Esko and switched on his computer. He was sitting in his office at the station, though it was a Saturday and he had a headache. He had come in to sort out the piles of papers that were now so numerous he wouldn't have time to analyse them during normal working hours. The ingredients for a turf war were ready, right there in their quiet little city. The Cobras moving in on the Hell's Angels' territory would produce a wave of violence – and maybe even a few bodies, as had happened in Copenhagen. Sometimes it was as though the Danish capital was engulfed in a civil war, with firearms and shootouts and innocent victims right there in the city centre. It seemed incredible: this was Scandinavia, not Soweto. The Finnish authorities and all the tree-hugging humanists should visit Copenhagen and Malmö and take a look at what an open-door immigration policy really means, thought Esko.

Marko Halttu's death could well be the first kill in a gang war. Someone had whacked him over the head before his death, which otherwise looked like an overdose. Who had been in that apartment? None other than Sammy Mashid. The Paki kid was trying to play innocent, but Esko knew the gangs and the drug world. Nobody was innocent. Narcotics, money and power were the only things that mattered, and they made people do all sorts of things. Of course, Sammy could be a victim, too, just a pawn in the big boys' games, but he was still guilty, of that Esko was certain. Hell, if that bitch of a lawyer stops me from interrogating the boy again. Virkkunen had put a letter from Internal Investigations on his desk. Esko had thrown it in the bin unopened. He had done nothing wrong and wouldn't consent to any interviews or investigations. He'd rather hand in his notice. It was a tempting thought; he could slap his letter of resignation on Virkkunen's desk and get the hell out, leave behind the mundane cases and boring colleagues and do something new. He remembered the advertisement saved in his browser's bookmarks. How about it, he found himself wondering – to his own surprise. That would be something new. He had always believed that if you want to help refugees you should help them in their own countries and not haul them halfway across the world to be pampered at the expense of the Finnish taxpayer. The thought was tantalising.

Esko finished off his can and pulled another one from the rucksack beneath his desk. He organised the papers on his desk into new piles and sipped his beer. The material had originally been organised by theme: telecommunications, interrogations, house searches and so on. Now he reorganised events in chronological order. That would give him a fresh perspective on the situation, making it easier to establish how Sammy, Reza and Marko fitted into the murky world of the Cobras and the Hell's Angels.

The job took him five beers and six cigarettes. It was late. Esko decided to go into town and get himself good and drunk, and leave the job of reading everything until later.

11

ANNA WOKE to the sound of the doorbell. She looked at the alarm clock ticking on her bedside table; it was eight-thirty. She'd slept well, thanks to the skiing. The doorbell rattled again. Yes, all right, Anna shouted, reluctantly lifted the duvet, put on her dressing gown and went to the door. She was sure it would be Ákos.

'A twig for thee, a gift for me, a pussy from the willow tree; the time is here, to thank you dear, and give good tidings all the year!' chirped two little Easter witches standing in the stairwell, waving decorated willow branches.

A fene egye meg, Anna cursed to herself. She'd forgotten – again. She always forgot, every year. So why did the kids always come back without fail? It was Palm Sunday and the local children were wandering from door to door dressed as Easter witches. They always dressed the same way: a brightly coloured scarf round their heads, red freckles drawn with Mum's lipstick and a funny-looking skirt. Sometimes the witches were little boys. They had taken far less time over their costumes and generally looked like … little boys. To Anna they looked nothing like witches. For all their irritating sprightliness, these two were very cute, the younger probably not even in school. The children were carrying a large collection of pussy willows and a basket to fill with treats. At least they'd gone to the trouble of collecting the willows and decorating them with bright feathers. They were actually quite pretty.

'Hang on, I'll see if I've got any change in my wallet,' Anna told the children, though she was sure she didn't have any. She had no cash: no coins, no notes, no sweets, no biscuits. Absolutely nothing.

'Oh dear, I'm sorry, I haven't got anything to give you.'

The witches looked disappointed.

'Then you don't get a willow,' said the elder one.

'I suppose not,' Anna replied, embarrassed. *A francba*, I'm going to go out today and buy a packet of Easter eggs ready for next year, she thought. And all my Christmas presents; they're always left to the last minute too. Were the shops open on Palm Sunday? They were always open. Nothing was so sacred as to stop the constant exchange of money. Anna closed the door and squinted through the peephole into the stairwell. The witches moved next door. The elder one rang the doorbell and the smaller one turned to look at Anna's door. A small pink tongue poked out of his grimacing mouth.

Anna trudged back to bed but couldn't get to sleep. She reluctantly got up and made some coffee. She was just about to pour it into a cup when the doorbell rang again. There would be witches coming round all day. Best not answer the door. The letterbox screeched as it was prised open.

'*Anna, otthon vagy?*' Ákos's voice echoed through the hallway. Damn it, he must be completely drunk, thought Anna and ran into the hall to open the door. Ákos looked scruffy, but he wasn't staggering and didn't smell of booze.

'I've tried to call you,' said her brother as he stepped into the hall.

'Grandma is ill.'

Ákos took a deep breath. 'What's wrong with her?'

'She was complaining of stomach cramps about a week ago; now she's stopped eating altogether. Her back is sore too.'

'Has someone looked at her?'

'She's in hospital. They took X-rays and ultrasound images on Friday. At least they didn't find any tumours.'

'Good.'

'I know. But something's wrong. She's staying on the ward over the weekend and they'll continue testing her next week. She's in a bad way, because she hasn't eaten or drunk anything. She's being fed through a tube.'

'Poor thing,' said Ákos, clearly worried.

Ákos was their grandmother's favourite grandchild, regardless of the Mohican and his raucous behaviour. Grandma made her own ice cream; she always had a tub in the freezer and would give Ákos the largest portion. She also baked *pogács*, savoury little scones, especially if Ákos asked for them. Ákos had always been their spokesman whenever the children wanted something from Grandma. At the time, Anna had been terribly jealous of this favouritism, though on the whole she felt just as loved as her brothers. As an adult she'd once watched a sobbing little boy trying in vain to climb into his father's arms. In a flash she recalled how their own father used to reject Ákos, and at that moment she understood that Grandma was trying to make up for the faults of her own son.

'The doctors said she's in good condition on the whole, and they think she'll be able to go home soon.'

'Good. Should we go and visit her?'

'I can't get away at the moment. Work.'

'I could go.'

'Would you?'

'I've got to. I want to see Grandma again before she's in a coffin.'

'Have you got any money?'

Ákos stared at the wall, embarrassed. '*A rohadt büdös élet*, Anna, you know how it is,' he sulked.

'I can buy your tickets.'

'Again?'

'Yes. How did you like being back there? You haven't talked about our visit over Christmas. What did you get up to? We hardly saw you.'

'Look who's talking! I was mostly at home by myself or down at The Taverna playing billiards with Laci.'

'You weren't drinking?'

'No.'

Anna knew that her brother had wanted to show his mother and their other relatives that he was fine, and she was glad he'd managed it. Their mother had asked Ákos to stay on and wept as they prepared to leave. It was hardly surprising, as Ákos had only visited once since they'd left, and that had been over ten years ago.

'It would be nice to visit home again,' he said.

'Are you in good enough shape?'

'Everything's fine.'

Anna switched on her computer and booked the tickets straight away. Ákos would leave early on Thursday morning. He would be in Budapest before midday. Ákos didn't have a driving licence, so renting a car to drive to Serbia was out of the question, but there were several intercity trains between Budapest and Szeged every day. Someone would pick him up from there, Laci perhaps, or their cousin Attila. It wouldn't be a problem. Some years ago the old border crossing at Horgos had been moved a few kilometres to the west, once the road link between Budapest and Belgrade had finally been turned into a four-lane motorway. The distance from the customs control to Kanizsa was longer than before, but because the border crossing was considerably bigger the queues of vehicles seemed to move much more quickly. The journey didn't take any longer than usual. Anna thought of the winding lines of cars at the customs office, people agitatedly darting from one line to the next, people who always thought the neighbouring queue was moving faster. During the vacation rush around July and August, crossing the border could still take hours. The sun beat down on them, cars stood parked in line, the exhaust fumes were stifling, the chrome glinted, those who didn't need to sit behind the wheel wandered between the cars stretching their legs, wiping sweat from their brows. Now and then the queue edged a car's width closer to the passport control and freedom. People got hungry if they hadn't brought anything to eat. But now it was March and the queues wouldn't be too bad. Any one of their relatives would be happy to fetch Ákos from the Hungarian side. If only I could go too, thought Anna.

The morning was gradually starting to warm, the chill of night beginning to fade, but Esko didn't notice it. The taxi seat was juddering monotonously. Esko tried to focus his gaze on the delicate lantern hanging on the leafless crack willow. The lantern's white paint was flaking and dappled with rust. Bitch, he said out loud. The taxi driver glanced at Esko with a look of confusion, but didn't say anything; he was used to odd clients and knew to keep his mouth shut. Through the blur of alcohol Esko remembered how they'd planted the willow the summer the house was completed. They'd planted hundreds of perennials that summer too, and flower bulbs later in the autumn. The garden still blossomed every summer. Esko stared at the blurry snow verges that covered the floral bloom waiting to be released. Over there were the foxgloves and the peonies, and there the monkshoods, the creeping bellflowers, the greenhead coneflowers and the poppies. The roses in the front garden and along the garage wall, the plantain lilies beneath the hedgerow, the ferns.

I remember you all by name, thought Esko. I'm not as fucking callous as she said. He stepped out of the car and staggered as he pulled the lighter from his jacket pocket, lit a cigarette.

'Damn it,' he cursed. The cigarette fell to the ground and went out. 'Fucking piece of shit,' he slurred and lit another.

Esko couldn't explain why he'd called a taxi and driven out here. He'd popped into a bar in town, gone home and sat there drinking all night by himself, fallen asleep for a while, and as soon as he'd woken up, he'd called a taxi. Now he couldn't bear to look at the darkened house, the familiar garden, the flowers hidden beneath the snow, the trees and shrubs and empty lanterns, whose flickering in the darkening evenings had once meant something. Even less did he want to think of what was going on inside the house, that someone had moved in there, slept in the bed he had bought, woke next to his wife. His former wife.

'Let's go,' said Esko as he sat in the car once again. The car's motor breathed warm air into the interior. He felt sleepy.

'Where to?' asked the driver.

'Wherever you want. Just drive.'

Esko stared at the city through the taxi window. The landscape flashing past his eyes made him feel nauseous at first, before the sensation turned to a dull headache. If Esko had been sober or slightly more alert, he would have noticed the dark SUV driving behind them. The taxi driver noticed it, but guessed it must have been coincidence that the car was going in the same direction.

'Take me back home,' Esko said eventually. 'Dead tired. Got to get to work on Monday morning.'

The taxi driver looked at the stocky, dishevelled man in the front seat and glanced at his watch. It was almost ten o'clock. The sound of church bells could be heard somewhere. The dark SUV disappeared into the growing flow of traffic and the taxi driver forgot all about it.

12

'YES. It's my father.'

Anna looked carefully at Juha Karppinen as he stood in the morgue next to Vilho's body. He looked sad and shocked. His hair had thinned on top and it had been a while since his last haircut. He was wearing a suit that, though not bespoke, fitted him well. His grey tie added to the business-like, inconspicuous impression. The epitome of a tax officer going to work, a pen pusher. From his hands Anna could tell he didn't do physical work. They were too smooth, his fingers long and slender, almost feminine. It looked as though he wanted to touch his father, to take him by the hand and caress him. Anna noticed he wasn't wearing a wedding ring. She looked for signs of a hangover, but there was nothing. Maybe he really had been skiing after all. Because of Ákos, I look for signs of alcoholism in everyone, she thought, maybe because of Esko too. I'm turning into a cynical woman, an uptight cow. This weekend I'm going to drink myself blind drunk, that's settled, and I'll smoke as many cigarettes as I want.

'What happened to him? Why does he look like that?' asked Juha Karppinen.

'He was run over by a car. According to an eyewitness and judging by his injuries, he was lying on the road when the car hit him.'

'Somebody saw it happen?'

'Well, the driver,' Anna clarified.

'Who was it?'

'A young girl, a foreigner. She was within the speed limit and hadn't been drinking, but the road was very slippery. We're pressing charges for reckless driving and causing death by dangerous driving.'

'And he was just lying there?'

'Yes. Did your father have any underlying illnesses?'

'He had this and that, but nothing serious. For his age he was in pretty good shape.'

'Dementia?'

'No, he was sharp as a tack. Sometimes a bit too sharp,' said Juha Karppinen with a stifled chuckle. 'For his age, I mean. He was eighty-two,' he continued.

'Any heart problems?'

'Probably. Don't all people that age have something? I have to admit, we weren't very close.'

'When was the last time you saw him?'

Juha Karppinen thought hard. 'I'm ashamed to say it, but probably three or four months ago.'

'Any phone calls? Were you in the habit of calling one another?'

Juha looked even more uncomfortable. 'Not really. I think I called him at Christmas.'

You think you called him, thought Anna. That means you didn't.

'Do you know whether your father had any friends that we could ask about him?'

'I don't really know them either, I'm afraid. He had a few friends. Just a minute … I remember one of them. Niilo Säävälä was his name.'

Anna wrote down the name.

'Where is your mother?' she asked.

'Mother died when I was twenty. Aggressive pancreatic cancer. My father never remarried, and as far as I know he didn't have any serious friendships with women after that. Of course, I can't be certain. As I said, we weren't very close.'

'And you?'

'What about me?'

'Do you have a family?'

'I have two children; they're adults now. Their mother and I divorced years ago.'

'And are you close to them?' Anna couldn't help asking.

'That has nothing to do with this,' he replied. 'My father has died. We weren't the best of friends, but he was still my father. I'm upset. Can I be alone with him for a moment?'

'Of course,' said Anna and left the room.

Linnea Markkula was waiting outside the morgue and gave Anna an inquisitive look. Anna gave an affirmative nod; the body had been identified.

Linnea seemed relieved. 'It'll save us a fortune not having to get the dentist involved.'

'Quite. What about Marko Halttu, the junkie kid?'

'You won't believe how much work I've got. It's as though the whole city has decided to kick the bucket in suspicious circumstances this week, so I haven't got round to him yet. He's on my list for tomorrow. Coming to watch?'

'I haven't been assigned the autopsy.'

'It was an overdose, right?'

'Most likely, but there could be something else too. The kid had a gaping wound in his head. You'll have to find out for me.'

'And I will.'

'It's a strange case though. Somehow there's an illegal immigrant and a criminal gang mixed up in all this too.'

'That was quite a seizure you pulled off.'

'I know. Of course, the case will eventually be handed over to the NBI, but we're doing our bit.'

'I'll email you by ten tomorrow with my preliminary findings. I should be done by then.'

'Good.'

The stairwell was tagged with graffiti; the broken window in the door was patched together with duct tape. If possible, the suburb of Vaarala was even more destitute than Rajapuro or Koivuharju. The houses were older, and no new houses had been built in the vicinity. The suburb had sprung up in the early 1970s, when people leaving the countryside needed cheap housing, and factory workers needed homes, a place to sleep between shifts. A few decades ago the gardens and playgrounds of Vaarala had been filled with kids of all ages; nowadays the place looked more like a large-scale immigrant reception centre. Women in burqas hauled shopping bags back home, dark-skinned children clinging at their skirts. A few trendily dressed black guys loitered around in the car park and in front of the houses, but for the most part the suburb seemed quiet and deserted.

Esko rang the doorbell. There was no name on the letterbox. The interpreter, a young man in spectacles carrying a fake-leather briefcase and wearing a badly fitting suit, stood next to Esko with an air of importance. The young man told Esko he studied economics and that he'd come straight from a lecture. That's right, Esko had thought. You come here to study courtesy of our taxpayers, and once you're finished you'll probably disappear and help develop your own country. He managed to quell his desire to comment on the matter out loud.

The door opened. The woman from the online news item Esko had found stood in the doorway. Her black, heavily made-up eyes looking at Esko unblinkingly; her cheerless, beautifully shaped mouth asked the men to come in. The woman had made coffee in a small, decorative tin pot. She was quite tall and slender, and was wearing a pair of loose black trousers and a tunic embellished with sequins. A beautiful, embroidered scarf was wound round her head, though it didn't cover everything, as it had in the photograph. An attractive woman, Esko had to admit. The woman introduced herself as Naseem, placed coffee cups on the table and asked them to sit down.

'Why do the police want to speak to me? Have I done something bad?' Naseem asked in a low, pleasant tone. Esko listened so intently to the exotic cadence of her voice that he almost forgot the presence of the interpreter.

'Your telephone number appears regularly in calls made by a person we are investigating,' Esko explained. 'That's what I'd like to ask about.'

'It must be Reza. He's my son.'

Esko's heart gave an extra beat. The mother. How the hell was there no mention of Reza's mother in the paperwork he'd received from the NBI? Having said that, the documentation hadn't told him much about Reza either. That's why he'd been given the assignment in the first place. His job was to dig up that information.

'Where is he now?'

'If only I knew.'

'Doesn't he live here, at home?'

'No. Well, officially, yes, but he's not here very often.'

The woman's face was taut with anxiety. Her beautiful black eyes were overcast with a shadow of fatigue.

'But he still phones you,' Esko stated.

The woman smiled joylessly. 'He tries to be a good son. He calls and asks how I'm doing.'

'When did you last see Reza?' Esko asked.

'Yesterday.'

Esko sat upright. The boy had been on the police's radar for weeks, and now it turns out he'd been here only recently.

'Why are the police interested in my son?'

Esko could hear the distress in the woman's voice, though he didn't understand the words until the interpreter spoke.

'We believe he may be mixed up with a criminal gang. Do you know anything about that?'

Naseem shook her head and nervously glanced in turn at the floor, the interpreter and Esko.

'What did he do when he visited? What did he say?' Esko asked.

'He fetched some clean clothes and brought his dirty laundry. He ate, slept for a few hours. He didn't tell me anything about himself.'

'Didn't he tell you where he's staying? Who he's hanging out with? What he's up to?'

'He doesn't tell me these things. He turns up out of the blue and disappears again.'

'Does he call before he turns up?'

'Sometimes. Not always.'

'Are you worried about him?'

'I'm very worried. Reza dropped out of school. No good will come of that.'

This woman can help me, thought Esko. Keep focussed, man, for crying out loud. This is your opportunity. He forced a friendly expression on to his face and began asking about the woman's family, her life, her past, her work in Iran, life as a refugee, about how her son, Reza, had come to Finland by himself as a minor years ago. She spoke beautifully. Her face was expressive; delicate hand movements paced her speech. Esko noticed that her nails were long and painted red. After a while Esko had to admit to himself that he admired her powerful narrative. Her speech, its rhythms, inflections and choices of words revealed the kind of education that you rarely encountered in Finland; she spoke in a manner profoundly different from most Finns. She didn't seem embittered, though she had been through a lot. Her husband had been killed, and her son had fled soon afterwards. She had stayed behind to work for her women's organisation, putting her own life at risk. Eventually she too had been forced to head to a refugee camp when the danger became too great. Through the family reunion programme she had come to Finland to be with her son. Esko began to ask her about conditions in the camp, almost forgetting the reason for his visit. The woman told him how she had organised lessons for the little children every morning, how she had taught them to read and write, and how in the evenings she had seen patients – all for free, of course. She didn't stay there very long, unlike many others who spent their entire lives in refugee camps, who were born and died there. Esko was astonished to learn that some people truly spent their whole lives moving from one refugee camp to the next, that only a tiny fraction of people in camps ever managed to get away.

Pull yourself together, he commanded himself. We're supposed to be talking about Reza, I'm supposed to be shrewd. This woman is the key to finding Reza, and I'm damn well going to unlock that door.

'I'm afraid I have to tell you straight up that I think your son is in grave danger,' said Esko.

'Really?' Naseem looked shocked. 'Why?'

'These gangs are violent. Life with these people is dangerous and presents a lot of potential threats, including drugs.'

'I couldn't bear it if anything happened to my son.'

'Perhaps you can help me.'

'How?'

'For instance, you could tell me when you know he's coming home. If he calls, you could ask him where he is, who he is with and what he is doing.'

'He won't tell me things like this.'

'Think about it. Your son really is at risk. The police want to help him.'

Naseem said nothing. She looked hesitant and nervous. Esko gave the woman his card and asked her to call him through the interpreter if she heard anything from Reza. It must be difficult, thought Esko. What must it feel like for an adult, a highly educated and intelligent person, to have to conduct even the simplest matters with the help of someone else? And how much do all these interpreters cost the taxpayer? It's crazy.

As Esko was in the hallway pulling on his coat and the interpreter was standing in the doorway ready to leave, Naseem came up to Esko and handed him a crumpled scrap torn from a pad of squared paper.

'I found this in the pocket of Reza's jeans when I was loading the washing machine.'

On the scrap of paper was scribbled a standard mobile-phone number. Esko felt his arms tingle. There was a pinch in his chest. The interpreter tried to peer over at the number, but Esko folded the piece of paper and put it in his wallet.

Anna called Niilo Säävälä soon after Juha had left. An old man with a pleasant, deep voice, he was clearly shocked to hear of his friend's death. He fell silent for a long time, and Anna could hear the sound of suppressed sighs on the phone. Then the man briefly explained that he and Vilho were former work mates and had known each other since they were young men. Nowadays they tried to meet once a month at the local swimming baths, where they would sit in the sauna, catch up and reminisce about the past. In the pool they stretched their frail bodies and looked at the women, Niilo explained with a weepy chuckle. Vilho had quite an eye for female beauty. They'd last met only three days before Vilho's accident. Vilho had been in good shape and high spirits. Niilo knew that Vilho collected knives but couldn't say what kind of knives were in the collection. He wasn't the sort of person to show them off all the time, said Niilo. He told her that there was often a third old friend at the swimming baths, Hermanni Harju, who was an enthusiastic knife collector. He'd be able to tell you something about Vilho's collection.

Anna took down the man's contact details, but apparently Hermanni would be in Spain until the beginning of May and might have switched off his Finnish phone. When Anna asked about Vilho's son, Niilo fell silent. He said all he knew about Juha was his name and profession. Vilho hadn't often spoken about his son – or his grandchildren. It was a bit strange, but what of it? Each to his own, said Niilo. 'We don't poke our noses into other folk's business. Plenty of men my age have a difficult relationship with their children. We worked ourselves into the ground, so we didn't have time to look after the kids like young men these days.' Anna could hear a new sadness in Niilo's voice; he was clearly talking about himself too. She remembered reading research about what dying people regretted most in their lives. At the top of the list was the lack of time spent with their children.

Anna gave Niilo her contact details and asked him to call her if he remembered anything else. On the spur of the moment she asked him about the Oriental rug, just as Niilo was winding up the conversation. He laughed and said that Vilho was a strange man. He never bragged about things, though he liked to invest in quality. 'Peace be with him,' Niilo said with a low sob.

After returning to the police station, Esko called the number on the scrap of paper.

'Pizzeria Hazileklek, Maalik speaking.'

'What the bloody hell…?' Esko cursed.

'Pardon me? Who is this?'

'Senior Constable Esko Niemi from the police. Good afternoon.'

'Afternoon,' Maalik answered cautiously.

'This telephone number was found in the pocket of a man suspected of some very serious crimes.'

'Oh? I don't know anything about that.'

'Ever heard the name Reza Jobrani?'

'No.'

'So why was your phone number in his pocket?'

'I don't know. Maybe he order a pizza.'

'Somehow he's linked to you and your business. Start talking.'

'Probably a customer. I don't know them all.'

'I'm coming down there today to talk to you and your boyfriend. And I might just check to see that all your licences and tax returns are in order while I'm at it.'

'For all means. We have nothing to hide.'

'It's *by* all means.'

'Very well. By all means. Is that all?'

'For now. You'll hear from me again soon.'

Esko ended the call, flustered. The queer was lying so much his nose would start growing. That pizzeria is probably a front for money laundering, hiding stolen goods or something. It couldn't be pure coincidence that their phone number was in Reza's trouser pocket. Reza Jobrani isn't the sort of guy that orders pizzas, thought Esko angrily. Though it was possible. But given that Sammy was their apprentice, their bum boy or whatever, there were simply too many coincidences in this mess. In a police investigation coincidences like this provide credible leads. Esko could feel the pieces of the jigsaw moving closer to one another. Soon they would lock together, and as soon as that happened he would make his move.

'You know the pizzeria pansies.'

Anna raised her eyes from the computer screen and looked at Esko, who had appeared at her office door without knocking.

'Come in. Nice to see you too,' she said sourly. She had tried to call Hermanni Harju and was forced to accept what Niilo had suspected: Hermanni was using a Spanish prepaid phone. Now Anna was trying to establish the part of Spain in which he spent the winters and whether there was any way of reaching him. It shouldn't be too difficult, Anna thought, if only this jerk hadn't come and disturbed me.

Esko closed the door behind him and sat astride a chair on the other side of the desk.

'Don't you think it's time you decorated this room?' he asked and looked around with an air of distaste. 'You've been made permanent now. You could bring in some flowers or...'

'What do you want?'

'Someone's in a mood. Time of the month?'

'Do you want something? I'm a bit busy.'

'What are you working on?'

Anna explained about Vilho Karppinen's collection of knives. Esko thought about this for a moment.

'I think you're taking this a bit too far,' he said eventually. 'How the hell could the knife found in Ketoniemi be from the old guy's apartment? You reckon Old Granddad stabbed someone, then lay down in the road on the other side of the city – in his slippers and pyjamas? Hardly. Anyway, the knife is Nils's job. Ask him to look into it.'

'You're probably right,' Anna admitted, though she didn't entirely agree. 'So, what did you want?'

'The gays are somehow mixed up in all this gang business.'

'Who do you mean?'

'Come off it. You know.'

'They are people. They have names. You mean Maalik and Farzad.'

'I talked to the mother of Reza – you know, the gang leader. Anyway, the mother found a scrap of paper in her son's pocket with a phone number for their pizzeria.'

'Even a gang leader can order a pizza. It doesn't mean anything.'

'Think about it. Sammy is connected with the pizzeria, and now this. It can't be coincidence.'

'Yes, it can.'

'You're biased because you're friends with the immigrant poofters.'

'Yes, I am. And I know them well enough to know that there's no way they're mixed up with any gangs. They're intelligent, grown men.'

'Often as not those pizza places are hotbeds of illegal trade.'

'Hazileklek isn't one of them.'

'Listen, are you a criminal investigator or what?'

Anna felt flustered. I must learn to control myself, she thought. I'm unable to take professional distance when I'm emotionally involved, and I let Esko wind me up.

'I was going to ask for your help, but now I'm not so sure,' he said.

'What do you need me to do?'

'Nothing. I don't think you're up to it.'

'Esko. I'm sorry. I was wrong,' said Anna and wondered at how easy it felt to admit her mistake.

'Okay. I called the pizzeria and this Maalik of yours answered the phone.' Esko said his name in a mocking, simpering voice. 'Of course, he wouldn't tell me anything.'

No wonder, thought Anna.

'I thought you might go there and talk to them, because you get on with them.'

'If they really are mixed up in criminal activities, do you think they'd tell me anything either?'

'Of course they won't, but they'll still talk to you. You'll notice if there's something not too kosher going on.'

'I don't think it's a good idea. I want to excuse myself from this one.'

'Recuse yourself if something comes up.'

Anna thought about it for a moment. She remembered the first time she'd gone into Hazileklek for a pizza while Ákos had been on work experience there. She had got on with Farzad and Maalik from the word go, but she noticed they didn't think much of Ákos. It was hardly surprising; Ákos turned up late, his breath stinking of yesterday's liquor. He would do nothing on his own initiative, not even the simplest tasks, like loading and unloading the dishwasher, but always waited to be told. She couldn't imagine them letting him loose front of house. Maalik and Farzad stoically put up with him until the end of his contract and wrote him a politely neutral reference. Anna had kept in touch with Maalik and Farzad; Ákos hadn't set foot in the place since leaving. Later on Farzad told Anna that Ákos was a good young man: funny, friendly and with a good sense of humour, but a lousy employee.

Perhaps I'll have to talk to them, thought Anna. Besides, this Reza could simply have ordered a pizza, no matter what Esko thinks. She nodded at Esko. He gave her a friendly pat on the back.

'Good one, mate. I knew I could rely on you.'

Anna felt embarrassed again. Esko left the room and Anna stood up, stretched her shoulder blades, stepped to the window and squinted out into the city below. Am I his mate for doing the right thing? Or am I his mate because that's just the way I am? And since when did I start worrying about something as insignificant as myself?

The sun shone like a smouldering disc in the cold, blue sky. Anna closed the venetian blinds. Every year the speed with which the days got longer took her by surprise; after the months of oppressive darkness it felt astonishing suddenly to notice dust gathering in the corner of the room, greasy fingerprints on the windows. The sun seemed to penetrate everything, make everything visible again. There was something almost distressing about it. Though Anna wholeheartedly enjoyed following the progress of spring and waiting for the onset of summer, she fully appreciated why some people felt almost tormented by the light. Rooms and windows weren't the only places where dust and grease stains collected.

13

THE REPORT on the Opel belonging to Marko Halttu's mother had been marked as urgent and important. Anna clicked the email attachment with a sense of expectation. More drugs or signs of gangs, she quickly presumed, but the findings revealed something altogether different. Anna carefully read the report twice, once quickly skimming through, then a second time, one word at a time, as if to make sure that the text in front of her eyes truly existed. There was a surprise in the boot of the car. Human traces: a bloodstain, a few hairs, epithelial cells. Call ASAP, Kirsti signed off her email. *Úr Isten*, said Anna out loud. What else has the junkie boy been up to? Who transported people like that? Only dead people got stuffed into the boot of a car. Or prisoners, victims of torture. Nobody travelled in the boot of a car by choice. What on earth has been going on in that ghost house?

Anna got on the phone to Kirsti, who sounded excited and agitated when she picked up.

'The hairs found in the boot of Halttu's car match the hairs from Vilho Karppinen, the old man found on the road at Taipaleenmäki,' she said. 'Same colour, same length, same structure. You'll have to cross-reference the DNA, but the forensics team knows a thing or two about this. I'll bet my fifteen years' experience that old Mr Karppinen was in the boot of that car.'

'It can't be!' Anna exclaimed. What did this mean? Why on earth was Vilho in the boot of the car?

'Looks like it, I'm afraid.' Kirsti's voice had become serious.

'If he'd been driven there by car, that would certainly explain why there were no footprints on the road.'

'It also complicates the investigation considerably.'

'I know. This means that Marko Halttu is somehow involved in Vilho's death. *Jebiga bassza meg.*'

'What?'

'Nothing.'

'Besides, we found other hairs in the car too. Black ones, definitely not Finnish. On the headrest in the passenger seat.'

'Really? This gets more and more interesting.'

'Don't you have an illegal Pakistani boy in holding?'

'Yes. I'm scheduled to interview Sammy today.'

'Good. Ask him about the car.'

'Damn right I will.'

Anna felt troubled. She didn't want to ask Sammy about the car and any hairs they'd found there. She wanted to get him out of police custody, sort him out with an apartment and get him into school, treat his drug addiction and offer him the possibility of the life every young man should have. Esko would strangle me if he knew, she thought. And after Sammy she was due to interview Maalik and Farzad. Am I fit to conduct these interviews at all, she wondered.

Linnea had sent Anna an email too. She had completed Marko Halttu's autopsy and submitted the preliminary report. Linnea estimated the time of death at around two days before they had found the body. That means Sammy had been in the apartment with a corpse, helping himself to drugs. Halttu's body displayed contusions that had been caused around twenty-four hours before his death. The bruises were on his chest and arms, and there was one large bruise on his left thigh. In addition to the contusions, there was severe blunt-force trauma to his left temple, and this he sustained around the same time as the other injuries. Halttu had lost a lot of blood from the wound. Linnea said the injuries were consistent with a fight. However, none of them was serious enough to kill him. There was no internal bleeding. Linnea had sent blood samples off to the forensics laboratory to be tested. Despite the signs of violence, the death looked like a routine junkie overdose. They would have to wait weeks for the results of the blood samples and forensic confirmation of the hairs from the Opel,

Anna estimated impatiently. She told Virkkunen the news and asked him how they should now proceed with Sammy's interview.

'How are you feeling?' Anna asked Sammy in the interview room.

The boy looked wretched. The tremors had gone, but the sedatives and all the placebo drugs pumped into him made Sammy look like one of Madame Tussaud's waxworks. His face was unresponsive; he was awake yet asleep.

Sammy shrugged his emaciated shoulders.

Anna had asked Esko to join her, but he politely declined. Naturally Ritva Siponen was present too. She was sitting at the back of the room, behind Sammy's back.

'Let's go through once again what happened in Marko Halttu's apartment. Tell us everything you can remember.'

'Too tired,' Sammy replied.

'When did you first meet Marko?'

'End of January.'

'Where was this?'

'Can't remember. On a street somewhere.'

'Did Marko try to sell you some Subutex?'

'No. I asked him for some.'

'Had someone told you to ask him?'

'Yes.'

'Who?'

'Can't remember. It might have been the same guy that gave me my first tabs.'

I must go and talk to that guy, thought Anna.

'Then what happened?'

'At first Macke said he didn't have any subs. Then we chatted for a while; he asked where I'm from and why I'm in Finland – the same shit that you probably know all about.'

'I do. Then what?'

'Then Macke said he might have something back at his flat. We went there. That was the first time I slept there.'

'Was there a lot of gear in Marko's flat at that time?'

'No. Only subs, and not very many.'

'Do you think Marko was mixed up in something bigger back then?'

'He only ever had the same amount of gear as a regular user, nothing more.'

'Where in Pakistan do you come from?'

Sammy swayed almost imperceptibly in this chair, glanced up at Anna for the first time. The boy's eyes were so terribly mournful that she felt a sting inside.

'From the suburbs around Quetta.'

'What kind of place is it?'

'I can't remember.'

'A river runs through my home town,' said Anna.

Sammy stared at her.

'Where do you come from?' he asked suddenly. A glimmer of interest flashed in his eyes.

Got you, Anna thought contentedly.

'The former Yugoslavia. I came here as a little girl, to escape the war.'

Sammy continued staring at her. Anna could almost see the cogs turning in his head. A police officer who was almost like him. Could such a thing really exist?

'Quetta is surrounded by beautiful mountains and fruit groves. There's lots of dust and sand. It can be dangerous.'

'Why is it dangerous?'

Sammy gave a cheerless smile. 'It's near the Afghan borderlands. The place is full of crazy people, the Taliban, communists, the tribes, smugglers, you name it.'

'I lived near a border too.'

Anna thought of the restless atmosphere in the border areas. Her mother had taken liquor and cigarettes across the border into Hungary, sold them in lay-bys straight out of the car window, then treated herself to something special in one of the Jugend-style cafés in

Szeged. Western liquor, so widely available in Yugoslavia, was once a desirable commodity in Hungary under communism. Nowadays she felt a strange sense of release as she crossed the EU border and entered Serbia, as though a belt pulled tight around her waist had suddenly slackened, as though she'd taken off her seat belt. In her childhood, Hungary had been a drearier, poorer place than Yugoslavia; now their roles had dramatically switched, at least superficially. But the sense of a somewhat freer atmosphere in her former home country hadn't gone away. In Serbia she still breathed and laughed differently from in Hungary, regardless of the shameful stains of the wars, the break-up of the country and the rise of nationalism. Anna often thought about this. How much does it take to crush a person once and for all? Why was it that, for all its welfare, Finland often felt so unbearably bleak?

'Tell me about your family,' she urged him.

The boy swayed again. It was a good sign. I'm touching a nerve, Anna thought.

'What do you want to know?'

'What about your father?'

Sammy thought about this for a long time, chewed the fingernails of his left hand.

'My father was an electrician,' he answered sullenly. 'He had a good job with one of the big construction firms in Quetta. He worked hard, and people liked him.'

'And your mother?'

Sammy said nothing; he stared ahead, a distressed gaze in his bleary eyes.

'Did your mother have a job?'

'She was a seamstress. She made her own clothes and mended torn ones. It brought in a little extra income. We weren't rich, but we were never hungry.'

'What kind of woman was she?'

'I'm tired. I want to go back to my cell and sleep.'

'I still have a few questions. We don't have to talk about your mother if you don't want to.'

Sammy gave a barely audible snort.

'When he died, Marko had bruises on his body and a head wound. Did you two fight?'

'I don't remember.'

'Try to remember.'

'I don't think we fought. His head was bleeding when I arrived.'

'Did Marko tell you where he got the wound?'

'No.'

'Did you ask him?'

'Can't remember.'

Anna sighed. The trivial answers were beginning to annoy her.

'You were in Marko's car,' she said, changing the subject.

'Was that a question?' Sammy asked.

'We found black hairs in the car. Why were you there?'

'I wasn't.'

'We also found hairs belonging to an old man who lives in the same building as Marko. Do you know anything about that?'

There was a flash of panic in Sammy's eyes. He turned and looked helplessly at his lawyer.

'I'm tired,' he said once again.

Ritva Siponen jumped to her feet and informed them that the interview was over for now.

'We'll continue tomorrow,' said Anna and smiled at Sammy. He didn't smile back.

Sari and Esko were in a patrol car driving towards Rajapuro. They had a warrant to search an apartment where at the weekend there had been a sighting of a man tattooed with gang insignias. The police were throwing all their resources at this operation; this time they were joined by a group from Special Branch and reinforcements from Patrol. Esko had high hopes for the operation. The more the police were able to disrupt the Cobras, the more swiftly their activities in the city and throughout the country could be snuffed out. Also, he wanted to get in before the Angels had a chance. For once, the police and the bikers had the same objective, but the Angels' methods were somewhat different from those of the police; they resulted only in more violence, more law-breaking, chaos and fear. Esko remembered only too well what it was like when the Angels and the Bandidos fought a turf war in the late 1990s. A repeat of those events was the last thing anyone needed.

The building in question was one of the ten-storey blocks in Rajapuro. Its red-painted concrete walls stood tall, stretching up towards the sky, which was gleaming with bright blue spring light. It was a few degrees below freezing. The forecourt had been badly gritted and was glazed with patches of black ice. The search would be carried out without delay. A group of officers in blue overalls crept into the stairwell. A few of them remained outside to guard the forecourt; a couple stood at the door. The field officer was standing next to his car, overseeing the operation and giving orders and instructions over his police radio.

The apartment door had to be broken down, because nobody answered. The occupants clearly had better things to do, as from inside the apartment the officers heard shouts, stamping footsteps, the flush of a toilet. The police burst inside. Three men were waiting for them, their hands already above their heads. They were all arrested; two officers conducted an initial search and found a pistol and ten packets of Subutex. Enough to press charges, thought Esko, satisfied with himself. That's three snakes out of action, at least for a while. The pack of Cobras was shrinking. Once they had Reza in custody, the group would disappear altogether and he could move on to other things.

Esko went into the stairwell, called the lift and ordered a nosy neighbour peering out of his door to get back inside. The man looked Asian, black hair and squinty eyes, his mouth set in a permanent smile, like a mask hiding his true face. Where the hell do they all come from, Esko thought as he stepped into the lift. Once outside he lit a cigarette, filling his lungs with long, satisfying drags that induced a coughing fit. Esko noticed he'd been coughing more and more all winter. Sometimes he coughed so much that his ribs ached.

'Esko, look!' one of the officers shouted and pointed at the neighbouring building.

Esko saw the figure of a young man peering round the corner at the squad cars parked outside. Then he disappeared. It was Reza.

'Tell the field officer. We've got to bring him in,' said Esko and began running after Reza and the two officers who were in pursuit. He saw the boy turn back on himself and slip behind the apartment blocks with the uniformed officers on his tail. A moment later one of the officers walked back and said the boy seemed to have vanished into thin air.

'He's gone inside,' Esko shouted and told the field officer to call for back-up.

The police surrounded the building and quickly filed inside.

But Reza was smarter. Once most of the officers were inside the building and Esko was just about to go inside too, out of the corner of his eye he saw something move by the side of the opposite building.

'Over there,' Esko bellowed and dashed after the boy.

Esko ran as fast as he could. The scarf he had carelessly thrown round his neck flew into the air and Esko almost fell on the slippery pavement, but sped up regardless. Reza's shiny puffer jacket and his head, covered in a hoodie, bobbed about fifty metres ahead of him. Damn it, I'm going to get you, thought Esko and right then felt the strength drain from his legs, and his lungs clenched so tightly that he was forced to stop. Reza disappeared from view. Esko's chest stung and ached; the pain was excruciating. He pressed his palm against his chest, coughed and gasped for breath, heard the sound of the patrol cars speeding off after Reza, their sirens wailing. He didn't have the strength to alert them.

Sari arrived on the scene.

'What's the matter?' she asked.

'Out of shape … Age … it's nothing,' he stammered between fits of breathlessness.

'Is it your heart?'

'No, it's bloody not. I should cut back on the fags. My lungs can't take running like that.'

'Well cut back, then.'

'What?'

'Cut back on the fags, if that's what you've got to do.'

'For Christ's sake, don't you start,' he scoffed and lit a cigarette, but couldn't smoke it. He propped his arms against his thighs, tried to catch his breath and grimaced. The cigarette smouldered between his forefinger and middle finger. He had nearly caught the boy. Nearly. He'd screwed up, missed his chance. Big time. Fucking hell.

'Esko, your lips are blue. I'm going to call an ambulance,' said Sari, worried.

'Don't you bloody dare,' said Esko. 'I'm fine.'

'Then go straight to the doctor at the station. I'll tell the squad to give you a lift.'

'No need, I can get there myself. I'll be right as rain.'

Sari stared at him with a look of concern.

'Are you fit to work? I mean, in general?' she asked after a moment. 'Maybe I should have a chat with Virkkunen.'

'Have a smoke and relax, will you?' said Esko, still trying to steady his breathing as he held out the packet of cigarettes. Sari glared at him angrily and walked off towards the flashing blue lights and the group of onlookers that had gathered at the scene.

Perhaps I really should go to the doctor, thought Esko and noticed that the chest pains still hadn't subsided.

Once again there were only a few customers in Pizzeria Hazileklek. Sturdy white candles had been lit on the tables. The atmosphere was calm and beautiful, very unlike the average pizza parlour. Maalik was standing behind the counter and didn't look at all surprised to see Anna, though she only rarely visited the place after lunchtime. They were expecting a visit from the police, she thought. I shouldn't have come here; I don't want to be at work when I'm here.

'Hello Anna. How are you?'

'Very well, thank you.'

'And how is Sammy?'

'Physically he's better; mentally things are taking their toll.'

'Will he be granted asylum?'

'I really don't know. I haven't had time to look at the case. There are many things to sort out here, not only regarding Sammy.'

'That's why this man call here? Esko?'

'Yes. Your telephone number was found in the pocket of one of our suspects. His name is Reza Jobrani.'

'Never heard of him. Lots of people order by phone.' Maalik's voice sounded very worried.

'I know that, and I know you're good people. But you understand that the police have to look into this thoroughly?'

'Who is this Reza?'

'He's associated with a very dangerous street gang from Sweden and Denmark that's trying to set up in Finland. They're called the Black Cobras. This is his picture.'

Maalik fell silent. He stared at the photograph, then turned to look towards the kitchen, where the sounds of clattering dishes and the rush of a tap could be heard.

'I'll get Farzad,' he said eventually.

It took a moment before the men returned. Farzad dried his hands on a towel and greeted Anna, his expression tense and nervous. There's something going on after all; Anna's pulse started to rise. I can't bear it if they are involved with the gang too, she thought. They can't be.

'We want to be honest with you, Anna,' said Farzad. 'But we are very frighten.'

Anna waited for him to continue.

'A month ago two young men came in. Iranians. At first they were very kind, very friendly, they ask things, chat to us,' said Maalik and looked at Farzad, as if to check for assurance. Farzad nodded.

'But then they start to threaten us. They said if we don't pay them, there will be trouble, but if we do, they will protect us.'

'Protect you from what?' asked Anna, though she knew the answer.

'These men were Black Cobras, they said they protect us from Hell's Angels.'

'And, more to the point, from themselves,' Anna surmised.

'Well, yes. They tried to speak friendly, but they were very threatening. They said Hazileklek might catch fire or something might happen us, if we don't pay them.'

'How much are they asking for?'

'One thousand euros a month.'

'Did you pay them?'

'At first we didn't agree. We threw them out and said we call the police, but the same evening a car almost run into Farzad as he was leaving work.'

'What kind of car was it?'

'A black SUV. New and expensive. We didn't see the make.'

'What about the registration number?'

'No, we were so shocked.'

'What happened next?'

'We think about it over night and decide to pay them.'

'I'm glad you're telling me this.'

'They said if we talk to police, they kill us.'

'I will have to consult my superior, to see how best to deal with these kinds of situations,' said Anna. Protection rackets are new to me. I doubt anything like this has ever happened in this city before, she thought.

Maalik and Farzad looked at one another.

'The motorbikers have done things before. Not to us, but we know a few people.'

Well, thought Anna. So the Cobras are stepping on the Angels' toes in this matter too. Anna promised to contact the men as soon as she knew how to proceed and told them to be on their guard.

'It might be best to shut the restaurant and go home,' Anna suggested, but the men would not hear of it.

'This is our livelihood. We cannot simply shut the door in the customers' faces,' Farzad said proudly.

'Besides, it would look strange if we suddenly disappeared. They will guess we have talk to police.'

'You're right,' said Anna. 'But make sure you call us straight away if anything untoward happens. Okay?'

The men promised they would. Anna left the pizzeria, accepted that she would have to put in more overtime and strode briskly through the freezing city towards the police station and straight into Virkkunen's office to discuss how best to protect Maalik and Farzad.

Ákos was excited. He picked T-shirts and hoodies from the clothes horse, folded them and packed them carefully into the suitcase Anna had brought. Anna sat on the unmade bed and watched her brother. She felt angry. Gabriella had called just as she was leaving for her brother's flat and demanded to come with her. At first Anna had tried to refuse, but the girl went on and on, complaining about how lonely she was, until finally Anna relented. Now she wished she hadn't. She didn't need other people witnessing this moment. It felt bad enough that her brother was leaving, her grandmother was ill, and Anna had to stay here.

'Should I take a coat?' asked Ákos.

'I didn't think to ask Mum what the weather was like. It's always warm there, isn't it? I'll check the weather in Budapest,' said Anna and opened up the web browser on her phone.

The doorbell rang.

'That'll be your au pair,' said Ákos and went to open the door. The hallway was filled with the happy sounds of Hungarian chit-chat; Gabriella didn't seem remotely fazed by Ákos's slightly dishevelled appearance, and the two seemed to get on right away. That was all she needed.

'It was 18°C today in Budapest,' she heard Gabriella say. Anna switched off her phone. She was annoyed at Gabriella's intervention.

'Your place is further south, so it could be even warmer.' Gabriella appeared in the doorway and looked at Anna. '*Szia. Te is akarsz menni?*'

'I want to go, but I can't. I've got too much work on, it's best to stay here.'

'Shame. I'd go at the drop of a hat if my grandmother was ill.'

'You're not going anywhere while a certain investigation is still pending.'

Ákos stared at the women in disbelief but said nothing. Gabriella just smiled.

'Do I need to pack all my liquids in a plastic bag?' Ákos asked.

'No. I paid for you to check a bag into the hold.'

'Great.'

'You can bring back some presents then, some *pálinka* maybe,' Gabriella giggled. 'They make really good *pálinka* down your way.'

'Oh, Ákos knows all about that,' Anna quipped bitterly.

'What's up with you?' asked Gabriella.

'Nothing,' Anna replied and wondered what really *was* the matter with her.

'We're still allowed to distil it at home; that's why it tastes so good. Our dad used to make hundreds of litres of peach and apricot *pálinka* every summer,' Ákos explained.

'But he doesn't any more?'

'No. Well, for all I know he might still make it, but not in this world. He passed away.'

'Oh, I'm sorry. Still, I bet the *pálinka* was good.'

'We weren't allowed to taste it back then; we were too young. But Mum kept a few bottles, so we got to taste them later. It was good, especially the apricot.'

'In Hungary you can only get mass-produced stuff. Sometimes it's quite good. I like the plum-flavoured one.'

'The factory stuff is shit; you can't compare it to the real thing.'

'You'll have to bring back a few bottles. I want to taste it.'

'We'll see about that,' said Ákos, somewhat embarrassed, as

though he'd suddenly remembered that his relationship with alcohol wasn't entirely normal.

Ákos continued packing. His clothes didn't even half fill the large suitcase. Gabriella chatted away unperturbed, telling them amusing stories about her student days and holidays with her family, paying not the slightest attention to Anna's sulky mood. Ákos asked Gabriella about her life, about coming to Finland, how she liked it here, and cracked jokes that made Gabriella laugh like a bell. Anna had to admit that her brother was a smooth operator. She had utterly forgotten this side to Ákos, his quick sense of humour and his ability to chat with almost anybody. But, she supposed, good company is always best in your native language. That's what it is. Ákos is withering away in Finland. It's great that he gets to visit home again; it'll do him good, she told herself

Anna closed her eyes and let the gentle hum of chit-chat flow inside her like a dram of apricot *pálinka*. She felt suddenly warm and cosy. Let Ákos go, she thought. I'll get there in the summer. It's not long now; only a few short months away.

Someone had etched a poem into the concrete wall. There was a lot of other graffiti too, initials, dates, genitals, tags, the word 'Mum', the same outbursts as on toilet doors, only more tragic. People defaced toilet doors as a drunken prank, then they opened the doors, had another drink and went home. Here nobody staggered around drunk and nobody left without permission. Is this my home now, Sammy wondered. Surely this too can be a home: a nest locked away from the outside, bars on the windows, a place where the residents don't have a key. At least it felt safe here, especially when he contemplated what awaited him on the outside.

Sammy didn't understand a word of the poem; it was in Finnish. Still, he read the text many times every day, tried to absorb the incomprehensible words and took a strange comfort from them. Why must everything have a meaning? he pondered. He didn't need to understand the words for them to flow in and out of him, pure and bright. Language is only an image of what is happening inside us, he thought, of what we observe around us, but those images are universal. The Tower of Babel hasn't scattered them yet. I read that poem as though I'm looking at an image, he thought as he lay on the hard mattress of the police bunk. It has a rhythm, a shape; I just can't understand the content – but that doesn't matter at all.

The nurse would be coming in an hour. Sammy was already waiting for her. She was so beautiful. She brought him wonderful pills. He was finally starting to feel human again. In fact, for the first time in a while Sammy felt almost good. Only the continual fear of being sent home perturbed him. It gnawed at his insides like a rat, at times filling him with a terror that snatched his breath and almost choked him. He had no permits, no paperwork. He was illegal. What does it mean to be an illegal person? Did he have the right to build a life for himself, to work and start a family? Did he have the right to exist? At least he didn't have children yet. Sammy knew of some illegal families whose children were at school in Finland, who had already learnt Finnish, made friends, integrated themselves in Finnish life while their parents were waiting for an answer from the authorities that would give them leave to remain. Then, after years of waiting, they were refused and deported. The fact of disrupting the children's schooling or the stress caused to the whole family didn't count for much in the decision-making. The Immigration Office simply stared at reports on the security situation in each country, and if someone somewhere had decided that the country was safe, then it was safe.

Just like Pakistan, Sammy scoffed. He knew all there was to know about the safety of his home country. Besides, safety was always relative. If you only looked from the perspective of the majority of the population, every country was safe. Insecurity was a problem for minorities and the poor. And what kind of madman would risk themselves and the lives of their children to escape their home country, usually by becoming indebted to unscrupulous smugglers? Who would want to spend years in a life of uncertainty, being sent from one country to the next, unless the dangers at home were very real? It was all very well to deal out – like raffle tickets – apparently carefully considered judgements on an individual's legality or illegality in a place like Finland, a country where the most pressing minority issue is whether learning Swedish at school should be compulsory. Sammy's Finnish teacher had told him about this. He couldn't believe his ears. Social inequality was so great that it made him feel ill. He tried not to think about it, but couldn't do it. Though physically he felt better than he had for a long time, he was exhausted by the small cell, the lack of exercise, the interviews and the effect of the drugs.

That policewoman was strange. Her seemingly insignificant questions felt like a punch in the face. After their interviews Sammy always felt drained. The situation wasn't helped by Ritva Siponen's debriefings. His lawyer was intent on going through every detail of the case every time they met, and she always advised him what to say in the following interviews. It irritated him. He felt like nothing but Ritva's marionette, the involuntary focus of a set of legal procedures. He tried to forget about Ritva and the interviews, the drugs and his past, everything that he had clung to far too tightly. He tried to forget his fears, let things progress as they were meant to.

Sammy read the poem on the wall one more time. He was overcome by a strange sensation. Restlessness, a longing for home, for his mother, all the pain and loss whirled inside him like an oppressive gale, but at the same time something new flickered within him. He heard the wind blowing across the Afghan borderlands, sensed its humid gusts right here, far away amid the snow and frost, felt the touch of dust and sand against his cheek. The wind found a hole in his body and blew right through him. Agitated, he stood up from his bunk. His heart was thumping so hard that the veins throbbed in his head, he clenched his fists, opened them again, paced back and forth across the floor of his cell and smiled, for suddenly he knew exactly what to do.

*

Esko went home late that evening, tired and in pain. He'd been looking forward to an evening on the sofa watching television shows, munching on sandwiches and knocking back a few comforting beers. He was ashamed, and it wasn't a nice feeling. He had made a fool of himself in front of his colleagues by being so out of breath after a short run that he'd almost choked. And the worst of it was that he hadn't even caught the little fucker. He would be the laughing stock of the station.

Esko flicked on the lights in the stairwell and called the lift; he didn't dare take the stairs. He really was beginning to worry; it was perfectly possible that his heart was about to pack up. He belonged to every risk group there was: he was an almost sixty-year-old male who smoked, drank and didn't exercise. The lift appeared in front of him with a hiss. A few years ago the rattling old model with the concertina door had been replaced by this brightly lit metallic box. Esko stepped inside and jabbed the number four with his finger. The number lit up, green. A digital screen counted the floors as though he were in a much fancier building. Esko stared at himself in the mirror on the back wall. The pallid light in the lift made his face look old and haggard. Do you really want to die of a heart attack? he asked his reflection. It didn't respond but stared back at him dejectedly from beneath sagging eyelids.

When Esko opened his apartment door and switched on the lights in the hallway, he knew instantly that something wasn't quite as it should be. At first he thought it was probably because of his fatigue after an exhausting day, the shock caused by the fear of death, but almost at once he realised that there was something else too. It was as though the hallway gave off a strange smell, the faintest hint of something sweet, perfume or aftershave. His old copper's instinct told him to remain on the threshold and not to shut the door. Everything was quiet. From inside the apartment he could hear the tick of the clock; a dull thump behind the neighbour's door; somewhere someone blew their nose. The lights in the hallway went out. Esko held his breath. He heard the fading sound of footsteps one floor below, then the front door clicked shut. In his aching chest his heart beat faster than the clock. He closed the door and ran to the window. He couldn't see anyone in the yard. For Christ's sake, don't start losing your mind, he told himself, sniffed the air in the living room without sensing anything out of place, but remained by the window watching the yard for a moment longer. After at least ten minutes had passed and he still hadn't seen a soul outside, he gave up, cracked open a beer, switched on the television and slumped on the sofa with the remote control in his hand.

The American comedy show with canned laughter couldn't catch his attention; his restless thoughts were still on the events of earlier that day: Naseem, Reza, his own health, the incident when he'd arrived home. Esko wondered whether his nose was playing tricks on him. Someone had been in the hallway, that much was certain, and there was nothing out of the ordinary about that. In apartment blocks people were always moving around in the stairwells. The sweet smell must have come from that passer-by who had decided to take the stairs instead of the lift. The man had just walked past Esko's door, and the scent molecules were still hanging in the air. Yet still Esko felt as though someone had been inside his apartment. Why? Was it fear? Esko allowed his experienced eyes to scan across the living room; everything was as it should be. He went into the kitchen – nothing out of the ordinary there either. I really am becoming paranoid, he thought as he walked into the bedroom. The computer screen was black and lifeless, his papers in a neat pile, as always. The top drawer of his desk was slightly ajar. You must have left it like that yourself, idiot, he thought and felt the hairs on his arms stand on end. A tightening sensation gripped his chest so hard that it was difficult to breathe.

14

'LET'S CONTINUE,' Anna said to Sammy. That was too abrupt a start, she thought instantly. The boy withdrew into his shell.

It was early in the morning. Once again Sammy was in the interview room, Ritva Siponen sitting next to him like a dour shadow. The sun had already risen, pale fluorescent light banished the eternal dim of the windowless room, cups of coffee stood steaming on the table. Anna had asked Esko to join them, but he'd declined, muttered something indistinct about being too busy and looked right past her, from which Anna deduced that Siponen had been true to her word and Esko had received an official warning.

Anna urged Sammy to drink something. The boy carefully raised the mug to his lips and sipped, then replaced the mug on the table and didn't look at it again. Ritva Siponen hadn't wanted coffee or anything else to drink. Still, the woman's podgy figure revealed that she too was partial to treating herself. We all have our vices, thought Anna, our own private business that we think nobody else notices.

'We are going to compare the black hairs found in Marko's car to your DNA sample. Rest assured, we will establish whether or not you were in that car,' said Anna. It was best to lay down the facts straight away without beating around the bush. Maybe it would encourage him to talk a bit more quickly.

Sammy tried to look impassive, but Anna noticed that he was building up to something. There was a new intensity about him, an enthusiasm that she hadn't seen before.

'They are my hairs,' said Sammy. 'You don't need to compare samples.'

Ritva Siponen adjusted her posture.

'When were you in his car and why?'

'We drove around one night, that's all,' Sammy answered and looked Anna right in the eyes. The fear, fatigue and despair had vanished from his eyes. Was the boy on new medication for his withdrawal symptoms, Anna wondered.

'Why?'

'We had to take something, fetch something.'

'Drugs?'

'Maybe.'

'Be more specific.'

'We went to pick up some subs one night. I can't remember where it was or when it happened. It wasn't long ago, a few weeks maybe.'

'And was Vilho Karppinen already in the boot of the car?'

Ritva Siponen gave an involuntary stammer. Sammy didn't look at her. A minute passed. Anna could sense Sammy's composure transforming right there in front of her. Still he stared at her fixedly, almost defiant. His posture was dignified, his expression bright and cool.

'No,' he said eventually.

Ritva Siponen sighed, but Anna knew this wasn't all.

'That was only later.'

'Why was the old man in the car?'

'Because we had to get rid of the body.'

Sammy drew a breath and looked in turn at Ritva and Anna with a look of determination in his eyes.

'I killed him. I murdered him. And I murdered Macke too.'

'Why?' Anna tried to remain calm though her heart was thumping and she could feel the blood rising to her cheeks. Sammy exuded self-confidence. Ritva Siponen started frantically scribbling down notes.

'I wanted the drugs. Macke wasn't going to give me anything.'

'Whose drugs were they?'

'No idea, but they didn't belong to Macke, that's for sure.'

'What happened then?'

'We got into a fight. I caused those bruises. I hit him over the head with something; I can't remember what. Macke was unconscious, then I injected him with a shitload of Subutex.'

'That's enough,' said Siponen. 'That's quite enough for today. I need to consult with my client in private before we continue.'

'The boy admitted to killing Vilho Karppinen and Marko Halttu,' Anna told her colleagues who had all gathered in Virkkunen's office.

'What the heck?' Nils gasped.

'His lawyer terminated the interview there and then. I couldn't ask him anything after that.'

'What's going on here?' asked Sari. 'I can almost understand murdering Halttu, but why on earth would Sammy kill the old man?'

'I don't know. But the fact is we've found hairs from Vilho Karppinen in the boot of Marko's Opel and Sammy's hair in the passenger seat, so they're both mixed up in this one way or the other.'

'We mustn't forget the woman living opposite. Riitta Vehviläinen is still missing,' said Virkkunen.

'The gangs must be behind this,' said Nils. 'The old pair saw something they weren't supposed to see.'

'It certainly looks that way,' said Virkkunen. 'Siponen won't allow us to interview Sammy again until tomorrow, so by then we need to gather all the information we have and plan how to proceed with the investigation.'

'I'm guessing this Sammy is one of the main suspects in the gang cases. Esko will have to find watertight evidence and a link to the Black Cobras,' said Nils.

'We need everybody on board with this investigation. Where is Esko?'

'I haven't seen him,' said Sari. 'Probably at home sleeping off a hangover.'

Virkkunen frowned. 'We also have to step up the search for that old lady. And we'll have to take a closer look at Vilho's affairs – bank details, telephone calls, everything.'

'Got it.'

'Anna will continue interviewing Sammy tomorrow. And we'll have to inform Vilho's son of the turn of events. This also puts the dangerous-driving charges against that young girl in a new light.'

'She always maintained the man was lying in the road when she approached,' Sari commented.

'Gabriella,' said Anna and felt a tinge of disappointment. If what Sammy said was true, all the charges against her would be dropped. Why was that so disappointing? It was good news; the girl was innocent of Vilho's death. Virkkunen's wife and children stared at her from a golden picture frame on the desk. Why did Anna always think his wife's stare was trying to warn her of something? And why did she have a niggling feeling that the innocent party here was Sammy, not Gabriella?

'If you see Esko, tell him to come and see me at once,' said Virkkunen. Sari gave a gloating smile.

The waiting room was empty, but twenty minutes after his appointment time Esko still hadn't seen the doctor. He flicked through health magazines and twice had to go outside for a cigarette. The chest pains had stopped and his lungs were no longer stinging. He'd had a light cough in the morning, but that too had passed. I'm probably sitting here for nothing, he thought. If the bloody doctor isn't here in five minutes, I'm going to work, he resolved and tried to concentrate on an article about the health benefits of blueberries. Five minutes had almost elapsed when the doctor's surgery door opened and Esko was called inside. Nobody had come out of the room, Esko noted. This was all deliberately to piss him off, he thought, working himself up even further.

The doctor was a young woman. Not bad looking, thought Esko, but is she any good at her job? Looks like she's barely out of college. The doctor asked about Esko's general state of health, his lifestyle, and she was particularly interested in what had happened when he chased after the suspect. Was the pain sharp, constricting, dull or pulsating? Where exactly was the pain? Did it seem to radiate outwards? How long had it lasted? Had he experienced anything like this before? Esko fibbed about the number of cigarettes he smoked, said he only drank now and then, but admitted that regular exercise had fallen by the wayside lately. He played down the pain. He'd never experienced it before, he said, and it hadn't been all that bad while he was running. The doctor looked at Esko, somewhat sceptical. She asked him to take off his jumper, then listened carefully to his heart and lungs. The verdict was blunt. They would have to examine his lungs more closely as the doctor could hear extraneous sounds, and they would take him up to A&E straight away to perform a cardiograph. She urged him to quit smoking, printed off the appropriate referrals and wrote out a prescription for medication to alleviate the initial shock of giving up smoking. Esko reluctantly took the papers from her. The young doctor gave him a firm, jovial shake of the hand and said it was high time he started looking after himself. If he changed his lifestyle, he would have plenty of life in him yet.

Esko stepped out of the health centre and immediately lit a cigarette. He felt old, too old to take care of himself. Did anything matter any more? There was nobody at home waiting for him and the younger ones were speeding past him at work – he couldn't even run after a crook any more.

Esko's phone rang in his pocket. He flicked the cigarette to the ground and answered quickly.

'I need some money,' said the breathless voice at the other end. The connection was bad, the line crackled and hissed. In the background he could hear the sound of traffic.

'I haven't got any on me.'

'I need three hundred, fast. I've got some information; it's fucking important.'

'Okay, you'll get your money. Now talk to me.'

'Where can I get the money and when?'

'Tomorrow. Come to the Hesburger on Rautatienkatu. What is it?'

'I need it today.'

'No can do. Tomorrow.'

'All right then, for fuck's sake.'

'Well?'

'You'd better watch your back,' said the voice.

'Why?' asked Esko and instinctively scanned the car park outside the health centre. There was nobody there.

'You're on the Cobras' radar.'

'They wouldn't dare touch a copper.'

The voice on the telephone chuckled.

'Killing the bastards in blue is the highest honour there is.'

'How do you know this? Have you got any details? Where? When?' Esko asked and gazed around him. His chest had started to ache again. He lit another cigarette.

'I know something. I'll tell you once I get the money. You'd better have eyes in the back of your head.'

'I have. See you tomorrow. Ten o'clock.'

'Does it have to be so early?'

'Christ, if it's not good enough, you'll get two hundred at eleven o'clock.'

'All right, all right, ten it is.'

You'll get two hundred anyway, thought Esko angrily and ended the call. He felt an unpleasant tightening sensation in his throat. It was fear, pure, chilling fear. Fuck me, when did I become this pathetic, he wondered. I've got to talk to someone about this. But who?

Anna was going over the files on Vilho Karppinen. According to his bank statements he was a man who took good care of his finances, and over the years he had saved a small but significant amount of money. He owned the apartment in Leppioja, a cottage in the countryside and a stretch of woodland in Kainuu, and he had enough money in the bank to last him many years to come. He wasn't fantastically rich but wasn't poor by any means. Anna didn't really know why she called the skiing resort at Kero to verify that

Juha Karppinen had really been there. Perhaps it was because Anna didn't believe Sammy's story or because as a police officer she was used to double-checking everything. With deaths in suspicious circumstances, it was always worth finding out if anyone would benefit from the death. The receptionist at the resort confirmed Juha's story. Besides, the size of his inheritance wasn't out of the ordinary.

Anna forced herself to call Juha, though she wasn't in the mood to do any more work that day. Fatigue had hit her straight after the meeting. She'd noticed before that intensive interviews and immediate debriefings with colleagues zapped her energy, making her head feel leaden and empty. Anna briefly outlined the recent turn of events regarding Vilho's death, Sammy's confession and the investigation that would now ensue. Juha seemed unable to take in what Anna was saying. She had to explain twice who Sammy Mashid was and how a refugee drug addict had anything to do with his father being run over on an icy stretch of road. Once things became clear to him, he fell silent with shock and couldn't utter a word. Anna explained that the police would be in touch with Juha as and when they were able to confirm the details of Sammy's story. Juha swallowed and thanked her for the information. Anna ended the call. The hierarchy of death, she thought as she stared out across the city, where people hurried from one shop to the next buying things they didn't need, where the headlights of the streams of traffic caressed the black surface of the road and where neon signs glowed in all imaginable colours, making the cityscape seem artificial and cinematic. The manner in which someone dies isn't irrelevant, though the result is always the same. A violent death is more difficult to come to terms with than an accident, and an accident is harder to accept than illness. A so-called natural death was best, the most desirable death of all. It was no wonder Juha Karppinen was in shock.

I really don't care how or when I die, thought Anna. In fact, I'm not afraid of death. What difference does it make whether I exist or not, in the greater scheme of things? We are nothing but tiny specks, though we think ourselves so important and unique. Anna's eyes fixed on a woman in the street below, carrying a heavy bag of shopping in one hand and dragging a child behind her with the other. The child was writhing and resisting, trying to wriggle free of his mother's hand, but the woman held on to him tightly.

When Esko arrived at the station, Virkkunen was waiting for him. He had been keeping an eye on his office door to see when Esko turned up.

'Where have you been? Breathe.'

'For crying out loud,' said Esko and breathed towards Virkkunen's face so hard that a bead of saliva flew on to his cheek. Good job I didn't drink too much yesterday, he thought contentedly.

'I hear you got into a spot of bother during yesterday's raid.'

'I wasn't in any flaming bother.'

'Apparently you looked like you were about to have a heart attack.'

'Sari told you that, did she?'

'That's irrelevant.'

'Sari's got something against me. She's been behaving like a right bitch recently.'

'You didn't have the strength to run.'

'Listen, the suspect is a lad in his twenties and I'm 56. Is it any wonder I didn't catch him?'

'How long are you going to lie to yourself, Esko?'

'Lie about what?'

'By telling yourself you're fit as a fiddle, that you can carry on with all your bad habits forever.'

'I've just come from the doctor's. I'm fine.'

'Is that so?'

'Yes. I'm supposed to stop smoking, but they all say that, don't they?'

'If I'm honest, you don't look very well. How about the drink?'

'For Christ's sake, Pertti, just drop it. You know I do my job far better than many people round here. Did they catch the bugger?'

'No,' said Virkkunen. 'He managed to get away though there

were at least ten officers after him. But at least we've been able to disrupt the Cobras good and proper. At this point, that's what's most important: making it impossible for them to operate.'

'Right. And that's exactly what we're going to do.'

Virkkunen looked at Esko, puzzled. 'Is something the matter?'

'What do you mean?' Esko snapped.

'You seem worried.'

'There's nothing the matter. I'm a bit tired, that's all.'

Virkkunen gave Esko a friendly pat on the back. 'Come round for a sauna some weekend. You haven't visited for ages. Raija's always asking after you.'

'Sounds good,' said Esko. 'I'll do that.'

Esko went into his office to write up his report on yesterday's operation, but it was hard to concentrate. He kept thinking about the phone call from his informant. He hadn't said anything to Virkkunen, because he didn't want to believe what he'd heard. The guy was only after some money; he'd probably invented the whole story. These gang members wouldn't dare kill a policeman because it wouldn't do them any good; it would bring them nothing but trouble. The Black Cobras were brutal, but they'd never touched an officer, not even in Denmark. At least, not on purpose. Still, Esko had to admit he was ruffled. Maybe it would be best to remain on his guard, just to be sure. He listened to his heart, to the sensations in his chest. Nothing. Everything felt normal. The cardiograph could wait. Esko looked at the prescription the doctor had given him, tore it in half and threw it into the rubbish bin. He thought of his father, who had smoked like a chimney and lived almost to the age of ninety. I've got good genes, he thought and started to write. He wondered how to describe events so as not to draw attention to his own failure. Even an idiot could see that Reza was simply too young to be chased by someone Esko's age. After typing a few lines he remembered something. He clicked on the bookmark menu. The advertisement was still there, top of the list. He googled the name of the organisation mentioned in the advert. Construction projects in national parks, teaching in slums, care in orphanages, security work in refugee camps.

You had to buy the flights yourself, but once you were there you were looked after. It's all a bloody scam, thought Esko. If these people needed a work force so badly, why did you have to pay for your own flight? And God knows what kind of shack you'd have to live in once you got there. You'd doubtless have to share a room with ten sweaty hippies, and the food was probably the cheapest corn gruel imaginable. Esko clicked open the section about security work in refugee camps. *We are looking for security professionals to assist UN troops at refugee camps around the world. Are you looking for voluntary work that offers you real challenges? Are you used to working under pressure in demanding conditions? Do you have experience of the security business? We are looking for people with plenty of first-hand experience in military, police and security positions. Placements from three to six months. Ability to carry a weapon is compulsory.*

At least this sounded like something worthwhile. Esko began searching for information on refugee camps without really knowing why. He was surprised. There were lots of camps around the world sheltering a staggering number of people. New camps were springing up all the time, especially in the Middle East, which was going through yet another period of turbulence. For some reason he thought of the Karelian refugees evacuated to Finland during the Second World War.

Esko snapped out of his daydreaming when someone knocked on the door. Virkkunen stood in the doorway looking puzzled, behind him two dark-haired figures, a man and a woman. Esko was taken aback. He hadn't imagined Reza's mother would ever get in touch with the police again. He asked Naseem and the interpreter to sit down, asked whether they would like coffee or tea. They both refused, though this didn't stop Esko fetching himself a fresh cup.

'Who are they?' Virkkunen asked him in the corridor.

'I'll explain as soon as they've gone,' Esko replied.

'You're not up to something I don't know about, are you?'

'Of course not. The woman is Reza Jobrani's mother. I've only just tracked her down, but we still haven't got any significant information out of her.'

'Come to my office as soon as they leave.'

'Okay.'

Esko poured himself a cup of coffee and went back to his own office, where a frightened-looking Naseem was sitting next to the interpreter.

'Has Reza come home?' Esko asked eagerly. Had the boy taken a scare after the chase and gone running right back to Mummy?

'I still haven't seen him,' Naseem replied and fell silent. She looked uncomfortable, as though it was difficult to talk.

'What has happened?' Esko asked, trying to sound friendly.

'I know something,' Naseem said quietly.

Right, Esko, keep calm, he frantically told himself.

'Would you like to talk about it?' he asked gently.

Naseem nodded and looked at Esko. Tears gleamed in her beautiful dark eyes. Esko felt a wave of pity, a sensation that he didn't like one bit.

'I know about the gang. The Black Cobras.'

'What do you know about them?'

'It started the first time Reza visited relatives in Denmark. This happened a few years ago, soon after I arrived in Finland. After that trip, he somehow changed.'

'In what way?'

'He became secretive. He wasn't at home very often. Then he dropped out of school.'

'What was he studying?'

'He wanted to be a restaurant chef. Not the best career choice, but a career all the same. I wanted him to go to university.'

'Quite.'

'In any case, it was a blow to me when he quit school. I tried to talk some sense into him, asked our friends and relatives to talk to him, but it was futile. It was as though he slipped from our hands, and that's when things started going downhill.'

'What happened in Denmark?'

'His cousins told us that Reza was mixing with the wrong crowd. You know the situation in Denmark; gang warfare is out of hand. That's when Reza first met the Black Cobras.'

'Did he tell you what he was up to?'

'Of course not.'

'Do you know anything about it?'

The woman looked at Esko with a look of near amusement in her mournful eyes.

'I'm not stupid. I have my own contacts in Denmark, and besides, I am a mother. Mothers can see everything, if only they open their eyes.'

Esko didn't respond but waited for her to continue.

'Reza established the Black Cobras here in Finland – he and his new friends brought it with them like the most prized Danish export. They started putting their operations together at least a year ago. Reza recruited his friends from Vaarala, Rajapuro and across the city.'

'Why didn't you contact the police then? And why didn't you tell me this when I asked you?' Esko was trying to suppress the note of exasperation in his voice.

Naseem wept. Her tears had created a black blotch of mascara beneath her left eye.

'It's not that easy. Perhaps you find this hard to appreciate, but to me, to people like me, the police force does not represent protection – on the contrary. We are all weaned on notions like this, and it's difficult to change one's perceptions no matter how much the Finnish authorities try to convince you to trust them.'

'I understand,' said Esko, though he didn't quite understand.

'I've thought about this day and night since your visit. My son is in real danger. I came to the conclusion that I would rather see him in prison than in a coffin. And that is why I want to help the police, to help you, now.'

'I understand,' said Esko, and the interpreter relayed this.

For a moment Naseem was silent. She looked at her well-groomed hands, then at the floor, and seemed hesitant once again. A faint blush rose to her cheeks.

'This really isn't easy,' she said and glanced at Esko. Again he noticed the tears welling in her eyes.

'Of course not,' Esko said and cleared his throat. 'Especially when it's your own child in question.'

'You are a wonderful man,' said Naseem and looked Esko full in the eyes. 'You remind me of my husband.'

Esko was taken aback. He felt suddenly aware of the presence of the interpreter, though the man knew how to sit in the room as though he weren't there at all. Again Esko cleared his throat, tried to muster something approaching an encouraging smile though he could feel sweat beading on his brow, his cheeks burning. He glanced over at the interpreter, who looked as if he hadn't noticed a thing.

'I think I know where Reza is hiding,' Naseem continued.

'Where?' Esko's voice sounded hoarse.

'He has two close friends, and they are both involved in the gang. Here are their addresses and their parents' addresses. Four different places, but Reza is certainly in one of them.'

'Thank you,' said Esko. He could say nothing else.

'There's no need to thank me. I want to help my son. I don't want him to end up on the wrong path, or worse, to die. I am trying to tell myself that the police are my friends in this matter.'

'You are a very wise woman,' said Esko, to his own surprise.

Naseem dried her tears and smiled at him.

15

THE AIRPORT CHECK-IN LOUNGE was surprisingly quiet. The spring break was over, and now planes were filled mostly with slick business passengers whose companies hadn't heard of such a thing as a conference call. Anna had never understood how a meeting could be so important that it was worth flying people halfway across the planet. The world needed a wake-up call, something to stop it in its tracks and make it realise how crazy things had become. As long as the money kept flowing, there was no incentive to slow down. But right now it didn't concern her; the main thing was that Ákos got to visit their grandmother.

Her brother looked shaky. Yesterday's high spirits were gone. Had he hit the bottle once Anna and Gabriella had left? At least budget airlines no longer serve free alcohol, she thought with relief. Once he was back home, surely Ákos wouldn't dare hit the booze. He wanted to show them he'd changed. Besides, he was genuinely worried about their grandmother. They had agreed that Ákos would call as soon as he arrived.

Ákos checked himself in at the machine in the lobby, or rather Anna did it for him, because Ákos's hands were trembling too much. Then she accompanied her brother to the relatively short queue at the security gate. Anna stayed behind, watching her brother's back as he took off his jacket and belt and placed them in a white plastic box, and removed his shoes to reveal an endearing pair of odd socks. As he stepped through the metal detectors, Ákos turned and waved with a smile. His exhausted face lit up with excitement. Anna felt a wrench of longing inside her. I want to go too, she thought and glanced at the clock. Sammy's interview was scheduled to recommence in an hour. I'll take my summer holidays there, she vowed. I won't spend a single day in Finland.

Hesburger hadn't yet opened for the day when Esko gripped the handle and tried to pull the large glass door open. A man dressed in a security uniform walked across the room trying to find the right key from a heavy key ring. His figure merged with Esko's reflection in the glass door; for a moment they were one and the same. The guard found the correct key and ushered in the first customer of the day. Esko mumbled something in reply. Again he chose a spot far away from the windows that looked out on to a busy shopping street. Maybe this isn't the best meeting place in the world, he thought – but so what? Behind the counter a young girl with a ponytail was waiting, clearly peeved, for Esko to order something, but he never ate hamburgers or drank Coca-Cola. If only they would serve me a cold beer, he thought.

Two teenage girls came in dressed in tight jeans and short jackets, with thick scarves wrapped round their necks like tyres. Their faces were heavily made up and their hair dyed, one bright white, the other light purple. The girls went to the counter and giggled over what to order. Shouldn't they be at school, thought Esko. Skivers. He looked at the time: five past ten. The damn guy was always late. I should have turned up an hour late, let him wait for once. Esko ordered a coffee and slowly sipped from the paper cup until it was empty. At twenty past ten his informant finally arrived.

'Am I late?' he asked first off, then without waiting for an answer informed Esko that he was hungry.

Esko bought him a double cheeseburger and a glass of soda. Here I am, keeping him fed yet again. Jesus, this information had better be worth the trouble, he thought. The man tore into the burger as though he'd never seen food before.

'You said I'm in danger,' said Esko, as the man wiped his dirty beard on a napkin and glanced up at the menu above the counter displaying enormous burgers that looked completely different from the ones that customers stuffed into their mouths.

'Can I have another one?'

'No. You tell me what the hell's going on or I'll leave right now and you can wave goodbye to any food and money.'

The man glared at Esko. Beneath his dishevelled exterior he gave off the certainty of having the upper hand.

'Whatever, mate,' he said. 'You're the one who's losing out, not me.'

The two men glowered at one another for a moment. The informant smirked with satisfaction; Esko had to force himself not to punch him.

'Fine,' he said eventually and stood up. 'As you wish. Thirty years in this job means I'm not fazed by anything, least of all a bunch of brats getting too big for their fucking boots. Before long I'll have rounded up those Paki gangland runts, every last one of them. Then it'll be time for you lot. Starting with you. I'm sure the Angels would be very interested in your relationship with the police.'

Esko shunted his chair beneath the table with such force that it almost toppled over. He marched out into the street, felt the touch of the chilled spring air on his face, the fug of exhaust fumes in his nose, the incessant hum of the city in his ears. He dug a cigarette from his pocket, lit up and strode off towards the police station.

'Wait!' came a desperate voice behind him.

Esko didn't stop. Let the little fucker run after me. What a satisfying situation.

'Wait! Hang on, really!' the man shouted as he ran to catch up with Esko. 'Have you lost it? Someone's bound to see us now,' he gasped and grabbed Esko by the arm.

'In there,' said Esko and pointed to a bar across the street, the only place downtown where gang members sometimes enjoyed a morning pint. Not the best place, but it was their only option.

'Not there,' said the man in a panic.

'Get in there. Now,' Esko commanded him.

Esko bought two bottles of beer.

'So, now will you talk?' he said and placed the bottles on the table with a clink.

'Yeah, but not here,' said the man, peering nervously around.

'We're here now. I haven't got all day to piss around.'

'A couple of our guys had a little chat with some of the Cobras the other day. I was driving.'

'Well, well. A little chat?'

The man smiled. 'That's right. A nice, friendly chat, that's all, to suggest they get the fuck off our turf. Well, during our little chat it turned out they're planning to take you out. Killing you would be a test of loyalty or something, a dare.'

'Are they that stupid?' Esko scoffed, though the idea chilled him.

'They're out of control, man. They've got so much gear on the streets, new members coming up, back-up from Denmark, money, you name it. It's starting to go to their heads. They think they're the fucking Godfather. The Angels are pissed off.'

'Who was it you talked to?'

'Reza and his mate from Denmark.'

'Where are they now?'

'Dunno. We met up with them out of town. Far away from beady eyes.'

'How do they get about?'

'I didn't see their car. They'd parked well out of view.'

'I don't think they'd tell you something like this. You're lying.'

'I'm not.'

'If they're planning to kill me, why the hell would they tell the Angels? Something's not right here.'

'Well, if you want the truth, we met up to try and bury the hatchet, to suggest we work together.'

Christ almighty, thought Esko. That's all we need.

'And you're not on our Christmas card list either. We lost a shit load of money because of you.'

'And how's that?'

'The gear at that small-time junkie's place belonged to us. The kid was supposed to sell it on to the Cobras, but you lot organised a raid before either of us could get our hands on it.'

'And who was it gave me the address?' Esko asked. 'If you ask me, they've got the wrong man in the firing line.'

The young man swallowed, took a gulp of beer. Suddenly he seemed to notice something. A look of panic spread across his face and he quickly lowered his head.

'Can I have the money? I've got to get out of here.'

Esko took an envelope from his jacket pocket and slid it across the table. The man snatched it, peered inside, stuffed it into his own pocket and disappeared into the crowded street without looking back.

Esko calmly finished his beer. He heard the drone of drunken conversation at the next table. Esko glanced over at the people sitting there and recognised at least one of them, an old acquaintance of the police. The man nodded towards him. I hope he's not involved with the Angels these days, thought Esko. If so, I'm not the only one in danger. Well, my snitch makes his own choices; I can't be responsible for his safety round the clock. He certainly seemed to be telling the truth, though he clearly hadn't told everything he knew. I'm just one policeman among many – I'm not even a gang liaison officer. I shouldn't matter a damn. Why the hell would the Cobras want to take me out? Could this be part of the plan they'd hatched with the Angels? Am I getting too close to something important? He thought of Naseem.

'You have confessed to the murders of Marko Halttu and Vilho Karppinen. Would you like to change your statement?' Anna began yet another interview.

Sammy still seemed keen. A little too keen, Anna thought.

'No. I killed them.'

'Tell us exactly what happened, in the correct order, in as much detail as possible.'

'The old guy turned up at Macke's flat and started sounding off.'

'When was this?'

'One night I was there. A few weeks ago. I can't remember the exact date.'

'And why was he "sounding off"?'

'Because Macke had the music up too loud.'

Anna recalled that one of the neighbours had made an official complaint about the noise. *A fene egye meg* – was Sammy telling the truth after all?

'What happened next?'

'The old codger stood there shouting and I lost my temper. I told him to shut it or I'd kill him. He wouldn't stop. I hit him in the face and he fell over, then I smacked his head a few times against the corner of the table. And he died.'

Anna looked over at Ritva Siponen. She shook her head with a look of resignation.

'Sammy, you don't understand Finnish,' said Anna. 'How could you have talked to Vilho?'

Sammy appeared to think about this for a moment. 'That must be why he didn't realise I was serious.'

Anna shivered. 'Then what?'

'Then Macke and I threw him from the balcony, dragged him into the car, drove him far away and dumped him in the road. It served him right.'

'Had you taken any Subutex at this point?'

Ritva cleared her throat, trying to get Sammy's attention.

'No. I was completely sober. I only took some once we got back to the flat.'

'This is a very serious matter.'

'I know,' he answered.

'And what about Marko? Why did you kill him?'

'I already told you. He didn't want to give me any subs, even though the flat was full of the stuff. I tried to grab some from him and we got into a fight. He threatened to call the cops and tell them what I'd done to the old guy. I gave him a good beating, punched him in the head, just the way I'd done to that old man. I don't know whether he died there and then, but I decided to make sure with a little extra Subutex. I injected him with quite a lot. It would have killed a horse.'

'Why are you telling us this now?'

Sammy seemed pensive. He pouted his red-brown lips, and for a moment he looked like a little boy. Then his expression turned to one of sadness. He lowered his eyes and stared at the floor as though in shame.

'My conscience has started to plague me. I am a Christian. I want to atone for my sins.'

'Very well, Sammy. I am arresting you for the murders of Vilho Karppinen and Marko Halttu.'

'How long will I get?'

'I don't decide that. But it'll be many years.'

'Ritva, how long?'

Ritva Siponen didn't answer. She simply stared at the floor in disbelief.

After concluding the interview, Anna called the forensics team and told them to take a closer look at Marko Halttu's apartment and balcony. Then she telephoned Linnea Markkula to ask about the contusions on Vilho's head. Linnea believed the injury was consistent with Sammy's story about the coffee table.

'I was puzzled by that wound from the start, do you remember? It didn't look like something sustained in a car accident,' said Linnea with satisfaction.

Anna remembered. The two incidents had happened so close to one another that the forensics team hadn't been able to differentiate the wounds. So it seemed that Sammy really was telling the truth. Everything he had said matched the evidence. Anna didn't understand why she was so upset, angry even. Despite everything, she didn't want to believe Sammy's version of events. Sammy wasn't a killer. The boy could never bring himself to smash a defenceless old man's head against a table, no matter how many drugs he'd taken; of that Anna was almost certain. Or was she completely mistaken? The most dangerous psychopaths could often seem charming and innocent, more so than genuinely charming and innocent people themselves. Maybe Esko was right after all and Sammy was the main suspect in the street-gang case too. Maybe Sammy was the reason for the vast quantities of drugs they'd found in Halttu's apartment.

Anna looked at the clock on her office wall. In a few hours Ákos would land in Budapest and step out of the airport into eighteen-degree heat, into the land of *pálinka* and the *puszta*, surrounded by relatives. The sun shimmered behind the window, the frosted trees glittering in its raw, penetrating light. Why won't the sun warm us properly, she wondered. The sub-zero temperatures went on and on; that morning it went down almost to -10°C. She'd scraped the car windows so vigorously that her arm ached. The seat had been ice cold, freezing Anna's bottom. The car had only properly warmed up once they reached the airport. I'll probably get a urinary-tract infection or something even worse, she thought. I'm sick of this freezing weather. I'm sick of snow, still heaped around the city at the beginning of May. I'm sick of the frost permanently stuck across the car windows, of skiing and the northern wind that seems to rip through everything. I'm sick of the slippery pavements, sick of always feeling cold outside, then sweating beneath layers of winter clothes the minute I step into a department store, only to feel even colder when I walk outside again. I want to look out across the open sea, not a sheet of ice.

I don't even want the sea. I want to get away. Somewhere. Anywhere.

'*Szia, itt az Anna*,' she greeted Gabriella, who giggled upon hearing Anna's voice.

'*Szia, Anna. Hogy vagy?*'

'I'm pretty busy. Some new information has come to light about the death of Vilho Karppinen.'

'Well?'

'It seems he was very likely already dead when you ran over him.'

'Really? Well … oh my goodness … That's great! Oh God, should I even say that?'

'This is unofficial for the moment. We still have to verify a few matters.'

'Brilliant! I was so worried I'd never be able to go home, that I'd have to stay here forever.'

'Think back to the time of the accident. Can you remember exactly what position he was lying in before you hit him?'

'I've already told you. He was across the road on his side, facing towards me.'

'Did you see anyone else further down the road?'

'I can't remember.'

'Did you see any oncoming cars at all?'

'I really don't know. I don't think so. It was so dark.'

'Are you absolutely sure? This is very important.'

'There was traffic in town, of course, but once I got out into the woods I don't remember seeing anyone at all. How did he die? Why was he lying in the road?'

'I can't tell you any details as the investigation is still pending, but the charges against you will be dropped regardless.'

'Was it a heart attack?'

'I'm afraid I can't tell you.'

'Anna, *légy szíves*,' Gabriella whined. 'I'm dying of curiosity.'

'I'm sorry.'

'We had such a good time last night.'

'That was a private matter; this is a work matter. Try and understand.'

'All right then,' said Gabriella, disappointed. 'Shall we meet up at the weekend? I'd like to show you some photos from home.'

'I'm probably going to be working all weekend.'

'I should have guessed. You know, sometimes I think you're downright jealous of me.'

'And why's that?'

'Because I've got a family and a home, a place to go back to.'

'So do I,' Anna replied, somewhat baffled.

'Do you? Do you really? The same way I do?' asked Gabriella pointedly.

'Yes!' Anna shouted.

'Where exactly? Yugoslavia? Serbia?'

'I'm not listening to this rubbish any more. Don't call me again.'

Anna hung up. Her heart was beating in her chest, and she noticed she was out of breath. Then she hurled her phone to the floor. The back cover sprung off and the battery slid along the waxed floor and stopped beneath her desk. Anna ran into the toilet but wouldn't allow herself to cry.

The police had ordered round-the-clock surveillance at Hazileklek. In practice this meant a security firm checking the building every hour and a civilian police officer visiting the restaurant's forecourt once a day. Nobody had seen or heard anything of the blackmailers. Still, Maalik and Farzad were on their guard. Despite Maalik's objections, Farzad had bought a baseball bat and placed it behind the counter, on a stand he'd cobbled together. Isn't that going a bit too far? Maalik had asked. This sort of thing only happens in films. That's where I learnt this little trick, Farzad answered and tested to see how quickly he could grab the bat. Anna walked across town to meet the Afghan men. She wanted to tell them of Sammy's confession; after all, they were the only so-called normal people with whom Sammy had any contact. The temperature had risen rapidly throughout the day. A warm breeze blew in from the south, rooks gathered in the trees outside the town hall and melting snow soaked her shoes.

'Hello, Anna, come on in,' Farzad greeted her, though not as jovially as usual. 'Would you like some food?'

'I could have a cup of tea. Mint, please, if you have any,' she replied, took off her coat and scarf and hung them on the coat rack.

'Yes, we do. I'll make some. Maalik, Anna is here,' Farzad shouted on his way into the kitchen.

Maalik appeared in the dining room. He looked tired. The understated style and tidiness, so characteristic of both men, had not entirely disappeared, but a small crack seemed to have ripped through it. Their jaws were dark with stubble, bags had appeared beneath their eyes and the worry lines across their brows had deepened.

'How have you been coping?' Anna asked.

'Not very well. Customers don't like the security guard here all the time. It make the place seem unsafe. The customers can sense it.'

The dining room was almost empty. Only two tables were occupied: one by a young family, father, mother and two school-aged children, and the other by a couple talking intensely over a bottle of wine.

'Things will get better once we sort out these gangs,' Anna tried to comfort him, though she realised that at that moment nothing could have comforted Maalik. 'The main thing is that they haven't shown up here.'

'Have you arrested them yet?'

'A few. We are constantly trying to disrupt their operations, patrol squads stop certain cars and certain people and we'll organise a house search for the smallest offence. We know who the ringleaders are, so we'll soon sort things out.'

'We are afraid. They see that this place is being watched. They will take revenge.'

'If they see that the restaurant is guarded, they won't dare do anything,' said Anna, though she doubted this herself.

'They will attack us at home. That's what we are afraid of.'

'It won't be long before we've got them all rounded up,' said Anna. 'Then there will be nothing to worry about.'

If only that were the case, she thought. And even if they managed to wipe out the Black Cobras, there were still the Hell's Angels, the Bandidos, United Brotherhood and the rest of them. The threat would never go away completely. But this she didn't say to Maalik.

Farzad came out of the kitchen carrying a pot of steaming mint tea. He poured cups for everyone and sat down to join them. The tea was sweet and fresh.

'The reason I've come is because I want to talk about Sammy,' said Anna.

'Poor boy. Have they filed his appeal yet?'

'Probably, but I'm afraid it's unlikely to change anything at this point.'

'Why?'

'Sammy has confessed to two counts of murder.'

'What?' the men gasped almost at once. They began speaking hurriedly in Farsi, shaking their heads and gesticulating frantically.

'This cannot be true,' Maalik said eventually. 'We don't believe this for one minute.'

Anna had hoped to hear something like this.

'Why not?' she asked.

'Sammy is a good boy, very polite. He would not hurt even a fly.'

'He is also a drug addict, and drug addicts will do almost anything to get their hands on more drugs.'

'Not Sammy. For sure not. He has worked for us, cleaning, washing dishes, little things. The cash register is right there, always open, but we are never missing a penny,' said Maalik.

'Our wallets are always in the staffroom. Sammy could have stolen money any time, but he never did,' Farzad continued.

'And don't drug addicts normally steal – not kill?' asked Maalik. 'Sammy doesn't even steal.'

'That's true,' said Anna. 'But he told us himself that he killed those two men.'

'Who did he killed?'

'Kill,' Anna corrected him and regretted it instantly. As a child she'd always been infuriated whenever people corrected her Finnish. 'One was an elderly man and the other was a young substance abuser. Both victims lived in the same building.'

'And why he kill them?'

'Because of a row over drugs. One of them, at least.'

'We cannot believe this is true. Sammy is always very polite and respectful. He is not a killer.'

'If he is found guilty, will he stay in Finland?' Farzad asked suddenly.

'Convicted felons are generally deported,' Anna replied.

'Sammy does not know this. That's why he is lying. He doesn't want sent home, where he will be killed.'

'Or perhaps that's precisely why he killed those people,' said Anna.

Esko was sitting in a civilian car parked outside Ruiskukkatie 10 in Rajapuro. The building rising like a grey box in front of him was home to a member of Reza's gang, and Naseem suspected her son might be hiding out there. Esko had been sitting in the car for two and a half hours, but nothing had happened. He still hadn't told Virkkunen about the warning his informant had given him, or anyone else for that matter, because if he did he would almost certainly be taken off the case and possibly even moved into hiding for a while. He didn't believe he was in any serious danger, and besides, he wanted to bring Reza in by himself. We've already managed to put a spanner in the bastard's works, Esko surmised. The confiscation of the drugs in Halttu's apartment will have been a huge setback both to the Angels and the Cobras. Halttu was mixed up in a dangerous game; it's no wonder he got himself killed. And no matter what Anna says, the Paki kid killed the old boy and he's probably one of the Cobras' dealers. We've arrested three wogs in raids and confiscated their office equipment, so they'll be feeling the heat, he thought to himself but didn't feel any sense of satisfaction.

I am sick to death of this job, thought Esko. He felt a chill, though the Webasto car heater was switched on. He looked up at the dark windows on the second floor and waited for someone, Reza or his friend, for anyone to arrive. From time to time he smoked a cigarette in the car, only opening the window slightly. He tried to sense the feelings in his chest and listen to the sound of his breathing. Nothing. He felt normal. His little episode must simply have been because he was out of shape. Maybe I really should cut back on the smokes, he thought and flicked his half-smoked cigarette out of the window. There was nobody in the yard. Esko yawned. He thought of the advertisement still waiting for him in his bookmark browser.

Should I ask Naseem about conditions in these camps, he thought, just out of curiosity? Naseem probably knew a fair bit about security and safety at these camps. She was a smart woman and she'd worked there herself. He couldn't see himself working in a refugee camp, but what harm could there be in asking? Still, he had to admit that there was something very attractive about the idea, something different. We should help people, that's for sure, but we should help them in their own countries, where the need for help is most acute. That's precisely what he could do. He still had time to experience something completely new. Or did he? He'd thought like this once before and managed to screw his life up once and for all. Maybe I should get that cardiograph done after all. Just to be on the safe side.

Esko waited in Rajapuro until midnight and only smoked one more cigarette, and as nobody had yet turned up at the apartment he started the car and drove home. On the way he stopped in at a petrol station open round the clock. Two large trucks were parked outside. A man was filling his old, metallic-grey Fiat with extortionately priced petrol; a few night owls sat inside flicking through the tabloids, truck drivers on their obligatory breaks. The station's bright-orange interior stung Esko's tired eyes. He wondered whether he would ever buy anything here during the daytime. There were at least three counters, which made the layout seem confusing. Thankfully only one of them was open at night. There was ten centimetres of thick brown liquid at the bottom of the coffee pot; Esko poured it into a paper cup, picked an old and dry-looking white roll with cheese from the vitrine, went to the counter and paid. He pressed a lid on to the cup and decided to drive home and eat there.

As he stepped outside, Esko noticed that between the trucks on the forecourt a large SUV had appeared, a brand-new Kia Sorento. Its lights were switched off and its windows were so dark that he couldn't see inside. Esko's heart began to thump. Nobody had come into the station after him. He surreptitiously tried to get a look at the vehicle's registration as he walked past, but the plates were covered in snow and mud. It was hard to take out his keys while holding his roll and coffee cup; he had to put the cup on the ground, the roll fell next to it. Esko snatched it up and stuffed it in his pocket, and just then the SUV's engine revved into life, it's over-the-top set of lights flicked on and shone right at him. Esko managed to open the door and quickly sat in the car. By now his heart was racing. I'm going to have a heart attack, he thought, turning the ignition and speeding away from the petrol station, his wheels spinning in the slush. The SUV began to follow him, but at the first intersection turned in the opposite direction. Esko took a few extra detours before returning home, but he couldn't see the car anywhere.

For Christ's sake, that snitch is turning me into a madman with all his nonsense, Esko thought, sitting in his darkened kitchen. He didn't want to switch on the lights. He opened a can of beer, lit a cigarette and realised he'd left the cup of coffee on the ground in the station forecourt. He peered out of the window into the empty yard. Only his neighbours' familiar cars stood in the floodlit car park, waiting for morning, for their owners to leave for work. The yard was quiet and sleepy. The Kia Sorento was nowhere to be seen.

16

'SAMMY?'

'What?'

The cell was bright. The light wasn't coming from the windows, because there were none, but from the light bulbs on the ceiling behind a protective metallic grille. Anna had come down to the holding cells. She wanted to talk to Sammy alone.

'I don't believe you killed those people. Why are you lying to us?'

Sammy was doing press-ups on the floor, counting in a foreign language, out of breath. Then he slumped to the floor and rolled on to his back.

'I'm not lying.'

'You won't be allowed to stay here. Convicted criminals are deported as a matter of course.'

'Ritva said that could take at least three years with the judicial process and all the bureaucracy. She said they won't necessarily send me back. She wants to make a legal precedent, so I can serve my sentence in Finland.'

'It sounds desperate.'

'I am desperate, a desperate murderer.'

'I talked to Maalik and Farzad. They said you wouldn't hurt a fly.'

'They don't know the real me.'

'I think they do.'

'Why are you here?' Sammy asked and sat up. He wiped sweat from his brow.

'I want to talk to you.'

'I mean, why are you in Finland.'

'I live here.'

'Yeah, I know that. But why? Why don't you go back to your home?'

Anna thought for a moment how to answer.

'My home is here now,' she said eventually. 'My work is here, my brother.'

'You see? I want a job here too. I don't have a brother any more.'

'Neither do I – well, one of them, that is. Or a father.'

And before long I won't have a grandmother either, she thought. Sammy looked at her with his friendly eyes, eyes that had seen so much, and edged closer to her.

'I saw straight away there was sadness inside you. It lives there and won't go away,' he said.

Anna closed her eyes for a moment, took a deep breath. You can't start crying now, she told herself.

'Sammy, even if you're allowed to stay and serve your sentence in Finland, you will be locked up for at least ten years,' she said quietly.

'That's plenty of time to study and learn Finnish. In ten years' time I'll still be young.'

'Please, Sammy. It doesn't work like that.'

'It has to work. Ritva said it might work out.'

'And is that why you're lying to us?'

'I'm not lying,' he insisted.

Anna left the cell. The guard opened the heavy metal door, and Anna stepped out into the corridor, which reeked of tobacco. Sammy's desperation had touched her profoundly. What fate could possibly be so terrible that years in prison felt like salvation in comparison? Why hadn't Sammy been awarded leave to remain when he first applied? If that had happened, he would be studying somewhere, he would have a future. Anna knew that Sammy's story wasn't at all exceptional. The world was full of stateless people, people who for one reason or another had been forced to leave their homes and travel far and wide, people whose hope of a better tomorrow, of settling somewhere and living in peace was not in their own hands but in the hands of the authorities, lawyers and politicians, the kind of people who after a hard day's work went back to their own homes, stretched their legs on the sofa, sighed with comfort and wondered who would take the kids to their various activities that evening, whether to go the Pilates or the kettle-bell class, whether to watch TV or go to bed early, and all this without once thinking that their secure lives, lives they took for granted, were in worldwide terms nothing but an illusion. Hands like that need to be washed regularly.

Anna went into her office. She tried to concentrate on writing up a few reports, but it was futile. She decided to drive into town.

Anna spent a while looking for the boy. First she asked the boy's mother, who suggested she ask his former girlfriend. The girl was living in a tiny council flat, a real dump, and she was in as bad a condition as the apartment. Her long blond hair was thin and greasy, her eyes were restless and her speech slurred and unclear. The floor was covered in litter and the bed stank of urine. Anna almost felt like searching the premises, or at least taking the girl into police custody to sober her up, but for the moment she had to keep a low profile. She mustn't frighten the boy or piss him off.

The boy's name was Jani Huttunen, a regular guest at the police station, a small-time crook and drug dealer. Judging by Sammy's description, it was Jani who had given Sammy his first Subutex and got him hooked. A tall, thin boy, blond hair, acne – there were plenty of boys like that, but not very many Subutex dealers. Anna had interviewed Jani in relation to the death of a substance abuser just before Christmas. The death was eventually attributed to an overdose, but Jani had stuck in Anna's mind. The boy had seemed sharp. Anna told him she thought he was wasting his talent. He'd laughed smugly and said he'd always hated wasting his time at school.

Anna decided to check out the areas where drugs were in regular circulation: the shopping centre at Rajapuro, behind the supermarket in Vaarala and in the parks and car parks around Koivuharju. It was the first day of April and the sky seemed to hang over the city like a damp gauze. The cold front had finally gone; now she had to put up with puddles of melting snow, the streams of slush and the possibility of further cold snaps. She would still be able to ski out at sea for a while, until the wind from the south whipped water on to the ice and turned it into a sinking, floating mush that only the bravest skiers dared use. People like this were out skiing so long into the spring that Anna thought they must have a gift for walking on water.

In Vaarala she got lucky. Jani was just leaving the forecourt outside the supermarket, his long legs striding somewhere, a hoodie tightly pulled over his head, his hands deep in his jeans pockets and his shoulders hunched over as Anna pulled the car up in front of him.

'Get in. Now,' Anna ordered him and opened the passenger door.

Jani hesitated for a second, weighed up his chances of getting away, glanced in both directions, then eventually clambered into the car. Anna was surprised. The boy probably didn't have any gear on him, otherwise he'd have made a run for it.

'Remember me? Fekete Anna from the police. How's it going?' said Anna and shook Jani's hand. The boy took her hand, reluctantly squeezed it and didn't say a thing.

'I want to talk to you,' she continued. 'You and I are going for a little drive.'

At first Jani stayed remarkably calm, chewed gum, tapped his fingers against his thighs and whistled a rhythm playing in his head. As Anna drove out of the city without saying anything, the boy became visibly agitated. He squirmed restlessly in his seat, flicked on the car radio and turned the volume up full. Anna switched it off again.

'Where the fuck are you taking me?' Jani finally decided to speak.

'Ask me nicely and I might tell you,' said Anna.

The boy said nothing. Anna continued driving. When Anna slowed as they approached an intersection, he suddenly tried to wrench the door open and throw himself out on to the road, but Anna had locked the door from the inside and Jani could do nothing but feebly rattle the door handle. Out of the corner of her eyes Anna could see that the young man, who a moment ago was so cocky and self-assured, was close to tears.

'Where are you taking me?' he asked quietly.

'So, you can speak politely. Where would you like to go?'

'Home,' he replied even more quietly.

'I'll take you home as soon as you tell me a thing or two.'

Anna switched on the flashing lights and drove down a small track that she was sure didn't lead anywhere. After about fifty metres she brought the car to a stop in the middle of the woods and turned to look at Jani.

'I'm going to show you a few pictures. Look at them carefully and tell me whether you've seen these people before. Okay?'

Again Jani hesitated. He glanced around the grey woodland, clearly looking for an escape route. Anna could almost see the disappointment and embarrassment on his face. Outside the supermarket he might have had a chance; out here he could do nothing. Eventually he nodded. Anna handed him photographs of Sammy and Reza. Jani only looked at them for a second.

'I know them both. This one's an illegal, hiding from the police but uses quite a bit, and this one…'

Anna waited. Jani was clearly worried about talking to her.

'He's called Reza. Big-time crook. He's dangerous.'

'In what way?'

'He's violent, into gang stuff. He's got an army of immigrants working for him.'

'Was Sammy involved with him?'

'Not that I know.'

'What about this guy?' asked Anna and showed him a photograph of Marko Halttu.

Her telephone rang. It was Gabriella. What the hell did that girl want from her, Anna wondered. She thought she'd made it clear she wanted to be left in peace. Anna pressed the 'reject' button and turned again to Jani.

The phone rang again. *A francba*, Anna cursed to herself, can't she just leave me alone – but this number was unknown, and hesitating slightly she decided to answer.

'Fekete Anna,' she said and stepped out of the car while keeping a watchful eye on Jani in the passenger seat.

'Has there been any news about my mother?' asked an agitated female voice.

'Hello? Is that Leena Rekola?'

'Yes, it is. Why has nobody been in touch with me? What has happened to my mother?'

'You have a different number.'

'I changed my number because I was frightened. This number is unlisted.'

'Has something happened? I mean, do you suddenly feel unsafe?'

'Isn't this reason enough?' Leena almost shouted. 'Some confounded drug addict dies, his neighbour dies and my mother is missing – and it's all happened in the same building. Do you hear? The same building! You're only investigating that gang, but have you ever considered that my mother's disappearance could have another explanation altogether? Have you?'

'I am still convinced that we'll find your mother safe and sound,' said Anna without knowing why she wasn't telling the truth. Surely it was wrong to get the woman's hopes up? Wasn't it better to prepare relatives for the worst?

'And where do you imagine we are going to find her?' Now Leena was really shouting. 'Where? I've called everyone – our most distant relatives, even the ones on my father's side, though my mother had nothing to do with them whatsoever. I've been through her old school and work friends, even visited the place we lived when I was young and asked the old neighbours. Nothing. Nobody has heard a thing!'

'You have done a great job,' said Anna and noticed that Jani had switched on the police radio and was listening to it with a smirk on his spotty face. Anna mustered an irritated expression, gave the window a sharp tap and waved her finger. Brat, she thought.

'Quite. And what have the police been doing?' said Leena, her voice chilling.

'Missing persons are not technically a matter for the Violent Crimes Unit…'

'Nonsense. Tell me what the police has done.'

Now Jani was rummaging through the glove compartment. The hoodie had slid from his head to reveal his blond, unevenly shorn hair.

'Leena, I'm very sorry, I'm afraid I can't talk at the moment,' said Anna and opened the car door. Jani turned and looked at her with an infuriating grin. He was holding a bunch of papers.

'Stop it. Put them back right now,' Anna shouted.

'Excuse me?' said Leena.

'I'm sorry, that wasn't meant for you, but I really can't talk right now. Can I call you as soon as I've established what the police have found out about your mother's disappearance?'

'Very well,' said Leena and hung up.

'I'm sure you drove the teachers berserk,' said Anna and looked at Jani as he stuffed a petrol receipt into his mouth.

'I know Macke,' Jani said munching on the receipt. 'He was a total schizo.'

'When was the last time you saw him?'

'Hmm. When was it he snuffed it? A few weeks ago, right? It was just before that. I saw him selling gear in Rajapuro.'

Anna could see that he knew more than he was telling.

'Tell me everything,' she encouraged him.

'What's in it for me?'

'I won't search you for drugs.'

'Wow, how generous of you,' said Jani and looked at Anna with his blue-grey eyes. Their pupils were nothing but small, black specks. 'I haven't got anything on me anyway. I need some cash.'

'You'll get fifty, if you give me some decent information.'

Jani didn't answer immediately. He chewed his fingernails and stared out of the window. Anna could see the boy weighing up his options. Was it worth becoming a snitch for the police? Was it worth putting himself in danger for the sake of a few euros? With a bit of luck you could get a dose of Subutex for thirty; fifty might even get him two doses. He turned to look at Anna.

'Okay. There were a couple of Hell's Angels at the flat. They gave Macke a good kicking.'

The power of money is extraordinary, thought Anna. Especially when it was a question of drugs.

'Do you know why?'

'I don't know anything about that. But it's been harder to get any subs recently. There were rumours Macke was trying to line his own pockets.'

Anna had already heard this from Esko, but the fact that Marko had been beaten up by the Hell's Angels shortly before his death was a new and significant piece of information. So Sammy hadn't caused Marko's bruises and injuries after all. This revealed Sammy's first lie, thought Anna contentedly, and it almost certainly wouldn't be his last.

'Do you know anything else?' she asked in a friendly tone.

Jani thought about this for a moment. His eyes were bleary, his jaw covered in wispy fluff and riddled with acne. Poor boy, thought Anna.

'You should talk to his girlfriend,' Jani said eventually. 'She reckons Macke topped himself.'

'Really? That would be very important information. Who is she?'

'She's called Hilla, best mates with my girlfriend. I can tell her you want to talk to her.'

'That's my boy, Jani. Thank you.'

'Don't mention it,' he said and looked out of the car window. Anna noticed a restless and anguished look in the boy's eyes.

'Can we talk again some time, if I think of any other questions?' asked Anna.

'We'll see,' Jani replied.

'Well, here you go for now,' said Anna and handed him a fifty-euro note. 'Whatever you decide.'

He snatched the bill quickly, like a fledgling whose mother has brought food back to the nest.

Anna drove back into town. She chatted with Jani about all sorts of things, asked about his life, tried to talk to him the way she would to any young man his age. He answered reluctantly. It seemed as though he was ashamed of himself. Anna dropped him off where she'd found him, outside the supermarket in Vaarala. A security-firm van was parked outside. The shop had been the target of numerous attempted robberies and the employees were frightened without a constant security presence on site.

'See ya,' said Jani, opening the door and running off towards the apartment blocks.

Anna felt her heart racing. A smile crept across her face. I've got my very own informant, she thought, exhilarated. Just like all real criminal investigators.

17

HE DIDN'T HAVE TO LEAVE. He could stay, spend years in a secure room safe from the world outside. Sammy felt a rush of inexpressible joy. If he went to prison, he would be free. If he was charged with murder, he might receive a life sentence, Ritva Siponen had said, trying to frighten him. She didn't understand that this was precisely what he wanted. A life sentence. In Finland that didn't mean spending the rest of his life behind bars, but it would be at least eight or ten years. That was enough for Sammy. He would even be happy with the worst possible scenario – deportation – because that would take years to put through the courts. Without any charges, he would be deported straight away.

In a few years anything could happen in Pakistan, the situation for Christians might improve or worsen, but that didn't matter, because over time people would forget him and his name. Perhaps he too could forget himself, forget his past. He would try to, at least. He could change his name to something that didn't give away his Christian background. Mashid meant 'Messiah', and almost all the Christians in Pakistan were called Mashid. He could take a Finnish name. What could it be? Juhani Virtanen – the most common men's first name and the most common surname in Finland. One of his Finnish classes had been about names. Sammy thought it was strange that names in Finland often didn't mean anything, though he recognised that many of them had Christian origins. Sammy stood up from his bunk, assumed an official expression, held out his hand, said 'my name is Juhani Virtanen' twice, in the best Finnish he could muster, and shook an imaginary hand in front of him. The name tasted strange.

He would kick the drugs, finally. He thought of the opium dens in Karachi, the Subutex market on these frozen northern streets. How different they were, and yet how similar. Disaffected people on the margins of society, the living dead, recreational users that needed something to liven up a life that's just too easy, people who think they're in control of themselves. Maybe some people can stay in control, but Sammy knew how rapidly the drugs can take over, how abruptly everything can change. People will do anything for money: prostitution, theft, begging, pay-day loans. Despair, withdrawal symptoms, a heightened level of tolerance, desensitisation to the drugs, deepening addiction, getting involved with a dangerous crowd, depression, self-loathing, suicides. All this was as true in Finland as it was in Pakistan. He banished from his mind the thought that he would have to give up his best friend, and swallowed the saliva that had formed in his mouth. After ten years behind bars I'll no longer remember what it feels like to slowly press down on a syringe, thought Sammy. I'll forget what it feels like when the subs or heroin or any drugs flood into my bloodstream, so dazzling and intense that angels strum their harps in heaven out of sheer blissful happiness. But why can't I forget that sensation? I should think only of dirty mattresses on the floors of darkened rooms, junkies who would kill you just to get a fix, chilling nights in this frozen city, desperately walking the streets looking for someone selling bupe, scavenging for money, a place to stay, trying to escape everything. That's what I mustn't forget, he thought. I'm going to study. I will learn this language so well that they won't be able to throw me out. Ritva told me that prisoners here can retake their high-school exams and learn a trade. I'm going to do all that.

Sammy looked up at the poem on his cell wall. The poem burned his retina like the beating sun. Perhaps his interpreter could translate it for him.

The scan only took a moment, but still Esko felt the urge to tear the electrodes from his body and run away. Except that he didn't have the strength to run. He wanted to curse out loud. Cables and meters were attached all over his body: his chest, wrists, ankles, everywhere.

A machine sketched a fidgety graph in time with his heart, but he couldn't see it. All he could see was the depressing blue curtain pulled in front of him. Behind the curtain another patient was giving a blood sample. What a palaver, thought Esko, no privacy whatsoever. The machine beeped. A young nurse in a white coat pulled back the curtain and slipped inside the cubicle. She calmly removed the electrodes. Her fingers were small and cold, ringless, her nails neatly trimmed. The chill of her touch tickled Esko's skin. It didn't feel bad at all. For a moment he imagined her caressing him, stroking his greying hairs and pressing a light kiss on his chest. The nurse reminded him of his former wife when she was young.

'Right, you can get dressed now. I'll take this to the doctor. If you could go and sit in waiting room number three, he'll call you from there.'

'Will it take long? ' Esko asked as he pulled on his shirt.

'It shouldn't take very long. We're not too busy at the moment.'

Esko went into the waiting room and sat down on one of the red plastic chairs. He pressed a piece of nicotine chewing gum from the packet and started chewing it; a bitter taste flooded into his mouth. He thought of the list of all the Kia Sorentos in town that he'd pulled from the database. Judging by the names of the owners, two were registered to immigrants and one belonged to a rental firm. Esko had called them all. The rental company gave him a potential lead. The car had been rented to a man called Rasul Alif, and it turned out that his personal details, including his name, were fake. Esko told the traffic police to stop and search every black Kia Sorento that they saw. He looked at the other people waiting in the room: three old ladies, a man, and a woman with a whinging kid. They all looked lost, as though they had ended up there by accident. If my heart is in good nick, I'm going to go and work in a camp after all, he thought. You bet I will. Nothing is going to stop me.

'Niemi,' came a voice from the door of room number five. Esko stood up stiffly, walked to the door and shook hands with the doctor, a man approximately his age but who exuded an annoying aura of excellent health.

'Please sit down,' said the doctor and placed the cardiograph on his desk. 'When did this episode of breathlessness take place?'

'On Tuesday,' said Esko.

'Tell me what happened.'

Now Esko felt even more annoyed. His paperwork doubtless showed what he'd said about what had happened during the chase, how he'd felt and everything else. Why did they have to go over the matter again and again? He briefly explained the course of events, doing little to hide the note of irritation in his voice. The doctor looked at him intently.

'I'd like to listen to your lungs again.'

For crying out loud, the nurses had already listened to his lungs. We already know there's a funny sound in them. Just tell me whether everything's okay on the bloody scan, he thought. He started to suspect that everything might not be okay after all. That's why the doctor wanted to examine him again and was asking all these questions: he couldn't bring himself to tell Esko straight up that he'd had a heart attack, that he was going to need coronary angioplasty, that he didn't have long left.

The doctor took his stethoscope and listened closely to Esko's chest and back, at times telling him to take a deep breath, at times asking him to hold his breath.

'Well,' he said finally and prised the stethoscope from his ears. 'The cardiograph doesn't show anything out of the ordinary. Your heart seems to be fine.'

'Really?' Esko gasped. He felt as though he rose a centimetre above his chair.

'It would certainly show us if you'd had some kind of heart attack. But as for your lungs … I understand you're a smoker?'

'I've cut back quite a bit,' said Esko and showed the doctor the chewing gum in his mouth.

'I'm afraid cutting back won't help at this point. I recommend that you stop altogether. It seems likely that you are developing a condition called chronic obstructive pulmonary disease.'

'What the hell?' Esko blurted.

'Of course, we'll need to do more tests. You'll receive notification by post once we've scheduled an appointment. But please, stop smoking immediately. COPD is a very serious condition. Here's some information about it that I've printed for you. I can write you a prescription for something to help you stop…'

'Yes, I've already got one of those, thank you very much,' said Esko and took the bunch of printouts.

When he got out of the hospital he crushed his half-full packet of cigarettes and threw it in the bin. He glanced around the car park but couldn't see a black SUV or anything else suspicious, and decided to see whether he could find Reza at the other address his mother had provided.

The bar was full. Anna pushed her way through a crush of punters and almost knocked a young woman's drink over her chest. A few hours later, and that girl would have started a fight, thought Anna. She ordered a bottle of lager. The beer was wonderfully chilled; it tingled in her mouth and had a pleasant bitterness. I needed this, she thought. Being around other people, relaxing, having fun. I've buried myself at home and at work, obsessed with skiing on the ice. This weekend I'm not going skiing at all. I'm going to have a two-day hangover, laze around in bed and drink a couple of beers to steady myself through the day. She sent Réka a text message. For once she plucked up the courage – and on a Friday. She left out the bit about being out on the town by herself. Anna looked across the crowds of people. She quickly finished her bottle and ordered another. Today I'm not holding back, *a kurva életbe*.

'Look who's here!'

Anna jumped at the voice behind her back and turned to look. 'Nils! How's it going?'

'Not bad. I came straight from work. In fact, technically I'm still at work. I've been looking into that cloakroom tag. I suppose I should be getting home.'

'Don't go yet. Any news on the tag?'

'Not yet. I've been round about half the bars and restaurants in the city and still haven't come up with anything. It's a bit frustrating, especially as the tag could have come from anywhere. It could be from another city.'

'We'll find out sooner or later.'

'By yourself, are you?' asked Nils and stepped closer to Anna.

'Yes.'

'Me too. My wife couldn't be bothered to join me.'

'Is your wife Sámi too?'

'Gosh, Anna. You're really direct. I like it. The whole Sámi thing is a bit of a taboo, you know. It's like asking, is your wife a mongoloid too.'

'Surely not?' Anna chuckled.

'Well, maybe not quite, but still. It's a difficult issue for some people.'

'I had no idea. Seems some good comes from being an outsider.'

'You're not an outsider. You speak Finnish better than me.'

'Really?'

'I'm serious. I only started speaking it properly when I joined the police academy.'

'Wow. Where are you from originally?'

'Near Inari. A tiny village in the middle of nowhere. Only three huts.'

'Excuse me?'

'It's a village with only three houses. My journey to school was forty-five kilometres each way.'

'Terrible.'

'At least I didn't have to live in a hostel somewhere. Do you want a drink?' Nils asked and pointed to Anna's bottle, which again was almost empty.

'I'll have another one of these, thanks.'

Nils stood in line at the bar. Someone turned the music up louder. Anna could feel the alcohol making her dizzy. Nils was a full head taller than most other people at the counter, and his back muscles were defined beneath his shirt. One hell of a good-looking guy, thought Anna. And nice with it. Anna gripped the bottle Nils handed her and took a long swig, looking him fixedly in the eyes. Nils looked back at her just as fixedly.

'Have you got children?' Anna asked for want of something to say.

'Yes, a girl. She's five.'

'Where do you live?'

'In the new area of Leppioja.'

'Oh, doesn't Rauno live there too?'

'Yes. Quite nearby, in fact.'

'Do you know how he's doing?'

'The physiotherapy seems to be progressing well. Nina has decided to stay with him for the time being.'

'Good. That's great news.'

'I know. It would have been too much if he'd lost his health and his wife all at once.'

'Quite.'

'Of course, financially an arrangement like that can be tough, but Rauno's got good insurance, so apparently they'll survive for at least six months.'

Anna couldn't think of anything else to say. She looked across the crowd again, spotted a few people checking her out and eyed them back for a moment. Tonight I'm going to pull myself a man, she thought and turned back to Nils. He avoided meeting her eyes.

'It looks like Esko's back on the booze,' he said eventually.

'Hmm. I suppose that makes two of us.' Anna didn't want to talk about it.

'Have you noticed him drunk at work too?'

'I don't pay attention to things like that.'

Nils smirked. 'I thought as much. How are things otherwise?'

'Not much to tell. Work, mostly.'

'Do you visit your former homeland often?'

'I don't have a former homeland.'

'Oh, right. What does it feel like that the country where you were born no longer exists?'

'You get used to it. I don't think about it very often. The idea of the fatherland never meant much to me anyway. I think I lack the brain receptors to appreciate something like that.'

'I sometimes feel the same way, though of course Finland is a fatherland of sorts for the Sámi people.'

'The town, the house and the people who live there are all the same, though the name of the country has changed,' said Anna.

Well, in some respects, she added to herself. Worry about her grandmother washed over her mind. Ákos had called from the hospital and said that Grandma was very weak.

'There's never been a separate Sámi country, so in that respect my situation is even worse than yours,' said Nils.

They both laughed. Anna looked at Nils. She was interested and she felt a wave of drunken wooziness in her head and legs. It's incredible that, deep down, this man from the far north is very similar to me, she thought.

'Listen, I've really got to go. My wife will have a fit if I stay out too late.'

'Okay,' said Anna, trying to hide her disappointment.

'See you on Monday.'

'See you. Say hi to your wife.'

To her surprise, Nils touched Anna's cheek. His hand was warm and rough.

'I will. You behave now,' he said, winked at her and left.

Anna downed the rest of her beer and glanced at the people around her. Everyone seemed focussed on their drinks and their own conversations. Anna suddenly felt herself shut out. The music had been turned up again, the yell of conversation blared above it.

Her ears ached from the cacophony. Anna decided to change bars. I'll find a place where single, horny men are out looking for prey, a place where desperate women swing their hips on the dance floor for the gratification of the hunters – and I'm going to pick up the most handsome of the lot, she decided. The beer fizzed inside her and warmed her. Though Anna never danced, the early-evening tipsiness sped up her decision to go to the hottest nightclub in town. She lit a cigarette as she stepped out into the frosted street.

There wasn't yet a queue at the cloakroom of the Dorian Nightclub, or at the bar. As she left her coat in the cloakroom, Anna noticed that the tags were black and that they bore the word KARHU. Good, I'm not on duty this evening, she thought. This is my free time. She bought a beer. Was this her fourth or fifth? She instantly checked herself, relieved and almost defiant: I wasn't supposed to count tonight. The nightclub's tables were hidden in booths, lascivious-looking velvet curtains draped above them. Golden beams of light circled the dance floor and the monotonous disco music was at a bearable volume. Propping up the bar were men, and girls in miniskirts drinking brightly coloured drinks through a straw. A steady flow of revellers poured inside. Nobody wanted to be caught up in the queue that would shortly form outside the front door.

Anna wandered around the labyrinthine bar. Each corridor seemed to open out into another dance floor, new bar counters, new men with interest in their eyes. What an awful place, she thought, before correcting herself. This was a one off, she resolved and fetched another beer. In a dim corner of the final room she saw a roulette table. A young man dressed in a tuxedo was deftly handing out playing chips to people standing around the table. The roulette wheel spun into action. The players, three men and one woman, held their breath, trying to look uninterested. The ball came to a halt on one of the numbers. The players' shoulders slumped a fraction. The croupier handed out new chips. The players' muscles tensed again. Anna stood watching the game. There was something magic about the moment. The dimmed lights, the concentrated bodies standing like statues around the table covered in green fabric, the whirr of the table as it spun towards the jackpot – or perhaps not. One of the players turned round. Anna recognised the face. The man's expression flickered for a fraction of a second, like a child caught doing something naughty. Then he said something to the croupier, handed him the remaining chips and left without looking at Anna.

18

ANNA AWOKE in a set of unfamiliar sheets. Her mouth was dry and her head ached. She felt sick. Where am I, she wondered and sensed movement beside her. The room was dim, the venetian blinds were firmly shut, and the sheets smelt of someone strange. Another movement beside her. A burning sensation on her skin. *A francba*, I can't remember anything, she thought and quickly pushed the man away from her, got up and looked for the bathroom. The apartment was large, clean and decorated with masculine simplicity. This shag certainly didn't have money problems, she thought as she rinsed her face in the stylish designer sink. The bright bathroom tiles gleamed, the walk-in shower was like something from a luxury spa, the boards in the sauna that she could just make out behind a glass door were probably not your average abachi wood. Anna thought of her own bathroom, the pallid blue plastic flooring, the shower with the white hose and only two settings: on and off. She hadn't even bothered buying matching bath towels. The ones she had at the moment probably dated back to her days as a student; they were threadbare and the fabric hangers had snapped long ago. When was the last time I bought anything new for my apartment, she wondered. Something beautiful? She looked at herself in the mirror. Her eyes were red and bleary, and the bags sagging beneath them didn't make matters any better. She felt dizzy.

Meanwhile the unknown man had got up and started making some coffee – naked. Anna looked at his muscular, gym-toned body, which seemed to stand in contrast to his greying hair. How old is this guy, she wondered, and who is he? The man asked whether she took milk or sugar, whether she'd like a sandwich. Anna nodded.

She wanted everything. When the man went into the bathroom, Anna quickly rifled through the pile of post on the kitchen counter. Markku Leinonen. The address was downtown. At least it's easy to get home from here, she thought, relieved. I won't have to call a cab. Where on earth did I pick this guy up? Or did he pick me up? Anna tried to think back to the events of the previous evening. She remembered standing by the roulette table, buying some playing chips, fetching a glass of rum … and that's when everything got hazy. When would she learn not to touch hard liquor – at least not when she couldn't count how many beers she'd drunk? She thanked her lucky stars that she hadn't been raped or beaten up or worse, but *a picsába* – I really can't remember a thing.

The man strode out of the bathroom with a smile, still naked.

'That was quite a game we played last night,' he said with a sparkle in his eye.

'Well, yes…' Anna replied. 'Could you remind me exactly what kind of game it was?'

'Hah, has our police officer forgotten already?'

'Yes, and it's not amusing.'

'Sorry. I hope you don't normally drink that much.'

Anna's stomach ached. She tried to hold back the grimace spreading across her face.

'Only on my nights off, a few times a week,' she replied sourly.

For a moment the man looked at her, puzzled, then laughed. 'There's something fascinating about you. It must be your sense of humour.'

'That's nice. Well, are you going to tell me?'

'Tell you what?'

'How we ended up here, for a start? Who are you? What have we done? That kind of thing.'

'You really can't remember? We met at the roulette table. You won quite a bit of money and said you'd treat me for the rest of the evening. I've never heard a pick-up line like that before. You really made an impression.'

'Aha. And what happened then?'

The man took a step closer to Anna, looked at her intently and gave her a meaningful smile. 'And you really did treat me.'

'I have to go to the bathroom. I feel sick.'

Anna went into the bedroom, gathered her clothes from the floor, couldn't find her underwear – had the man added them to a sick collection of trophies? – got dressed quickly and came back into the kitchen.

'I'm going home. My husband's probably wondering where I've got to. He gets pretty jealous.'

'But you told me you were single.'

'Well, people say all sorts of things when they're drunk. And I'm not really a police officer.'

'What are you then?'

The man seemed suddenly adrift in his own kitchen, lost without a map.

'A nursery-school teacher.'

'The way you asked about the other roulette players, I was sure you were a cop.'

'I was just having you on,' she said calmly, though she felt a wave of disquiet: what the hell have I been telling this guy?

'But why?'

'The same old story. My husband cheated on me, so I took revenge. But nice to hear you had some fun.'

Anna turned and stepped into the hallway, twisted the lock on the front door. A click echoed round the stairwell. A sense of panic tingled in the balls of her feet. Someone was breathing down her neck, inside her head. A two-headed eagle, a girl raped, left for dead. The river. *A kurva anyád*, will this never end? Anna noticed her legs were trembling uncontrollably.

'Anna, don't go yet.'

'My name's Mirva. Just forget the whole thing, okay?'

Anna ran down the stairs and out of the building, and though she could still taste the previous night in her mouth, she lit a cigarette.

It didn't make her feel any better. She smoked the cigarette, trying to calm herself down, and checked the time on her mobile. It was ten o'clock. I haven't slept much, she thought and walked off in search of a bar that had already opened for the day.

19

'ANNA AND ESKO, in my office,' said Virkkunen from the staffroom door. Anna had just poured herself a cup of coffee. Esko was reading the morning papers with a sulky expression on his face. Anna wanted to ask what was wrong with him. Esko had been strange and distant these last few days. Anna guessed it had something to do with the suspicion of an underlying illness, which she had only heard from Sari; Esko never told anybody anything about his health or well-being. But there was something else going on too. Esko seemed somehow troubled.

Anna took her coffee with her and followed Virkkunen into his office, trying to avoid the eyes of his pretty wife staring at her from the desk.

'I've just got off the phone with the finance division,' Virkkunen began.

'Yes?'

'They've been investigating a case of large-scale illegal construction, and it turns out our beloved Hell's Angels are somehow involved. Everything about it is dodgy: receipt fraud, money-laundering, you name it.'

'And what's this got to do with us?' Esko grumbled.

'Kari Haapsaari, that's the caretaker from the house in Leppioja, is suspected of being behind the receipt fraud. The house underwent an extensive pipe and window refit a few years ago.'

'Damn.'

'I've met him,' said Anna. 'Slimy bastard.'

'Of course, this might have nothing to do with recent events in the house, but alarm bells have started ringing. At the very least we'll have to bring this Haapsaari in for a good grilling. We're not all that interested in the receipt fraud, the guys from finance will take care of that, but I wondered whether Vilho and Riitta might have found out something they shouldn't.'

'The caretaker told me that Vilho had complained about noises from the pipes after the renovations,' explained Anna.

'Maybe he had other things to get off his chest too,' suggested Virkkunen.

'Sounds a bit far-fetched,' said Esko. 'How would ordinary residents find out something like that?'

'I don't know. But that's what you two are going to find out,' said Virkkunen.

Heikki Hiltunen was driving a large rubbish truck towards the tip at Mustikkamäki, or the refuse reprocessing centre as it was called these days. He steered the truck, full of stinking household rubbish and the packaging materials of a hysterically consumerist society, past the compost bins and the incinerators burning rubbish for energy, and towards the landfill site, the rush of Green Day blaring through his headphones at full volume. He didn't spare a thought for how sick the landscape looked. JCBs wobbled on top of mountains of rubbish, slowly compressing it into a smaller heap to make room for even *more* rubbish. He didn't once think why there was so much of it, because he had been born in an age when amassing all kinds of needless junk was seen as an unavoidable, even aspirational part of life.

Heikki enjoyed his early shifts; they meant he could get home early and take his car for a spin. He'd just bought his first car, an old Toyota in pretty good condition, with money he'd earned and saved. He was so proud of it. The old Toyota didn't exactly turn the girls' heads, but it was far more impressive than a bicycle. He'd even picked up in it once. Kaisa. Heikki remembered Kaisa, her chubby thighs and soft tummy. He reversed the truck towards the mountain of trash. *I'm coming home*, Green Day yelled in his ears. One press of the button and the back of the truck began to rise up. Kaisa was a sweet girl. Heikki tried to behave like an experienced Casanova with women, but he wasn't really up to it. The reality was that Kaisa had taken his virginity. Not on the backseat of the Toyota, but in Heikki's shabby, rented bachelor pad. That was the ride of my life, Heikki thought with a smirk. Her thighs, her stomach, her arms … I could call Kaisa after work.

What the hell's that? He took a closer look in the rear-view mirror. Something strange had tipped from the truck amongst the bin-liners and plastic bags. A leg. A thigh.

Heikki jumped out of the cabin and ran through the stinking air towards the foot of the tip. Yes. A leg jutted out of the mountain of trash. Not a chubby, soft leg like Kaisa's but a white one with varicose veins. Heikki's primal scream rang out over the whirr of the truck's engine and across the tip.

Anna went into Esko's office. She needed a cigarette. She'd received another email from Béci, and the craving for nicotine hit her again. That's what partying at the weekend does to you. *A francba*, everything falls to pieces the minute you loosen your grip. She'd deleted the message without replying. But Béci was certainly persistent. He'd been nice and relatively good in bed, but Anna had her reasons for not responding to him. The idea of a Hungarian man, and especially one from Kanizsa, seemed quite tempting, at least in theory, but in practice, in reality, it was something altogether different. It was a culture that reared boys into a world in which women could never become their equals. And if by some fluke they did, the men simply took off. In that culture, a woman's role was to cook, serve drinks, clean and entertain; she had to be pretty but sufficiently in the background, funny but not too intelligent. The man was the one who shone, the one with freedom, who did as he pleased, the one that people doted upon, looked after and admired. There wouldn't be anything wrong with it if the same was possible for women, but it wasn't. That, in a nutshell, was the Balkan male mentality that

Béci had been talking about, though he'd probably meant something rather different. Anna could never put up with a relationship like that. Still, so many Finnish men seemed far too nice and soft in comparison. Nothing's ever good enough for me, she thought.

'I haven't got any,' said Esko. Anna was surprised but didn't have time to comment before Esko continued. 'They've found a body in Mustikkamäki. That's means more overtime for us.'

'You won't have any time to go out on the piss,' said Anna.

'Look who's talking,' Esko retorted.

'Who is it?'

'Some woman.'

'*Bassza meg*. Do we have to go straight away?'

'Yes.'

'Where can I get a cigarette before we leave?'

'Ask Peltola on the second floor. You should probably cut back too.'

Anna smirked, stuck her tongue out at Esko and told him to meet her in the car depot in ten minutes.

What must this place smell like in the summer heat, thought Anna as she tried to hold her breath. Esko parked the car outside the modern-looking refuse reprocessing centre, behind which the mountains of rubbish seemed to extend as far as the eye could see. The area was surrounded by a tall fence with electric barbed wire twisting around the upper edge. Rummaging and scavenging were forbidden here; what has been thrown away must stay thrown away. If you want something, you buy it, preferably something plastic wrapped in two layers of polythene packaging, so that there's something to leave behind. This was the fingerprint of modern man; it was the future of our city and our planet, thought Anna. Rubbish that will never go away. In the warm spring air, the stench of the thawing tip was nauseating.

The site manager, Samuli Kenttälä, led Anna and Esko past the ridges of trash to a valley where a solitary rubbish truck stood with its tipper raised into the air.

'That's where we found her,' Kenttälä explained and pointed towards the bottom of the ridge. A panicked young man stood beside the vehicle.

Anna saw the leg. It jutted grotesquely from amid the trash. She and Esko stepped closer. They carefully began moving strips of plastic to one side, juice cartons, yoghurt tubs and other rubbish from around the leg. Beneath the rubbish they unearthed a large, black bin-liner tied securely with a tight knot. The lower edge of the bag was torn, and the leg protruded from the hole.

'Let's wait for forensics and the coroner,' said Esko and turned to talk to the young driver.

What do you know – he's not lighting up, Anna noted.

'Where did you pick up this load?'

'Mostly around Mellunniemi. That's where I was on my round. Some of it's from Vesala.'

'Have you any idea where you picked up that bin-bag?'

'No. I don't much look at what comes tumbling out of folk's bins. Only if there's something wrong, mind, if the mechanism gets stuck or something.'

'Did anything get stuck this morning?'

'No. Everything was working normally.'

'Still, that bag is so big that I doubt it came from your average-sized bin,' said Anna.

'I couldn't say,' said Heikki. 'Vesala is mostly all detached houses, and the bins are pretty small. But there are terraced houses in Mellunniemi; they have bigger bins.'

'I want you to think through your route this morning and try and imagine where there's a bin big enough to hold that bag.'

'I could go through the log on the satnav. That has all the addresses and other information.'

'Do that,' said Esko.

Three cars arrived. The forensics team and Linnea Markkula. Anna and Esko explained what they already knew about the situation and the investigators got to work. First they cordoned off the area; even the rubbish truck remained behind police tape. Then they painstakingly photographed the scene. Once this was done, they carefully opened up the bin-liner. A deathly white face spattered in bloodstains stared back at them. The mouth was frozen in a terrified grimace and there was a gaping wound on the neck; the victim's throat had been slit. Everything was covered in dried blood.

'It's Riitta Vehviläinen,' Anna told Esko.

'The dead junkie's neighbour?'

'Yep. The dead Vilho Karppinen's neighbour too.'

'Jesus Christ.'

'Your repertoire of swear words has softened lately.'

'Go screw yourself.'

'Esko, not in public.'

'Vehviläinen didn't live anywhere near where this trash was picked up,' said Esko.

'No, she lived the other side of town.'

'Could she have been killed where the teenagers found that knife? Out in Ketoniemi?'

Anna was frustrated that she hadn't thought of this immediately. But Esko was surely right. Riitta's throat had been cut with a sharp instrument. In Ketoniemi they had found a knife and lots of human blood. It couldn't be mere coincidence.

'It's very likely. And there were signs that somebody had dragged a heavy bag through the snow too.'

'But the rubbish truck didn't drive through Ketoniemi either.'

'No, but it's easy enough to move a body in a car. There were tyre tracks from an SUV in the forest.'

Esko hesitated a moment. 'I think I'm being followed by an SUV.'

'What? Why didn't you say something?'

'I'm not a hundred per cent sure. Besides, it's not that important.'

'Yes, it is. It's very important, and frightening.'

'You visited Riitta's apartment.' Esko changed the subject. 'Were there any signs of a struggle?'

'Nothing. The rugs were neatly placed; the chairs were all upright.'

'She must have been lured out of the apartment, then killed and dumped in the rubbish bin.'

'It's cold-blooded.'

'Perhaps Vehviläinen did her own spying through the peephole. The gang kids might have noticed and decided to shut up a potential witness once and for all,' said Esko. 'She must have seen someone really important, one of the Cobras or the Angels. These guys are capable of just this kind of brutality.'

'You might be right,' said Anna.

'She must have seen Reza,' said Esko with a glint in his eye.

20

NILS HAD FINALLY ESTABLISHED the origin of the cloakroom tag. He eagerly told the team what he had found out at the analysis group's weekly meeting of all police divisions. The tag came from the Millennium Club, the biggest nightclub in the downtown area. The doorman couldn't remember when it had gone missing or who had taken it, because hundreds of people visited the club every night and cloakroom tickets disappeared all the time. The doorman showed Nils a box full of spare tags. People lost all kinds of things when they were drunk.

'But that's not all,' Nils added mysteriously. 'The doorman looked familiar, so I looked into his background.'

Nils paused. He looked at Anna.

'He's a member of the Hell's Angels,' he said eventually.

The conference room was filled with a hubbub of conversation. Anna glanced at Esko, who nodded knowingly to himself. Sari whispered something into Anna's ear, but Anna couldn't make out what. Virkkunen stood up and asked for silence.

'Right, everyone,' he said, cleared his throat and lifted his spectacles. 'It now seems clearer than ever that the gangs are somehow implicated in the events and deaths at the house in Leppioja. This is an extremely serious matter, particularly as two civilians have lost their lives. We must find out everything we can about Riitta Vehviläinen's life and her death. We mustn't rule out other lines of enquiry, though the Black Cobras and the Hell's Angels are now our prime suspects. Riitta knew something about what was going on in that house, and she paid a heavy price. I want that caretaker interviewed immediately. Keep your eyes and ears open. And be careful.

These are hard-boiled criminals we're dealing with. An officer's life is worth nothing at all to these people,' Virkkunen emphasised, and looked at Esko.

Anna was given the task of breaking the news to Riitta's daughter, Leena Rekola. Leena and her family lived in a post-war, prefabricated house on the outskirts of the city centre. Anna stepped cautiously across the icy car park. The yard hadn't been gritted and her feet kept slipping. Beneath the apple tree was a heap of snow with tunnels and windows dug into it and brightly coloured plastic buckets and spades scattered nearby. A child's bike was lying on the path, skis and poles were propped at the side of the house. Though she couldn't see Leena's children, the yard was so full of happy, chaotic life that Anna felt almost faint having to walk across it bearing such terrible news. I won't get through this, she thought and rang the doorbell.

Leena opened the door. Her expression said it all; she already knew what Anna had to say.

'Come in,' said Leena. Anna stepped into the cosy house, which had been renovated with painstaking reverence for the old-fashioned feel of the building. Leena took her coat, put it on a clothes hanger and hung it in the closet.

'Tea or coffee?' she asked.

'Tea, please.'

They went into the kitchen. There were no sounds of children, and the television and radio were silent. The atmosphere in the house was peaceful. It would be nice to live here, thought Anna.

'I don't have cake or anything,' said Leena as she put some water on to boil and set cups on the table. 'I've been trying to lose weight, so I don't want to fill the cupboards with temptation.'

'It doesn't matter. I don't really feel like eating,' said Anna.

Once the tea was ready, Leena sat down across the table from Anna.

'Have you found my mother?' she asked.

'Yes,' said Anna. She could feel a lump in her throat, and it wouldn't go away no matter how much she tried to swallow.

'Where?'

'At the landfill site at Mustikkamäki.'

'So she's dead?'

'Yes.'

'How?'

'The coroner will release a statement about your mother's death once she has examined the body. But what we do know is…'

Anna had to take a breath. She couldn't put this into words. This was the worst thing about police work, meeting victims' relatives, telling them what had happened to their loved ones.

'Is what? Just say it. I sensed all along that something terrible had happened.'

'Her throat had been slit with a large knife. We found a knife some time ago in the woods near Ketoniemi, but the police will have to compare the blood found on the knife to a sample from your mother before we can say with any certainty if it was the murder weapon. At present that is our assumption.'

Leena sat still and quiet. She looked at Anna unblinking as large, round tears formed in the corners of her eyes, ran down her cheeks and dropped on the table and into her teacup. Then she began to tremble. The weeping wrenched her body so strongly that Anna thought she might fall from her chair.

'I'm very sorry,' said Anna. How meaningless it sounded. 'My sincerest condolences.'

'I'm glad she's been found. At least now we know what happened. Uncertainty is the worst thing of all, or so they say,' said Leena through her sobs. 'I'll have to call my husband. He's out skating with the children. I want them to come home straight away.'

'Of course, by all means,' said Anna.

Leena went into the other room; her weepy voice could be heard in the kitchen.

'They'll be here soon,' she said when she returned. 'My husband is in shock. I hope he's able to drive safely.'

'I'm afraid there are a number of things I still have to ask you.

Are you able to answer now or would you prefer me to come back tomorrow?'

'Let's do it now,' said Leena and rubbed her eyes, smudging mascara across her cheek. 'I want the killer found straight away.'

'Good. Do you have any idea how your mother could have ended up in Ketoniemi? We believe that's where she was stabbed. Did she have any friends there?'

'No. I've already said she didn't have many friends. How did she end up at the landfill site?'

'We still have to establish that. Her body was placed in a large plastic bag. The driver noticed her as he was emptying the rubbish truck.'

'Good God. It's sick, completely sick. How can I tell my children something like that?'

'Don't tell them any details, not yet at least. Perhaps when they're older. For now it's enough just to say their grandmother has died.'

'Mother didn't know anyone in Ketoniemi,' said Leena quietly and started crying once again.

'We looked into the number your mother had called shortly before she disappeared.'

'Villy. Is he the killer?'

'Villy's full name is Vilho Karppinen. He was your mother's neighbour.'

'Why on earth would she call him?'

'Can you tell us anything about that? Did your mother know Vilho well?'

'I don't know. She never spoke about anyone called Vilho.'

'Somehow their stories are linked, and so are their deaths.'

'This is all so shocking,' Leena gasped.

The front door rattled and the sounds of people taking coats off came from the hallway. A tall, bearded man, his eyes bleary with tears, stepped into the kitchen and took Leena in his arms. Three children looked at their parents in shock. Anna thought of her own grandmother, whose condition had worsened. She felt like one of those children.

'I'll leave you in peace,' said Anna. 'We'll be in touch, and please call me immediately if you think of anything that seems important, anything at all.'

'Yes,' came Leena's stifled sob from within her husband's arms.

Anna returned to the police station with a heavy heart. It would be best to go straight home, climb under the duvet, eat some chocolate and listen to music, forget all the terrible things that had happened and sleep for at least ten hours, she thought, exhausted. But she had work to do, so she would have to struggle on for a few hours yet. Esko was already waiting for her.

The caretaker from Leppioja had been called in for questioning. He seemed nervous and frightened, almost childlike as he sat squirming on a chair at the table in the interview room. All his arrogance had disappeared somewhere along the way, Anna noted contentedly.

'You can start by telling us where you were on the twelfth of March,' Esko boomed.

Esko was always stern and intimidating in interview situations, but now Anna noticed that he could be downright terrifying.

'At work,' Kari Haapsaari answered abruptly.

'What, all day? We're particularly interested in your movements that evening and night.'

'After work I went home. That evening someone called me out because of a burst pipe, so I had to take care of that.'

'Where?'

'In Vesala.'

Anna and Esko glanced at once another. The rubbish truck had driven through Vesala.

'What time was that?'

'Around eight o'clock. Why are you asking?'

'We suspect your involvement in the recent deaths at the house in Leppioja. You already know about Marko Halttu and Vilho Karppinen, and now Riitta Vehviläinen has been found dead.'

'How can you think I had anything to do with it? I haven't done anything,' the man said in a panic and fidgeted with his shirt buttons, his eyes wide with fear.

'Because you're already involved in some illegal activities, aren't you? We know all about the construction and renovation projects you've managed, the receipt fraud and your links to a certain motorbike gang.'

'What the hell?' yelled the caretaker.

'Yes, what the hell?' Esko snapped. 'But we're not interested in your dodgy finances. Don't worry. Officers from the fraud squad will want to talk to you about that shortly. We're interested in what's been going on in Leppioja.'

'I don't know anything about that. You can believe what you like.'

'We don't believe a word of it. Did Vilho and Riitta find out about your little side business? Is that why you had to shut them up?'

'What are you talking about? Of course I didn't!'

'You told us earlier that Vilho had complained about noises coming from the pipes and that you'd visited his apartment. Was that the real reason you went there? Was it something else he wanted to talk about?'

'Like what?'

'Something to do with the pipe renovation, for instance. Had Vilho realised that what he'd read in the documents handed out by the housing association didn't quite match what he'd seen, heard and calculated for himself?'

'He complained about a noise.'

'How could brand new pipes have made such a racket?' Anna asked.

The caretaker glared at her. 'That's what I thought too.'

'Besides, Marko Halttu, another resident at the house, was involved in a drug racket operated by the Hell's Angels. Might it be the case that during this pipe renovation you ended up owing the Angels some money, and they started asking you to do them little favours in the house where everything had started going wrong?' Esko suggested.

'You're wrong. That's not what happened,' Haapsaari shouted.

'So what did happen?'

'I haven't killed anybody. I went straight home from Vesala at around ten o'clock. My wife can verify it.'

'And we will verify if you're lying,' Esko added chillingly.

21

THE AIR SMELT of the thawing earth, dog's droppings and last autumn's rotten leaves revealed beneath the melting snow. Snow buntings flew in a wild flock across the ice-covered shoreline, their white wings fluttering like small, happy fans. How magnificent the migratory birds are, thought Anna. This was something she loved about her northern city and the surrounding countryside. With the proximity of the sea, you couldn't help noticing the return of the birds. They came in waves; like the sea itself. First came a few solitary birds, daring and cautious, the rooks, seagulls and snow buntings, soon to be followed by the geese, swans, ducks, then the waders and smaller birds that eat insects, and the air that had been so silenced by the winter months was suddenly filled with the birds' agitated cries and calls, squawks and singing. Anna wasn't a passionate bird-watcher, she could only identify a few of the most common species, but there was something fascinating about migratory birds. They lived in the north and the south, flew tirelessly back and forth, and always found their way home. It was incredible.

Anna was walking towards the forensics laboratory. Streams of water trickled into the drains; the crunch of footsteps on snow had turned to a squelch. Her phone rang in her pocket. It was Gabriella. She had told the girl not to call her again.

'*Szia*,' said Anna after wondering whether or not to answer.

'*Szia. Hogy vagy?*'

'*Jól, köszi. És te?*'

'Listen, Anna. I need to talk.'

'Well?'

'I'm sorry I was so rude last time.'

'Apology accepted,' said Anna curtly. Though it isn't really, she thought.

'I must have been really worn out.'

'It's all right,' said Anna.

'Really?'

'Let's just forget about it.'

'Thanks, Anna. Listen, I've been thinking about things, and you know what, I'd really like to stay in Finland for another year. I thought I could study Finnish at the Open University; it could come in really handy when I go back to Hungary.'

'*És?*' asked Anna, slightly puzzled.

'I thought you might be able to help me out. I'd like to find another family that needs an au pair.'

Anna thought about this for a moment. She'd been horrible to Gabriella for no good reason; she was the one that should be apologising, not the other way round. Anna had been avoiding her, though the girl just seemed in need of a friend. Again she thought of the migratory birds that always find their way home. Gabriella was like one of them, but Anna … Gabriella was right; Anna really was envious. It was hard to admit, but it was the truth.

'I might have an idea,' she said eventually and heard Gabriella gasp with excitement. 'One of my colleagues might be interested. I could talk to her.'

'Oh, Anna, thank you! Great. You're a treasure.'

'Well, not quite,' said Anna, embarrassed.

'*Hogy van a nagymamád?*'

'Not very well. Her condition has worsened.'

'I'm sorry. Tell Ákos I said hello when you next talk to him. When is he coming back?'

'I don't know,' said Anna. A sense of yearning gripped her stomach.

Anna said goodbye to Gabriella and stepped into the large, white building through the heavy front door. She took the lift down to the basement where Linnea was already waiting for her.

Riitta Vehviläinen was lying on her back on the metallic gurney.

She was small and thin. It would have been easy to drag her out of the woodland and throw her in a rubbish bin. What a gruesome end to a human life, thought Anna. To end up in a tip amongst bags of rubbish.

'I've done the preliminary autopsy, measured and weighed the organs, that sort of thing,' said Linnea. 'We can concentrate on the wound to the throat and other signs of violence, and the *livor mortis*, of course. I'll try and estimate her time of death as precisely as possible.'

Anna shuddered. Riitta was so ghostly pale. Anna had seen plenty of bodies during her time with patrol. It was an unavoidable part of police work, but it still felt terrible every time. She took out her camera and began photographing the body.

Linnea leaned over to examine the neck and spoke her findings aloud into a dictation machine.

'Slightly curved, almost horizontal wound at the front of the neck, clean-edged and sharp at both ends, twenty-one centimetres in length. The wound is gaping, and without pulling back the skin its width from top to bottom is around five centimetres. Blood has flowed from the wound, drying around the neck and chest area. The wound is around three centimetres deep. Horizontal wounds severing the carotid artery and surrounding veins are visible on both sides.'

Anna watched, captivated, as Linnea worked; she listened to her voice, which had become cold and matter-of-fact.

Finally Linnea switched off the Dictaphone and spoke to Anna. 'So, in layman's terms, this slit was caused by an extremely sharp weapon and probably in a single motion. The victim would have died from blood loss very quickly.'

'Surely the killer must have been covered in blood,' Anna wondered.

'Not necessarily. The easiest way to slit someone's throat is from behind. That means only the hands would be covered in blood spatter.'

'True.'

'Judging by the level of *livor mortis*, I estimate that death occurred some time ago. The marks are a brownish-red colour, because of the sub-zero temperatures we've had lately. What's more, the body has begun to dry out slightly.'

'When?'

'As you know, I can't say for sure, but I imagine some time at the beginning of March. The first two weeks. I'll be in touch straight away if I can make my estimate any more specific.'

'Vilho Karppinen died on the twelfth,' said Anna.

'This woman died around the same time. It could even be the same day.'

'Interesting. That fits our theory. Did you find anything else?'

'Let's see. There are no defensive marks on the hands, and there are no other stab wounds on the body.'

'So she went off with her killer without being coerced and walked into the woods like a lamb to the slaughter.'

Linnea smirked. 'You probably won't believe it, but I'm a country girl at heart. We had lambs at home, and they don't walk calmly to the slaughterhouse either. They struggle and fight back as much as they can. Believe me. I know. But you're right; this lady wasn't taken anywhere by force.'

'Okay,' said Anna and switched off the camera. 'Let's be in touch when anything new comes to light.'

'Join me for a drink on Friday night,' Linnea suggested.

'I don't think I'll have time,' said Anna, somewhat frustrated. Did she always have to ask?

'Somehow I knew you'd say that. Have a good weekend.'

Anna tried to smile, but she noticed Linnea seemed hurt. Once this case is tied up, I must ask her out for an evening, Anna resolved.

Nils called Anna as she was walking back to the station. The sea opened up before her, white and grey. The snow buntings had flown elsewhere. Nils had established the route the rubbish truck had taken and had examined all the bins in the area. In only three places were the bins large enough to hold something the size of a human body.

'But none of them is anywhere near Leppioja,' said Nils with disappointment.

'The killer was moving by car. They could have dumped Riitta anywhere. As far away from her own home as possible, of course.'

'One of the bins was in a well-hidden place. If I needed to dump a body, I'd use that one. None of the surrounding houses has a direct view out to this bin.'

'But have a chat with the neighbours anyway. Maybe one of them saw something.'

'I'll get on to it.'

'There were tyre tracks at the crime scene. Have we learned anything else about the vehicle?'

'No, but those gang members drive around in an SUV.'

'Get Esko to look into the car.'

'Have you got any new information?' asked Nils.

'I've just been to the autopsy. I'll tell you all about it at the meeting tomorrow morning and show you the photographs. Riitta probably died at around the same time as Vilho.'

Nils whistled at the other end of the telephone. It stung Anna's ear.

'Sari and I are going to Leppioja later on. We'll have to talk to the neighbours again.'

'Good luck with that. See you in the morning.'

'You too,' said Anna. Something pleasant flared in her chest. Nils was a really nice guy.

The sound of children playing came from behind the Kumpula family's door. Their mother opened the door, and Anna could see that a box of Lego had been emptied across the hallway floor. The children were sitting on the rug, building something with great concentration, and only glanced up at the police officers standing at the door before continuing to play, as though nothing in the world could have disturbed them. Anna felt a fleeting sense of longing, a desire to go back to a time that had been lost forever. She thought of her grandmother, who always fetched a box of toys from a bedroom cupboard every time Anna visited, battered old Barbies with tangled, fuzzy hair, rubber figurines with gnawed heads and legs.

'It's a bit crowded here at the moment, but do come in,' said Virpi Kumpula apologetically. 'Let's go through to the kitchen.'

Anna and Sari followed her, stepping over children and pieces of Lego.

'I've heard about the other terrible things going on here, not just that Halttu,' said Virpi as they sat at the kitchen table. 'Would you like some coffee?'

'No, thank you,' said Sari. 'You're right. Two other neighbours have died in suspicious circumstances. Vilho Karppinen and Riitta Vehviläinen.'

'It's shocking. We're frightened here,' said Virpi.

'That's perfectly understandable, but I don't think you're in any danger. It seems the elderly victims had one way or another got themselves mixed up with the same group of organised criminals that is somehow responsible for Halttu's death. They possibly saw something they weren't supposed to see,' Anna explained and looked at Sari.

'We haven't seen anything, thank goodness,' said Virpi and glanced at her children playing in the hallway.

'Have you had any problems with the pipework since the renovations?' asked Anna.

'No, why?' Virpi seemed perplexed.

'Vilho Karppinen had complained to the housing association about noises from the new pipes.'

'I haven't heard any noises.'

'How well do you know the caretaker of this building?'

'I've never actually seen him. I only know his name from the paperwork given to us by the housing association.'

'Did the pipe renovation go as planned, as far as you know?'

'Yes. Everything happened on time. We had no complaints. It was expensive, of course, but there's nothing you can do about that. Why do you ask?'

'We're looking into a line of enquiry involving the caretaker here. Have you heard any rumours about him?'

'No. He's never here really.'

'Good. Did you know Riitta or Vilho?'

'I knew who they were. I mean, we said hello to one another in the stairwell, sometimes had a chat out in the yard, the way neighbours normally talk to one another, nothing more than that. We've never visited one another's flats, for instance. Riitta hardly ever went out in the yard, but Vilho was in much better shape. He spent a lot of time outdoors.'

'Did you ever notice anything strange about them? Did they seem worried, afraid?'

'No. But I did notice Riitta ringing Vilho's doorbell fairly frequently. And she went inside his flat too.'

'Really? When did you last see Riitta?'

'Maybe a couple of weeks ago, a month perhaps. She was standing at Vilho's door when I came back from work.'

'Did you talk to her?'

'No. Hang on … yes. Riitta seemed a bit flustered and explained that she'd run out of salt and had to borrow some from Vilho. How did they die?' Virpi looked worriedly at Anna and Sari.

'I'm afraid we're not at liberty to reveal any details at the moment.'

'Did anybody else ever ring Vilho's doorbell?' asked Sari.

'Well, I don't spy on all my neighbours' guests. It's not as if there was a constant flow of people in and out.'

'The scary lady upstairs,' said a bright little boy's voice. A blond boy of around eight had appeared at the kitchen door.

'What?' said Virpi. 'Those children of mine are always listening in to grown-ups' conversations,' she continued apologetically.

'What about the lady upstairs?' asked Anna and gave the boy an encouraging smile.

'She was always ringing Mr Karppinen's doorbell too.'

Mrs Lehmusvirta opened the door with the same sour expression as before.

'What is it now?' she snapped, opening the door only a few centimetres.

'Can we come in?' Anna asked as jovially as she could muster. 'We're interviewing everyone in the house again.'

'Why?'

'Because two of your neighbours, Vilho Karppinen and Riitta Vehviläinen, have died.'

'They were old.'

'That's true,' said Sari. 'But both died in suspicious circumstances, so if you wouldn't mind...'

'Very well, come in,' Mrs Lehmusvirta groaned, opened the door a few centimetres more and disappeared inside the apartment.

It was dark inside. The hallway was heavy with stagnant air and the thick stench of food, meat and gravy. Anna felt sick. She suddenly felt a craving for mushroom soup. I must have some later on, she thought and wondered what had brought on this sudden urge. Normally she never ate mushrooms.

'How well did you know Karppinen and Vehviläinen?' Sari asked in the drab kitchen fitted with dated, dark-brown wooden cupboards. The curtains were pulled shut; only a faint light came from the lamp above the stove, making the pedantically scoured hob gleam.

'Not very well. I knew Riitta better than Vilho.'

'Witnesses say you have been seen at Karppinen's door regularly. Why did you visit him if you didn't know him very well?' asked Anna. The woman's cocky, uptight attitude was beginning to annoy her.

The woman didn't answer straight away. She began angrily

scrubbing the kitchen table with a cloth, muttering something about the crumbs that were taking over the whole house.

'Something terrible is happening in this building,' said Sari. 'It's very important that you tell us everything you know.'

'Something terrible has been going on in this building for a long time,' Mrs Lehmusvirta snapped.

'What do you mean?'

'That Vehviläinen woman was knocking around with Vilho like a brazen little girl.'

Anna looked at Sari. Were Riitta and Vilho having a relationship, her eyes tried to ask.

'It serves them right, the both of them,' said Mrs Lehmusvirta and stared at each officer in turn. Though her eyes were small and wrinkled, her gaze was hard as steel.

'That's a very harsh thing to say,' said Sari. 'Why would you think a thing like that?'

'What they were up to was sinful. This place is full of sin. Drugs, sex, the lot. It's a good job it's finally come to an end.'

'Were Vilho and Riitta involved with drugs too?' Anna asked, incredulous.

'For goodness sake, no,' said Mrs Lehmusvirta. 'But what would I know? Perhaps they were. What they were up to was filthy enough.'

'What's filthy about that?'

'At their age! It's ridiculous.'

'Maybe they were just lonely,' Anna hazarded.

'What they were doing was sinful. That's all there is to it. I won't allow something like that in this building, right in front of my eyes.'

'And what exactly were they doing?'

'Cavorting. Spending the night together, fornicating. Kissing each other goodbye.'

'But that's wonderful,' said Sari and attempted a smile.

'It's disgusting.'

'What were you doing on the twelfth of March?'

The woman's expression sharpened. She vigorously rinsed the kitchen cloth under steaming hot water and placed it over the tap to dry, wiped her hands on the hem of her black dress and stood stiffly by the kitchen table.

'I was here.'

'Did you see Vilho and Riitta that day?'

Mrs Lehmusvirta's eyes narrowed into two cruel slits. Her thin lips tightened even more, pinching her mouth into a set of deep, angry furrows.

'Am I supposed to remember that? Well, I doubt it. I despise that man.' Mrs Lehmusvirta spat the words from her mouth.

'Why?' asked Sari.

'I despise sin and sinners.'

'Do you despise them enough to kill them?' asked Sari.

Air hissed between Mrs Lehmusvirta's lips. She took a glass from the drying cupboard, filled it with water and drank slowly until the glass was empty.

'Of course not. Though I might have been tempted.'

For a moment Anna and Sari were silent. There was something intimidating about Toini Lehmusvirta. The old lady stood stock still in front of them, gripping her glass.

'And do you know the caretaker for this building?' Anna asked, as if to lighten the mood.

'No.'

'Have you ever heard noises from your pipes?'

'No.'

'Did you notice anything untoward going on during the pipe and window renovations?'

'Like what?'

'Well, like something that didn't quite go as planned?'

'The renovations went perfectly well. Horrid waste of money, if you ask me.'

Anna and Sari left Leppioja somewhat baffled. If Vilho and Riitta had found out something involving the caretaker, they were the only people in the block to do so. The matter now seemed clear. The caretaker wouldn't have needed to get his own hands dirty; he probably got one of the Angels to take care of the elderly couple. These building renovations involved such large sums of money that the lives of two pensioners would mean nothing to ruthless criminals like this. People were murdered for far less. But what exactly had Vilho and Riitta discovered and how? Had they seen something they weren't supposed to see?

Later that afternoon the police received two important pieces of information. According to the forensic tests, the blood found in Ketoniemi was a match for Riitta Vehviläinen, and the knife belonged to Vilho. Nils had been in touch with Hermanni Harju's relatives and tracked him down in Spain. He had emailed the man a photograph of the knife and Hermanni identified it without hesitation.

Anna telephoned Hermanni to ask about Vilho and Riitta. The man was excited; he was clearly enjoying being able to help the police.

'Vilho and I belonged to the Finnish Knife Club. Well, I still do…' explained Hermanni.

'That's interesting,' said Anna.

'I can't for the life of me remember where he found that knife. It must have been on a trip abroad.'

'I don't think that particularly matters,' said Anna. 'We need to establish who could have used the knife to kill Riitta Vehviläinen.'

'Terrible things going on back home. Poor old Vilho, and Riitta. I had to go to the doctor's yesterday when I heard about all this,' Hermanni's tone became more sombre. 'There's a Finnish doctor here, and Finnish shops too with Karelian pies and liver casserole. It's mighty handy.'

'That sounds nice. Do you know whether Vilho and Riitta were … involved in any way?'

'Blimey, you didn't know about that? They were very involved.'

'Could you tell me about it?'

'It was very passionate,' Hermanni chuckled. 'Would you believe me if I told you people my age can have a passionate love life?'

'Absolutely. In what way was it passionate?'

'Jealousy, you name it. It's only a shame Riitta was so frail. They wanted to travel together. I invited them out here.'

'Why were they jealous of one another?'

'Because Vilho had another woman before Riitta. She lived in the same block. Toini, her name was. I can't recall her surname. It started with an L, I think.'

'Lehmusvirta?' asked Anna.

'That's right. Toini Lehmusvirta. I never met her, but Vilho told me she could be terribly jealous.'

Anna had a frightful hunch. Could Mrs Lehmusvirta really have killed Riitta? How could she have lured Riitta out to Ketoniemi? Anna recalled Mrs Lehmusvirta's figure. She was a relatively large woman, but still. Did she own an SUV? Surely an old woman wouldn't be able to drag a body in a bin-liner and throw it into a bin – even though Riitta was small and thin. Could Toini have an accomplice and, if so, who could it be? The caretaker? Anna wondered where to look next and what to look for. It was as though the answer was right in front of her but her eyes couldn't focus on it. It was like firing arrows into the fog. All she could do was hope that one of them hit their target.

22

THEY DON'T BELIEVE ME. That woman officer doesn't believe me at any rate. What can I do now? Sammy was frantically pacing round his small cell, up and down, round and round. He had lied about everything, that was true enough, but you'd think someone like him would be the perfect scapegoat, a real treat for the police, who could now take all the credit for getting to the bottom of these brutal crimes. No, it wasn't all lies. Everything he'd told them about home was true. If they don't believe him, he'll have to go back. It would be his final journey. Perhaps he should at least try to be grateful. He had spent two years in a reception centre, free from persecution, he hadn't once fallen ill after going underground, he didn't have children to look after, he hadn't ended up in one of the polluted immigrant concentration camps in Greece and hadn't drowned in the Mediterranean. He was alive, he had almost completely kicked the drugs and he was young. He would be able to live in this cell by himself for at least a while yet. The pretty nurse visited him again, caressed him. Should I try and convince myself everything is fine? What should I do?

Just then Sammy remembered seeing a man in the stairwell the night he had gone to Macke's place, the same night Vilho had died. That man could prove Sammy had been there. Maybe then the police would believe him. I'll have to tell the policewoman about it. She can find him. Maybe there's still hope, Sammy thought.

Sun and ice, the glare of bright piles of spring snow like a flame burning into her eyes, a hint of the approaching summer warmth in the wind from the south. Anna skied slowly, following the horizon.

The wind tickled her cheeks; it no longer bit into her skin. The willow trees along the shore had finally thawed and jutted leafless from amid the snow verges like brooms. Anna skied up to them to see whether they already bore soft, white pussy willows. The snow was hard as stone; it crunched beneath her skis. Firm snow, finally. She headed along the shoreline towards the woods, zigzagged between the trees and thickets as quickly as she could, and felt the wild joy that freedom brings. Since the snow had fallen, the woods had been virtually inaccessible, and now the melting snow would soften the terrain so much that skiing would soon be impossible. Firm snow was a rare pleasure, something she couldn't enjoy every year. Now the string of cold nights had been sufficiently long, and they too would soon be gone.

After half an hour Anna realised that she was lost. She had never skied so deep into these woods. Where was it she had veered off the ice? She took her bearings from the position of the sun, turned and began slowly retracing her own tracks, which she could just make out on the rough surface of the snow. The snow protected everything living beneath it: new shoots, moss, moles' warrens. She could feel the wordless anticipation of spring melting the snow from beneath, struggling to keep up with the sun. Here and there her tracks disappeared, but she always found them again. Anna wasn't frightened. She quite enjoyed the feeling of not knowing where she was, the feeling that she had to find her way home, that she couldn't simply follow her tracks, that there was a protective layer of dimmed light between the snow and the earth. Sometimes she got lost on purpose. Sometimes she felt like she was constantly lost. Perhaps that's why the sensation of being lost felt so liberating.

Finding the car wasn't quite as easy as she had imagined. She had accidentally started following someone else's tracks – how could she have lost concentration like that? – and ended up doing an extra hour's trek through the woods. Eventually she found her way back to the shore and the rest of the journey passed smoothly. Navigating out across the sea only required knowing the points of the compass.

By the time she got home Anna was tired and hungry, but there was nothing to eat in the fridge. Will I ever learn to fetch at least a week's worth of food at once, she wondered as her stomach rumbled, and realised it was unlikely. I could eat at Hazileklek, ask how they are getting on, check that everything is okay with Maalik and Farzad.

But Anna didn't make it to Hazileklek or anywhere else that day. She forgot her hunger and her fatigue and couldn't get to sleep without taking some pills. Her mother called. Anna's grandmother had died that morning; her heart had simply stopped beating. Could Anna come to the funeral on Tuesday? She would have to book tickets straight away. Réka could pick her up at the border, or she could rent a car, as she normally did. Grandma had been in a lot of pain, so in that respect death had been a relief; now everything was well, now she could finally be with Grandpa once again. I've cried and I'm going to miss her, said Anna's mother, but no one can live forever.

Why not? Anna thought. Grandma should have been allowed to. I need her; we all need our own grandmothers, someone who represents continuity, someone who never leaves us.

Anna lay on the sofa for the rest of the day and felt the emptiness digging into her skin. She wanted to listen to Delay's *Tummaa* album, its melancholy sounds, comforting in their darkness, but she couldn't even bring herself to get up and put the CD on. Where do I belong, she wondered. Where is my home? Is it here in this almost unfurnished one-bedroom apartment where the walls echo and the floors are cold, in this freezing country where I've spent the majority of my life? Or is it there, Serbia, the place I still called Yugoslavia when I left, and if so, where? My mother's house? The rooms filled with the ghosts of my father, Áron and now my grandmother, rooms in which the presence of the dead is greater than that of the living in the memories, objects, photographs on the mantelpiece? Is that where my home is? Is a home a building? A city? A country or family? A person?

A person. At that moment Anna felt with chilling certainty that

Ákos would never return to Finland and that she'd be left here all alone. It was a strange feeling, as she and Ákos hadn't been close for years. Anna had studied on the other side of the country and hadn't wanted anything to do with her alcoholic brother. Let him drink, she'd thought, let him ruin his life and his opportunities by himself. Once Anna had moved back north, where the family had settled after fleeing from Yugoslavia, they had become closer again. And though Anna reluctantly looked after some practical matters for her brother, they had become friends, more even. Ákos was the only person in the world who shared something with Anna, something that words could never describe. I can't bear the thought of having to lose Ákos too, she thought. She buried her face in a cushion, but the tears would not come. They hardened into a lump in her chest where years of unwept tears rattled against one another like stones.

23

'I SHOULD HAVE BOOKED TICKETS there and then and gone to the funeral,' Anna told Sari.

'Why is the funeral so soon? In two days' time?'

'I don't know. They tend to bury people quickly there. Maybe it has to do with the climate or the Catholic church. I don't know.'

'But how do relatives have time to find out about it and make travel plans?'

'They just do. I suppose.'

'Oh, Anna, I'm so sorry.'

'Thanks. The worst of it is that I can't get there.'

'You can visit her grave in the summer, and tomorrow you can have a private remembrance service all of your own,' Sari comforted her and gave her a hug.

Anna pressed herself against Sari's sturdy yet slender body, holding back her tears. How was it possible to feel so miserable? So empty and so wretched all at once, as though a limb had been violently ripped off. Anna swallowed back her sobs, let go of Sari and said she'd be fine, though she knew that none of her ghost pains would ease up or disappear. Her dear, eternal grandmother had died. Her visits home would never feel the same again.

'I've got my suspicions about Lehmusvirta,' said Anna, trying to return to the protection of her working persona and push the grief aside.

'She's a terrible piece of work. And what a relationship drama was going on in that building! I just had a chat with Niilo Säävälä.'

'Did he know anything?'

'Yes. He told me that Vilho and Riitta started seeing one another years ago. At first it was all quite innocent, having coffee together, going for walks, that sort of thing, but after a while they'd become closer. Apparently they hadn't wanted to tell their children.'

'Did you ask him why?'

'Of course. Niilo said that children often react strangely when they hear about their elderly parents' love lives. They think they're going to miss out on their inheritance.'

Anna involuntarily thought of her grandmother. It would undoubtedly have been a bit strange if she'd been having a passionate love affair in the last years of her life. But why should it have been strange? Isn't it wonderful to be able to enjoy the closeness of another person, no matter what age we are? Sometimes Anna thought young people were far more stuck in their ways than the elderly.

'Lehmusvirta had apparently tried to disrupt their relationship in every conceivable way, ringing the doorbell when Riitta was visiting Vilho, telephoning him, trying to stop them spending time together, dropping religious leaflets through their letterboxes,' said Sari.

'Perhaps she lost her mind.'

'She lost her mind a long time ago, there's no doubt about that. But is she capable of murder? I can't say.'

'She has no alibi,' Anna pointed out.

'You're right. And she has a motive,' said Sari and took Anna by the hand. 'Don't be sad, my friend. I mean, be sad, grieve, but remember that it will get better.'

Anna hugged Sari. At least somebody cares about me, she thought, holding back tears once again.

Reza hadn't been seen at any of the addresses Naseem had given. Neither had any other members of the Cobras. Esko had visited all four locations several times, sat in his car staking the places out for hours at different times of day, waiting for something to happen, but there was nothing. Nothing at all. It was odd. He entered the addresses into the police database and confirmed the gutting news that he had begun to suspect. There were no immigrants registered at any of these addresses. The residents at all four of the addresses had everyday Finnish names. One was a family with children, one a retired couple, one a student at the city polytechnic college and one was a single, middle-aged woman who worked as a cook at the primary school in Rajapuro.

Esko tried to call Naseem, but her telephone was switched off. What the hell did this mean? Naseem had deliberately misled him. Esko felt a sense of rage boiling within him. He'd trusted her. He had believed every word that had passed those beautiful red lips, and now it turned out to be nothing but a pack of lies. He should have guessed; liars and con artists every last one of them, even the beautiful, smart, educated ones. He pulled on his coat, switched off the lights in his office and headed for Vaarala. You and I are going to have a little talk, he thought agitatedly. Damn it, I'll charge you with giving a false statement.

But there was nobody home in Vaarala. Esko repeatedly and angrily rang the doorbell, put his ear against the door and listened for any movement coming from inside the apartment, but everything was quiet and the door remained shut. Fucking hell, Esko cursed out loud. He heard the front door click, the sound of footsteps. Someone was coming up the stairs; footsteps echoed round the stairwell. I hope it's Naseem, he thought as a woman dressed in a black burqa appeared on the landing. The woman's skin was dark and gleaming; her eyes looked frightened.

'Do you speak Finnish?' asked Esko.

'A little,' the woman replied nervously. A bright-yellow supermarket carrier bag dangled from her hand.

'Do you know the lady who lives here? Naseem Jobrani?'

'Yes, a bit.'

'Where is she? I must talk to her urgently,' said Esko and showed the woman his police badge.

The woman gave a start and seemed even more worried. 'I don't know. I haven't seen Naseem many days.'

'Where has she gone? Did she tell you her plans?'

'I don't know where Naseem is,' the woman repeated.

'Very well,' Esko muttered. 'Here is my telephone number. Call me if you see her. Is that clear? This is a police matter.'

'Yes, of course,' said the woman and took his card.

Right, you'll never call me, thought Esko, and he ran down the stairs, got into his car and drove back to the police station with no regard for the speed limits.

'Vilho Karppinen's case just got a bit more complicated,' said Linnea Markkula on the telephone as she tried to catch her breath.

'How so?' asked Anna.

'We got the results back from the NBI's forensics lab today. The old man's bloodstream contained an incredible amount of propranolol, almost five milligrams per litre.'

'What's that?'

'It's a beta-blocker used to regulate blood pressure. It's actually quite common in suicide cases. The name of the drug is Propral.'

'What does this mean?'

'Remember when I said the victim's heart was slightly enlarged? Well, he probably had a blood-pressure condition. You'll have to see what medication he was on.'

'I'll get on to it. Could he have taken a dose like that accidentally?'

'I doubt he could have taken this much. Unless he was demented, but he wasn't. The amount in his blood is over ten times the normal dose.'

'Could he have tried to kill himself before going to complain about the music?'

'Sounds a bit unlikely. I doubt the music would have bothered him if the intention was to die rather than sleep.'

'This doesn't make sense.'

'But the fact remains that Vilho's blood contained a deadly amount of the stuff.'

'Is there any way you can establish the order that these events happened? Did he die from the car crash, from being beaten up by Sammy or from the drugs?'

'It might be impossible. All three factors overlap one another so much.'

'Can you come to any conclusions?'

'Propranolol starts to take effect about an hour after ingestion. So he must have taken the drugs either around the same time he went to Halttu's apartment or just before.'

'Could Sammy and Marko have administered the drugs?' Anna wondered out loud. 'Sammy hasn't said anything about that. Only that he smashed the victim's head against the corner of the table. This doesn't add up. I'll have to interview Vilho's son again. Maybe he knows something about his father's medication.'

Juha Karppinen arrived at their meeting ten minutes late. Anna put it down to indifference, though he seemed genuinely apologetic and complained of a traffic jam in the city centre. It could be true; it was late afternoon.

'We have some fresh information regarding your father's death,' Anna began.

'Really? What?'

Anna watched his reactions but couldn't see anything flicker in his calm exterior.

'His blood contained a lethal dose of Propral.'

'What's that?'

'It's a blood-pressure medication. He had it on prescription.'

'Did my father have problems with his blood pressure? Well, it doesn't really surprise me – he was quite old. Didn't a junkie immigrant already confess to beating him up or something?'

'Yes, he did. And with that in mind, this new information doesn't fit what we already know about his death and the circumstances that led to it.'

'The boy must have given it to him. Drug addicts can get their hands on all kind of substances, can't they?'

'I doubt he would have used this particular drug. Of course, it's possible. In any case, we now have to investigate your father's death from a rather different perspective.'

'Of course, I appreciate that.'

'Did you know your father's neighbour, Mrs Riitta Vehviläinen?'

'No. Well, I remember seeing that name on the letterbox, but I don't think I ever laid eyes on her. Why do you ask?'

'She is dead too. She was murdered.'

'Goodness. Did the immigrant boy kill her too?'

'The immigrant boy doesn't know anything about Riitta. To be perfectly honest, I don't believe he's telling the truth.'

'But he confessed. Surely nobody is crazy enough to confess to a murder they didn't commit.'

'Could your father have committed suicide?'

'How should I know? I haven't had anything to do with him for years. But why not? It sounds like the only plausible explanation. Perhaps he was depressed. He never really got over the death of my mother. Maybe things like that start to bother you in old age, start to feel closer as you reach the autumn of your life.'

'We're going to be looking into your father's movements in the last few days and weeks before his murder. Telephone calls, bank details, purchases, friends, everything. I'm sure things will soon become clear.'

'Good. I want to know what happened to my father.'

Juha buried his face in the palms of his hands. Anna could hear his stifled sobs. Why don't I feel remotely sorry for that man? she wondered. I'm becoming a hard, cold, cruel person.

Anna left the station to call Juha Karppinen's former wife. She needed to move, having sat at her computer all afternoon. Her back was stiff and her neck ached. The temperature was around zero. Droplets of water trickled from the gable of the police station into a puddle on the street. The sky was bright, but dark-grey clouds seemed to be rolling in from the northeast – snow or even rain. If only it would rain, thought Anna. The snow will melt faster. Though the skiing season seemed to get shorter every year – snow stayed on the ground much later than before and the biting, sub-zero temperatures arrived later in the spring, only to end like a slap in the face some time in April as warm air blew in from the south – she yearned to go running on the bare earth, to pack her skiing equipment away in the basement until next winter.

Anna walked briskly to the area of parkland by the mouth of the river. Over there the sound of traffic wouldn't disturb her telephone call and the air was cleaner. Anna liked the park. It was so big that you had to leave at least ten minutes to walk from one side to the other. Hidden in the garden were old greenhouses, each with exotic plants that used to form part of the city's botanical garden. Now they were empty. During the summer months one of them housed a nice little café that served enormous butter buns. The snow-covered paths were pretty. The trees in the park were mostly tall maples and birches, interspersed with a few thick spruces and lindens. Anna could hear the twittering of a bird in the treetops. Could it be a chaffinch?

Juha Karppinen's ex-wife, Sirpa Heikkilä, lived in the south of Finland with her new husband. Anna began by explaining the circumstances of Vilho's death and said that she needed some information about Juha.

'Do you think Juha could have murdered my father-in-law, my former father-in-law, that is?' the woman asked, shocked.

'We are still working on a number of lines of enquiry, and we don't have a suspect,' Anna explained.

'What do you want to know about Juha? I'm not in contact with him at all these days, now that the children are grown up and getting on with their own lives.'

'Tell me what kind of man he is. Generally speaking,' said Anna.

'I doubt I know him well enough these days to say anything at all. When I first met him he was wonderful, then little by little he turned into a thoroughly nasty person. Well, I think I did too.'

'In what way was he nasty?'

'I don't think he's a murderer, if that's what you mean. He was never violent or anything like that. He just got caught up in gambling.'

Anna sat up, alert. 'What kind of gambling?'

'Cards, roulette, horses, you name it. I imagine in the age of the internet he's up to his neck in online gambling.'

The veins in Anna's temples started humming. She remembered something. How could I have dismissed it, forgotten the matter altogether, she berated herself. I wasn't at work, she conceded in her own defence. I was drunk. At some point I lost my memory. And I was playing too.

'I once saw him at a roulette table,' said Anna, instantly deciding to ask Virkkunen for a warrant to seize Juha Karppinen's computer and search his house.

'I saw him quite a few times. That's what eventually brought our marriage to an end. Juha screwed up our finances, he was always on edge, everything was going to pot. Thank God we had a prenuptial agreement, or I would have ended up having to pay his debts. Still, he might have changed, come to his senses. I really don't know what he gets up to these days. Thankfully.'

'Thank you for this information, thank you very much,' said Anna and ended the call. The twittering of the bird could be heard again. Yes, I think it is a chaffinch. I hope it doesn't die of hunger out here; it's still so cold.

24

'WHAT EXACTLY are we looking for?' Sari asked Anna. Vilho Karppinen's apartment was quiet and expectant. Anna felt sick at the thought of going inside. At first she was puzzled at this feeling but understood later that it must have to do with the knives, still on display in the glass cabinet in the living room. More to the point, it was the knife that was missing that unnerved her. It was still a mystery how Vilho's rare collector's item had ended up in the woods in Ketoniemi where it was used to slit open Riitta Vihviläinen's throat.

'Let's just look around. We've got to find the medication and the prescriptions.'

'Which pharmacy did Vilho use? They would have copies of the prescriptions.'

'His son didn't even know about his father's blood-pressure condition, so I doubt he'd know which pharmacy he used. Let's find the medicine cabinet and see what else he's got.'

They quickly found Vilho's collection of medicine on the middle shelf of the cupboard above the counter. There wasn't much there. A few packets of painkillers, a tub of moisturising cream and some Vitamin D.

'There's no Propral here.'

'There was a packet in Riitta's cupboard though,' Anna remembered.

'Let's check that out too. Karppinen seems like a relatively healthy man, judging by his medicine cabinet.'

'Where might he keep his prescriptions?'

Anna and Sari began going through his boxes and cupboards.

They worked slowly and methodically; if there was still any evidence of what had happened to Vilho, they mustn't compromise it. Finding that evidence was someone else's job. The collection of knives in the living room looked grotesque and frightening. The bottles of spirits in the next cabinet made everything look even more chilling. The classic Finnish combination at the root of most homicides: blades and alcohol. Normally it was an axe and alcohol. Could Vilho have killed first Vehviläinen then himself, carried out a shocking murder on the spur of the moment, then realised the horror and finality of what he'd done and been unable to live with it?

A box in the bookshelf gave them what they needed. It contained a plastic envelope full of prescriptions dating back many years. There were at least three prescriptions for Propral, but they had all long since expired. The latest prescription was missing.

'The current prescription isn't here,' said Anna.

'Either Vilho recovered from his blood-pressure condition and no longer needed the medication, or the prescription and the drugs have all been removed,' Sari suggested.

'Let's check Riitta's medicine cabinet straight away. Something's not right here.'

'Okay.'

Sari and Anna left the apartment and took the stairs down to the ground floor. Anna went straight to the cabinet in Riitta's kitchen, picked up the bottle of Propral and read the label.

'This is Vilho's medicine,' she said.

'What?'

'This was prescribed to Vilho. It's a bottle of a hundred tablets, and it's almost empty, though it was only bought at the beginning of March.'

'So why is it in Riitta's cabinet?'

'That's the question. This was purchased at the University Pharmacy on Kirkkokatu.'

'We'll have to go there right away.'

'Could Vilho really have murdered Riitta?'

'Or could Riitta have murdered Vilho?'

'Good God,' Sari gasped. 'They could have killed one another. Riitta poisoned Vilho with Propral and Vilho stabbed Riitta before the drugs kicked in.'

'There was no blood on Vilho's hands.'

'He washed himself thoroughly and died shortly afterwards. Or something.'

'I don't know. Vilho didn't have a car. How could he have transported a body?'

'True. This all sounds a bit far-fetched,' Sari sighed. 'Will we ever work this one out?'

Anna thought of the conversation she'd had with Mrs Vehviläinen's daughter while she'd been talking to her informant. We only see what we expect to see, she thought, and more to the point we don't see what we don't expect to see. What should we be seeing now? What direction should we take? The obvious direction or the direction you'd never think of? What can we see out there? What is there to see?

That evening Zoran called and asked whether Anna was happy with Ritva Siponen's work. Anna didn't want to discuss work matters with Zoran, and she told him this upfront. Have it your way, Zoran laughed it off and suggested they meet up. Nataša had taken the children to a friend's place, and Zoran could spend the night at Anna's place.

'I've missed you,' he said in Serbian in that soft, deep voice of his. Though Anna was repelled by Zoran's macho attitude, she found it hard to resist his self-assured, almost aggressive masculinity, a trait that Finnish men always seemed to lack. But now she thought of Nataša. She recalled how they had first met. Anna had been thirteen, Nataša fourteen. It was winter then too, the school playground was dark and cold. It all happened one morning. Anna had just stepped into the playground and seen a group of loud-mouthed, heavily made-up girls forming a circle around a strange-looking girl.

A new pupil, poor thing, Anna had thought and tried to slip past as though she hadn't noticed anything going on, but then she heard the words 'Yugoslav bitch'. She stared at the ring of girls and caught the new girl's eyes. They were cold and hard, the girl was beautiful and fearless, and Anna knew that this irritated Tiina, the ringleader of the bullies.

It wasn't Anna's style to get involved in other students' business, she preferred to keep herself to herself, to the point that she was almost pitiable. Acting assertively was something she'd only picked up at the academy. But that time she stepped in. She pushed through the ring of bullies, took the girl by the hand and said *ajde, idemo*, come on, let's go. Then she took the girl to the staffroom, told the teachers what had happened in the playground and left the girl to be looked after by the school nurse. When Anna was walking home after school, the girl ran up to her and spoke furiously.

'*U pičku materinu*, you should have let me fight them,' she shouted at Anna. 'Fucking do-gooder, you had to go and tell the teachers. I'll never be able to set foot in that school again, thanks to you.'

Anna didn't understand everything the girl was shouting, her Serbian wasn't very good, but she got the point: this girl could look after herself without the help of a teacher's pet like her. They'd gone to Anna's place for a cup of hot chocolate. She introduced herself to Nataša. They never became the best of friends, though they often spent time together. Nataša found a kindred spirit in Tiina's gang. Anna had a secret admiration for Nataša's boldness, and that's why she'd been so surprised when only a few years later Nataša started dating Zoran, married young, dropped out of college, stayed at home to look after the kids, and turned into a quiet little wife, there only to please her husband. What's more, Anna had complicated her relationship with Nataša by spending the odd night in Zoran's arms, and in doing so she'd lost a friend.

'It's not on,' said Anna.

'Why not, honey? We haven't seen each other properly for ages. My lovely lady,' Zoran tried to charm her.

'I mean it. We can't do this. Don't call me again if all you can think about is cheating on your wife. I'm not sleeping with you again.'

'*Jebiga*, Anna, what are you raving on about?'

'I'm not raving. We should have stopped this thing years ago. We should never have started it.'

'What's the matter with you?'

Anna held back the tears. She told Zoran about her grandmother's death, how Ákos had gone to the funeral but she hadn't been able to get there.

'Honey, I'm sorry. Let me come round there and comfort you.'

'Haven't you understood a word I've said?' she shouted. 'I'm not sleeping with you again. Ever.'

Anna hung up and wiped a tear on her sleeve. In a rage she opened a can of beer and went out to the balcony for a cigarette. Why can't some men ever give up, she wondered. Béci was still sending her emails, though she had only replied to one or two, and with nothing but a few words. And at that moment the loneliness hit her, attacked her like a pack of ravenous wolves. Anxiety gnawed at her insides, punched and pummelled her, making her body feel heavy and sore. Now I don't even have Zoran, she thought and felt another wave of tears welling to the surface, but she stopped it in its tracks, swallowed it back to the hidden place full of other forgotten miseries.

She went back inside and opened another beer. She tried to call her mother on Skype. She wanted to talk about Grandma, her final days, her funeral. She wanted to tell her mother about the pain, her sense of longing, to talk about Zoran, to ask her mother why breaking up with a married man, with whom she hadn't officially been together, could feel so terrible. There was no answer. Thank God, she thought. I don't normally talk to Mum about my feelings, and certainly not about my sex life. Besides, her mother would have seen straight through it all and said that Anna needed to be in touch with her roots, whatever form that touch might take.

She tossed and turned in bed for hours waiting for sleep to come. The apartment around her felt cold and solitary. She fetched a spare blanket from the closet, put *Westernization Completed* on low volume and decided to take some sleeping pills if she hadn't fallen asleep in half an hour. The thought seemed to calm her. She quickly drifted to sleep, dreamt dreams punctuated by the rhythms of AGF, dreams of which by morning she could remember nothing at all.

25

ANNA PICKED UP an unmarked Ford from the depot beneath the police station and drove through heavy traffic towards the main road leading east out of the city. The traffic was backed up, the lanes weren't moving, someone was nervously beeping their horn at the traffic lights. Anna looked at the cars in the lines of traffic. Almost every last one of them contained only one person, the driver. It's strange that car sharing hasn't caught on here – especially given the sky-high price of petrol, she thought. Perhaps it's for the best; the sooner we run out of oil, the better. At least then we'll be forced to come up with an alternative. The idea of running out of oil had been used to scare people as long as Anna could remember. She'd never understood what was so terrifying about it; humans had survived perfectly well without oil for the majority of their time on earth, so what was to stop them doing so again? And why are people always trying to frighten us into action? If it's not the oil drying up, it's a global pandemic, a financial crash, the mass retirement of the baby-boomer generation, a heat wave even. Was the propagation of such collective menaces a means of keeping people in check, of making them dutifully fulfil the roles society had assigned them as consumers and producers, of making that role seem so secure and satisfying a way of life that it wouldn't even occur to anyone that alternative truths might be possible?

An irate beep came from behind her. Anna snapped back to reality and noticed that the cars in front had edged forward and the lights had again turned red. It'll be evening by the time I get home, she thought. But what does it matter? There's nobody there anyway.

The skiing resort at Iso-Kero was like every other skiing resort in the country. A hotel at the top of the fell with clusters of log cabins around it, miniature villages of cabins at the foot of the fell, an overpriced village shop, lots of Russian tourists, a reindeer enclosure, a husky farm, trailers, ski boxes, drinks in the hotel lobby, one too many cocktails at the after-ski party. The slopes of Kero Fell were scored with downhill pistes and ski lifts. During the summer the place was empty and the deserted pistes looked like enormous gashes violently scratched into the fell's sensitive skin. The scars of this annual winter destruction didn't look quite as brutal when everything was white and covered in snow. Anna parked the car in front of the hotel and stepped outside. It was windy at the summit, and the air was fresh. The sky was overcast, the temperature a few degrees below freezing: ideal weather for skiing. I should have taken my skis with me and done a short trek after work, thought Anna as she stretched her legs. The hilly terrain would make a refreshing change from the sea ice, and it would be light long into the evening.

Anna looked at her watch. She'd carefully measured how long the journey had taken. From the city centre, it took between ninety minutes and two hours to drive out here, depending on the weather and the number of reindeer lazily trotting along the road. She had only seen one, standing in the verge of snow like a statue staring in the woods.

Anna went into the hotel. The foyer was full of Lapland trinkets and souvenirs for sale, though the centre wasn't actually in Lapland. For foreign tourists, the idea of Lapland was relative. You could buy the same junk in Helsinki department stores too. At the reception sat a young girl, her eyes glued to her iPhone. She didn't look up. Anna cleared her throat. The girl remained uncommunicative.

'Good afternoon,' Anna said eventually. The girl started and sheepishly slid her phone into her pocket.

'I'm sorry, madam, I didn't notice you there. Do you have a reservation?'

'No. My name's Fekete Anna, I'm from the police. I called this morning and said I'd be paying a visit,' she said and showed her badge.

'Oh yes, that's right. Welcome to Kero.'

'I've come to ask about one of your customers. I'd like to see the records you have for a Mr Juha Karppinen. It seems he arrived on the eleventh of March.'

'Our customer records are confidential, I'm afraid.'

'Don't worry, I've got all the relevant warrants. This is a criminal investigation,' said Anna.

'What if I call my supervisor?'

'You do that.'

The girl stepped out from behind the reception desk and gave Anna an awkward smile. She walked across the foyer to the restaurant, where a throng of tanned guests in brightly coloured skiing gear were lining up at the lunchtime buffet table. Anna recalled the skiing trip she'd taken years ago. She'd gone with the only serious boyfriend she'd ever had, a policeman who shared Anna's passion for sports and outdoor activities but who hadn't understood her need to spend time alone, nor her reluctance to start a family. They'd spent a week skiing through the wilderness without seeing anyone else. They carried their food and all their equipment on sleds that they pulled behind them. The layer of snow was thick and soft. Lunch was mostly rice with dried mincemeat, macaroni with dried mincemeat. Every morning they put the dried meat in a sealed plastic bag with a dash of water so it could rehydrate. They prepared their food on a portable stove, sheltering from the wind. Dessert was a cup of instant coffee and some chocolate. How delicious it had all tasted.

She hadn't hiked like that since their break-up. Anna noticed that she missed it. Would Béci make a good hiking companion? Anna guessed he would rather spend his nights between a set of clean sheets than in a sleeping bag in a shack in the woods and would rather eat gourmet hotel food than simple hiking fodder, but she would never know the truth. She had no plans to ask him.

The hotel manager was a man of around sixty. He shook Anna's hand firmly and showed her to his office. Anna declined the offer of coffee and asked to see the details of Juha Karppinen's visit immediately. The manager signed into the computer system and quickly located the records in question.

'That's right. Juha Karppinen checked in on the eleventh of March at 2.15 p.m. He stayed in Room 173. He stayed with us for a week and a half. I don't remember him myself; I don't deal with the customer-service side of the business.'

'Could you tell me who was working that afternoon? And the next day, the twelfth of March.'

'Let me see. We had the same reception staff on both days: Inkeri in the morning and Janne in the afternoon and evening. To cut costs we don't have anyone on duty during the night.'

'What time does the evening shift end?'

'Midnight.'

'How do customers get in if they come back after that?'

'Everyone is given a door code.'

Anna thought carefully. Vilho had died around midnight. Propral takes effect around an hour after being administered. If Juha had driven from here into town to kill Vilho, he would have had to leave at 8 p.m. at the latest.

'I'd like to talk to both receptionists.'

'Inkeri will be starting the evening shift at four o'clock. Janne is on his day off, but he lives on site in the dormitory for seasonal staff.'

'Could you ask them both to come up here now? I'll talk to the staff at the restaurant while I'm waiting.'

'That's fine. What has this Karppinen done?' asked the manager. His body language betrayed his almost childish curiosity.

'I'm afraid I can't go into details at this point in the investigation,' Anna replied, and walked through to the restaurant.

As she drove back towards the city through the monotonous forest landscape where small villages eked out a living far away from supermarkets, banks and one another, where clusters of slender fir trees disappeared the further she drove and the last vestiges of snow grew thinner the closer she came to the sea, Anna went over what she'd learned. The barman had remembered Juha. He'd been in the restaurant every evening and drunk quite a lot. Whether he had been there on the Wednesday evening in question, the barman couldn't be entirely sure. I think he was here every single night of his stay, but I can't be sure, he said. That Wednesday there was a dance and a band playing in the hotel bar. There had been so many people in the bar that it was impossible to remember anyone in particular.

Inkeri from reception clearly remembered Juha checking in. He had arrived dragging large suitcases and a bag of skiing equipment, quizzed her about the conditions of the pistes and skiing tracks, the breakfast and other hotel services, and booked the sauna between eight and ten o'clock the following evening. Janne had been on duty that night, and he remembered seeing Juha taking the stairs down to the basement with a towel over his arm just before eight o'clock. Juha waved hello and asked whether he could take his own bottles down to the sauna; Janne answered that that was fine, as long as he didn't leave the empties lying around. He didn't remember seeing Juha return from the sauna, because by then the restaurant and the lobby bar had started to fill with revellers. Juha's alibi wasn't watertight, and more importantly, Inkeri remembered that Juha was driving an SUV. Anna saw movement by the side of the road. She braked and flashed her lights at the oncoming car. A group of grey reindeer strutted into the road and began trotting in front of her. The reindeer zigzagged between the lanes of traffic until the large white male that had first run out into the road leapt over the verge and back into the forest; the rest of the herd followed him and the road was clear again.

Anna's phone rang. She switched on her hands-free device and answered. It was Sari. Apparently Vilho had been very active on the housing-association committee, and on several occasions he'd asked for more detailed documentation from the firm that carried out the pipe and window renovations. It seemed that Vilho had suspected that not everything about the company was above board. The firm never provided him with the documents. Anna told Sari that Juha drove an SUV.

'What if they were in it together?' asked Sari. 'Juha and the caretaker.'

'It's quite possible,' said Anna. 'And if that's so, we're going to find out very soon.'

'Excellent. We're nearly there. Oh yes. That Sammy has been asking to talk to you all day. He still maintains he killed Vilho and Marko, but funnily he didn't know anything about Riitta. He clammed up when I asked about her. Now he's saying there was a man in the corridor the night he killed Vilho and that this man could verify that Sammy was there.'

'Poor boy,' said Anna. 'I'll visit him tomorrow. We'll have to see whether anybody saw Juha's SUV somewhere other than in the hotel car park on the night of the murders, and we should check the GPS coordinates for his mobile phone.'

'I'm on it. Drive carefully,' said Sari and hung up.

Grandma's funeral had gone smoothly. The service was held at Kanizsa cemetery in a chapel with a stone floor so cold, despite the sunshine, that Ákos and her mother's feet had felt the chill. Lots of relatives from Hungary and Serbia had gathered for the occasion. Ákos, her mother and her father's brothers had greeted each of them in turn, standing in the small chapel. The service lasted several hours, the priest said a blessing and prayed for the deceased. After this the congregation had travelled to Békavár for a meal. The funeral had turned into a warm family reunion; relatives who rarely saw one another had a chance to chat and catch up with each other's news. Everyone except Anna. Grandma's obituary, complete with a photograph, was taped to every bulletin board in the town, on trees and streetlamps. Ákos promised to bring one back with him but couldn't say when he would be back. Anna felt a chill. What will happen when Mum dies? Who would she have left? What remains of home when those who live there are gone?

Anna went out to the balcony for a cigarette and drank a large can of beer. She couldn't bring herself to listen to music but leant instead on the windowsill in the darkened living room and stared out at the concrete walls of the houses opposite. The grey skies above the suburbs appeared to give off a faint glimmer of light. Anna had noticed it before. The combination of thick cloud cover and the landscape, as it turned towards the spring, seemed in some strange way to light itself. The pitch darkness had gone. Then she put clean sheets on the bed, took a sleeping pill and curled up beneath the blankets.

26

SAMMY WAS SITTING in police custody eagerly examining the photographs Anna had brought him. Anna looked at Sammy but thought of Ákos. How was her brother coping? Back home spring would already be well underway, the fruit trees would be about to burst into blossom and snowbells would rise like brilliant-white dapples from the brown earth. Here people would be trudging through slush for months to come. Would her brother be able to enjoy it? Or had he hit the bottle again?

Toini Lehmusvirta, the caretaker, Kari Haapsaari, Juha Karppinen, Reza, a couple of Hell's Angels and one person who had nothing at all to do with the investigation stared from photographs on the table. It seemed almost as though it was the job of the people in the photographs to identify Sammy, and not the other way round. Anna's stomach was rumbling though she had eaten a substantial breakfast. She'd been constantly hungry for the last few days, and there was a strange, unpleasant taste in her mouth that she couldn't get rid of no matter how often she brushed her teeth.

Sammy picked out one of the photographs.

'It's him,' he said.

Anna's skin began to tingle.

'Are you absolutely sure?' she asked.

Sammy nodded eagerly. A new glimmer of hope had lit in his eyes.

'Yes, I'm sure. I was waiting at the front door, trying to get up to Macke's place. I haven't got a phone and there are no doorbells outside,' he explained excitedly. 'That guy came out of the stairwell and let me in. We even exchanged a few words. He can prove that I was there. And that night I killed Vilho Karppinen.'

'Good,' said Anna. 'This is very important information.'

Sammy chuckled with happiness. His face lit up. Oh Sammy, you poor thing, thought Anna. This information is more important than you know.

Hilla was pale and gaunt. She was wearing a camouflage army jacket, a pair of scuffed fake-leather boots, no hat and no gloves. She was shivering and constantly shifted her bodyweight from one leg to the other. Her eyes looked empty, as though she couldn't properly see ahead, as though there was nobody behind them. Anna's informant, Jani, had told her where to find the girl, and Anna had left immediately. Jani made Anna swear not to frisk her for drugs, and Anna had promised. But I will be filing a report with the drug squad and social services, she thought. This girl's still a child.

'Aren't you cold?' asked Anna and tried to give the girl an encouraging smile.

Hilla scowled angrily at her and didn't answer. 'D'you want something?' she asked in a slurred, lacklustre voice.

'Was Marko Halttu your boyfriend?'

The girl scuffed the grit on the ground. For a moment Anna thought she hadn't heard the question; she was quiet for a long while and stared at the dirt.

'Yes,' she answered eventually.

'Were you together long?'

A tear ran down the girl's cheek. 'Six months.'

'Do you know anything about Marko's death?'

She raised her weepy eyes, looked up at Anna and nodded. The shivers seemed to rattle her birdlike body all the more powerfully.

'He topped himself,' she said quietly.

'How do you know that?'

The girl took a phone from her pocket, fiddled with it for a moment and handed it to Anna. 'See for yourself.'

On the screen was a text message from Marko, sent on the day he died: *This mess is too big man. I can't do it no more. Don't blame yourself. Thanks for everything, babe. This is it. See you in junkie heaven.*

By now Hilla was sobbing out loud. Anna handed her a tissue.

'Why didn't you call an ambulance?' she asked.

A tortured moan escaped from the girl's throat. 'I only read the message later on, once the cops had already found him. Back then I was totally out of it all the time.'

'And now?'

'I've cut back a lot. I'm trying to kick it.'

'Good. Are you getting treatment?'

'No, I'll be fine on my own. I'm not that hooked no more.'

Of course not, Anna thought with sadness. You lot never are.

'Well, thanks for this information. It's really important to us. I think Macke would have wanted people to know the truth, don't you?'

'Yeah,' she said and blew her nose. 'I miss him.' With that, Hilla turned and lumbered off, her hands in her pockets, her head lowered. For a moment Anna stood watching her, then she called the city's social services and made a report to the child welfare officer.

The results of the spirometry test weren't alarming, but they weren't great either. Esko had visited the hospital that morning for further tests, again fearing the worst. He sat there sweating and had been convinced he was going to receive a death sentence, and was taken aback when that wasn't the case. You seem to be developing chronic obstructive pulmonary disease, said the doctor, but you can still prevent it. In other words, he was nearly healthy. It was a miracle. Esko looked at the cigarette cabinet by the supermarket checkout, hidden behind a rolling door. Out of habit he almost ordered three packets of Norths but instead asked for two packets of nicotine chewing gum and a nicotine mouth spray.

He'd asked the doctor what was causing his chest pains. The doctor speculated that it could have something to do with tense muscles around his ribcage. He asked about Esko's exercise regime and ordered him to the gym, to do aerobic exercise, swimming or yoga. He'd then given Esko a referral to a physiotherapist and suggested he try using a chiropractor. Yoga, Esko scoffed. Jesus Christ, the things these people come up with. Isn't it enough that I'm trying keep off the fucking smokes, he thought, as he stepped out of the shop and into the warm spring weather. A flock of geese flew overhead. See you in the autumn, he thought. Hunting those things down will give me plenty of exercise. Just then he noticed a Kia Sorento parked outside the shop. Esko turned on his heels and walked quickly away. He glanced over his shoulder and saw a foot stepping out of the car. A man dressed in a black hoodie jumped out. It looked as though he had something in his hand. Was it a gun? Christ, it looked like a pistol. Esko started running. He slipped round the corner of the house behind the shop and took a sharp left towards the next building. From there a cycle path led into the park where he might be able to find a hiding place. Again he peered over his shoulder. There were two men. No, three. They all had black hair, the same black hoodies, and they were gaining on him fast. Now I'll have to be crafty. If I run, I'll never get away, thought Esko and decided not to take the cycle path but dashed into the gulley between two neighbouring apartment blocks. His heart was beating like a hammer. That familiar old pain started to clench around his chest.

He stood right against the building's concrete wall and edged forward. As he reached the corner he pulled his pistol from the holster beneath his arm, and with the gun in his hand he peered round the corner. There was no one in sight. He ran towards the next building as quickly as his legs could take him. He was out of breath, and for a moment he felt as though he was about to choke, but carried on along the side of the building. From there he called Virkkunen and told him to send reinforcements. How long would they take to get here? He tried to calculate it in his head. Five minutes, or ten? Will I be able to hide between these buildings that long? He glanced once more round the corner and thought he might have shaken the hooded men from his heels, then saw one of them appear from behind the building in front. The guy was stocky and he was striding confidently towards Esko with the weapon in his hand. The other two were nowhere to be seen. Shit, thought Esko. Did he see me? He leant against the concrete wall; its rough surface scratched the back of his head. He gripped the pistol in his hand and held his breath.

Grit on the path rustled around the corner. The man bellowed something in an incomprehensible language, probably calling for his buddy. There came the sound of brisk footsteps, and Esko heard the man burst into a run. He didn't have time to think about anything as the man suddenly appeared round the corner pointing his gun. Esko instinctively grabbed his arm. I'm going to die, he thought. The gun went off, a yellow plastic bullet shot upwards and the pistol flew in an arc to the ground. Esko twisted the man's arm so hard that he slumped to his knees in the slush. It's a fake gun, he thought, gasping frantically for breath. It's a fucking toy. What the fuck are these guys playing at? Esko pressed his own gun, genuine and lethal, against the man's temple.

'Hands behind your head.' he shouted. 'Now, you piece of shit!'

The man slowly raised his hands. The melting snow soaked into his light-coloured jeans. The lunging cobra on the back of his hoodie didn't hiss and didn't bite. Esko looked at the white logo printed on the black fabric and smiled with satisfaction.

The two other men were approaching from a distance.

'Stop right there or I'll shoot,' shouted Esko. The men stopped in their tracks. So the fuckers understand Finnish when they need to, he thought.

'Hands up! Move an inch and I'll shoot this waste of space here,' he hollered at the men. They raised their hands. The sound of police sirens could be heard in the distance.

'Stay right where you are,' he shouted at them. 'You don't fucking play around with me, got that? I could shoot your mate by mistake. It wouldn't be the first time.'

Two squad cars swerved on to the scene. Officers in uniform

charged out of the cars. One patrol picked up the men standing in the distance, the other ran up to Esko and the man kneeling on the ground.

'*Salaam alaikum*, mate. Nice gun,' Esko said to the man once the patrol officers had cuffed him. 'Where's Reza?'

The man, who up close turned out to be nothing but a teenager, barely eighteen, stared at Esko with a look of loathing in his black eyes. Then he noisily hocked a glob of mucus from the back of his throat and spat it at Esko's feet.

Esko raised his hand to slap the boy in the face but controlled himself at the last moment. 'You don't need to tell me,' he said. 'I'm going to find him myself.'

The boy smiled in mockery, all the while staring unblinkingly at Esko.

'You wanna bet?' he said.

27

THE SAUNA STOVE HISSED fiercely as the water struck its stones. The thermometer showed almost 90°C. The fire fizzed in the sauna's hatch. This was the only source of light in the dim garden sauna, which featured only the bare minimum of comfort, no specially shaped boards, no shower, no glass doors. Cold water came from a tap in the wall, and it was warmed in a bricked cauldron above the stove until it was boiling hot. Virkkunen had taken a birch sauna whisk he'd made in the summer out of the freezer and thawed it in the lukewarm water in the washing basin.

'*Betula pendula*. Silver birch,' said Virkkunen, handed Esko the whisk and cracked open a can of beer.

'It's not, actually,' said Esko sniffing the thawed twigs. It smelled of summer. It brought something to mind. The first time he'd shared a sauna with Anneli.

Virkkunen threw water on the stove; steam leapt up from the black stones and hit the boards so ferociously that the men had to hunch their shoulders and shelter their heads between their knees.

'What is it then?'

'I can't remember, but it's not *pendula*.'

'Wanna bet?'

'Fine. Five euros.'

'Ten. We'll settle it at work on Monday,' said Virkkunen and emptied his can in a single gulp.

Esko moistened the whisk in the washbasin and began lashing himself. He covered his whole body, firstly whipping his back until it was red, then his arms, legs and stomach; one cubic centimetre at a time he whacked his skin in silence. The only sounds were the slap of birch twigs against his body, the angry hiss each time Virkkunen threw more water on the stove and the men's groans. Leaves flew from the whisk, stuck to Esko's sweaty back and on the sauna boards; the entire sauna filled with the aromas of Midsummer.

'Damn good sauna you've got here,' said Esko and put the beater back into the bucket of water. He stretched his legs across the railing, leant back, rested his head against the black logs in the wall and closed his eyes. Everything was silent. The fire in the hatch was beginning to die down; its murmur and crackling had quietened. His skin tingled deliciously from the birch twigs. The warmth relaxed him. There is something almost holy about a moment like this, something that only a Finn can truly understand, thought Esko and sipped his warm beer. The can singed his lips.

'Have you put your flat up for sale yet?' asked Virkkunen, and rinsed his face with cold water.

'No,' Esko replied.

'Why not?'

'It's not that simple. Nobody would buy it these days.'

'Surely smaller flats like yours get snapped up.'

'The location isn't great; it's too far from the city, too far from the university. Besides, I'm not sure I want to go anywhere after all. Yesterday it somehow struck me.'

'You did a heroic job out there. Christ, there's plenty of fight in you yet.'

'I just did what needed to be done,' said Esko and stepped down from the boards with a puff. He poured a bucket of cool water over his head, washing the birch leaves to the floor.

'We've hit the Cobras hard. They've lost so many big players that their operations are drying up as we speak.'

'Reza is still on the loose,' said Esko and rubbed himself with soap. Time to do something about this belly, he thought. Before long I won't be able to see my own dick.

'Alone Reza is nothing. Esko, you did a fine job. The NBI sent a personal note of thanks. We're all really proud of you.'

Esko huffed with feigned modesty, but he felt a heat burning inside him, a sense of victory and gratification; it was as though his entire body was vying to outshine the spring sunlight.

Virkkunen threw more water on the stove. The stones hissed and heat spread through the sauna.

'Time for a break,' he said eventually.

'I think the laws in this country need changing,' said Virkkunen once the men were sitting on the porch outside the sauna with towels wrapped round their waists, steam rising from their skin, cooling themselves with fresh cans of ice-cold beer. Streetlights glimmered out by the road. A few cars were parked along the street, but by now there was no traffic. People had returned to their homes to start the weekend or had gone into town to celebrate, to their cottages or to visit relatives. There were no lights on in the neighbouring houses. Out of force of habit Esko glanced across the row of cars and peered at the hedgerows surrounding the garden. The shadows beneath them were black. Nothing moved.

'The police should be given greater powers to deal with organised crime,' Virkkunen continued.

Esko snorted in agreement. He didn't want to talk about this, not now that the sauna had relaxed his tense muscles, the birch twigs had scoured the dirt from his skin and the beer was nicely going to his head.

'We can't even agree what organised crime is, so the police are unable to act promptly.'

Virkkunen stood up, staggered slightly, went into the sauna dressing room. There came the sound of knocking and rattling, then he returned with a bottle of brandy. He handed the bottle to Esko, who took a deep swig of it. The brown liquid stung his throat. Esko gave the bottle back to Virkkunen.

'There should be longer sentences for the ringleaders. They're the worst of the bunch,' Virkkunen said, becoming increasingly animated. The drink made his voice sound slightly hazy.

'You're right there,' Esko muttered and emptied his bottle of beer.

He thought of Naseem and Reza. He had a hunch that he might never catch the guy. Something rustled in the bushes at the end of the garden. Esko looked up but couldn't see anything. The wind, he thought, and the bush rustled again.

'We should have far greater authority to tackle organised crime and the gangs that cause it.'

'One more soak in the steam?' said Esko, and looked once more at the thick bushes, which were now silent.

Virkkunen cracked open another two beers, then picked a couple of birch logs from the palette beneath the porch and chucked them far into the stove. The logs flared up, the orange glow of the flames danced across the floor and walls. It was Esko's turn to throw the water. He filled the bucket with cold water, drizzled some beer across the hot stones and threw three ladles of water on the stove. The soft vapours filling the sauna smelled of baking bread; the heat burned their skin and the men grimaced.

'Have you heard from Anneli?'

'Nope,' said Esko and stared at the condensation that had gathered on the sauna's small windowpane. Patterns emerged beneath the steam, flowers and smiley faces drawn by Virkkunen's children. In the middle of the darkened garden, a lantern illuminated a circle in the sodden ground where last autumn's lawn, revealed beneath the melting snow, lay slimy as seaweed.

'Raija mentioned she'd seen her in town. They went for coffee, apparently.'

Esko muttered something.

'Raija wants to renovate the kitchen. Well, I'm the one that's going to have to do it, of course,' said Virkkunen, trying to change the subject, took a long swig of beer and burped.

'You're joking?'

'No. She sits up reading decorating magazines and complains about what weather-beaten kitchen units we've got and how everything should be more *ergonomic*. What an irritating word. Ergonomic, my arse.'

'Sounds like you'd better get to work.'

'Christ, when am I supposed to do something like that – and with what money? If I were rich I'd just get the builders in to do it.'

'You could ask the Angels for a quote.'

The men burst in hearty laughter, clacked their warmed cans of beer together and drank.

'Someone's coming,' said Esko and pointed into the garden. A dark shadow flickered through the light from the lantern. Esko felt his heart clench tight. He leapt down from the boards. Will this never fucking end, he thought, looking for something to use as a weapon. He picked up the ladle and raised it just as the sauna door opened.

A blond woman, well preserved for her age, peered inside.

'Esko, a woman called Naseem has been trying to contact you. It's vitally important, apparently, and she needs to talk to you right now,' said Raija and held out Virkkunen's work phone to the ruddy, drunken men, dripping with sweat, one wielding a ladle with a look of profound embarrassment on his face.

The letter was short and to the point. It was written in English. I should have known, Esko slurred to Virkkunen. Of course she could speak English, she was a doctor after all. That interpreter was a waste of public money. Virkkunen nodded beside him, his eyes blurry. They had taken a taxi to Vaarala, told the driver to drive as quickly as he could, that he had two police officers in the car and they'd sort things out if he got into trouble. The driver had put his foot on the gas with the excitement of a teenager who'd just got his licence. They told him to wait in the car park. The two men charged up to Naseem's door where a neighbour with a set of keys was waiting and opened the door.

The letter was on the kitchen table.

Esko, I am sorry I've lied to you, it began.

Esko sat down at the table. The room was swaying unpleasantly, and the text on the page of squared paper torn from a notebook came in and out of focus.

When you first visited me, I finally realised that my son was in very grave danger. I couldn't bear to stand by and watch him go to prison or worse, end up dead. He is a good boy at heart and I love him. I want him to have another chance at a decent life. I have taken him to safety. We have left the country. You will never find him, and you will never find me.

You must know that nobody ever wanted to harm you, not really. I am sorry that I have caused you to fear for your safety. This was part of my plan to play for some extra time, as were the fake addresses that I gave you.

Once more, I am truly sorry.

There was nothing else I could do. I hope you understand.

Naseem.

'Damn it,' said Esko and handed the letter to Virkkunen, who staggered as he took hold of it. This is the first time I've worked with Pertti blind drunk, Esko mused, and the thought would have been funny had the situation not been so dismal.

'So what do we do now?' asked Esko.

'Now we get ourselves good and drunk,' Pertti Virkkunen replied.

The silence of the apartment didn't invite her to step inside. A pile of advertisements had appeared on the hallway mat. Anna stepped over it, closed the door behind her and walked into her brother's bedsit, with its tiny kitchen set into one of the walls. Anna had been out running when her brother had sent a message asking her to fill out his unemployment benefit forms on his behalf. Anna wasn't in the mood but had agreed nonetheless. It seemed her role as a primary carer continued, even though her brother was far away and, according to their mother, had stayed off the booze. The empty apartment looked abandoned. The few items of furniture were old, bought at the flea market: a sofa, a low shelving unit, an unmade mattress in the corner, a dirty pot and plate in the sink. The television that Anna had given him had disappeared. Ákos had probably sold it the day before his trip for a bit of money, or to spend it on drink.

Anna washed the dishes. Water filled the sink. She couldn't find any washing-up liquid. There was an empty beer can in the drying cabinet. Anna opened up the other kitchen cupboards; they were all full of empty cans and bottles, the cheapest brands available. She felt a pinch at the bottom of her stomach and was happy she'd remembered to put on a sanitary towel. Her period generally took her by surprise and stained her underwear, though she recorded it in her diary. And so starts another five days of being in pain and pissed off, she thought and went to the bathroom, which was the size of a small kennel. The toilet bowl was dirty, and so was the floor. Anna cleaned the bowl and sat down. Her towel was still bright white. Then she mopped the floor and scrubbed the worst of the stains from the walls. What the hell is wrong with me, she wondered. I shouldn't have to do this. Still, she decided to fetch the vacuum from her own apartment and give the place a thorough spring clean, wash the sheets and air the mattress. Her brother probably wouldn't even notice the difference when he came back, but Anna was calmed by the thought that Ákos could live like other people, even for a moment.

As she dusted the shelves, Anna found an old, reddened photograph placed face down beneath a pile of books. Dad, Mum, Áron, Ákos and Anna as a baby in her father's arms. They were standing in the yard outside their old house, its whitewashed walls gleaming in the background. Everyone was looking at the camera with posed expressions on their face – everyone except Dad, who was smiling at the baby in his arms. The baby's hand reached out towards Dad's face. Anna felt a quiver of emotion run through her body. Or had she caught a chill from the sweat caused first by her run and then the cleaning? My family, she thought, my torn-apart family, back when everything was still fine. What do I have left of this? A lonely life in a strange, faraway country. Can my father's loving eyes reach me here? Do his arms still carry me? Would my life have been different if he hadn't died? Would Mum have felt so insecure, would she have fled, tried to salvage what was left of the family by tearing it from its roots? Probably not. And what would have become of me back there? What would have become of Ákos in the country that no longer existed? It was hard to imagine. Perhaps I'd be married and have children, like all proper women in the Balkans. Perhaps Ákos would have continued his studies, become a vet, maybe he wouldn't drink, wouldn't be so isolated. He too might be married and have a family.

Now there's only Mum and Ákos left, thought Anna. And me. My stump of a family, its members so estranged from one another. The distance, the Skype calls, the homesickness. Anna swallowed back the tears, put the photograph back beneath the pile of books, put clean sheets on Ákos's bed and left, completely forgetting about the unemployment benefit forms lying on the table.

28

THIS TIME THEY MET in a park on the edge of the city centre, near the sea. Fog rose above the water like a thin, moist gauze. The gentle breeze carried in the smell of seaweed, fish and the recently tarred hulls of boats. It was early morning and the city hadn't yet woken up. It was still yawning beneath the blankets in warm bedrooms; it pattered into the kitchen to switch on the coffee maker, its hair tangled from sleep, fetched the newspaper from the hallway mat, or rolled on its side and continued sleeping, content that it was a Sunday. To Esko's surprise, his snitch had contacted him and asked to meet him right away. Esko had glanced at his watch and saw it was just after seven o'clock. Last time he'd barely been able to keep an appointment at ten, he thought sullenly but agreed to meet up, as he could hear from the man's voice that something was wrong.

'I'm in trouble,' he told Esko. No good morning, no how are you, no how's work been going. These conversations didn't need meaningless chit-chat, and that suited Esko fine.

'Life's a bitch, but it's hardly surprising in your line of work.'

His informant coughed and lit a cigarette, offered one to Esko. He shook his head.

'A guy saw us in that bar. I'm going to have to get out of town for a while.'

'Where are you going?'

'My brother-in-law owns a plumbing firm out in the sticks, far away from here. I'm going to work for him, at first just to earn my keep, then I can think about the future.'

'Sounds good.'

'I'll be well off the gang's radar.'

'You can get anywhere quickly on a Harley Davidson.'

'I never told no one I had a sister. They'll never find me; they won't even come after me.'

Is that so? thought Esko. Still, he felt content. This might be the man's first and last chance to turn his life around. Esko hoped with all his heart that he could make it work out.

'But that's not all,' he said.

'Well?'

'The Cobras are done and dusted. At least for now.'

'Really?'

'Yep. You brought in all the big players, and now Reza's gone underground. The normal members, the kids on that estate, they can't do nothing without Reza and the others. The whole operation dried up before it even got started.'

'Good thing too,' said Esko. Nothing in his voice, expression or body language betrayed the thrill of success flaring within him.

'Right, I'll be off then. Probably won't be seeing you again.'

'Hopefully not. Take care of yourself,' said Esko.

They shook hands, and Esko gave his former snitch a friendly slap on the back. Then they parted company and went their separate ways. Esko noticed a silver-grey car waiting for the man at the edge of the park. A woman was leaning on the bonnet smoking a cigarette. That must be the sister.

Once the man had stepped inside and the car had disappeared from view, Esko leapt into the air like a young foal, ran a few steps and kicked a clump of ice, sending it flying in a magnificent arc through the air.

I'll have to call Anna right away, he thought, and tell her she doesn't need to worry about the Afghan poofters any more.

A seagull squawked nearby. It felt good to breathe in the sea air, moist from the fog. Nothing in his body hurt.

Bloody hell, I did it, he thought, and stopped to greet the sun slowly rising behind the curtain of mist.

*

Sammy was sitting in the interview room with Ritva Siponen. He was tired and hoped he would soon be able to go to court, receive his sentence and finally find peace. Over the past weeks his doses of Subutex had been gradually reduced; he'd had some withdrawal symptoms, but in the hands of that pretty nurse they'd felt almost bearable. Sammy was happy to be kicking the drugs one day at a time. Whatever happened, he would never touch them again. And yet the thought of this made him feel a strange sense of longing. The membranes in his mouth started throbbing, right by the saliva glands. Sammy knew it was an aching desire that would live within him for the rest of his life, something that would always try and tempt him, though he knew only too well the dangers of giving in. The drugs were both his friend and his worst enemy; addiction was a treacherous mistress who first seduced him with her charms only then to destroy him.

'Sammy, it seems you've told us some very serious lies,' said Anna.

'What do you mean? I have not,' he said, panicking.

'Yes, you have. We now know that Marko Halttu killed himself. His girlfriend received a suicide note from him by text message. Marko's life was in a terrible mess.'

Sammy thought carefully what to say.

'Very well, I admit I didn't kill him, but I killed the other one. You can't prove I didn't.'

'I'm afraid we can. Vilho Karppinen's blood contained a lethal dose of a particular medication. He was already dying when he arrived at Marko's apartment.'

'What? That can't be true.'

'It is true.'

Sammy's face drained of all expression. He sat motionless, staring blankly at the wall. That's that, he thought. There goes my final chance. I can kiss goodbye to a life now.

Ritva Siponen cleared her throat.

'The authorities have processed our appeal, and I'm afraid it was unsuccessful. The fact that you have been mixed up with drugs while here in Finland was a serious factor in their decision. Sammy, you're being sent back to Pakistan.'

Sammy buried his face in the palms of his hands but didn't make a sound. The first thing I'll do is find some heroin, he thought, inject myself so full of the stuff that I won't feel anything when they come for me, so that the drugs will kill me before they can do it. Let that be my final journey, he thought. And I'll take that journey just like Macke did.

'I'm so sorry,' said Anna.

Sammy looked up at her. She always looks so sad, he thought, even though her life here is fine. Sammy felt the urge to comfort Anna, to take her by the hand and say something beautiful. But he couldn't, and it would have felt strange. She was clearly trying to comfort him.

'So am I,' was all he could muster.

29

THE DAY BEGAN GREY and overcast, though seemed to hint at warm weather to come. Heavy clouds rolled across the city, hiding the disc of the sun behind them, and the air was moist like just before rain. The roads were wet with rapidly melting snow; running water collected in underground tunnels, puddles dotted the surface of the pavements. Anna had wondered about this before: the chill of spring with the sun shining from the bright sky above, then the sudden rise in temperature, the southern winds bringing clouds and rain to the north, melting the snow far more efficiently than the sun. That spring the freezing temperatures had continued longer than usual. Anna didn't mind the slush, because it meant that summer was on its way.

Juha Karppinen was sitting in the interview room at the police station wearing a suit and tie. Anna and Virkkunen scrutinised him for a moment before beginning the interview. Anna was looking for cracks in the man's self-assured exterior, places to aim her line of attack. She'd noticed a flash of agitation in his eyes as he stepped into the room, but it had soon disappeared behind the arrogant grin that told them he thought the interview was an utter waste of time.

'You are being interviewed in relation to the murders of your father, Vilho Karppinen, and his neighbour, Riitta Vehviläinen,' Anna began. She sensed a nausea welling in her stomach and felt like vomiting. She'd had the same sensation earlier that morning and worried that she might be coming down with something, but the feeling had passed once she'd eaten two tubs of sour yoghurt. She took a sip of water from the glass on the table and hoped it would make her feel better.

'We have a witness who saw you in the stairwell at your father's house on the night he died, the twelfth of March,' said Virkkunen.

Juha took a deep breath and sucked his lips.

'Who? It's not true,' he said.

'That's for us to know,' said Anna. 'You told us earlier on that you were at the Kero skiing resort, a hundred kilometres away. However, the hotel staff cannot definitively verify your alibi. You were there, of course, but you could easily have driven into town on Wednesday evening without anyone noticing, murdered your father and Riitta Vehviläinen, and returned to the skiing resort as though nothing had happened.'

'Indeed I could, but I didn't. Why on earth would I do something so terrible?'

'For your inheritance, of course.'

'I don't need an inheritance. I have a regular job and my finances are in order. Besides, my father's estate wasn't worth killing him for. It wasn't that big.'

'Unless you were up to your ears in gambling debts, then it would come in very handy. You gamble a lot, don't you? Have done for some time.'

'So what? It's not illegal,' he said quietly.

'I think you've got a gambling problem.'

'Of course I don't. It's just a bit of fun, a bachelor's way of spending time. You dabble too,' he said and gave her a smarmy smile. Virkkunen looked at Anna in bewilderment. Anna dismissed Juha's jibe as though she hadn't heard it and continued.

'You gambled while you were married. According to your ex-wife that was the main reason for your divorce.'

'That bitch will say anything to ruin my reputation. I didn't play much at all, just a bit now and then. And that's how it is today, too.'

'Your creditors would disagree with that statement.'

Juha said nothing. That shut you up, thought Anna.

'I've been looking into your finances, and I know of at least three loan companies that have already sent you final demands. And we're not talking about peanuts here.'

'Those online companies are con artists. I've been meaning to make an official complaint about them.'

'So why didn't you?'

'I haven't got round to it. Something like that always takes a lot of time and effort.'

'How much are you in debt?'

'Not all that much.'

'How much?'

'I can't remember the exact amount.'

'I can tell you the exact amount. I've added it up, you see, and subpoenaed information from across the world. You are in serious debt to numerous international online gambling companies. On top of that, you have a mortgage, a loan for your car and two credit cards, both of which have been frozen for non-payment. And your maintenance payments to your ex-wife are in arrears.'

'You can forget about them,' Juha shouted. 'Sirpa doesn't make me pay them any more.'

'Lucky you,' said Anna. Sitting beside her, Virkkunen gave an approving nod of the head.

'You can't seriously believe I gave my father an overdose and dumped his body in the road on a freezing night?'

'You administered the drugs but you didn't dump the body. The poor junkies downstairs took care of that for you. For a moment there I imagine you must have been quite pleased with the mess they'd accidentally caused. As if by magic, the gangs got mixed up in things and took all the attention away from you.'

'You're crazy,' said Juha. But his voice didn't have as much pluck as before. His shoulders had slouched and his posture, a moment ago so belligerent, now seemed slumped. The room was silent for a moment. Juha was calculating what to say, his head lowered; the police officers waited patiently. Eventually he snapped out of it. His eyes seemed to sparkle, tears of rage glistened in them.

'I haven't had anything to do with my father for years. I don't know anything about his wealth, his illnesses or his medication, not to mention his death,' he shouted and tried to stand up. Virkkunen pushed him back into his chair by the shoulders and told him to calm down.

'This is absolutely outrageous. You spend your time like this, pestering decent taxpayers. Investigate the bloody Pakis that were going in and out of that building dealing drugs. They're the real criminals, not me,' Juha muttered.

'Your father had a sizeable estate. The inheritance would have had quite an impact on your life, what with all your debts. Isn't that right?' asked Virkkunen.

'Yes, it would,' Juha whispered. 'But I didn't kill him or the woman next door.'

'You lied to us when you said that you hadn't visited your father for years. And what do you know, you were seen at his apartment on the night of his death. You'll appreciate that this fact alone makes you look very guilty?'

'I do appreciate that, but I was at the resort in Kero. I sat in the bar all evening drinking. There was a party going on, a band and lots of people. Surely someone can confirm that I was there? Besides, I couldn't have driven anywhere. I was drunk.'

'Well, perhaps your mobile made the trip by itself,' Anna suggested.

'What are you talking about?'

'Remember, the police can trace your mobile phone's GPS movements. If you didn't come into town that evening, your phone must have done so without you.'

Juha fell silent. The muscles in his face twitched. He took deep, fitful breaths through his nostrils, propped his elbow on the arm of his chair and rested his forehead against the palm of his hand.

'What's more, an assistant at the University Pharmacy in town remembers that you came in at the beginning of March, bought a one-hundred pack of Propral with your father's prescription and asked specific questions about the side-effects and dosage limits. And that's not all. At the site of Riitta Vehviläinen's murder we found a set of tyre tracks that exactly match the wheels on your SUV. We also found a cloakroom tag from a bar where you often play roulette. So it seems everything wasn't quite as well planned and executed as it might have been.'

Juha began to tremble. He started to cry. His pathetic wails filled the interview room. He howled and sniffled and spluttered, and couldn't stop. Anna handed him a tissue. She almost felt sorry for the man crumbling in front of her.

His inconsolable sobs lasted for several minutes. Juha's shoulders shuddered and snot ran on to his trousers. The officers waited patiently. They knew that the game was up, and so did Juha. Once the surge of emotion was over, they would learn in detail what had happened in Leppioja on the night of the twelfth of March. Gradually the crying subsided. Juha was breathing in fits; pitiful, hiccupping gasps came from his throat, like a child after a powerful tantrum. A few seconds more, perhaps a minute, and he would start talking. Juha blew his nose and asked Anna for another tissue. He wiped his tear-stained face.

'Very well,' he said without raising his eyes. 'I confess.'

Anna and Virkkunen looked at one another but still didn't say anything. The moment was charged and strangely volatile. They had to give the man's regret enough room to breathe; pressing or pushing him would have been like lighting a fuse, igniting a bomb that could implode, damaging or destroying outright everything that had yet to be said.

'I don't know what happened to me,' Juha began in a small, thin voice. Anna had to concentrate to hear what he was saying.

'Years and years in a cycle of debt. Every day another final demand waiting when I got home from work, and no chance of ever paying them off on these wages. My nerves were constantly on edge, I never had money for anything nice. Bills from debt collectors and demands from bailiffs. Once someone even threatened to kill me. For real.'

Juha raised his head. Anna saw that his tension had gone. On his face now was a look of pure sorrow.

'My wife left me, wouldn't let me see the children. The debt grew and grew. After a while I didn't want to see the kids; I couldn't even afford cinema tickets for them,' he continued and wiped the trickle of tears that had run down his cheek. He began to whimper again.

'Just imagine what years of hell feel like,' he said through his tears. 'I desperately wanted to find a way out. Besides, my father was an old man. He often said he wanted to die and join my mother. Well, he's there now. It's not such a bad thing, is it? I'm not a killer. Not really.'

'What about Riitta Vehviläinen? What happened to her?' asked Virkkunen.

'I might as well tell you everything. I've got nothing left to lose.'

'The more you cooperate with us now, the better it will be for you in the long run,' Virkkunen encouraged him.

Juha took a sip of water. He looked at the floor, his feet, the walls, anywhere but at Anna and Virkkunen. Then he closed his eyes, leaned his head back as though trying to muster the strength to continue.

'I dissolved the Propral into my father's coffee and cognac. I was worried that he might taste it, but everything went well. He didn't notice a thing.'

'Very well indeed,' Anna couldn't stop herself from commenting.

'I was already driving back to Kero when I realised I'd left the bottle of Propral on the coffee table in the living room. I decided to go back and get rid of it, and the prescription. When I went into the apartment, that woman from next door was there. It frightened the life out of me. The old bat asked whether I'd heard any noise from downstairs because the junkies were making a racket, and she asked where Vilho was, whether I'd taken him somewhere. I was out of my mind with fright. I realised she was screwing up my plan, that she could undermine my alibi. I quickly made up a story, saying that the junkies were dangerous and that she'd had to leave the house and get to safety. I took one of Dad's knives from the glass cabinet and encouraged her to come with me. I didn't really have to talk her round; she was as freaked out as I was. I told her I'd take her to my father. We went to her apartment to fetch a coat. That's when I slipped the bottle of Propral into her cupboard.'

Juha paused, took a deep breath and rubbed his forehead.

'Well. Then I took her out to the woods and killed her.'

'Slitting her throat was particularly cruel,' said Anna.

'I thought about strangling her, but I didn't want to touch her with my bare hands. There was a lot of blood, but somehow it all seemed cleaner this way.'

'What did you do with your bloodied clothes?'

'I went home, changed and washed myself. I dumped them in the bin at my house.'

'You dumped Riitta in the bin too.'

'There happened to be a roll of bin-liners in my car. That's where I got the idea.'

'It sounds very cruel. You say you're not a killer. After everything you've told us, what does that make you?'

Juha began to cry again. An inconsolable whimpering bubbled from his throat, tears ran down his cheeks, but Anna no longer felt remotely sorry for the man in front of her.

The mood in the staffroom was flat. Anna, Esko, Sari, Nils and Virkkunen quietly drank from their mugs, nobody had taken any cake, and the stale canteen biscuits didn't seem to appeal either. Juha had been charged with one count of murder and one of manslaughter. The caretaker had had nothing to do with events. He had been able to prove that he was with his family at the time of the killings. Everything felt somehow unreal. Anna recalled the feeling of emptiness that had engulfed her after wrapping up the Hummingbird case. She'd expected a sense of elation and relief but it didn't come. Now she felt the same again. Perhaps these investigations were so intensive, so all-consuming, that bringing them to a conclusion didn't offer instant relief after all. It was as though the air inside a balloon was slowly fizzling out through a tiny hole. The relief would come later. It would take a few days or weeks to get back to normal. She hoped that another case, at least not one this big, didn't present itself for a while. Fatigue pressed heavily on Anna's shoulders; the sense of nausea hadn't passed. She wanted to go home and sleep for at least a day.

I'm not going anywhere. The whole idea was stupid. Where would I go – and why? Esko looked out of his apartment window into the yard, with nothing but a car park and the communal rubbish bins, not a soul in sight. The mountain of snow, piled up behind the car park by the snow trucks during the winter months, had shrunk to nothing but a pile of slush with great puddles at its foot. Nobody would buy this apartment, and even if they did, what then? What would happen if I wanted to come back? I'd have nowhere to go, I'd have to build everything from scratch, and I'm not young any more. When I divorced Anneli and went on my way, I thought that everything would change, that I'd change, that life would change. But it didn't. Not for the better anyway. For a moment it felt like being free, like the rope round my neck had slackened a little, the same damn rope that's so tight now I can barely breathe. They haven't gone anywhere, the ropes, the shackles. I'm the one that put them round my neck in the first place and now they've grown stuck. Besides, these people make me sick, refugees, the sick and frail, all benefit scroungers. Let them fix their own problems. Even Naseem turned out to be a fucking fraud.

What if I called Anneli, he thought, and knew that he wouldn't. I could ask how she's doing, tell her about my plans. What would she say to that? Would she laugh? Say, 'that's a great idea, go for it'? That's what she'd always said, and still the noose round my neck seemed to tighten all the more. I've been a damn fool. But I sorted out the Cobras. Christ, the NBI wouldn't have been able to do anything without me. In practice, it was me who stopped the gang setting down roots in Finland. Damn it, I deserve a medal for this. I'm still up to this job, oh yes. There's still blood running in this old cop's veins. Only another few years till I retire. Then. Then I'll be free, thought Esko, though he knew that wasn't true either. He fetched a bottle of Koskenkorva and slumped on his bed. Nobody is ever free, at least not while they are running from themselves, he thought and took a swig from the bottle. Vodka ran down his chin and on to the sheets, and burned his throat like fire.

That evening Anna stopped at the pharmacy on the way home. She made a cup of tea and paced up and down the apartment, ate a sandwich and listened to Delay's *Tummaa* album, thinking about Grandma. Then she steeled herself and fetched her purchase from her bag. She opened up the small, light-blue cardboard packet and read the instructions carefully, twice. The procedure seemed simple. She went into the toilet and urinated into an empty yoghurt pot that she had washed and saved for some reason; she had no recollection why. She placed the testing stick in the yoghurt pot and went out to the balcony for a cigarette. The evening was warm. Earlier that day the temperature had risen above zero and it hadn't yet dropped though the sun had set long ago. It'll be even warmer tomorrow, thought Anna and looked at the concrete walls sprawling in front of her.

After her New Year's Eve party, she had gone straight from Béci's parents' place to visit her grandmother. Grandma had made some coffee and asked her about the party, and she'd been very interested in how Anna's former school friends were doing. Anna had enjoyed talking about them, though she imagined her grandmother had far better knowledge of the goings-on in Kanizsa than she did. Anna told her about Béci. She'd always been able to talk to Grandma about her boyfriends and relationship problems. She told her about their evening by the Tisza, the rusty swings and about how good Béci's company had felt, how different he was from Finnish men. So what's the matter, Grandma had asked. Anna wondered how her grandmother knew that anything was the matter; Anna hadn't said anything to that effect. She thought for a moment about what to say and wondered whether Grandma would understand.

'It's stupid,' Anna said. 'We were talking about Finnish houses, how they are warm inside even in the winter, how you can walk around with bare feet even though it's freezing outside.' Yes, Grandma had said inquisitively and poured more coffee. The old porcelain cups clinked prettily as Grandma stirred in her sugar. Anna loved that calming, familiar sound. 'So then I tried to explain how the houses are insulated, how all the floors and walls and ceilings are lined with thick layers of insulation, the windows are triple-glazed so that the cold and the wind never come through them – but I couldn't remember the word for "insulation".'

Anna had been ashamed; she'd felt stupid and boastful, a fussy snob for whom nothing was ever good enough.

'Béci said, maybe you don't need to know,' Anna told her grandmother without looking her in the eyes. 'He'd said that women don't need to know words like that. Am I being an idiot, Grandma?' Anna whispered.

No, her grandmother had responded instantly. I understand you perfectly well, she said with a resolute smile and rubbed Anna's head.

Anna stubbed out her cigarette and returned to the bathroom. Her heart was pounding as she lifted up the yoghurt pot. I can't bring myself to look, she thought. But there was nothing for it. There in the middle of the testing stick, in a small square window, were two clear, red lines.

Anna stared at it, felt a tear rolling down her cheek. She looked at the plastic bathroom walls, at her own face in the mirror spattered with toothpaste. Oh Grandma, dear Grandma, she thought. As much as you would have wanted your family to continue and your son, my father, to have grandchildren, I cannot keep this child. I don't know its father. I'm not ready to be a mother. I can't look after a child, raise a child, can't take on such a responsibility for the rest of my life. I simply cannot. Anna burst into tears, slumped to her knees. Red and black circles swirled in her eyes. A girl lay abandoned on the riverbank, dead, a two-headed eagle tearing at her insides with its bloodied beak.

30

'ANNA, WHAT'S THE MATTER?' asked Sari and gave her a worried look. It was early morning. They were driving towards the airport with Sammy Mashid in the back of the car. Sammy had asked to be escorted by Anna and the immigration authority had agreed. Ritva Siponen had asked to be present, but Sammy had refused.

'Nothing,' Anna answered. The phone in her pocket beeped; somebody had sent her a text message.

'Look, I can see something's wrong. Have you been crying?'

How the hell does she notice everything, Anna wondered.

'No, I haven't. I was so tired that I forgot to wash my mascara off last night. My eyes were completely swollen this morning.'

'How are you holding up?' Sari asked Sammy in English, though her sceptical eyes remained firmly on Anna.

Sammy didn't answer. His olive skin was pale. He was resting his forehead against the car window, staring with empty eyes out at the northern city that was not to become his home, whose morning traffic was a joke compared to the Karachi rush hour, a city where there were no opium dens but where you were sure to score some Subutex, a city whose cobbled streets gradually turned to motorways and intersections that now spat him out.

Anna clicked open the text message. It was from her mother. Ákos had hit the bottle and wouldn't be able to come back to Finland, said the message. *I'm taking him to a treatment centre. I'll call this evening.*

Anna started to cry. She thought of the tiny collection of cells growing in her womb. Ákos would become an uncle. Her mother would become a grandmother. I'll be a mother. But it won't work. It can't work; I can barely look after myself. Anna felt an immeasurable solitude surrounding her, enveloping her, wrapping her in a parcel that nobody would ever open. Why can't Ákos control himself? Why am I here all by myself at a time like this?

'Anna, what's wrong?' asked Sari.

'It's nothing. I'm just worried about Sammy,' said Anna and struggled to hold back her tears.

'He's frightened to death.'

Anna tried to banish her gloomy thoughts and glanced at Sammy on the back seat. The sight of him didn't comfort her.

'No wonder. You'd be frightened too.'

'Will he be killed back home?'

I'm about to kill my own child before it even has arms and legs, thought Anna.

'Sooner or later,' she answered.

'Bloody hell. Aren't there restrictions on travelling to Pakistan?'

Anna sighed. She too had thought of this almost every day since they'd found Sammy.

'That's only for Finns. Tourists should avoid travelling to certain areas and the whole country is considered dangerous, according to the foreign office.'

'So we send back a local resident whose life is in real danger?'

'Yes. Apparently a Finnish life is more valuable than a Pakistani life, not to mention the lives of Pakistani Christians.'

When will it start to kick, Anna wondered.

'Bloody hell,' Sari sighed again.

Anna and Sari escorted Sammy on to the plane before boarding began. They waited until all the other passengers had boarded and the stewardess gave the signal. Anna wanted to hug Sammy, but he continued staring out of the window, silent and limp. The officers left the aeroplane and stood outside to make sure nobody got off after the doors were secured. Their colleagues would be waiting in Helsinki to escort Sammy on to the next flight.

A warm breeze was blowing from the south. The sky had clouded over. One at a time, cool droplets of water began to fall on Anna's face, her shoulders, the ground. A couple of swans flew overhead beneath the low cloud cover. The contours of the white birds blurred against the heavy, grey rainclouds, the roar of the aeroplane's engines drowned out the squawk of the birds as it sped along the runway, rose lightly into the air and soared towards the clouds. Heavenly Father, or whoever you are, let Sammy find his way home, Anna said to herself. And forgive me, forgive me for terminating this pregnancy.

Once the mass of clouds had swallowed up the disappearing plane, Anna and Sari walked back to the car and drove into town in silence. The rain got heavier and the piles of snow seemed to melt before their eyes. They picked up a couple of large, filled rolls at a local bakery and went back to the station to make some coffee. Anna gave Sari contact details for Gabriella and her host family, told her that the girl wanted to remain in Finland for a while and find another au pair position. Sari was thrilled. You'll have a new friend, she said to Anna. You've probably missed having Hungarian friends. Anna didn't answer but admitted to herself that that was probably the case. Without much discussion they agreed to call it a day; a free afternoon was the least they deserved after weeks of hard work. Once she got home, Anna made an appointment with the gynaecologist. She lit a candle on the kitchen table though it was still light outside, listened to *Tummaa* by Delay and looked out at the shrinking piles of snow in the yard, now grey with sand and grit.

A humid wind pushed back the hazy threat of the Afghan borderlands up ahead. Everything was silent; the horizon shimmered like a mirage in the glow of the sun. Suddenly something appeared from the rippling air, at first only a speck, growing rapidly. It was a car, a dirty-green jeep full of men. The barrels of rifles jutted like extensions of the men's silhouettes towards the sky, Mosin-Nagants and Kalashnikovs with bayonets inherited from the Second World War, but still functioning and deadly. The vehicle kicked up such a thick gauze of dust and sand that the glare of the sun dimmed behind it. The car was hurtling at full speed towards a solitary whitewashed building standing at the edge of the desert. Now from amongst the men on the trailer at the back, a smaller figure came into view; black and slightly hunched. The jeep came to a halt. Two men with rifles jumped to the ground; one of them held out his hand and helped from the trailer the woman shrouded in a burqa. She cautiously lifted her veil, a sliver of black lace covering her eyes. She didn't look around, simply followed the riflemen towards the building. They walked into a small office where men in uniforms stood smoking cigarettes and drank tea from chipped porcelain cups. The air was thick with smoke. The men stared at the new arrivals. The woman lowered her head and tried to convince herself that she had nothing to fear. Her cousin was standing beside her. Thank God she'd found him. Without a male relative she would never have made it. Without a male relative she would have no chance at all.

Behind the battered table sat a chubby official, his cruel, gleaming eyes fixed on the woman. Her cousin had said that the man was one of them, that there was nothing to worry about. Everything would work out just fine. Then why did he look so mean? Was the man showing off in front of the other soldiers? Or was her cousin mistaken after all? The woman choked back her fear and stood beside her cousin, silent and humble. We'll get through this. The man is one of us. He has to be.

‘What is your cousin’s wife’s name?’ the official growled from behind the table, addressing his question to the man standing next to the woman. Her cousin had said he would do the talking, but she could feel the words bubbling up within her, she wouldn’t be able to hold them back for long, for the certainty that her words were true had grown and grown within her for a month now, like a storm gathering pace, and now those words were wrenching at her, overwhelming her, tearing at her so much that soon nothing would be able to hold them back. If the man is one of us, he will understand. Dear God, let it be true.

‘Iqra Mashid.’

‘And where is she going?’

‘Karachi.’

‘Why?’

The storm whipped up, its first ferocious gust pushing out the words that had so tortured the woman; the force of those words filled the room with their energy, the official groped for a pen to sign all the relevant documents.

‘I know that my son is there. I know that I will find him,’ said the woman and cautiously raised her head.

Acknowledgements

Thank you to Maija, Jani, Jaakko, Risto, Paavo and Satu for all the expert advice.

I would like to take this opportunity to thank everyone at the Otava Publishing Company, particularly Leenastiina Kakko and Aleksi Pöyry, for their constant guidance and encouragement. Thanks also go to the panel of judges at the Petrona Award 2015; it was an honour to be shortlisted for this award in such prestigious company. And finally, thank you to the indefatigable Karen Sullivan at Orenda Books and to translator David Hackston for all their hard work in bringing my work to an English-speaking public.

Mum and friends, thank you for your support.